TERROR BELOW

Ethan turned to go back to the ship, and suddenly fell flat on his face.

Three . . . no, four, tiny cream-white tendrils had erupted from the ice and locked around his right ankle. Now they were stretched taut, pulling him downward. Ice began to crack in sheets around his prone form. He fought for a grip. His hips were already vanishing beneath the surface when he managed to lock both arms around a pika-pedan stump. Then the stump broke off in his arms.

And the pulling from the deadly ice worm below continued . . .

MISSION TO MOULOKIN

ALAN DEAN FOSTER

A Del Rey Book

BALLANTINE BOOKS • NEW YORK

A Del Rey Book
Published by Ballantine Books

Library of Congress Catalog Card Number: 78-70603

ISBN 0-345-29661-3

Manufactured in the United States of America

First Edition: April 1979
Third Printing: November 1980

Cover art by Michael Herring

For Mike and Helen Green,
beloved Uncle and Aunt always,
and damn the indifferent genetics of it all . . .

Meckleven

*lifeboat crash site

Wannome

*

Sofold

Ayhas

Priory of the
Brotherhood *

Pika-pina/
Pika-pedan
fields

Great Sea Ocean

prevailing wind

Detail of Moulokin

First
Gate

Second Gate

cliffs

land of the
golden
saia

*shipyards

harbor

town

forests

castle

PORTER

Brass Monkey

Arsudun

Place-Where-The-Earth's-Blood-Burns

fortified outpost

Poyolavomaar

Pika-pina/Pika-pedan fields

Equator

Ice Pressure Ridge

Continental Plateau

Moulokin

N
W   E
S

PROLOGUE

It all began with a bungled kidnapping.

The two men who'd attempted to abduct the wealthy Hellespont du Kane and his daughter Colette from the KK-drive liner orbiting the ice world of Tran-ky-ky had been forced to take along two witnesses, a diminutive schoolteacher named Milliken Williams and a salesman, Ethan Fortune.

They hadn't counted on the additional presence of the white-haired giant who'd been sleeping off a drunk in the back of their intended escape lifeboat. Skua September had not taken politely to being abducted. His resultant action caused the lifeboat to crash thousands of wind-swept kilometers from the only human settlement on the frozen planet below. Those actions also caused the death of one kidnapper and the immobilization of the other.

Crossing the perpetually frozen oceans of Tran-ky-ky, with their subfreezing temperatures and unceasing winds, seemed impossible until a party of curious locals from the native city-state of Wannome reached them. Cautious and wary at first, human and Tran soon became friends, aided by the actions of one remarkable young Tran, the knight Hunnar Redbeard.

The arrival of the humans and their lifeboat of rare metal on metal-poor Tran-ky-ky served Redbeard well. It enabled him to use it as a sign that Wannome and its island of Sofold should resist the coming depredations of Sagyanak the Death and her Horde. Such wandering tribes of nomadic barbarians, whole cities living on their icerafts, periodically visited the permanent towns and city-states of Tran-ky-ky demanding tribute and ravishing all who dared refuse payment.

With the aid of crossbows and one other critical invention concocted by the teacher Williams and the local court wizard, Malmeevyn Eer-Meesach, the

1

Horde was defeated utterly. Then reluctantly, Torsk Kurdagh-Vlata, Landgrave and ruler of Wannome, agreed to keep his promise to help the shipwrecked humans reach the Commonwealth outpost of Brass Monkey.

Using duralloy metal from the ruined lifeboat to provide unbreakable ice runners, and employing designs adapted from the ancient clipper ships of Terra's seas, a huge raft rigged for ice running was constructed— the *Slanderscree*.

With Sir Hunnar and a crew of Tran sailors, the survivors set out on the dangerous, lengthy journey. They surmounted the threats posed by the remnants of the Horde, perilous local fauna such as guttorbyn and rampaging stavanzers—some the size of small spacecraft, a monastery of religious fanatics and the explosion of a gigantic volcano.

More troublesome to Ethan were his relationships with Elfa Kurdagh-Vlata, the daughter of the Landgrave who had stowed away aboard the *Slanderscree*, and with the affectionate but sarcastic and domineering Colette du Kane.

None of which prevented the *Slanderscree* from reaching the island of Arsudun, its human outpost and shuttleport of Brass Monkey, where they hoped they would find immediate transportation off the hellishly cold, windswept world of Tran-ky-ky . . .

I

Ethan Frome Fortune leaned over the wooden railing and screamed. The wind mangled his words.

Below the railing, the tiny two-man ice boat strained to maneuver close to the side of the racing icerigger. One of the men inside leaned out an open window to shout querulously up at Ethan, who then cupped both hands to the diaphragm of his thermal survival suit and tried to make himself understood. "I said, we're from Sofold. Sofold!"

Spreading both arms, the man in the boat shook his head to show he still couldn't understand. Then he had to use both hands to clutch at the window edge as the little craft swerved sharply to avoid one of the *Slanderscree's* huge duralloy runners.

Five curving metal skates supported the great ice ship: two nearly forward, two nearly aft where the arrowhead-shaped vessel's beam was widest, and a last at the pointed stern. Each towered nearly four meters, large enough to slice the cautious patrol boat in two if its driver wasn't careful or quick enough to stay out of the path of the two-hundred-meter ice ship.

Ethan slid back the face mask of his survival suit without shifting the glare-reducing goggles he wore beneath and reflected on what he'd just yelled. From Sofold? He? He was a moderately successful salesman for the House of Malaika. Sofold was the home of Hunnar Redbeard and Balavere Longax and other Tran, natives of this frozen, harsh iceworld of Tran-ky-ky. From Sofold? Had he grown that acclimated to the unforgiving planet in the year and a half he and his companions had been marooned there?

Blowing ice scoured his burnished epidermis like a razor, and he turned to shield the exposed skin. A glance at the thermometer set in the back of his left glove indicated the temperature a balmy −18° C. But then they were not too far from Tran-ky-ky's equator, where such tropical conditions could be expected.

A furry paw rested on his shoulder. Glancing around, Ethan found himself looking into the lionesque face of Sir Hunnar Redbeard. Hunnar had been leader of the first group of natives to encounter Ethan and his fellow shipwreck victims where they'd crashed, several thousand kilometers distant. Ethan studied the lightly clothed knight, envied his adaptation to a climate that could kill most unprotected humans in an hour.

The Tran bundled up in severe weather, but more temperate conditions allowed Sir Hunnar and his companions to shed their heavy hessavar furs for lighter attire, such as the hide vest and kilt the knight currently wore. Although he stood only a few centimeters taller than Ethan, the Tran was nearly twice as broad, yet his semihollow bone structure reduced his weight to little more than that of an average man.

Slitted black pupils glared from yellow feline eyes; shards of jet set in cabochons of bright topaz. They were split by a broad, blunt muzzle which ended above the wide mouth. Pursed lips and twitched-forward triangular ears combined to indicate curiosity. Hunnar's right *dan,* a tough membrane extending from wrist to hip, was partly open, bulging with the force of the wind, but he balanced easily on his *chiv,* the elongated claws which enabled any Tran to glide across ice more gracefully than the most talented human skater.

While Hunnar's reddish beard and rust-toned fur caused him to stand out in a crowd of his steel-gray fellows, it was his inquiring personality and natural curiosity that raised him above them in Ethan's estimation.

"They want to know," Ethan explained in Tran while gesturing at the small scout boat skittering alongside and below them, "where we've come from. I told them, but I don't think they heard me."

"Mayhap they heard you well, Sir Ethan, and simply do not know of Sofold."

"I told you to stop calling me sir, Hunnar." The titles the Tran of Wannome city had bestowed on the

4

humans after the defeat of Sagyanak's Horde still made him uncomfortable.

"Remember," Hunnar continued blithely, "until you and your companions landed near Sofold in your metal flying boat, we had neither seen nor heard of your race. Ignorance is a two-edged sword." He waved a massive arm at the scout boat. "It would be surprising indeed if your people here in this nearby outpost you call Brass Monkey, the only one of its kind on my world, had heard of so distant a nation as Sofold."

A cry from above and forward interrupted them. It came from the lookout's cage set atop the patriarchal tree which served now as the *Slanderscree's* mainmast. Many months of living among the Tran had given Ethan the ability to rapidly translate the lookout's words. After half a day's careful travel down the frozen inlet from the vast ice ocean beyond, they were finally coming into the harbor of Arsudun, the Tran city-state where humanity maintained its shivering outpost on this world.

Ethan and Hunnar stood on the helm deck. Other than the three masts, it was the highest point on the ship. Behind them, Captain Ta-hoding hurled rapid-fire directions at the two Tran wresting the great wheel connected to the duralloy runner which steered the *Slanderscree*. In accordance with the captain's orders, other Tran were manipulating the two huge airfoils at bow and stern to slow the icerigger still more.

Meanwhile the laborious and dangerous process of reefing in sails was proceeding rapidly. Ethan marveled how the Tran crew had mastered the rigging of the enormous ice ship. Only their claws and thick chiv enabled them to hold their footing on the icy spars above.

Though Hunnar slid easily over the icepath bordering the ship's railings Ethan struggled to remain upright as they moved forward for a better look. The helm deck reached as far as the broad end of the main arrowhead shape of the *Slanderscree*. Standing just above the muffled screech of the port-aft runner, they could now look straight at the harbor, since from where they stood the icerigger narrowed to a point some hundred and seventy meters ahead.

Arsudun was a bubble-shaped harbor located at the end of the long strait leading from the ice ocean. Like the ocean, the strait, and all other free-standing water on Tran-ky-ky, the harbor was frozen solid. It was a flat sheet of many shades of white, covered with a thin layer of snow and ice crystals. Where the snow had been blown away, grooves marked the routes other ice ships had taken.

Ethan was eighteen standard Commonwealth months late arriving. Brass Monkey was just another stopover on the new territory he'd been assigned to cover. But his involvement in an abortive kidnapping aboard the interstellar liner *Antares* and the subsequent crash-landing near Wannome, Hunnar's home city, had lengthened his stay considerably.

Arsudun was an island, larger than Sofold, probably smaller than some. As far as Ethan knew, Tran-ky-ky was a world of islands set like metamorphic hermits in a cluster of frozen oceans. Somewhere nearby was the humanx settlement of Brass Monkey, with its shuttleport and promise of passage off this inverted hell of a world. Andrenalin—Arsudun . . . they went together. What a pleasure it would be to stop playing explorer and return to the simple, gentle business of purveying manufactured goods from warm world to warm world!

He wondered about his companions, fellow survivors. Excusing himself, he left Hunnar and went to find them, searching the deck before entering the two double-tiered cabins set forward of the helm.

The would-be kidnappers who had abducted him were now dead. The individual principally responsible for their death was standing up forward, looking out over the bowsprit. Distance reduced even his impressive frame to a perpendicular spot of brown against the deck and the white ice ahead.

Of all of them, Skua September seemed most fitted for this world. Over two meters tall, massing nearly two hundred kilos, with his biblical-prophet visage and flowing white hair offset by the gold ring in his right ear, he resembled something that had slid off the front

6

of a glacier. There having been no survival suit on the *Antares'* lifeboat large enough to fit him, he'd resorted to native clothing. In hessavar fur coat and cape and trousers he looked very much like one of the natives, his glare goggles notwithstanding.

In the lee of the fore cabin, Milliken Williams stood chatting with his spiritual and intellectual soul brother, the Tran wizard Malmeevyn Eer-Meesach. The diminutive schoolteacher's manner was as dark and quiet as his coloring. September might be suited physically to Tran-ky-ky, but Williams melded into it mentally. There was more he could teach here than in any Commonwealth school, and more to learn than from any tape. Williams possessed a silent soul. If the weather was not to his liking, the tranquillity of intellectual adventure surely was.

Somewhere in one of the two cabins slept Hellespont du Kane and his daughter Colette, the objects of the kidnapping. Colette was also the reason for Ethan's present personal distress. She had proposed marriage to him; recently, bluntly. Despite her gross physical appearance, Ethan was seriously considering the offer. The prospect of marrying one of the wealthiest young women in the Arm was sufficient to overcome such superficialities as a lack of physical beauty. She was supremely competent as an individual, too. Ethan knew she ran the du Kane financial empire during her father's periodic attacks of senility.

But one had to consider her acid tongue, capable of verbally slicing one into neat little fragments of shrunken ego. And hers was a very high-powered personality, accustomed to manipulating corporation heads and ordering about Commonwealth representatives. Spending one's life with such an overpowering individual was something to be weighed carefully.

Somewhere below also slept the drugged Elfa Kurdagh-Vlata, daughter of the Landgrave of Sofold, who was Hunnar's ruler/chief/king. The royal stowaway had snored through much of the dangerous and eventful voyage from Sofold, but when she awoke Ethan would have another problem to deal with.

Despite certain obvious differences in physiology, there were enough similarities between human and

7

Tran for Elfa to have developed a distressing attraction to Ethan, much to his discomfort. It had caused unspoken but obvious pain to Hunnar. Both he and Ethan had managed to lay a veneer of honest friendship over that potentially explosive situation. The problem would crop up again when the royal offspring awoke.

Ethan had made his feelings in the matter known to Elfa. But that hadn't discouraged her from attempting to change his mind. If she would sleep just a few days longer, he would be off the planet and spared the problem of dealing with her personally. That would be just as well, because despite his declared feelings, there was an unavoidable feline animalness about Elfa that . . .

Using information relayed from the masthead lookouts and the bowsprit pointer, Ta-hoding skillfully directed the *Slanderscree* toward an open dock protruding from the harbor shoreline. The dock was simply a wooden road built out onto the ice. Its pilings were necessary to raise it to iceship deck level, not to keep it above the frozen water.

Smaller ice boats were beginning to cluster curiously around the *Slanderscree*. They complicated the task of maneuvering the colossal ship up to the dock. But Arsudun owned a wide harbor, much wider than the *Slanderscree's* home port of Wannome. Ta-hoding did a masterful job of maneuvering around and through the curious locals.

A few awed sightseers were warned off by the icerigger's crew. Their stupified amazement was justified, Ethan knew. The *Slanderscree* was likely twice the size of any ice ship they had ever seen.

No doubt the crowd gathering on the shore included admiring shipwrights and envious merchants. They would be hard to keep off the ship, once it docked. Their natural curiosity would impel them to inspect the strange rigging arrangement, a modification of ancient Terran water clippers adapted by Williams for Tran-ky-ky's ice oceans. Surely they would clamber all over the five massive duralloy runners on which the icerigger rode. Metal was a scarce commodity on

Tran-ky-ky. The other, smaller ice ships Ethan had seen were outfitted with runners of wood and, more rarely, of bone or stone.

Some of the ship's sailors cursed when the docking crew was slow to help them. The dockworkers too were dazed by the size of the *Slanderscree*. Mates had to direct their men to jump over the railings and down to the dock to man the cables and braces themselves, but once the process of tying up had begun, the land crew swung into action and began to help.

It was a tricky process. The *Slanderscree* was nearly three times the length of her dock, and no other docks in view were longer. There was no need for them. Ships the size of the *Slanderscree* simply did not exist on all of Tran-ky-ky.

Ta-hoding, however, was prepared to cope. As soon as his vessel's bow was secured he ordered the stern ice anchors released. They locked in place and would keep the huge vessel from swinging tail-first with the steady aft wind.

Wind, wind and cold. Ethan slid the protective face mask back down over his goggles to shield his delicate human flesh. The lee of an island or indoors were the only places you were out of the wind on Trank-ky-ky. It blew here the way the sun shone on paradisical New Riviera or on one of the thranx worlds such as Amropolous or Hivehom. It blew steadily, varying but never wholly ceasing, across the empty places and frozen seas. It blew steadily down the strait against his back now, sucked inward by the rising, slightly warmer air above the island.

A few clouds scudded in puffy formation across a sky of cobalt blue. Ethan turned his gaze as he moved forward. Grizzled and goggled, a seamed face turned to look back and down at him, to smile with teeth white as chips of the harbor around them.

"Upon my word, young feller-me-lad, if we haven't gone and made it in one piece!" Skua September rubbed one side of a nose as big in proportion to its face as the ship's bowsprit was to the hull. He turned away to study the town, its winding icepaths forming shiny ribbons between the buildings, the busy Tran walking or chivaning along them. The locals who didn't

9

stop to gawk at the icerigger held their arms out-
stretched parallel to the street, the wind filling their
membranous dan and scooting them along effortlessly.

Smoke curled skyward from a thousand chimneys.
Multistoried gambreled structures swelled haphazardly
up the gentle island slope until they crested against the
stark gray bulk of a substantial castle.

While Arsudun seemed to contain a population
considerably larger than Wannome, Ethan noted with
interest the smaller size of the castle. Its diminutive
proportions bespoke either the relative impecuniosity of
the local government or the becoming modesty of its
Landgrave.

Sir Hunnar offered a third possibility. "It looks not
more than a dozen years old, Sir Ethan . . . Ethan.
And it appears unusually well built." Hunnar clambered awkwardly over the railing and down the
boarding ladder. He relaxed visibly when he was able
to step onto the icepath covering the center portion of
the dock. Like all Tran, he was much more at home
on the ice than on any unslick solid surface.

Ethan and Skua joined the knight and his two
squires, Suaxusdal-Jagger and Budjir. The latter were
discussing the town and the assembled crowd in suspicious mutters. They kept their arms tight at their
sides, lest a gust of wind catch their dan and send
them unexpectedly rocketing forward.

A voice called from the ship to the landing party.
Squinting reflexively into the wind, although the suit
mask kept his eyes safe, Ethan made out a rotund,
survival-suited figure waving down at them from the
bow.

"When you get to the port, use the number twenty-
two double R if the authorities give you any trouble!"
The voice was crisp, insistent, yet feminine for all its
controlled power. Colette du Kane paused to murmur
something to the wavering figure alongside her, then
put an arm around her father to support him.

"That's our family code. Any processor unit will
recognize it instantly, Ethan. From a personal cardmeter to a Church ident. It will give us priority booking
on the next shuttle off here and cut through any red
tape."

"Twenty-two double R, okay." Ethan hesitated when she seemed about to add something else, but then her father bent over suddenly and she had to attend to him. They couldn't hear anything, but the figure's movements hinted at wracking, heaving coughs.

They turned, started for the town. Hunnar and the squires kept their speed down to a crawl to keep from outdistancing the humans. They were nearly reduced to walking.

"Strong woman," September murmured easily. Hunnar spoke to a local who directed them to the left. Following the harbor, they turned in that direction.

"Yes, she is," Ethan agreed. "But she tends to be a bit domineering."

"Why fella-me-lad, what do you expect from a scion of one of the merchant families? 'Course, it ain't fer me to say. You're the one she proposed to, not me."

"I know, Skua. But I respect your opinion. What do you think I should do?"

"You want the opinion of a wanted man." September grinned broadly. Then the smile vanished and September became unexpectedly, unnaturally solemn.

"Lad, you can ask my advice where fighting is concerned, hand-to-hand, ship-to-ship, machine-to-machine. You can ask where politics are concerned, or religion, or food or drink. You can ask my advice on any hundred matters, any thousand, and though I don't know amoeba-spit about half that many I'd still venture you a reply.

"But," and here he looked at Ethan so sharply, so furiously intent that the salesman missed a nervous step, "don't ask my advice where women are concerned because I've had worse luck with them than fighting or politics or any of the thousand others. No, feller-me-lad," he continued, some of his perpetual good humor returning, "that's a choice you'll have to make for yourself.

"I *will* tell you this: never confuse physical form and beauty with the capacity for passion. That's a mistake far too many men make. Beauty ain't skin deep ... it goes a damn sight deeper.

"Now let's hurry up the pace a bit. Sir Hunnar and his boys are practically fallin' asleep trying to hang

11

back with us, and I'm as anxious as you are to get to the port . . ."

They topped a slight rise. Below and just ahead lay the humanx community of Brass Monkey. At the moment, Ethan had eyes only for three concave depressions scooped from the frozen ground and neatly lined with opaque, ice-free metal. Shuttleboat pits. Just their metal linings, those three perfect bowls, contained a fortune in Tran terms, yet none of them seemed disturbed or in any way vandalized. Of course, he reminded himself, that might be due to the fact that the Tran didn't possess tools strong enough to cut through duralloy or metal-ceramic crystalloids.

Aligned in one of the pits was a small metal shape that bore a remarkable resemblance to the *Slanderscree,* save for the absence of masts and its more aerodynamic design. The little boat made Ethan's stomach flip. He could be on it very soon.

An enormous wall of frozen earth and blocks of ice and snow had been heaped up east of the community to shelter it from the steady wind off the harbor. The port buildings lay close by the near end of the harbor, and the group started down toward an L-shaped, two-story edifice. Two glowing signs shone in recesses above the snow-free main entrance. One read: BRASS MONKEY—*TRAN-KY-KY* ADMINISTRATION. In jagged local script below it were words translating roughly as SKY OUTLANDER'S PLACE.

An intermittent stream of bundled humans and an occasional Tran were presenting themselves at that entrance. Glassalloy windows, thick enough to be used in starships, offered the building's inhabitants views of the frozen world outside. Ethan could see in. Something was keeping the inside of such windows free from condensation.

"What do we here, Ethan?" Hunnar sounded uncertain. No doubt he was wondering if the strange humans in this place would have icepaths within their structures or if he would be forced to walk any distance.

"We have to book passage off your world. Back to our homes."

12

"Your homes," Hunnar echoed. "Of course." The knight's tone indicated a contradictory meaning. Ethan understood the language well enough now to discern such nuances. Hunnar was expressing sorrow at their imminent departure and at the same time, a profound gratitude. Or maybe he was just thinking of the sleeping Elfa Kurdagh-Vlata back on the *Slanderscree*.

Once more Ethan thought to reassure Hunnar that he had nothing to worry about in the way of competition for the favors of the Landgrave's daughter. But booking passage should provide sufficient reassurance.

There was an icepath ramp leading to the entrance, bordered by smooth metal for human use. It was grooved for traction despite the present absence of ice. Two sets of doors barred the way in.

They passed the first easily enough, despite the rise in temperature. But when they passed the second set and entered the building proper, Sir Hunnar reeled and the moody Suaxus nearly fell. The cause was immediately apparent. The Tran liked to maintain the temperature in their dwellings perhaps five degrees above freezing. The temperature inside the building, set for the human optimum, was devastatingly higher.

It was then that Ethan noticed there were no Tran inside the building itself. Those they had seen entering had stopped in the area enclosed by the two sets of doors, a small lobby lined with windows. There, Tran exchanged packages or held conversations with humans at windows installed for the purpose. The area was kept cool there for them, and tolerably warm for the humans behind the windows. Even so, the Tran there concluded their business hurriedly to rush out into the comforting arctic air outside.

"With . . . your permission, friend Ethan, friend Skua. . . ." Hunnar staggered erect. Without waiting for Ethan's acknowledgment, the knight and his two companions turned and stumbled outside. Through the transparent doors, Ethan could see Suaxus sit down hard, holding his head with both hands, while Hunnar and Budjir gulped deep icy breaths and ministered to him.

"I can see where they'd get heat stroke quick enough

13

in here." September was rapidly divesting himself of his hessavar furs. Ethan didn't have that problem. He simply slid back his face mask and goggles, plus the hood of his survival suit. The suit itself automatically adjusted for the warmer air inside the building, the suit material being naturally thermosensitive.

They walked to the information grid. Politely, a voice informed them of the portmaster's name and the location of his office. Directions were displayed on the map set alongside the grid.

A small, olive-skinned man with tightly curled black hair greeted them in the office. He displayed an air of relaxed efficiency. His eyebrows rose slightly at their entrance, otherwise he didn't appear too surprised at their presence. His gaze stayed mostly on September, which was no surprise at all. Skua had to duck to enter the office.

They were on the second floor of the building. Broad windows opened on side and back, showing the launch pits and the roofs of Arsudun. The contrast of frozen medievality and sleek modernity gave the windows the look of solidos, artificial and unlikely.

"Good morning, gentlesirs, good morning. Carpen Xenaxis, portmaster. We had a report from one of our harbor scouts that a large native vessel with humans aboard was coming in." He stopped, awaiting confirmation.

"Yes, we were aboard." Ethan introduced himself and September, then launched into a rapid explanation of their presence on Tran-ky-ky, the failed kidnapping of the du Kanes . . . and was cut off at that point.

"Just a moment . . . sorry." Xenaxis turned to the tridee screen set into one side of his desk, chatted briefly and softly to someone unseen. Then he turned back to them with a pleasant smile.

"It was assumed the du Kanes had died during the misfunction of the lifeboat, which you now tell me was no misfunction. I just reported them alive and well. We've had many inquiries. A large number of individuals will be most interested in this news." Xenaxis appeared suddenly uncertain. "They *are* alive and well?" Ethan nodded.

"The kidnappers themselves are dead," September

added. "I killed one of 'em myself. If there's a reward I'd like to lay claim to it."

"Naturally. That is your right." The portmaster touched another switch, prepared to make a fresh recording. "If you'll just give me your name, world of origin, home address and financial code I'm sure we..."

"Actually, that wouldn't be the fair thing to do." September gestured at his companion. "It was this here lad who was responsible for most of what happened. He deserves any credit."

Ethan turned a startled look on September, opened his mouth to comment. An experienced salesman is a specialist in reading expressions. A multitude of meanings were available for interpretation on the big man's face just then. To his credit, Ethan picked up most of them.

"If there is any kind of reward, I'll worry about that later." September relaxed ever so slightly. "The main thing we're concerned about is getting off this place as fast as possible."

"I can imagine." Xenaxis sounded properly sympathetic. "I do not myself find the company of the natives particularly pleasant. One can do business with them, but it is next to impossible to socialize. Besides the differences in temperature each race is accustomed to, they are argumentative and combative by nature." Ethan said nothing, maintaining a blank expression.

"The local trade is profitable then?" September somehow sounded as if there was more behind his question than just polite conversation.

Xenaxis shrugged. "Keeping the commercial end of this post open is my principal task, sir. There are three large warehouses here in Brass Monkey whose contents change frequently. Of course, I'm only a civil employee, straight salaried." Ethan thought he detected a note of envy in the portmaster's voice. "But some companies or individual entrepreneurs are certainly making money off this frozen wasteland."

"What kind of trade?" Xenaxis shouldn't find that question suspicious, Ethan thought. It was his business.

"What you'd expect." The portmaster leaned back in his chair. Ethan heard the faint hiss of posturic com-

15

pensators. Xenaxis had a bad back, it seemed. But he appeared anxious to talk. New faces were no doubt an infrequent sight in Brass Monkey.

"Mostly luxury goods: art works, carvings, furs, gemstones, handicrafts, some of the most remarkable ivory sculptures you'd ever want to see. The natives look clumsy, but they're capable of fine work." Ethan thought of a stavanzer tusk and what a good local artist might make of one.

"You know all about such things, of course," the portmaster continued. "When a civilization grows as modern as that of the Commonwealth, excellently crafted machinery and the mechanisms necessary for day to day living become cheap. People have a lot of excess credit to dispose of. So they spend on luxuries and art works and other nonessentials." His chair returned to the vertical, his tone to businesslike.

"As far as your taking passage off-planet, I'm assuming you require shuttle space for the both of you and the du Kanes."

"And one other, a teacher, name of Williams," Ethan said.

"Five. Should be able to manage that, given your unusual circumstances. I don't know a shipmaster who'd refuse you space." He turned to his tridee screen again and pushed buttons. "I'll put out notification of your survival to anyone you want to know about it, place it on the outpost bill. You've probably both got friends and relatives who'll be happy to hear you're still around. Maybe you're not as important to others as are the du Kanes, but you're important to yourselves."

Despite his possible dislike of the Tran, Ethan decided he liked the little portmaster very much. "I was told by Colette du Kane to use the code 22RR. She said it might help you expedite matters."

"If that's the family financial code, I'm sure it will," agreed Xenaxis. He checked a hidden readout. "The next ship due in stop orbit is the freighter *Palamas*. I'll make your boarding arrangements via satellite relay as soon as the *Palamas* is in range." He sounded apologetic. "We're not nearly big or important enough here to qualify for a deep-space particle beam. The

16

Palamas is a border-run ship, if I remember right. But she eventually orbits Drax IV, and you can make passage to anywhere from there."

"When's she due in?" Ethan was startled by the lack of enthusiasm in his voice.

"Oh, six fifteen on the twenty-fourth." Xenaxis studied the two blank faces a moment, then smiled slightly. "Sorry. I forgot you probably haven't been aware of local time since you touched down."

"A couple of us had chronometers," Ethan explained. "They didn't survive the crash. Those that did didn't survive the climate. Mine survived both, but didn't survive . . ." He held out his right hand, showed the portmaster where the gash in his survival suit had been patched from hand to shoulder.

"Lost it to a stavanzer."

"You mean those shipsized herbivores that weigh a couple of hundred tons each? Never seen one myself, only tridees taken by the scientific survey."

"We had to turn one around."

"Yes." Xenaxis eyed them both respectfully. *"Palamas* should break out of space-plus in a couple of days. Leave another two days, three at most for her to decelerate and insert. I'm sorry I can't offer you passage out of here any sooner. We don't even have a habitat station I can ferry you up to. But if I can break away from my own duties, I've a request to make."

"What's that?"

Rising and walking around his desk, the portmaster moved to the side window, stared out across the roofs of Arsudun. Snow skipped like fat white fleas across the insulated transparency. "I can see the masts of the ship you arrived in from here. It's much bigger than anything we've recorded so far. I'd love to have a close look at it."

"Talk to her Captain, Ta-hoding," Ethan advised him. "I'm sure he'll be glad to show you around. He's proud of his ship."

"He has reason to be." Xenaxis turned reluctantly from the window. "I suppose I'd better get back to work. Forms to fill out." He made a face.

"If you like, you can stay the five days until departure here in the post. We'll make room for you."

17

"Can't speak for the others." September was moving toward the door. "Myself, I think I'll stay with our Trannish friends."

"As you like." Xenaxis resumed his seat, turned toward Ethan. "Just a moment, Mr. Fortune. As I recall, there are two or three small cases consigned to you waiting in Number Three warehouse."

"My sample goods. One of them contains a dozen or so small, inert-element heaters. A year ago I'd have given a thousand credits for one. I guess I'll try and sell a few over the next couple of days. Thanks for reminding me." Odd, he mused as they exited from the portmaster's office, how he'd completely forgotten his sale goods. For some inexplicable reason, things such as profit margin, customer acceptance and territory expansion seemed childish to him now. Had Tranky-ky modified more than his tolerance to cold weather?

II

When they reached the first floor, September put a restraining hand on Ethan's shoulder, halted him. "Sir Hunnar and his companions won't mind waitin' a bit longer, feller-me-lad." He pointed down the corridor, in the direction away from the main entrance. "Let's go have a gander at your samples."

"Skua, I've got so much fighting for attention in my skull right now I really couldn't care less about those cases."

"I don't want you to open up shop in front of me, lad," September spoke softly. "I've another reason for wantin' to get inside that warehouse."

Ethan eyed him curiously, but the big man had already turned and was moving down the hallway. Ethan hurried to keep up with him.

"Should be a heated tunnel taking us out to the storage complex, once we find the right lift. Warehousing should be above surface like everything else."

Warehouse Three was a utilitarian rectangle of windowless metal. September was right about its location. Despite the cold, it was cheaper to build above ground on Tran-ky-ky. Easier to put up a prefabricated structure that could withstand the wind than to excavate the permafrost and frozen ground.

The warehouse was insulated but not well heated inside. Ethan would have been shivering without his survival suit. A glance at a wall thermometer indicated the interior temperature was just above freezing. Outside, that would amount to a severe heat wave.

Two guards were posted at the warehouse doorway. When pressed for an explanation of their rather incongruous presence, one explained readily. "There've been stories about the natives stealing anything they can get their paws on." The man looked indifferent. "It's a cold job, but what the hell ain't on this world?"

"Have you ever caught a local stealing?" Ethan couldn't keep the anger out of his voice, and the guard noted it.

"Hey, look, I don't make policy, friend. I just enforce it, me and Jolene here." The other guard put a self-important hand on her beamer. "Let's see your authorization slip."

"Call the postmaster." Ethan wasn't feeling too cooperative. Maybe the Tran weren't the most outgoing people in the galaxy, but it didn't seem to him that anyone here was making much of an effort to learn otherwise.

"Oh, *dierd!* What's your name or crate code?" Ethan told him. "Yeah, your stuff's about four rows back, then turn right. Section twenty D." He stepped aside. September gave him a pleasant smile, his coguard a larger one. She didn't smile back.

"I don't understand this," Ethan grumbled as they made their way back through the tall shelves of crates and packages. "All the Tran we've encountered have been honest; in fact, I never heard Hunnar or anyone else even mention thievery in Wannome."

"They haven't had sufficient interaction with the corrupting influence of an acquisitive civilization," September commented half-seriously. They turned right at the fourth row.

19

Ethan found his three small seamless plastic crates. Only his sealkey could debond the molecular structure of the blue material forming the square shapes. The house of Malaika overseals looked intact and untampered with.

"I can pick them up anytime, Skua. What did you want to look at in here?"

"I'm already looking at it, lad." September's gaze was taking in the ceiling-high stacks of crates. "I've seen what I wanted to. Time to go."

They left the chilly chamber, passing under the hostile eyes of the guards. September didn't speak until they were nearly back to the main port entrance.

"Something bothered me about Xenaxis' comments concernin' the local trade," he explained. "Now that I've seen inside, it bothers me more. According to the markings on those crates, the trade going on here strikes me as awfully one-sided." -

"One-sided how?"

"Lad, those crates back there were new moldings, and the markings on them confirmed it. There's a lot more going off this world than is comin' in. Course, it's hard to measure how many duralloy or ceramisteel knives equal one carving. But I don't think the Tran know the value of their exports. How much is a hundred liters of water worth to a man in a desert? For that matter, how much is a hundred liters of dirt worth to a man in an ocean?

"Someone's making a lot more than an honest profit here, feller-me-lad. Your packages were the only ones I saw in the whole place with a merchant family crest on 'em. Someone else, maybe unlicensed, is running a fine little monopoly here, and cheating the Tran in the bargain. Of course, they don't think they're getting cheated, because they don't know any better. But *I* know, and it makes me mad, lad. These folks are my friends."

"Our friends," Ethan said quietly.

"Sure, our friends . . . for another five days."

"So what can we do about it? No, wait. I do represent the House of Malaika. I've never met the old man himself, but from what I know he's a bit more honest than many of the family heads. The injustice of the

20

situation here wouldn't move him to action. Profits would. I'm sure he'd be willing to come in and make the Tran a better deal."

"I'm thinking of something a bit different from spreading the lucre, lad. Tell you about it later." With that the giant lapsed into introspective silence as they made their way toward the entrance.

Just before reaching the doors they passed a pair of thranx. The meter-tall insects who with mankind co-dominated the Commonwealth were bundled almost beyond recognition in survival suits designed for their eight-limbed bodies. Even within the building they wore specially woven fur-lined sleeves over their feathery antennae. Apparently they were willing to forgo a loss of sensitivity for acceptable warmth.

Hailing from hot, humid worlds, the thranx were especially uncomfortable here on Tran-ky-ky. They walked past, muttering to each other in High Thranx. Ethan wondered what horrible misdemeanor the two had committed to be assigned to this world. Tran-ky-ky would be a fair realization of the thranx concept of Hell.

"Wonder what's going on?" September pointed outside as they passed the inner set of doors.

A crowd had gathered on the entryway ramp. There seemed to be an argument taking place in its center. The two men hurried through the outer doors.

It seemed as if a million lumens hit Ethan's eyes photons-on. The exterior doors were chemically tinted to make the outside glare bearable. Passing through, Ethan had neglected to pull down his goggles. Quickly he lowered them, opened his eyes. Gradually his sight returned and he could discern something besides white. It still felt as if someone had taken a file to his optic nerves. He lowered his face mask, not quite fast enough to prevent a couple of tears from freezing solid on his cheeks. The face shield melted them away.

Words of the argument reached him as he followed September forward into the crowd. Some of them he couldn't translate. The ones he could embarrassed him. A couple of Tran were expressing enormous dislike for one another.

One of them was Hunnar. The other Ethan didn't

recognize. The combatants faced each other in a small open space, exchanging imprecations with unfaltering volubility. Suaxus and Budjir stood nearby, fingering the hilts of their swords nervously, their teeth half showing. Those in the crowd nearest them were murmuring threateningly.

". . . off-spring of a crippled k'nith!" the strange Tran growled at Hunnar. Ethan noted with some surprise that the stranger was taller than the knight, though not nearly as muscular. In fact, he looked soft. Green and gold metal-fabric sashes were draped importantly across his chest in diagonal pattern, shoulder to hip below the dan.

Metal-fabric: imported trade goods, he knew. Strapped to the richly-dressed Tran's left leg was a short sword made of stelamic instead of the barely adequate local steel that formed Hunnar's blade. Its handle was made of intricately molded plastic.

"I will not fight with you." The stranger tried to muster some officious dignity. "I do not fight with . . ." The last word he used had an ambiguous meaning, one which could identify any outlander, or indicate the lowest form of peasant.

"I hight Sir Hunnar Redbeard," the knight replied with a half-snarl. "Conqueror of Sagyanak the Death, destroyer of the Horde, and knight of Wannome of Sofold."

"Never heard of either," someone in the crowd snickered. There was degrading laughter all around. Suaxus and Budjir tried to spot the quipster, failed.

"You will hear soon of it," Suaxus muttered. "It will make a fine inscription for your wandering time."

"Speaking of fertilizer," Hunnar continued, "that is undoubtedly what your family trades in, to obtain those shiny trappings you wear and that flashing new sword. So new, in fact, it seems not to have seen use. But then what use has one who dabbles in shit for a sword?"

The Tran opposite stiffened. Ethan knew that on Sofold, at least, natural wastes froze instantly as soon as they were exposed to the outside air. They were then collected by people who dealt in such produce and resold to various farmers, to be reheated and spread as fertilizer. The precarious island ecologies of Tran-ky-ky were kept in balance only by rigorous recycling of any available soil nutrients. The necessity of the profession, however, did not mitigate the offense of Hunnar's remark.

Everyone in the crowd recognized the insult. Snickers and comments gave way to angry mutterings and the movement of hands toward weapons. No adult Tran and few cubs were ever seen without at least a dirk attached to outer thigh. Though Hunnar and the squires were considerably more battle-trained and experienced than the mob of citizens, they were badly out-numbered.

September and Ethan stepped into the circle. "We are visitors here and we wish no trouble." Ethan studied the assemblage. "These three are our friends."

At that announcement a remarkable change came over the mob. The one Tran who had been arguing with Hunnar made apologetic gestures to Ethan. His manner changed abruptly from offensive to obsequious.

"May my cubs be taken by guttorbyn if I have offended you, sky outlanders! I did not know that these," he almost used the word for peasant again, "*others* were your personal friends. Had I so known, this would not have happened. I beg my family's forgiveness."

"Well," Ethan began, a bit confused by the unexpected speed of the other's apology, "I forgive you, if that's what you want."

"Tell Hunnar you're sorry." September grinned.

The brilliantly bedecked Tran stared at September. For an instant Ethan saw a glimmer in the native's eyes of something other than respect. It vanished quickly. "As the sky outlander desires." He turned to Hunnar.

"I ask forgiveness, friend." The last word was forced out like a recalcitrant belch.

"Finish it properly." Ethan threw the giant a warning look. They'd obtained an apology, for heaven's sake! What more did September want?

"My . . . my breath is your . . . your . . ." He looked

23

uncomfortably at September, avoiding the eyes of the crowd.

"Tell him," insisted September coolly.

Assuming a remarkable expression of distaste, the native put out both arms and approached Hunnar. Placing a hand on each of the knight's shoulders, he exhaled toward his face. "My breath is your warmth," he said quickly. Then he retreated into the crowd.

The sympathy of the onlookers, Ethan decided, lay with the departed and not with Hunnar. The knight wrinkled his broad muzzle. "*Pagh!* That smells of *falf* lard."

"Anyone else have anything to say?" September stared at the crowd. With murmurs and mutterings, the assembled citizens began to move off. Like crumbs falling from a cake, they fell away in different directions and smaller and smaller groups. The murmurs included distinct apologies, but all had been directed to Ethan and September.

"What was that all about?" Ethan asked the knight.

Hunnar looked upset. "We were waiting patiently for you and friend September. Local people were going back and forth from the building you entered. Many of them made comments to us. None were pleasant to hear, Ethan. Some would have caused blood to freeze in the streets of Wannome." He took a deep breath.

"But this is not Wannome and we did not wish to do something that might give you trouble or embarrassment. It was very hard, but we ignored all such comments. At least, we did so until that last *pash* made a reference upon my family line which could not be ignored.

"Had you not intervened, Ethan, I would have decorated the street with his insides."

"You are quick to forgive," Suaxus said softly. Hunnar turned and glared at him, but the squire looked back defiantly. Suaxus had always been fast to take offense, Ethan recalled.

"We hardly intervened," he said, trying to mollify any discomfort Hunnar might feel for not having fought his opponent. "We were ready to fight alongside you if need be. Why did they all simply apologize and melt away as they did?"

September began scratching the earring-decorated ear. "I'm not sure myself, lad. None of the Tran in Wannome acted like that toward us. They were polite, but independent."

Hunnar gestured at the locals chivaning to and from the building. "Not warriors." He said it disdainfully.

"Skua, did you notice the other's clothing?" Ethan asked.

"No. All I was watching was his face and sword arm."

"He was wearing metal-fabric sashes and other off-world decorations, and his sword was stelamic."

"Apologetic in proportion to commerce. Interesting." September looked thoughtful.

"They think," Suaxus said bitterly, "they are superior to us because of their association with your people here."

"That's ridiculous." Ethan felt acutely uncomfortable. "Why should they?"

"It's happened often enough in our own past, lad." September divided his attention equally between Ethan and Suaxus as he spoke. "When the great, rich explorers from beyond, wherever beyond happened to be at the time, set up a trading post, the local natives were quick to consolidate the trade monopoly on their own behalf. Nor were they averse to showing off their trade wealth in front of their excluded brethren.

"So though someone else is making the big money off the Tran-ky-ky trade, the Arsudunites are quite content with their own small corner on the market. It makes them feel big and important, just as Suaxus claims."

Budjir was as quiet as his companion squire was talkative, but when his spit hit the ground it possessed a certain nonverbal eloquence admirable in its conciseness.

They started back to the ship. The three Tran kept slightly to themselves, moving just ahead of the humans.

"I said inside the port, lad, that something else has got to be done to open up this world so all the locals benefit." He nodded back in the direction of the port

25

complex. "That little altercation back there between Hunnar and one citizen is going to form the pattern for inter-Tran relationships unless this local monopoly is broken. Both of 'em. The one the Arsudunites enjoy, and the bigger one behind it."

Ethan slipped slightly, just catching his balance on the frozen ground paralleling the icepath. "You told me you had something in mind. Me, I'd set up another trading post with shuttlecraft facilities somewhere else, maybe on Sofold. From there trade could be conducted that would be fair to all Tran, giving them fair value for their goods while still making an honest profit in return."

September shook his white-maned head. "No offense against our friends up ahead," and he gestured at Hunnar and the squires, "but as much as we may've come to like 'em personally, inside they're no different than any other Tran. Pretty soon Sofold would be just like Arsudun, jealous of its little monopoly. Oh, maybe Hunnar wouldn't go for it, but there're plenty of merchants in Wannome who'd fight to preserve it.

"No, something else is needed. Something that'll prevent any fiscal insularity from even getting established. And something that'll just incidentally slice this present unfair setup into pieces the size of those the *Slanderscree*'s runners cut out o' the ice.

"Young feller-me-lad, the Tran need Commonwealth representation."

Ethan halted. "That's impossible, Skua! It would've been done by now if survey had thought it possible. Sure, associate membership would be wonderful for them. They could deal with traders on a world-wide basis, spread the wealth and advances they could obtain evenly across the entire planet. But it's just not feasible."

"Better to try than to leave them open to the kind of exploitation that's goin' on here, lad. I think it can be done. First we've got to talk to the local Commissioner. "But you're leaving in a few days. No need to worry yourself about something you're convinced is impossible anyway."

"I've got a few days, like you say." Ethan resumed

26

walking. "It won't give me a depressex if I tag along and see the Commissioner with you."

The office of the Resident Planetary Commissioner was located in the main administration building, north-west of the port complex. Privately, Ethan thought it too ornate for a world where humanx population and interests were comparatively slight.

Five single-story buildings projected outward like the spokes of a wheel from the central structure, a three story pyramid of white and black stone done in checkerboard pattern broken only by windows. The five subsidiary structures were living quarters for the administrative staff.

The main entrance to the pyramid was another double-door arrangement with the halfway climate maintained between for interaction between human and Tran. That section was smaller than the one they'd previously encountered, and logically so. There was little need for Tran to come here, since all trade and commerce were handled at the port.

Inside the circular main lobby a small, glowing directory hung suspended in midair. The Commisioner's office was located on the third floor. They had to wait their turn at the small lift.

At the top they discovered that the Commissioner's suite *was* the third floor. They stepped from the lift directly into busy outer offices occupied by a great many large machines and two subsized humans, one male, one female. No one else was in sight.

Ethan's first impression of excessive ornateness was reinforced by the carpet. A glance showed his trained eye that it was strictly luxury material, an import—probably from Mantis or maybe Long Tunnel. Genetic manipulation had produced a natural substance with the look and feel of grass, the resistance of rubber, and the durability of dilyonite. The result was a pleasant-smelling and remarkably buoyant floor covering. It was very expensive. And though he wasn't conversant with diplomatic purchasing guidelines, somehow he didn't think that *verdidion* weave was standard decor for minor offworld offices, even that of a Resident Commissioner.

A young man who looked as if he could stand a

27

dozen good meals occupied the desk nearest the lift. His fingers danced over and across machinery and consoles with controlled jerkiness.

Ethan's eyes rose ceilingward, encountered the expected mosaic. Four circles of equal size met to form a crude square. The two nearest him were marked with stylized representations of continents, showing both hemispheres of Terra. Tangent to these two, the other pair had similar maps inlaid. These represented the two hemispheres of Hivehom, the home world of humanity's partner in the Commonwealth, the insectoid thranx.

Centered among these four larger circles and tangent to all of them was a single smaller circle. A vertical hourglass of bright blue, symbolizing Terra, was crossed by a horizontal hourglass of brilliant green signifying Hivehom. They formed the shape of the ancient Maltese cross, and where they merged the colors blended into aquamarine, the signet hue of the United Church. Since this was a Commonwealth and not a Church installation, the cross was surrounded by a field of crimson, the color of the Commonwealth.

The straw man seemed to take notice of them. He turned, greeted them indifferently, hands still jerking and darting as if hunting for a rest never to be granted.

"May I help you, sirs?" His eyes narrowed slightly then and he concentrated a touch more intently on them. "I don't think I know either of you." He had assumed a faintly disapproving air. "I thought I knew everyone in the outpost."

"We didn't arrive via the usual channels," September said.

Ethan tried to make himself sound important. "We'd like to see the Resident Commissioner."

The man wasn't impressed. "Concerning?" He spoke to Ethan, but his gaze remained fixed on September.

Ethan thought a moment. "Possibly crucial developments involving native affairs."

"What kind of developments? Are you two attached to the xenology team here?" A hand brushed back straight blond hair, rubbed at the side of a small sharp nose, moved down to pull at the hem of his shirt and

28

work up the other side to brush once again at the unruly hair.

Actually, the itch was concentrated not in hair, nose, or shirt: Instead, it was permanently located in the man's mind. Since he couldn't scratch that very well, he settled as did many others for rubbing parts of his anatomy that had nothing to do with his condition.

"We'd rather tell it to the Commissioner," said Ethan, trying his best not to sound difficult.

"Do you have an appointment? I don't recall any appointments scheduled for this afternoon."

"Blessed!" snapped the woman at the other desk, speaking for the first time. She was a stout lady who looked slightly older than September, and she sounded exasperated with her colleague. "If they're strangers here, then they must have come in on that big native ship." The straw man showed no reaction. "Didn't you hear about it?"

"I've been at my desk for the last several days, Eulali. You know I don't listen much to post gossip."

"No wonder you never learn anything," she sighed. "Anything they have to say could be important. Never mind that they came in on that ship. Just the fact that they're strangers."

"Okay," the man replied doubtfully. "I guess they can see Trell. But I won't break procedure."

"You and your damn procedure." Eulali turned back to her own complex instrumentation resuming her work.

"Procedure says you've got to have an appointment," the man insisted, rubbing the other side of his nose.

"Oh, all right." Ethan couldn't keep the impatience from his voice. "We'll make an appointment."

Turning back to the console before him, the man punched a button. Scribbled words appeared on a display screen. "Don't get excited. I said I wouldn't break procedure, and I won't. You can have an appointment for . . . five minutes from now be okay?" He smiled. It changed his face completely.

"That'll do," Ethan admitted.

"The nature of your business involves native affairs, right?" Ethan nodded once. "Names please?"

"Ethan Frome Fortune."

"Your home world or planet of origin?"

"Terra."

"Profession?"

"Salesman, general manufactured goods, small, representing the House of Malaika."

"Thanks." He glanced perfunctorily over at September. "Name?"

"Skua September." The words were grunted out, reluctantly.

"World of origin or birth?"

"I don't know."

"Now look here . . ."

"I'm telling you honestly, son. I don't know."

"Well, what does it say on your cardmeter?"

"It identifies me as a Commonwealth citizen. That's all."

"I've never seen an ident like that." The skinny interrogator chewed his lower lip, moved to tug the hem of his shirt and decided not to. "Profession?"

"Free-lance fehdreyer."

Again the youth hesitated. "That's not a Terranglo word, is it?"

"No, it's not a Terranglo word," September assured him.

"What is it in Symbospeech?"

"There's no Symbospeech direct equivalent. It's a phonetic rescription of an old Terran word from a language called yi'ish."

"Oh well, it doesn't matter anyway."

"When do we go in?" Ethan eyed the large wooden door nervously. September's replies were likely to provoke the skittish clerk if they continued much longer.

"I'll check." He touched another switch. "Sir?"

"I've been monitoring since you keyed me, Avence," a rich baritone responded. "They can come in. Be careful, Mr. September. You may have to duck. Our ceilings are designed for average human beings and thranx, not athletes or sifters."

Ethan looked startled, but September simply smiled, pointing to a spot in the ceiling between the Commonwealth symbols and the top of the wooden door.

"Don't worry. I'm used to duckin'. And I'm neither athlete nor sifter."

They rose and walked to the entrance. September's finger continued to point until Ethan spotted the spy-eye in the ceiling.

"Then he's been listening to and watching us the whole time?"

"Naturally, feller-me-lad. What do you expect from a good politician?"

The pyramid building had three sides, the room they entered three corners and walls. Both exterior walls were perfectly transparent, providing a sweeping and by now familiar view of the harbor and the city of Arsudun backed against uneven, white-clad hills. Between hills and harbor the steep-roofed houses looked like a vast spill of gray paint.

Much to Ethan's surprise, the usual desk was absent from the room's furnishings. Several large couches in freeform design were positioned around the three-sided chamber. Each was covered in a different variety of local fur. Without knowing anything about their durability, Ethan tried to estimate their worth on the open market based on color and thickness alone. It was substantial. Any life-supporting world as cold as Tran-ky-ky was bound to produce some extraordinary fur-bearing creatures. The treated skins in the room gave ample proof of riches no synthetics could match.

"I'm Jobius Trell," the room's sole inhabitant told them, moving to shake his visitor's hands in turn. He was tall, quite tall, standing midway in height between Ethan and September. His mouth seemed positioned naturally and permanently in a gentle, almost boyish grin. That saved him the necessity of worrying about when to smile in ticklish situations. Blue eyes, a square face, small if unlikely dimpled chin, and thick gray hair combed straight back. Ethan estimated his weight at around a hundred kilos, distributed on the build of an ordinary athlete. That is, one blessed with no athletic ability other than what was provided by more than usual size and weight, coupled with average coordination.

Between the Commissioner and September, Ethan

31

felt dwarfed in the room. A gesture directed the visitors to one couch. Trell took the recliner opposite. Ethan could now pick out numerous controls and devices, even thick tape files, set cleverly into the furniture.

A casual wave at September, and Trell spoke. "You noticed my small preview eye, Mr. September. Have you been familiar with espionage work and equipment in the past?"

"Nope. But I've been in the offices of a lot of politicians."

The Commissioner not only didn't take offense, his laugh sounded quite genuine. "So there's a sense of humor floating around inside that enormous frame of yours. Good. Let's see if I can save us some time." Leaning back into the couch, he ticked off points on his fingers as he talked.

"One: I've already heard the report you gave the postmaster, so I know everything you've told him. Rest assured I agree with him completely on expediting your passage off this world. After what you've been through, it's the very least I, as Resident Commonwealth representative, can do. You must've had a terrible time of it among the primitives."

"Not as terrible as everyone seems to think." September spoke easily, inviting challenge.

Trell chose not to accept, or perhaps didn't perceive the giant's comment as challenging. "Two, that ship you arrived in. I've had tapes made, solidos formed. Quite a piece of engineering." His voice altered, became slightly more intense as he inquired, "Where did the natives get the duralloy for five runners of that size? Surely the locals haven't mastered nuclear metallurgy somewhere out in the snow?"

"No." Ethan explained. "They cut them as best they could, with our help, from the hull of our wrecked lifeboat."

That apparently satisfied Trell. "I suspected something like that. While our Commonwealth charges here aren't stupid, they're much longer on muscle than brains."

"Yes, that's true," said September.

Ethan shook inside. Instead of the expected protest

32

at this slur on their friends, September had reacted with agreement and a beatific smile.

He thought furiously. Since September did nothing without good reason, it followed that he had one for concurring with the Commissioner. As Trell nodded in response, he saw that the Commissioner had been waiting for precisely the answer the big man had given him. But if their purpose in coming here was to convince the Commissioner that the Tran were worthy of associate Commonwealth status, they weren't off to a very good beginning.

Or were they? Come to think of it, reacting emotionally instead of with reason would be the worst way to get the Commissioner on their side. "Longer on muscle than brains, but not stupid", was an evaluation of the Tran with which Sir Hunnar himself might readily have agreed.

"Native affairs, you mentioned?" Trell looked at Ethan.

He rose. "We spent quite a number of months among them, sir." Pacing the plushly carpeted room, he felt himself relax. As always, he was most at ease when punching a product he believed in. He believed in the Tran.

"Environment and ecology have conspired against the natives, sir. They're widely dispersed, forced to cling to scattered, often barely accessible islands for survival. While they've adapted well to this harsh climate, their numbers don't seem to be great. I don't know why, but they aren't as numerous as they should be. That also works to their disadvantage.

"And yet," he continued enthusiastically, "Considering their extreme climate they've not only staved off extinction, but have advanced to a fair level of civilization. Their technology is unusually advanced in certain areas, such as iceship building and cold weather farming. Races inhabiting more pleasant worlds have not done as well"

"I agree with you." Ethan stopped pacing, astonished. First Trell described the Tran as having more muscle than brains, and now he was all but concurring with Ethan's optimistic assessment of their accomplishments.

33

"Well then?"

"Well then what, Mr. Fortune?" Trell was watching him closely.

Ethan was forced to discard all the arguments he had mustered mentally to build a case for the Tran's abilities and jump ahead. "If you agree with my assessment, sir, consider the benefits to this world of associate Commonwealth membership. They could send delegates to Council as observers. They'd learn a great deal and would be eligible for all kinds of government assistance for which they presently can't qualify. That would raise the planetary standard of living, which in turn would . . ."

Trell raised a hand, and Ethan stopped short. "Please, Mr. Fortune." The Commissioner's gaze switched from Ethan to September, then back again. "Don't you two realize that I would have been working for that very thing myself? Despite the natives' obvious drawbacks, I admire them very much." He gestured at his office.

"Look around you. I work here, relax here. Every item in this room not of an electronic nature is of local manufacture. The couches and chairs you rest upon, the decorative arts on walls and tables, everything. Personally I would enjoy nothing better than nominating my charges here for associate status. But," and he shook an admonishing finger at Ethan, "though I agree with you where the locals' scientific and artistic progress is concerned, let us objectively consider their handicaps. Social progress has lagged far, far behind everything else here." He stood, unconsciously exchanging pacing territory with Ethan, who resumed his seat. Except that Trell moved straight to the nearest window-wall and stared out over town and harbor.

"*You* wish the Tran to have associate Commonwealth status. *I* wish them to have it." He glanced back over a shoulder. "Which Tran, Mr. Fortune, do you refer to?"

Ethan started to reply, found his thoughts tangled by facts, and said nothing. September stared at him, silent and unhelpful . . .

III

"I see the problem has struck home." Trell turned from the window and the view beyond. "Arsudun was chosen to be the site of the Commonwealth outpost here because it was one of the larger islands located by first survey, and because it has a protected harbor which helps shield us here from the stronger winds off the ice ocean. However, further surveys could, I am certain, turn up forty other locations of equivalent suitability for Brass Monkey. Arsudun was lucky, not superior.

"Tell me . . . would it be fair to your friends from . . .?"

"From Sofold," September told him.

"From Sofold. Would it be fair to them if all the delegates from Tran-ky-ky to Council were to be elected or appointed from Arsudun?"

"Of course not," Ethan put in immediately. "All would vote and . . ." His voice trailed off.

Trell slumped back into his couch across from them. "Vote, Mr. Fortune? I don't know if there's a word in the Tran dialects for voting."

"They elect Landgraves from time to time," Ethan countered.

"Yes. When the offspring of former rulers are unacceptable. But you have a point, if what you say is true. I myself have never ventured from Arsudun. But if the sociologists who go out with the scouting parties are agreed on anything, it's the Tran's unwavering suspicion of his neighbor. They are belligerent and jingoistic." He shook his head slowly.

"No. I'm sorry, Mr. Fortune. If the Tran are to claim associate status in the Commonwealth, they must present such a claim in some united fashion. There is no planetary government to deal with here. In fact," he leaned forward, spoke with seeming ex-

35

citement, "I won't even require that. A dominant regional government would be sufficient, one comprised of a fairly diverse population and reasonable number of city-states. If that existed, then many of these other futile feudal states would fall into line. But you're not going to find any such organization on this world. You're just not.

"Hostility is a way of life on Tran-ky-ky. Not only don't the inhabitants of one state care a k'nith's hindquarters for their neighbors, what about these nomadic warrior groups?"

"We know about them," Ethan admitted, thinking back to the siege of Sofold by the horde of Sagyanak the Death in which he and September and the others had participated in the destruction of that ancient enemy of Hunnar's people.

"They're entitled by the Commonwealth charter to fair representation also." Trell stared expectantly at Ethan, as if the outcome of the discussion had already been decided. "Can you see the island dwellers allying themselves politically and culturally with those blood-hungry migratory bandits?" He shook his head again.

"No, I'm afraid not, gentlesirs. In a few thousand years, maybe even in a few hundred, they might mature enough to exchange breath with all their neighbors. But not now." He threw up both hands in an unnecessarily melodramatic gesture.

"As things stand now there is no way I in my position as Resident Commissioner can recommend them for associate membership. Or even for wardship. They are too independent and advanced to qualify as charity cases. A large regional government even—but these bellicose little island states, no. It's not workable or fair." He rose. Ethan and September did likewise.

"I thank you for your interest, gentlesirs. I think that on reflection you'll have to admit that personal emotion has played some part in your reasoning." He was chiding them gently. "You've spent considerable time among these people. It's only natural you'd want to help them. First, however, they must help themselves.

"Your ship will insert orbit in a couple of days, I believe. I'll be at the port to see you off personally.

If there's anything I can do for you in the meantime, any service I can perform, please don't hesitate to call on me."

"Thank you for your time, Mr. Commissioner." Ethan didn't try to hide his disappointment. They shook hands all around once more.

Trell spoke as they were halfway out the door. "You'll stay in the Administrator's quarters, of course. At government expense."

"That's right kind of you, sir." September smiled back at him. "Considerin' the distance and dangers our hosts have brought us through, however, I think they'd be downright insulted if we didn't spend our last few days with them. You understand."

"Of course." Ethan couldn't tell if Trell was displeased by this announcement or not. "Anytime you change your minds, want to switch from the barbaric to the civilized, your accommodations will be waiting for you."

"Thank you again," Ethan said, closing the door behind them.

Jobius Trell watched the door for a minute, then resumed his seat on the couch. Fur tickled the back of his neck and he shifted his position slightly. His mind was occupied by something other than the room's decor. Eventually he touched a nearby control, spoke into the room.

"Note: discuss visitor's psychoverbal orientation with compudex file. Compare intensity gradient with recording of conversation with portmaster Xenaxis. Request computation of likely action tendencies, based on available data."

Trell felt better after that, well enough to return to his real work. Always better to keep up with what he was supposed to be doing, so he could enjoy his apolitical machinations to the fullest.

Though the breeze off the harbor was comparatively mild, Ethan felt chilled through the artificial skin of his survival suit. Several local Tran sped past on the icepath they were paralleling. None turned to gawk. Humans were an accepted sight here on Arsudun.

"I guess that's that, Skua. Give him his due, his

37

arguments against granting status to Tran-ky-ky were strong."

"They sure were, feller-me-lad. For instance, he was right when he said we were emotionally involved in this matter. What he didn't add was that he's equally involved. More than emotionally, I'll wager. He said so with his face and his modukeys."

"Modukeys?"

"Every word can be pronounced a lot of ways, lad. Each way carries an emotional key. I can recognize a few of 'em. Enough to tell me our friend Trell wouldn't be too disappointed if the Tran stay just as divided and combative as they are now." He had the facemask of his suit up. September liked to have freedom to grimace. He did so now.

"Tell me, lad. Who would stand most to profit from the present situation, from keeping Tran-ky-ky backward and unrepresented in Council? Who could keep a nice, private eye on every bit of off-planet trade and regulate it to suit his own personal accounts?"

"I didn't get that impression from Trell at all, Skua." Ethan kicked at the icepath, sent a few pale splinters flying. "That's a strong accusation to make against a Resident Commissioner."

"There's an informal law, lad, about political appointees. The smaller the post, the less often they're inspected, and the more opportunity there is for foolin' around with the books." He clapped Ethan on the back, nearly knocking him down. "Wouldn't be the first time good manners have shielded a larcenous heart." He frowned. "Course, he's right about this feudal setup. We'll have to do something about that."

Ethan stopped, the snow swirling around him trying to find a way to penetrate his survival suit. "Do something about it? We can't do anything about it. What are you thinking?"

"I'm thinking, young feller-me-lad, that we've several days left to think about it . . ."

"Three there are it is not possible to do." Sir Hunnar Redbeard spoke with conviction as he gazed at humans and Tran seated around the long galley table of the *Slanderscree*.

"It is not possible to kill a stavanzer. It is not possible to stand against a westwind Rif. And it is not possible to keep the Tran from warring among themselves." He turned his feline stare on Ethan. His voice was as cold and asssured as the slight storm howling outside the ship, making squeaking sounds in the cracks between rafters and planks.

"What you propose, friend Ethan, cannot be imagined, far less can it be done. A union of islands, a confederation of states? A council of Landgraves?" His triangular ears switched nervously. "More likely it would be for water to run freely across the seas."

"It *has* to be done, Hunnar." Ethan was half pleading with the assembled knights. "Don't you understand how things have been set up here? The people of Arsudun and more importantly, their leaders, have a monopoly on all off-world trade and information. They profit tremendously, unfairly from it. It should be shared equally among all the Tran."

"Aye, the metal," a gruff voice added. Eyes turned in its direction.

Balavere Longax was Sofold's most respected living warrior. An older, stockier version of Hunnar, his gray fur turning to white in patches, he commanded silence on the rare occasions when he chose to speak. Though less excited than those of his colleagues, his words carried considerably more weight.

"The metal. Never have I seen so much metal as the people of Arsudun possess. Nor do they seem deserving of it." That brought irritated murmurs of agreement from several other members of the crew. "Not only their weapons, my friends, but yea too their household implements, water pots, and others are pure metal."

Ethan nodded enthusiastically. "And they're still being cheated, I think. Stelamic is cheaper than duralloy."

September pushed back his chair, making the floorboards creak. "Hunnar, if the Tran will spill blood for metal, why are you so damned sure they won't cooperate to get it?"

"It is considered degrading to cooperate with people from a less noble state," the knight replied, as if that explained everything. "Do you remember when

39

Sagyanak's Horde assaulted Wannome? The she-devil's tribe was a threat to all states. How much help was volunteered to us? How much aid did our neighbors provide to help fight the common enemy?" He sat down, mumbled, "Profit is not sufficient reason for forgetting old hatreds and suspicions. Your own Commonwealth-thing, there is no word for it in our language. The closest I can come is family."

"That's just how you have to start thinking of all Tran," Ethan interrupted excitedly. "You're a family. That's all any race is, an extended family. Like it or not, Tran-ky-ky is destined to take its place as a member of the Commonwealth. You can't go back to Wannome and look up at the night sky from your homes without realizing you're a part of something much bigger and grander than Sofold. You might as well gain the advantages that are yours by right, *now.*" A little out of breath and a bit embarrassed at the strength of his unexpected polemic, Ethan sat back down.

"Advantages which should be spread among all Tran," September added more quietly, but just as emphatically.

"My good friends with whom I share my warmth, I recognize the truth of your words." Hunnar looked despondent. "Would that I could will the spirit of this world otherwise. But the Tran are good at arguing with knives, not with words."

"Then you must achieve the same end with knives." Colette du Kane entered the room. She waddled gracefully to the far end of the long wooden table, placed both hands on it and leaned forward. "If reason and logic aren't enough to cement this confederation you must make, then do it with knives. The end is justified by what you will gain." She threw Ethan and September a rather disdainful look.

"Only profits have so far been mentioned, material things. Commonwealth membership will force you to mature as a people. Soon you won't need knives to discuss with. But if you fail," and she paused for emphasis, "you'll remain just as you are, frozen in ability and evolution as well as in daily life. You'll stay ig-

40

norant farmers and fighters and your cubs will grow up just as inefficient and deprived as you all are."

Wind hammered insistently at doorways and portholes, the only sound in the room.

Eventually Hunnar spoke, chosing his words carefully. "You have ventured enough insults to result in a shortened tongue, woman. Yet you did so, I believe, in the hope of benefiting us. What you say is truthspeak." Several of the other nobles now looked askance at Hunnar, then at one another. There were some unhappy mutterings and a few threatening looks in Colette's direction.

"Listen to you all." Ethan thought he had seen someone else behind Colette when she stepped through the cabin portal. Now that other person also entered.

Elfa Kurdagh-Vlata looked like a bewhiskered amazon in cloak and light robe. Her translucent dan caught the back light of oil lamps beyond and turned to curved sheets of orange flame when she raised her arms.

"You confirm what the human woman says every time you speak. She calls you ignorant and in response to her reasoning words you make stupid threatening sounds, like mewling cubs caught stealing vegetables."

"We grant the wisdom of her speaking," grumbled one of the other nobles at the table. "It was the manner of such speaking." While Elfa was the inheritor of the Landgrave's title, the noble had used no honorific in addressing her, Ethan noted. Such informality between rulers and ruled was one of the Tran's most heartening characteristics.

"But would Phulos-Tervo or any of our other border rulers do likewise?" the noble finished bluntly. There was murmur of agreement from around the table.

"Perhaps not." Elfa conceded the point readily. "But a total stranger might. Phulos-Tervo would be suspicious of anything my father might agree to. A stranger would know him not." She gestured at the humans in the room, pointing at each in turn.

"Here are our offworld friends, proof of the truths we will seek to convince others of. No one can dis-

41

pute their existence. Therefore it may be that others will accept their words as have we."

"That is possible," agreed a swaggering knight named Heso-idn. "If they will come with us." He eyed Ethan expectantly.

"Oh, I'll be staying." Milliken Williams sounded surprised that any other possiblity could be seriously considered. The ancient Tran seated next to him spoke through a white beard.

"Sir Williams and I still have much to discourse upon to one another. He could not leave now."

"Of course I couldn't." Williams' guileless enthusiasm did much to boost the confidence of the assembled Tran as he gazed blithely around the table. "You're much more interesting than any of my old pupils, and there's more here for me to learn. I couldn't possibly leave."

"You must realize, all of you, that as an educated citizen of fair achievement, citizen Williams is giving up a vote." September sounded as solemn as he could. "That is something no qualified inhabitant of the Commonwealth does lightly, I can assure you."

"What of you, friend September?" asked Hunnar.

"Oh, I guess I'll hang around a while yet." He picked at his teeth with a triangular fork left from the last meal. "Can't say much for your climate, but the food's good, the liquor is first class, and the company's agreeable. Can't ask for much more than that. Besides, nobody asks me too many questions." He turned to his right. "What about you, young feller-me-lad?"

Ethan found he was the object of everyone's attention, found himself wishing he was beneath the table instead of seated at its side. He gazed into his lap, fumbled for a reply.

"I don't know, Skua . . . Hunnar." His mouth felt like someone had suddenly substituted glue for saliva. "I have other interests, other obligations. There's my contracted job and . . ."

"All is understandable, friend Ethan." Hunnar smiled that simple Trannish smile, without showing his teeth.

For some reason, Hunnar's timely words of empathy made Ethan feel even worse. Wasn't he the sophisticated member of the advanced galactic civilization? Then why should he feel so devoid of worthwhile thoughts and meaningful feelings?

"Even if I could go with you, I'd only slow you down." Colette du Kane looked back toward the doorway. "My father's in our own cublicle, asleep. I can't turn him loose to manage the family affairs, not while he journeys from one island of sanity to another across an ocean of senility. There'd be too many who'd take advantage of him. Someone is obligated to take care of business. That obligation devolves upon my shoulders—and I've got the shoulders for it."

Even the Tran understood that joke, though Colette's width was no greater than the average native's.

"And there could be other obligations."

Ethan did not look up, but he knew exactly where she was looking when she said those words.

"I will tell you all this. If you have the good sense and the ability to organize enough of a government to qualify for associate Commonwealth status, then the House of du Kane will establish itself on Tran-ky-ky immediately and will treat fairly with all who treat fairly with it."

Elfa made a sign signifying agreement and compliments. The women had had run-ins before, both in Wannome and on the ship; but they could and had put their personal differences and feelings aside when logic dictated. Ethan wondered if the males in the room could do as well.

"It is settled then." Hunnar assumed a pose expressing determination and challenge. "We will try," he told Ethan, "because we believe in you and in what you say, friend Ethan. You have never lied to us in the past. I do not believe you lie to us now."

There was a rumble like that of an underground transport as chairs slid back from the table and the various knights, nobles, and squires broke up into smaller discussion groups. Some talked loudly and with considerable animation while others chatted in hushed tones. Every so often one or two of the debaters would exit through the door opening onto the deck, admitting the planet's eternal participant in all conversations—the wind.

Ethan left early, anxious for the solitude offered by his own cublicle. In a few days he could trade the poorly warmed box he shared with September for the cycle-heated atmosphere of a starship cabin. It was strange that the prospect no longer excited him the way it had when the *Slanderscree* had first entered Arsudun harbor.

Something like a hot summer breeze touched him on the shoulder, unnervingly warm and light in the chill air of the ship's corridor. Whirling, he found himself staring down at Colette du Kane. Behind him, the voices of the arguing Tran, September's intermittent bellow, William's gentle but persuasive murmur—all faded and merged to form a distant background hum. Small crystals of emerald focused unblinkingly on his own eyes, verdant craters in that moon face. Despite the survival suit face mask her pink flesh had been tanned umber from occasional exposure to Tranky-ky's harsh arctic sun.

For just a moment, he had a glimpse of sinuous beauty writhing to escape that gland-trapped coffin of fat. Only through the eyes could that exquisite self impinge on the world.

"Are you staying or coming?" No hint of coquetry there, no mock-embarrassed lowering of lashes. There was no room for it in a personality founded on bluntness. Though the door to the deck outside was closed, he felt something curl 'round him anyway, slowing his circulation, chilling his guts.

"Well? We've gotten along well these past weeks."

"I know, Colette." For one as perceptive as Ethan knew this woman to be, that should be answer enough. She elaborated anyway, rushing, hurrying her words so as to be rid of them as fast as possible.

"I asked you to marry me. Are you going to, or are you staying here?"

"I—I don't know. I suppose I need more time to think. I'm not stalling you, Colette, I'm telling you the truth."

She snorted derisively. "Every man I've ever known concluded any bad talk with that last homily."

44

"I'll tell you before the shuttle lifts, I promise." He grabbed her shoulders, held her as long as he dared. She was warm.

"If that's the way it has to be."

He let her go. "That's the way it has to be."

She forced a slight smile. "I guess that's better than an outright refusal. See you." She turned, flounced out the door. A gust of wind brought a few ice flakes swirling inward, dying even as they struck his face.

Two Tran knights followed her out, conversing easily as they ignored the bitter cold. To the natives they were reposing in a sheltered harbor, where they could stroll about outside almost naked. Only Ethan and the other humans had to hurry into their cabins before unprotected skin froze solid and crisp as a honeycomb.

It was an indication of the readiness with which the local Tran had accepted humanxkind and manifestations of its advanced technology that the natives in the shuttleport did not look up in awe when the shuttle's braking engines fired and it settled snugly into its berthing pit, tight as a snail withdrawing into its shell.

As the engines died, the internal supercooling elements built into the skin of the delta-winged atmospheric craft went to work. Soon hull and engines themselves were cool enough to touch.

Suspensors moved out from waiting bays. Businesslike words were exchanged between the shivering shuttlepilot and the landing crew. Packages and crates began to move from concealed storage bins into the shuttle, while in return the tiny ship gave birth to a multitude of smaller sealed shapes.

Local handicrafts were traded off for knives and lamps and stelamic weaponry. Fragments of poor quality but still immensely valuable green ozmidine bought radios and tridees and hand communicators. Ethan thought back to the immense volcano known to the Tran as The-Place-Where-The-Earth's-Blood-Burns and the cavern filled with ozmidine they'd discovered inside. He wondered what whoever was dominating the local trade would have thought of that breathtaking deposit of the ultraprecious green gem.

Nearby, Hellespont du Kane began chatting cheer-

45

fully with the physician the starship captain had thoughtfully sent down in the shuttle to attend his unexpected, famous passenger. Colette stood watching him, responding perfunctorily to September's gruff and somewhat obscene good-bye and Williams' more polite, deferential one.

Then there was nothing else to do, no one else to talk to, and Ethan found himself walking over. She moved to meet him.

Several silent moments passed. Perhaps the fact that his mind was now made up enabled him to match her stare more resolutely.

"How's your father?" he finally said lamely.

"As well as can be expected." She had to force herself to blunt her natural sharpness. "I keep trying to get him to consent to a body switch . . . he refuses additional revivifications. He won't do it. I don't think it's a death wish. The psychostics say it's not. But he won't agree to it even when he's senile, let alone during his occasional bursts of full lucidity. Keeps telling me it's time I took over, that he's held the reins long enough."

"You are ready to take over, Colette." Ethan spoke softly yet with enthusiasm. It was extremely difficult to sell Colette on herself. "I know how the merchant families work. I have to. I work for one myself."

"Ready or not, I have to." Her reply was so soft it was hard to believe it came from her. "What do you have to do, Ethan?"

He smiled. It wasn't easy. "I'm sorry, Colette. Truly I am."

"First they say they're telling the truth, then they always say they're sorry."

"Colette, . . ." Ethan fought for words. "I'm not a teller, I'm a told. You were raised, trained to give orders. I've matured learning to take them. Advice I can offer, but never orders. I don't think I'd be any good at it. I'd mess up any executive position you gave me, and then you'd be forced to cover for me. You'd have to explain me to my colleagues, the really qualified executives and compusymbs." He shook his head dolefully. "I couldn't handle the kind of snickering I'd be subjected to. And I won't accept a life as an ineffectual parasite."

"You have a peculiar conception of what being mated means." She sounded almost desperate without appearing to beg. "You could do whatever you wanted to, anything at all. Travel, hobbies . . . it doesn't even have to be with me." The gaze lowered just a little. "You could . . . even have other women on the side, if you so desired. I'd fix it so you could afford the best." She looked up again.

"You're a good man. You could do what you wish, so long as you . . ." she hesitated, "came back to me."

"No, Colette. I have something I have to see through, here."

For an instant something flared in her eyes. "It's that muscular teddy bear, isn't it?"

"No." Ethan's denial gained strength from his honest, obvious surprise. "Elfa's not a factor. I don't know what she sees in me, but she's a member of another race."

"That hasn't stopped people in the past," she countered accusingly.

"It stops me. Where Elfa Kurdagh-Vlata is concerned, any interest other than anthropological is strictly one-sided. Her side. I gave you the real reason. I could never be a professional student, professional traveler, professional hobbyist. Or a professional husband."

She seemed ready to leave, then grasped him so suddenly and hard he had to fight to regain his balance. She broke away just enough to plead, speaking so softly no one but Ethan could have heard. He found himself momentarily mesmerized by those metal-bright green eyes.

"You're the first man I ever met who treated me like a human being. You were good to me, and you were honest with me. I know I'm ugly."

"You're anything but that, Colette."

Her smile was full of pain. "For months I was the only human woman around. I enjoyed the isolation. I'm conversant enough with physiopsychology to read in your eyes my loss of five kilos for every month of that isolation. As soon as we reached any outpost of

47

human civilization you'd see me for what I am, for what no doctor can correct. It's happened since we've been here, at this outpost. I'm obese, sarcastic, and bitter to the point of dissolution."

"The last two you need to survive the important position you're going to assume," Ethan told her. "As for the first, that's an image you have of yourself." He thought of something September had told him. "Physical shape and attractiveness have little to do with each other. In the dark, all mankind looks alike.

"No, the reasons I can't marry you have to do with our mental makeup, not our physical."

She let go of him. His arms would show red where she'd gripped him. "House du Kane has businesses and branches on most of the populous worlds and many of the colonies. If you ever change your mind, Ethan Frome Fortune, you can get in touch with me." She grinned tightly. "Twenty-two double R, Ethan. It'll expedite anything."

"You'll find someone else."

"With my attractions? I can offer my cardmeter balance and my position. Those won't buy what I want. I've asked and pleaded, Ethan. I won't beg."

"I know. Begging's not part of your makeup, Colette."

A steward was gesturing from alongside the motion lounge her father was strapped into. A faint voice called her name. It came from the throat of a powerful human relic.

"Time to go. Good-bye Ethan. Remember me if you change your mind. Remember me if you don't."

She spared him the worry of whether or not to kiss her by turning and striding purposefully toward her father, toward the people and machines helping him stay alive. He watched as the motion lounge maneuvered itself up the rampway leading into the access tube of the shuttlecraft. Snow speckled the window he stared through.

Fifteen minutes died. Then the exchange of cartons and packagings was complete. A muted chemical bubbling sounded through the thick glassalloy window. Red-orange streaks, like spilled oil paint, emerged from the stern of the shuttle. It rose rapidly until it had shrunk to a size no bigger than any of ten thousand other bright ice flakes swirling through Tran-ky-ky's cold, cold atmosphere.

He rubbed his right arm where she'd clasped him, and thought.

IV

September let him stand like that for nearly an hour. Then he moved to join him.

"Not easy, feller-me-lad?"

"No, Skua. Not easy."

"Better this way, though," the giant said cheerily. "Money's not everything. She would have gotten tougher before sweeter as the years roll down. There's a universe full of fledglings waiting to try their wings who are a good deal softer."

"Skua."

"What is it, lad?"

"Shut up." He walked away, moving rapidly down the port corridor, hands jammed deep into his pockets. After a shrug, September followed, keeping the distance between them constant. There was a dark muddy wall raised around the young salesman, and it could only be taken down from within.

Sir Hunnar and his two squires were waiting patiently for them outside the shuttleport building. September had tried to argue them into coming inside to watch the liftoff of the shuttle from closer range. But the Tran had elected to forgo that pleasure, since it meant enduring the unbearably high temperatures inside.

"We saw it rise from out here, Ethan," the Tran knight said. "It was bigger than the skyboat you came to us in." A note of childlike wonder crept into his voice. "Does it truly chivan to a ship bigger still?"

"Much bigger, Hunnar." Ethan was reminded by the Tran's curious, open stare of the reason for his remaining here. One of those reasons, anyhow. "Let's find a place in town and have a tankard of reedle." At least the super pseudomead would salve his throat, if not his confused conscience.

The tavern they located had been smuggled in among more respectable looking two- and three-story structures on a narrow lane. It did not serve reedle, but they found an ample supply of nontoxic intoxicants. Most were derived from varieties of the omnipresent pika-pina or pika-pedan, a few from other plant life. All filled Ethan with an equally warm glow.

"How are we to proceed to form this necessary confederation, friend Ethan?" Suaxus-dal-Jagger sounded thoroughly discouraged, and the expedition hadn't begun. "We know nothing of this country. No one from Wannome or Sofold has ever been this far from home."

"So many *satch*," murmured his counterpart Budjir.

"That can be to our advantage." September hunched over the table. "The other states we will visit will know nothing of Sofold, but it's possible they will have heard of Arsudun, and consequently, of the humanx station here.

"We've already seen indications that there're entirely too many local goods goin' off-planet to have come from Arsudun alone. That means the Arsudunites are trading with the surrounding states. What better way for them to make themselves look big and important than to constantly claim extratrannish wizards—that's us—for allies?

"So how are they likely to react, when we show up and tell them they'd better confederate for their own good?"

Ethan put down the tall goblet of liquor, used the oversized spoon at his wrist to dip up another helping of the heavily spiced soup in front of him. He sipped at it carefully, the end of the spoon being too wide for his small human mouth. Soup had never been a favorite of his. He preferred more solid food. But Tran-ky-ky's climate could make anyone a lover of hot food in any form.

"I would rather," Hunnar replied petulantly, after considering September's logic, "begin in the neighborhood of Sofold." He pushed back in his chair, balanced on the two hind legs. Ethan knew the knight wouldn't fall. He'd never seen a people with such perfect, innate sense of balance.

"No. I think we'll have the better chance, Hunnar, here where we're all strangers to the folks we'll be tryin' to convert, and where humankind's dubious reputation has maybe preceded us."

"Ta-hoding should have voice in this too." Budjir put in a word for the *Slanderscree*'s captain. "It will be he who will bear considerable responsibility for taking us safely across uncharted ice, and for maneuvering us to safety should trouble arise."

"That's incidental," September countered vigorously. "I'll grant old Ta-hoding his piece, but it's more important that we—"

"I detect an odd smell in here, Baftem." Conversation at the table ceased.

The speaker was a richly dressed Tran standing very close to their booth. His dan spines were lacquered silvery chrome and pink, and he was nearly smothered beneath the impossibly thick fur of some slick white-striped and black-spotted creature. Next to him stood one of the largest Tran Ethan had seen, well over one and two-thirds meters tall and broad in proportion to a normal Tran physique. The latter had one paw resting lightly on the butt of some weapon banded to his left leg. It was dull white and gray and looked like the femur of some walking animal, possibly that of another Tran. Intricate bas-relief covered the club. Its knobby bottom end had been shaped into points.

"An offensive odor—I smell it too," said the giant, smiling unpleasantly. Ethan noted that conversation in the tavern had dropped to a steady, low susurration. Most eyes were on them.

The wealthy local performed an elaborate gesture through the air in front of his nose, accompanying it with much expressive grimacing. Continuing to shield his muzzle from some imaginary olfactory offense, he made a show of searching the area around the booth, peering beneath chairs, sniffing the table, checking the floor. On all fours he approached Hunnar's seat,

51

stopped sniffing, and stood. For effect, he sniffed once more, loudly enough for all the onlookers to hear.

"I believe I've found the source, Baftem," he told his companion. "Someone has had the bad manners to bring a castrated *bourf* into the room."

The quiet bcame total. When no one at the table reacted, the giant wrinkled his own muzzle distinctively, squinted at Hunnar and made a disgusted sound.

"You know how the enoglids drain once they've been neutered. Awful smell!" He looked around the table, exclaimed in mock surprise, "Yet the source seems to be more than one."

"Gentle, Baftem. It behooves a citizen to be polite, even to a fixed *bourf*." He bent over the table, leaning between Ethan and Hunnar. "Would you get out?"

Ethan admired Hunnar's control as the knight looked over his right shoulder, shouted. "Innkeeper, whose tavern is this; yours or his?"

With admirable prescience the innkeeper had already retreated to the vicinity of the cookroom doorway. In response to Hunnar's query he made some incomprehensible gabbling noises and ducked inside before further elucidation could be requested.

"Perhaps you are the innkeeper after all." Hunnar gazed nonchalantly up at the interloper. "Yet you look more like a rockworm to me." His gaze dropped to the other's feet. "But the slime you trail behind you leads from the entrance, not the back rooms."

Stepping back and pulling his sword in the same motion, the offended citizen slashed down. Hunnar was still balanced on the rear two legs of his chair. As the blade descended he shoved back. The sturdy back of the chair hit the attacker in the midsection, sending him stumbling away.

Ethan had managed to slide from behind the table and draw his own weapon. It weighed more than a cardmeter, but he'd been forced to learn how to use this new persuader in the past months. He didn't see the Tran who'd slipped up behind all of them, but dal-Jagger did. The would-be assassin threw Hunnar off-balance as he stumbled into him, clawing blindly at the squire's dirk which protruded between his eyes.

Everyone in the tavern, it seemed, charged them then. Ice swords and axes of bone and metal flailed wildly at the newcomers. Ethan found himself on the floor, trying to avoid the lance a husky customer was thrusting at him. He rolled, and the lance point struck sparks from the stone paving. The lance wielder tried raising his weapon for another strike when a table hit him in the face.

After throwing the table, September found himself wrestling with the giant Tran who'd backed up the wealthy insult-monger. The enormous bone club thrummed through the air. September skipped agilely out of its path. It took a head-sized chunk out of the wooden wall of the booth.

September moved in, hitting his feline opponent hard in the midsection. The giant grunted in surprise but didn't fall. He raised the club over his head, his expression turning from furious to foolish. September lifted the lightly-boned colossus into the air and threw him halfway across the tavern.

Knowing full well his own limitations where physical combat was concerned, Milliken Williams crouched low in the booth and did his utmost not to draw attention to his presence.

Ethan ducked a sword swing, grabbed the Tran by the neck and wrenched him off his feet. He struck the wall hard, went limp, and collapsed. Between the unexpected strength of the heavy-bodied humans and the professional fighting skill of Sir Hunnar and his squires, the large but undisciplined group of attackers was having a difficult time.

The aroma of blood began to be overpowering.

Ethan blocked a wide saber swing with his arm, felt the impact reverberate up to his shoulder muscles. Trying to bring as much of his weight to bear as possible, he swung his own sword over and down. His opponent parried, but the force of the blow knocked his blade from his hand. He knelt and recovered it before Ethan could strike again. But instead of resuming his assault, he backed away and hunted for help.

The most effective combatant of all proved to be not September, Sir Hunnar, or any of the rampaging citizens, but the innkeeper.

53

A massive circular band of black wrought iron hung from the rafters. It supported eight large oil-burning lamps. When September pulled it out of the ceiling and began to swing it as a weapon, the proprietor decided the time had come to make a stand for fiscal sanity. Being metal, the chandelier was the most valuable single furnishing in the tavern. It wouldn't do to have it broken and bent. Risking his life, he charged across the battlefield and emerged on the other side un-scathed.

The fight continued only a few minutes more, until, with admirable speed the innkeeper had located a group of constables. One of the combatants near the door announced their impending arrival and the inter-locked fighters instantly separated and began searching out unorthodox exists.

"The kitchen!" Hunnar shouted.

"Why?" Ethan wanted to know. "We didn't start anything."

A hand shoved him forward. "Police are usually the same everywhere, feller-me-lad. Best to avoid them when you can."

They raced through the malodorous cookroom, emerging into a back alley lightly carpeted with snow. Following Hunnar's lead they ran a short distance to the left, then slowed.

"Why are we slowing down?" Ethan looked back expectantly. But there was no sign of pursuit in the narrow passageway. "We're still fairly close to the tav-ern."

"They will not come looking for us this way, friend Ethan." Hunnar was panting steadily, his breaths much shorter and faster than that of the three humans.

"Why not?"

Hunnar indicated the surface they were traversing. With a clawed foot he kicked away the pale white ve-neer of snow to reveal stone blocks beneath. "There is no icepath here. No Tran in a hurry to go anywhere would leave a fast icepath. This idea I take from you." His breath condensed, vanishing with mathematical regularity in front of him.

"We do not think of 'running,' as you are naturally wont to do," he added. "Tran do not walk or run

54

where they can chivan. The local authorities will not think of this, and will pursue those who chose the ice-paths."

They continued to follow the stone-paving until they came to a wider road. There they blended into the daily traffic. Only their troubled thoughts distinguished them from the Tran moving busily around them, and they kept those as well concealed as their stained weapons.

Back on board the *Slanderscree* the other sailors and soldiers crowded quickly around dal-Jagger and Budjir, inspecting their slight wounds critically, all the while questioning them about the fight. Hunnar and the three humans moved off to the railing, staring back at the innocent harbor scene.

"They attacked us."

"That's pretty obvious, Milliken." The school-teacher shook his head impatiently.

"No, no—I'm not restating the obvious. I mean they attacked *us* . . . humans."

"What's so signif—" Ethan stopped, thoughtful. "I see. Ever since we've been here the locals have treated us with courtesy, even deference." He glanced up at September excitedly. "Skua, remember that incident a few days ago when we first went to visit the portmaster? The crowd that confronted Hunnar outside but backed off when we looked ready to intervene? What happened to that protection today?"

"I can only think of one thing, lad." September continued to stare at the town, one newly survival-suited hand picking at the ice on the wooden railing. "It was a preplanned attack. We were deliberately provoked. Or rather, Hunnar and his boys were, in the hope that you and I and Milliken would be drawn in—as we were. Somebody wants us dead, as well as Hunnar. I thought some of the customers fought awfully well for a bunch of spontaneously irritated townsfolk."

"But why?" Ethan's thoughts were as steady as the wind, which is to say, not at all.

"Have you not learned this truth by now, friend Ethan?" Hunnar glared at the city, his tone sardonic. "This is the kind of reception we will likely encounter everywhere we go with this plan of confederation. All

55

Tran have a natural suspicion of outlanders. Only your presence might mitigate this, and if it does not do so here in Arsudun where your people are known as benefactors, surely it will do us no good elsewhere."

"Sorry, Hunnar." September ran his gloved hand up from the rail to grip one of the thick pika-pina shrouds. "You're right about your people being naturally suspicious of strangers, but I doubt that's why *we* were attacked.

"Someone thinks we're dangerous—Ethan and Milliken and I. They'd like us out of the way. Why? That's pretty obvious, isn't it? Some folks here— maybe Arsudunite, likely both—have a nice little profitable monopoly on offworld trade. We've declared our intention of breaking up that monopoly. Some sailors must've talked." His voice dropped. "Wasn't sure it was important enough for someone to chance killin' us, though. Not til this afternoon."

"Then why don't we report that, Skua?"

"Feller-me-lad," September said gently, "don't be naive. What does it matter if a few humans are killed in a local brawl? Oh sure, you and I know it was no accidental encounter, but how do we prove that to a thranx judge?" He shook his head. "Not much we can do except be glad they weren't better swordsmen and step up our preparations for getting under way."

"It was a fight to speak well of." Hunnar's eyes gleamed. "Five against twenty-five."

Ethan looked with distaste at the blood-stained sword on his own suit belt. He'd tried wiping it clean in the snow, but the frozen red crystals adhered accusingly to the blade.

"You're too proud of killing, Hunnar."

The Tran knight cocked his head to one side, looking for all the world like an inquisitive tabby. "That be true, Ethan. I come not from your advanced civilization, though. You must find it in your heart to be patient with us." Wind rose and moaned around them as he gestured back down the strait leading out toward the ocean.

"My world is perhaps not so conducive to gentleness and understanding as is yours. Here we fight best with our hands and not our mouths."

"I didn't mean to be insulting," Ethan replied testily.

"That's enough." September looked disgustedly from human to Tran. "We're supposed to be forging a great alliance on this world, not testing the puny one we already have." He jerked a thumb at the harbor. Smoke rose from a thousand chimneys. "The sooner we leave here, the less we'll be disturbed, I hope." He eyed Hunnar.

"Where do we start?"

Hunnar grumbled a reply. "As it is so many satch back to Sofold, and since you are so set on beginning this great undertaking here, and since it is not my idea but yours, but most especially since I am certain we will have no better luck here than near home, I suppose we may as well look for our first allies in this part of the world.

"Besides, were we to return home with this bizarre conception, we would have difficulty keeping our crew. Men will not remain loyal when given a choice between reaching for a glorious madness or retaining their simple homes." He spun angrily and chivaned away.

"You shouldn't have made him mad, lad," September chided his friend.

"I know. I'm just not used to sticking things in people, and have a hard time sympathizing with anyone who does." He smiled crookedly. Odd, how the unexpected shoved its way into one's thoughts at the most unlikely moments. "Colette would be better at it than I am."

"If you feel so strongly about it, feller-me-lad, why are you staying here to help with this when you could be on your way to more civilized climes, where people only stick one another, as Hunnar said, with sharp words?"

Ethan thought just a moment. "So that some day Hunnar's grandchildren won't feel the need to pick up a knife to settle an argument." Behind and above them on the helm-deck, Ta-hoding was conversing with several mates. "Let's go arrange a course. We're going to bring maturity and knowledge to this world if it kills us."

"Which it very well is likely to, lad." They started aft. "Hunnar's probably right about the trouble we'll have tryin' to sell this confederation to the inhabitants of outlying city-states."

Ethan walked faster, more assuredly. "That's my business . . ."

Jobius Trell opened his mouth slightly inside the survival suit, listened to the candy laugh and smiled as he sucked. At the moment the flavor was persimmon, the laugh invitingly female.

The slim, mature Tran standing on the hillside next to him gave him a questioning look, puzzled by the obviously masculine human's ability to produce such a lilting chuckle.

Pausing in his study of the work going on in the little vale below them, Trell flipped back the face mask of his suit and turned his face from the stinging breeze. Using his gloved hand he picked the remainder of the candy from his mouth and showed it to his curious alien companion.

"Giggle drop. Sweet food," he explained.

"Igg-el drup." The Tran stumbled over the unfamiliar phonetics as the Resident Commissioner popped it back into his mouth and resumed sucking. "But the sound I heard, friend Trell?"

"Candy's formed in layers," Trell told him with a sigh. It was so boring, having to constantly explain the most common features of Commonwealth civilization to these barbarians, even one as curious and quick to learn as his companion of today. His attention wandered back to the work going on below.

The earthquake generated by the explosion of the great volcano known as The-Place-Where-The-Earth's-Blood-Burns had caused some damage, mostly to the native town but also a little in Brass Monkey. As Commissioner, it was his duty to supervise personally the necessary reconstruction work. Doing so also made him look good in the eyes of the locals.

That the collapsed native food storage house in the depression below constituted the only serious damage was a tribute to native engineering skills. But then, he reflected that even within Arsudun's comparatively sheltered harbor, a normal Tran structure had to be built well to stand up against the daily weather.

58

"How can food talk?"

"What? Oh. As each layer of the hard candy-stuff dissolves in your mouth, it releases a different flavor and a different laugh." He turned to face the Tran standing next to him.

He was slimmer than most of his brethren. In places —long streaky patches and spots—his steel-gray fur turned to coal-black. Other dark smudges colored his left ear, muzzle, and left cheek, running like a splotch of soft tar down his side to disappear beneath his brightly dyed blue cape and vest. His comparatively slender build was very similar to the Commissioner's.

These two had more in common than external construction, however.

Trell finished his explanation. "The laughs are recorded from real people—you've seen our recording devices throughout the port?" The Tran made a gesture of acknowledgment. "A computerized—a thought-smart machine—then sonically embeds the sounds in tiny bubbles of air which are not quite just air bubbles, as the candy food is being solidified. As each layer of encoded laugh bubbles is exposed to the air in your mouth, the sound is released." He grinned behind his mask at the obvious discomfort this explanation produced.

"Tell me, why shouldn't food sound as good as it tastes?"

"I do not know," the Tran responded gruffly, "but it is a strange thought to me, and not altogether agreeable."

"Perhaps, but we've brought many strange things to you and even the strangest have proven themselves profitable. We have an archaic expression—like my candy-food, money also talks."

The Tran brightened. "Something both our peoples agree upon, friend Trell. 'Money talking'—good, but I still think I like my own food to lie decently quiet."

Any onlooker could have told from the Tran's lavish attire—richly inlaid with valuable metal thread and thin, foil ornamentation in the vests, metal strips set in his dan that flashed when he raised an arm—that he was exceptionally well off even by Arsudun's standards.

59

What they might not have recognized as important was the band of metal encircling his neck.

From time to time a human aiding the locals below in the rebuilding of the storehouse would climb the slight slope in search of Trell's instructions or advice. Occasionally the questioner would be a Tran. And the inquiries were not racially exclusive. Sometimes a human would ask the Tran for advice, while a native would address the Commissioner.

The storehouse had been constructed partway down the strait and close to the ice's edge, where it had received more of the shock than comparable structures in the town. Several other buildings close by had been knocked slightly askew or had had windows cracked out. Only the storehouse had suffered complete destruction.

Trell knew that was because the Tran buildings were made mostly of stone and they had not yet mastered the art of constructing the dome. So any structure with a large open interior, such as the storehouse, was far less stable than those cut into smaller rooms and chambers whose inner walls served to support the roof. The Tran did not have the material for enclosing large areas.

Structural metals and plastics were required. The Tran knew nothing of plastics, and would never have considered wasting precious metal on construction, save for an occasional bolt or nail.

In fact, the only metal of consequence in any Arsudun building and possibly on all of Tran-ky-ky— except within the humanx station—was the double, solid brass door which now formed the entrance to the Landgrave's castle built back of the town. When the sun was right, one could see reflection down in the harbor.

It had been an inspired gift on Trell's part. The modest cost had been more than repaid in less tangible but far more valuable ways by the grateful Landgrave of Arsudun, Callonnin Ro-Vijar. Ways that ought to be preserved.

Trell turned to the Tran standing next to him. "I understand, friend Ro-Vijar, that some of my people, the newcomers who arrived on the great ice ship, were involved in a very nasty fight in a city tavern."

60

He indicated the harbor, where the towering masts of the *Slanderscree* rose above all other.

"I heard similar reports." The Landgrave of Arsudun performed the Trannish equivalent of a helpless shrug. "Outsiders are not popular here. Does this news disturb you?"

"It does disturb me," replied Trell. "It disturbs me, my friend, because it took place here, where news of it could reach other humans, including members of my own staff. If harm befell any humans so close to the outpost, it could create trouble. I could be discredited among my superiors. That could lead to disagreeable meddling by my government in the salubrious commercial covenants we have concluded here."

"That is to be avoided." Ro-Vijar kicked at the light snow. Sharp chiv sent bright flakes flying. "It is rumored that these newcomers talk of organizing a large number of independent states to apply for higher status within your government, your Commonwealth."

"So it's rumored." Trell smiled behind the face mask. Of course, it was he who had informed Ro-Vijar of the strangers' plans, but both men enjoyed their subtle word-play. It was a good habit, just in case anyone else happened to overhear.

"If they were to succeed in such an endeavor," the Landgrave continued, "would it not mean that any from the outlying regions could come and trade freely with many different representatives of your own island states?"

"Merchant families," Trell corrected him, "not island states. But the effect would be the same. Personally, I don't feel that's necessary. The present commercial arrangements are satisfactory to all concerned. Unless you think someone other than myself can supervise our trade better."

"I too, find the existing understandings agreeable."

They fell silent then, each absorbed in furious thinking while ostensibly concentrating on the construction which continued below them. Noisy crews raised the first new wall, bracing the unfamiliar prestressed plastic against the wind. Once it was molded in place, the work could proceed rapidly behind the windbreak it would provide.

"What then is to be done, friend Trell? Can you yourself do nothing?"

"I'm afraid not, my friend. I can conceal credits and crates and alter listings and manifests. Three citizen corpses would be dangerous to try and make disappear. Yet we must do something . . . and not clumsily visible, this time.

"These three humans are strangers to Arsudun, but not to your world, Landgrave. They have lived among the Tran for many months. They are intelligent. Their grasp of your language and nuances is firmer than that of my own specialists. While I am informed that a union such as they contemplate is extremely unlikely, they should not be given the opportunity to prove my xenologists wrong. They should be discouraged."

"Discouraged," echoed the Landgrave, mimicking the human vowels as best he could. "But not here. I understand. As soon as they are fairly on their way, I will muster the best arguments at my disposal."

"I'm sure they'll be effective."

Both turned back to watch as the second wall was raised into place and the human engineers commenced heat-sealing the corner where they joined. Nothing more was mentioned about the *Slanderscree*'s crusading crew. Nothing more needed to be. While they were of different races, they understood one another perfectly . . .

"What do you know about this Poyolavomaar?" Ethan held onto a shroud as he spoke to Ta-hoding. They were making their laborious way southward from Arsudun harbor, tacking into a stiff breeze.

"Only what the other captains on the icefront told me, friend Ethan. Four stars to port!" Responding to his command, the two burly helmsmen fought to turn the huge wooden wheel. A screeching sound slightly higher than usual came from the stern of the immense icerigger as the fifth duralloy runner, used to steer the vessel, cut sideways into the ice. Slowly the ship came around to a new heading.

For several days now they had been racing parallel to the island of Arsudun. They'd already covered, by

Williams' estimates, over a hundred kilometers. It was evident that Arsudun was many, many times the size of Sofold, Hunnar and Ta-hoding's home island.

The lowlands around the city and harbor had long since given way to cliffs which rose steeply from the ice to heights of thirty meters or more. Trees and shrubs grew to the edge of the cliffs, forming an uneven fringe at their tops, making the weaving cliffline resemble the spine of a nervous green cat.

"You told me," Ta-hoding went on, "we should begin our quest with some nearby yet important state. All of the captains and merchants I talked to agreed that Poyolavomaar was the most powerful in this region save Arsudun itself. It sounds like an interesting city to visit."

Safely clear of other ships, Ta-hoding was feeling conversational. "According to Zho Midan-Gee, the captain who was most helpful to me, Poyolavomaar is a cluster of ten or more closely grouped and very steep islands. He said they are so near to one another that all but the very youngest cubs can safely chivan from one to the next. Having made two trips there himself in past years, he most remembers that these islands form a circle, enclosed island to island by great walls much like the one which protects our own harbor at Wannome."

"It sounds very much like a place that could develop into a center of commerce," Ethan admitted.

Ta-hoding made a gesture of agreement. "Trade is the most important business there, Midan-Gee told me. If the walls all have gates, a captain could take his ship out of the enclosed harbor in any direction he chose, without worrying about where he would pick up a trailing wind.

"Still we must remember that many of these captains produce much of their own wind," Ta-hoding said portentously, blithely excluding himself from the company of ice-going prevaricators. "They like to boast of their abilities and expertise. This Poyolavomaar may be nought but a cluster of metal-poor villages. Yet I think Midan-Gee as honest as most and am inclined to trust him."

"We have to trust someone," Ethan reminded him.

Ta-hoding studied the setting sun. The thermonuclear candle was almost straight ahead, its flaming upper curve beginning to settle beneath the martingale of the ship. He glanced down at something set just behind the great wheel.

"According to compass, Ethan, we have been changing heading from south to southwest for the past two hours." He gestured at the land mass of Arsudun, which was still to port. Only now port had become north instead of west.

"We have rounded the southernmost part of the island," Ta-hoding continued. "As the winds on the open ice will become stronger and the day is almost done, with your permission I would suggest anchoring for the night."

"You're the captain, Ta-hoding. This ship is your charge. Do what you think best."

"Thank you, Sir Ethan." The portly Tran moved forward of the wheel, leaned over the helmdeck railing and shouted forward. Sailors turned immediately to listen. Ta-hoding was deferential and meek in private conversation. But when giving orders to his crew, he made certain his words were audible above the wind.

"Kilpit, Monslawic!" Two mates acknowledged. "Reef in all sails and prepare to anchor!"

These orders were voice-relayed back down the ship to the last sailor at the bowsprit. Each crawled his way up into the rigging. Once more Ethan marveled at the ability of the Tran sailors, who constantly had to set, adjust, and take in sails while walking on narrow spars in a perpetual gale.

When all the sheets were furled and the icerigger had come to a near halt, the fore and aft ice anchors were released. These clusters of metal thorns and spikes were usually set into a heavy globe of cast iron. Those of the *Slanderscree* gained additional holding power from the chips and shards of duralloy gleaned from the remnants of the cannibalized lifeboat in which Ethan and his friends had crashed.

There were nerve-tingling shrieks and crackings as the anchors snubbed themselves deeply into the ice fore and aft. The ship slipped slowly to the west, shoved by the persistent wind, until the pika-pina cables holding the anchors grew taut. The creaking and groaning ceased. The *Slanderscree* had come to a halt.

Immediately, blocking teams went over her side. They secured the ship by placing stone slabs in front and behind each of the five runners. Now the ship would not move unless struck by an abnormal wind. Guards at stern and bow were posted more to warn of such an approaching weather front than of any flesh-and-blood peril.

Ethan remained on deck, watching the last glow of sunlight shift steadily from yellow to red to purple.

"Not hungry, friend Ethan?"

Startled, his head jerked around. Yellow-framed black slits set in a furry face glowed back at him, flaming with sunset light.

"Not right now, Hunnar." He turned back to lean on the railing and stare out across the ice. Tran-ky-ky's two moons had risen. There was little snow or ice in the air tonight and just enough stratus cloud to mark the difference between atmosphere and deep space. Moonlight knocked double shadows off the trees clinging tenaciously to nearby cliff edges. The ice ocean itself had lost its daytime harshness, lay hard and unmoving while cloaked in ethereal blue-white moon glow.

Ethan glanced at his wrist thermometer. The exquisitely still landscape shivered in twenty-eight below zero C weather. By mid-morning dark, several hours before the sun rose once again, it would fall to minus sixty-two or three—plus the ever-present wind chill factor. He could remove his survival suit and blend fully with the land. His body would freeze in a couple of minutes.

Hunnar chose that moment to ask exactly the wrong question.

Pointing skyward, he inquired of Ethan, "Which of those is your home world?"

It was several minutes before the salesman could answer, and not all those minutes had been spent in studying the unfamiliar constellations overhead. "I don't know. It's far, unimaginably far from here, Hunnar."

"How many satch?" the knight asked guilelessly, his own gaze roving the night sky.

"Too many to count," Ethan told him, repressing a smile and wondering why they were both whispering. "The sun it circles is not a very big one." He gestured upward. "It's off in that general direction, too far and faint for us to see with our eyes. And there are other stars between yours and mine, some of which have worlds that my people and our friends the thranx inhabit.

He indicated a faintly reddish spot of light. "Far out from that star circles a land where water never freezes anywhere except in machines my people must make for only that purpose." Hunnar shook his head in wonder.

"So warm. A terrible-sounding place."

"My people don't like it much either, Hunnar. But our good companions the thranx thrive there. It's called Drax IV, and the land tries to eat the people. It's a strange place. I'll tell you about it some time." He returned his attention to the silent wind-scoured ice sea. Snow and ice particles were scudding about, tiny whirlwinds twisting them in the moonlight. Ethan saw invisible dancers in gem-studded gowns prancing beneath twin moons.

"I think I am a little hungry now." He slapped both hands on the railing. "I'll join you for supper."

They went down to the eating quarters for officers and knights inside the central cabin. When the door closed behind them, the only light on deck other than moonlight came from a few thick portholes. There was no movement except at opposite ends of the ship, where the weather watchers paced patiently, their faces muffled with furs. When the sun vanished, it grew cold enough in the night of Tran-ky-ky to chill even a native.

They were watching for dark clouds. They did not see the dark paws that grasped the railing amidships . . .

V

Alert, nervous eyes darted across the deck, looking and spying nothing animate. One hand temporarily let go its grip to make a gesture to figures below. Then the figure pulled itself onto the deck. It was followed by companion shapes, indistinct in the darkness.

They walked to center deck, between the two main cabins. Other shapes, coming up on the side opposite, met them there. Soft words were exchanged, firm intentions resolved. Several figures split off from the growing group and moved forward, another chivaned aft. It was quiet on the decks for several moments.

A choked scream sounded from the helmdeck. Within the large group amidships a leader cursed.

A door to the central cabin opened and a figure emerged, silhouetted in the light from inside. Looking about and seeing nothing, the figure turned to go back inside when a clanking sound stopped it. Drawing his sword, the sailor cautiously moved onto the deck to investigate. Then he saw something which made him shout.

"Boarders! The ship is boarded! Wind aboard, men of Sofold . . . ukk!" His screaming was silenced by a metal shaft which pierced him from sternum to spine.

But the alarm had been raised. In seconds the deck and cabins were filled with milling, cursing, shouting shapes. Figures continued to pour over the railings onto the decks. The situation looked bad for crew and passengers.

Three brown-suited shapes mounted the second story of the main cabin and surveyed the carnage taking place below them.

"Fighting too close-in to pick out friend from enemy," September declared above the awful sounds of murder, "but if we can keep the rest of them from getting aboard . . . You and Williams take the starboard side, feller-me-lad. I'll take the port."

"I don't like this." Nevertheless, Williams unlimbered his own small beamer. They had acquired the three hand weapons through unofficial channels in Brass Monkey, not because it was illegal for humans to carry modern weaponry on Tran-ky-ky, but because September had insisted they'd be better off keeping their capabilities hidden until they knew who was on whose side.

Three shafts of bright blue light jumped down from the cabin roof, struck the ship's railings and moved along them. The high-intensity coherent light beams swept incipient boarders from the *Slanderscree*'s sides, piercing one after another. They hardly had time to scream. They did not have time to get into the fighting.

Seeing this small victory produced a renewed surge of confidence in the crew, despair among their opponents. The sailors redoubled their efforts.

September shifted his beam from the charred top of the railing and played it intermittently on the ice. One burst revealed three ice craft mounted on bone runners waiting nearby.

Changing the intensity setting on his beamer he played it across the deck and sails of one icecraft. Flames lit the night, illuminating the other two craft and their now panicky crews. Those boarders still alive had to fight their way back to the railing. Some made their way back down the boarding ladders they had brought, others jumped and trusted to powerful leg muscles to absorb the shock of landing on the unyielding ice.

Ethan stopped firing, moved across the roof to grab September's shoulder. "Stop it, Skua, they're leaving."

September sighted carefully, fired again. "Just a few more bursts, lad." A distant scream penetrated the darkness. "I can get a couple more of 'em."

"Skua, stop it." Using both arms, Ethan managed to bring September's gun arm down. The giant gazed back at him. For a brief instant another person stared out of those deep-set eyes and Ethan took a couple of uncertain, frightened steps backward. Then the unearthly glare disappeared and September was himself again.

"Sorry, young feller-me-lad. Been in so many similar confrontations I tend to forget myself, sometimes." Ethan wondered if the giant meant it literally. "If we let them get away, they may try and kill us another day. However," he shrugged amiably, "I defer to your gentler sensibilities."

"Thank you." Both men looked back to see a disgusted Williams clipping on his own weapon and hurrying below.

Ethan and September used the exterior walks to make their way down to the deck. They found the Tran wizard Eer-Meesach in intense discussion with Hunnar.

"I don't recognize their trade insignia at all," the elderly Tran was saying.

Hunnar grunted, nudged a corpse with his foot. "That is not surprising, so far from home. Emblems and insignia would naturally be different and carry different meanings." He walked away, muttering to himself.

Hunnar joined the two humans as they moved to the railing. September used his beamer on low power wide beam to reveal an irregular path of crumpled hairy forms lying on the ice. Lightly stirred by the wind, they formed a grotesque trail leading toward the distant cliffs.

"The tip of this island would be a good place for raiders and pirates to lair," Hunnar declared. "Here they could ambush commerce traveling from the west side of Arsudun and lands lying thereto en route to Arsudun city. I would not have thought they would be so bold as to attack anything the size of the *Slanderscree*, through."

"Neither would I, Hunnar." September scratched at the back of his head, trying to run his fingers through his hair, then remembered the new survival suit he wore now. "Maybe it was too much of a temptation for 'em. They would've done all right, too, if we'd only had swords to fight with."

A mate approached Hunnar, chatted with him a moment, then moved on, holding a bandaged arm.

69

"Our losses are not severe," Hunnar informed them. "We may encounter more such assaults, friends. I would hope such sacrifices are not in vain."

"I hope so, too, friend Hunnar." Ethan was glad it was night. He didn't have to watch the sailors using meltwater to swab the blood from the decks.

Cleaning the decks produced three bodies who'd been offspring of Sofold. In accordance with custom, the deceased were carried into the body of the ship. They would remain in the unheated under deck until the *Slanderscree* returned home, preserved by the sub-freezing temperatures. Following departure ceremonies attended by their families, the corpses would be defrosted and reduced to a fine meal which would be spread across the cultivated fields of inner Sofold. Thus would the dead enrich the soil of their homeland which had supplied food to nourish them when alive. This was a necessary as well as spiritual tradition. The island states of Tran-ky-ky were not rich in natural fertilizers.

Tradition likewise deemed the bodies of the fallen enemy unhealthy. Being likely to spiritually poison the fields, these chilled torsos were unceremoniously dumped over the side. While the ship's shaman repaired fleshy wounds, her carpenter set about fixing the railings where the sky-outlanders' light knives had burnt through.

Repair operations under way, a far larger and more alert guard was mounted and the rest of the crew returned to their hammocks or supper, whatever they were doing when interrupted.

When everyone else had resumed downing cold food, an empty seat was noted in the chamber. The seat was the one located between Hunnar and Ethan.

"Who has last seen the Landgrave's daughter?" Hunnar's gaze met the curious stares of knights, squires and mates. Individual denials combined to create an air of anxiety in the room. It seemed that no one could remember seeing Elfa since they had first come to eat.

One sailor ventured that he'd seen her on deck fighting with the rest of the crew. Being occupied fully

70

with preserving his own life, he hadn't been able to watch her for long.

Hunnar rose. "Search the ship. Begin with the three cabins, then the interdeck storage bins, then the rigging."

For a second time the meal was abandoned as the inhabitants of the chamber spread out across the vessel. Every centimeter of wood was examined, every yard and sail locker combed. What the last areas searched lacked in likelihood, they made up for in the unanimity of response they produced.

Elfa Kurdagh-Vlata was no longer on the ship.

It was suggested she'd fallen or been knocked over the side. Scrambling over lines and ladders, the crew flooded the ice around and beneath the icerigger. September, Ethan and Hunnar quickly joined the search. Oil lamps carried by chivaning sailors suggested a conclave of fireflies, darting and weaving irregular search patterns over the ice. Several followed the line of inert forms stretching unevenly toward the nearby cliffs.

Once more all reports were negative. Elfa was neither alive aboard ship nor dead on the ice.

"They would not—" Hunnar paused, collected himself. "They would not have taken her corpse." His teeth showed and he was not smiling. "She would be of no use to anyone in any . . . capacity . . . if dead. We must assume she had been taken by those who escaped."

Senior warrior among all the assembled Tran, Balavere Longax half-grinned in the direction of the dark island. "Sympathy to them, then."

"Suaxus, Budjir, choose twenty crew, volunteers all, for an attempt." Hunnar glanced at the quiescent icerigger. "We can spare that many and still leave the ship safely protected, should this abduction be a diversion to weaken our defenses."

"You realize," September growled, raising his voice to make himself heard above the wind, "that if they hole up in any kind of fortified camp, we're going to have a helluva time worming her out."

"Would you think of not trying?" Hunnar spoke

71

calmly, but Ethan could see the knight was holding himself together with great effort.

"Of course not." Ethan couldn't tell if the big man was being sarcastic or not, and he couldn't see his expression beneath the survival suit mask. He tapped the tiny weapon attached to his waist. "If you're going to have any kind of chance, you'll need our firepower." Hunnar turned his attention to Ethan.

"This is not your fight, my friend."

"Hunnar, in the eighteen months I've known you, that's the stupidest thing you've ever said."

Hunnar's expression said thanks, his gratitude no less eloquent for being nonverbal.

"We must get the other things we brought with us from Brass Monkey," Ethan continued. "It won't take us a minute to get ready."

"It will take time to assemble the party," Balavere said.

The two humans reboarded the ship. On returning to the ice, they sat down and began to do strange things with their feet. Hunnar's curiosity took his mind off Elfa for a moment.

"Williams will stay on board," Ethan told him, puffing with the effort of what he was doing. "We should leave at least one beamer on the ship in case they try another attack."

"I do not think they will," said Hunnar, staring at Ethan's feet. "But it is a wise man who leaves one trap by the door of his house when he goes hunting." Unable to resist any longer, he gestured at September.

"What is it you do to your feet?"

Ethan stood, rocked awkwardly, but kept himself upright. "They're called ice skates, Hunnar." He bent, adjusted a strap. "They're artificial chiv, that fit over our own chivless feet. These are kind of special. We found out some of the workers in Brass Monkey had them made in the station metal-forming shop. They have gyroscopic compensators built into the soles."

"I do not understand this gyoscopek. But what do they compensate for?"

"For our clumsiness." He stumbled, seemed about to fall, when his feet suddenly shifted fluidly to help him regain his balance.

Hunnar wondered if they would compensate enough. Perhaps they needed more gysocopeks.

The assembled crewmembers wore uniformly grim expressions.

"I think this expedition will run smoother," September said, "if Ethan and I concentrate on just stayin' upright."

"I understand." Hunnar called up to someone leaning over the railing. Several lengths of pika-pina cable were tossed over the side.

One end of both cables were braided together. Hunnar handed the thick joined end to Ethan. Two sailors picked up the other two ends, opened their arms. Wind filled their dan, and Ethan found himself starting to move forward. September was alongside, likewise making use of the tow.

And suddenly they were racing toward the cliffs at nearly sixty kilometers an hour.

Ethan gritted his teeth behind the mask. If he lost his balance or his grip at this speed, a rough place on the ice ocean might rip even the tough material of the survival suit, admitting air cold enough to freeze skin on contact. Somehow he managed, though his bent knees ached and his hands throbbed.

Suaxus yelled at him from nearby. "Ready, friend Ethan! We are going to turn."

He tried to strengthen his grip, but his hands were numb from the strain and he couldn't tell if his grip was growing any stronger. On command, every Tran in the group dropped his or her left arm, leaned to the right, and swerved sharply in that direction.

Ethan worried about the strain on the cable as he snapped around like a rock on a string. But the cable held, and so did his wrists. They were running toward the cliffs in a wide arc. A glance between his feet showed they were following the ice paths cut by the retreating survivors of the assault on the ship.

It was nearing midnight, and the incredible cold of the Trannish night began to penetrate the immensely efficient thermotropic material of his suit. Once he slid open the face mask of his suit just a fraction, and a thin blast of air hit him like a ten-kilo boulder. He closed it immediately, shivering not from

73

the cold. How quickly out here his blood could freeze solid in his veins.

There were shouts from the head of the group. Suaxus, noting Ethan's curious stare through his face mask, pointed upward. They were nearly below the cliffs now. Twenty-five meters above, the irregular silhouette of trees growing at the edge thrust black spines into the moonlit sky.

A small fortress rode the edge of a spire of rock. It was separated from the main island by a five-meter-wide gap spanned by a wooden drawbridge.

The group swung off into shadow. "We'll try to go up an unguarded side," Hunnar was saying. "There should be only one walkway cut into the rock, and it is bound to be watched."

Such a walkway would be cut into the sheltered lee of the rock spire, on its eastern side. The little knot of armed Tran and humans decelerated on its dark, windswept, western flank.

Ethan let go of the cable, tilted his head back and struggled with feet intent on flying out from under him. The wall of the small fortress above was built of massive stone blocks. There were no turrets or peaked roofs for the wind to tear at.

"It does not seem possible," one of the squires finally declared. "It is too straight."

"No it's not." The squire stared at September.

"Do we fly up like the guttorbyn, sky-outlander?"

September walked—skated rather—to the base of the rock pillar. The stone tapered toward the top. "It's only about twenty meters. We could climb it."

"You mean, leave the ice?" Hunnar's eyes widened.

It occured to Ethan that the Tran, who moved so easily and gracefully across the ice ocean but found even walking burdensome, might find the concept of climbing an unprepared surface terrifying. While their sharp chiv would give good purchase on the wooden spars and masts of a ship, they would only slide on smooth rock. And their comparative inflexibility would keep them from probing for a foothold the way the ape-foot of a man could.

"All right. Then Ethan and I will go."

"Just a minute, Skua."

"I'm open to suggestions, feller-me-lad."

Ethan had to admit, finally, he couldn't think of anything better.

"We'll have surprise on our side, lad. Remember that."

"We will if we don't splatter ourselves all over the ice."

"You are both crazy." Hunnar exchanged shoulder grips and breath with both of them in turn. "We will trust your madness because we have no choice. Go with the wind."

"Thanks, Hunnar. But not this time." Ethan turned, removed his skates. Then he followed September up the first ledge, concentrating on where his feet and hands went and not looking down. The last thing he wanted was a steady breeze blowing him around while he was crawling like a fly up a wall.

But the wind turned out to be an ally. It blew steadily against his back, shoving him into the cliff. And the spire was not as sheer and smooth as it had appeared in the darkness. There were ample cracks and ledges where a human hand or foot could find a hold. They made steady progress upward.

Halfway up the granite wall Ethan waited while September hunted for an elusive handhold above. As he caught his breath and stared single-mindedly at the giant's backside he found himself wondering what a moderately successful salesman was doing glued like a bag of meat to cold rock on this frozen and inhospitable world, trying to rescue an argumentative princess who was more manx than man. Perhaps there had been more truth in Hunnar's appraisal of their scheme as madness than he'd been ready to admit.

September was moving again. Panting like an old engine, Ethan started up after him. It seemed the cliff extended, grew higher instead of shorter with each painful step upward. Once, he looked down. Dark blotches against the ice suggested the location of the waiting Tran. He missed a breath, forced his gaze skyward again.

He pulled himself up onto still another ledge, lay there for several minutes before he was aware that he was lying next to September's recumbent bulk and that the giant was motioning for him to be silent.

Ahead, he saw square-cut stones fitted carefully together.

The ledge was two meters wide, the wall of the fortress set that far back from the spire's edge. Looking up, he saw that the walls of the fortress, in keeping with its modest size, were not particularly high. There was no reason for them to be. The Tran would not consider a serious attack from this, to them, sheer side.

Holding tight to the stone and gravel ground, Ethan pulled himself to the edge and peered over the side again. Only bare ice was visible, which meant that the Tran had moved off toward the leeside stairway. According to plan, they would wait there until Ethan and September had cleared the way for them.

The two men moved to the base of the wall and began to crawl around the pinnacle, staying close to the stonework. The wall was five meters high, the drop off the edge considerably more.

Ethan considered their chances. Their assailants would still be treating their wounds. They should not expect an organized assault on their fortress so soon after their own attack. After all, as far as they knew, they'd only taken a single prisoner, and that was hardly worth risking a suicidal attack, was it? They should be tired from chivaning at top speed back to their base and climbing the stairway to it. They would have to have climbed, Ethan knew. No icepath could wind a practical course upward at the steep angle the hidden stairway suggested. Such a climb would be slow and painful for them to make. That same climb would also serve to discourage attackers. It would not have the same effect on more agile humans.

"We'll use our knives where possible, lad, beamers only if we have to." After disposing of the sentries guarding the pathway down to the ice, they'd signal Hunnar and the assault party, then hold the open walkway against any who might attempt to retake it.

So went the theory.

Five more minutes of crawling brought them around into the sheltered side of the fortress. They found themselves gazing at what had to be the top of the walkway.

On this side the pinnacle was several meters lower. Moving slightly away from the wall, Ethan could see stairs laboriously cut from the naked rock of the stone pillar wending their way down into darkness. Crawling to the edge of the cliff, he peered over. No sign of Hunnar and the others. That was as it should be. He felt confident they were waiting silently below, part of the shadows and hollow places, awaiting the human's signal.

Two armed Tran flanked the top stair. Their attention was directed down and out, their lances pointed threateningly at the stairway. From his position next to the edge, Ethan was able to obtain a good view of the parapet directly above the entrance.

"No sentries above," he whispered to the waiting September.

"Why should there be, feller-me-lad?" The giant was a brown-suited lump, just another rock buttressing the outer wall. "Sentries at the stairway and maybe at the drawbridge are guard enough."

Ethan reflected again on the Tran inability to climb smooth surfaces. There was no place to hide on the length of exposed stairway spiraling downward. One Tran could spot an attack party, give the alarm, have breakfast, and return before the fight began. A few soldiers with bows and arrows or spears could hold off an attacking army.

September was whispering to him again. "I'll take the fat one on the far side, lad. You take the other." He was fumbling for the small axe at his belt. Ethan would use a dirk. He hoped they wouldn't need to use beamers. Not that they would make any more noise than axe or knife, but the intense beams of light might be visible to someone within the fortress.

He crawled back next to the giant. Together they started to make their belly-scraping way toward the guards, keeping to the shadowy regions close by the wall. The wind helped to hide the noise of their passage; the Tran had excellent hearing.

Triangular furry ears flipped in their direction and

one of the guards turned, squinted. The two humans became part of the landscape.

"Be that you, Smigere?" The guard's double eyelids flickered against the wind. "You are not due on watch for three *vate*." Ethan held his breath. The curious guard took several steps toward them. "Smigere, are you sick?"

Although the sentry was staring straight at Ethan, he apparently still couldn't conceive of the possibility that any enemy could be *behind* him. The other guard was looking curiously at his companion.

There was no time for antique weapons. At such close range, it was impossible to miss with the beamers. Both Tran were punctured by thin ropes of azure light. Smigere's friend went down with an expression of surprise and hurt on his face, as if he couldn't quite believe what was happening to him. He looked down at the hole in his chest, dropped his lance, and stared curiously into the shadows. His eyes closed and he fell over onto his side. His beamed colleague had stumbled backward and tumbled over the side of the cliff.

After another glance at the moonlit ramparts above, September rose, walked over to the remaining body. He examined it briefly, then picked it up by one arm and leg. A single swing consigned it to the night and the ice. Wind and distance combined to prevent them from hearing the corpse strike the surface far below. That was fine with Ethan, though he wondered absently if the falling shapes had accidentally struck any of the waiting attack party. No time to worry about that now.

They ran to the doorway. Entrance to the fortress was blocked by a single outward-opening door of thick wood. It was large enough and wide enough for Tran to enter only in single-file. Any opponents fortunate enough to survive the stairway could be picked off one at a time if they tried to force their way into the keep.

Their task was only half finished. It was reasonable to expect a gatekeeper posted inside, if not another pair of guards. But no one had appeared to question the sudden manifestation of blue lights in the night sky. The sentries' demise had gone unwitnessed.

September had replaced the beamer at his waist,

78

redrawn his small axe. "No chance we can use beamers inside," he murmured. "We've been lucky so far, but someone's sure to see any lights inside the wall." Ethan had his knife out already.

"What now? Do we just walk in and check for guards?"

"Mebbe we do just that, lad. No reason for them to lock the door. Plenty of time to do that when the stairway guards give warning."

Ethan moved to stand with his back pressed against the wall flanking the door. September put a gloved hand on the horizontal lock bar of the gate, slid it out of its wall socket slowly. To Ethan it produced an abnormally loud screeching sound in the darkness. As soon as the bar was clear, September grabbed the single handle and pulled. When nothing happened, he pulled again, harder. Hinges creaked, but the door didn't budge.

"Locked from the inside after all. Damn!" He was heaving with the effort he'd expended on the handle. "One more good try." He handed Ethan his axe. Bracing his legs against the wall, he put both hands on the handle, pulled and shoved simultaneously.

Metal hinges groaned again. The door moved outward a couple of centimeters. Something went *ping* on the other side. The door came open a half meter, then a full meter . . . and metal flashed in a bath of moonlight.

"Look out!"

September let go of the handle, fell back onto the paving as Ethan stepped clear and fumbled for his beamer. No time for a knife, since he couldn't tell how many swords might be behind that gate. The giant was already on his knees, ready to confront whoever came charging out the forced door.

"I'm sorry . . . it's hard to see in this light." Elfa Kurdagh-Vlata put up the sword she was carrying, stared at the pair of startled humans.

"You!" Ethan blurted out.

She turned, glanced back at hidden sights, then looked anxiously from one man to the other. "I don't see anyone inside. Where are the two sentries?" When neither human replied, she made a curt gesture of understanding. "Good. I've been huddled inside for ten *vate,* trying to decide what to do. I knew they were out here and could not conceive of how to cut two throats at the same time without raising the alarm. The guard will be changed soon, but now we have time." She appeared to encounter a sudden thought.

"Forgive my preoccupation, Sir Ethan. I am remiss in manners. My thanks to you both for rescuing me."

"I wouldn't take credit for somethin' you seem to have practically pulled off by yourself," September replied. " 'Pon my word, you're a resourceful gal."

"I do my best, Sir Skua." But she was gazing at Ethan as she spoke, her yellow eyes glittering in the dim light.

He turned away hurriedly. "We'd better get moving. No sense tempting luck by hanging around."

"One moment." While Ethan and September exchanged questioning glances she vanished into the unseen courtyard. To Ethan's immense relief, she returned a moment later. Something bulky and indistinct was slung over her right shoulder. Two extensions hung slackly from the rest. Arms.

"What . . . who's that?" he asked.

"I was granted the opportunity to take a prisoner." If the weight of the body was troubling her, she didn't show it. "I believe he is a squire or higher. Would you not wish to learn who attacked us and why?"

"So you don't think it was common piracy either?" September smiled at her, though she couldn't see his grin behind the mask, not in the poor light.

"I do not know for certain, but I would like to."

"So would I." September started toward her. "Let me take him."

She glared at him. "Do you not think I can manage a simple load?"

"I wouldn't be surprised if you couldn't handle anything you wanted to, m'lady-cat. But you're not designed for descending steps, and we've a helluva lot of 'em to make our way down in the darkness. If we were on open ice, I wouldn't have opened my mouth. Do you not think," he finished, mimicking her, "that we can make better time?"

She hesitated only an instant before passing the

80

limp form over. "Rightness of your words, knight." Her attention turned back to Ethan. "So brave of you to challenge the fortress alone."

"We were the ones best built for climbing," he said uncomfortably. "Let's go."

It was Elfa who had the foresight to close and bolt the damaged door behind them.

VI

"Quiet." Hunnar made shushing gestures at the sailors assembled behind him. He peered around the curve of the pinnacle at the base of the stairway. "Someone comes."

The noise of feet on stone sounded for a few minutes more, inaudible to human ears but clear to those of the waiting Tran.

"I recognize Sir Ethan!" one of the squires said, and then they were all rushing from concealment to greet the Landgrave's daughter and her saviors. As they crowded around her, exchanging words and jokes, Ethan mused again on the informality between ruler and subject that was common among the Tran. In fact, he thought some of the joyful embraces between Elfa and sailors overly familiar. Hunnar didn't take exception to them, so Ethan kept his peace.

"So keep you all the glory of this adventure to yourself," the red-bearded knight said to Ethan. But there was no anger, only happiness in his voice as he spoke.

"Don't give us credit for anything except clearing the way." He indicated Elfa. "She was waiting for us at the door."

"With this." September dumped the unconscious prisoner onto the ice. At the sight of one of the kidnappers, angry mutters came from the fight-ready assembly. There was a gentle, dangerous surge toward the motionless shape.

Hunnar motioned them away. "If it is our pleasure

we can kill him later." He looked down at the unfortunate warrior. "And I think that *will* be our pleasure. A wise man can learn even from a burning book."

A pika-pina rope bound the captive's ankles together, a second tied his wrists in front of his groin. Two Tran picked up ropes attached to his feet, opened their dan, and started back toward the distant *Slanderscree*.

As they picked up speed, Ethan wondered at the strength and toughness of Tran hide. The prisoner's back must be feeling the effect of friction between body and ice. He remarked on his concern to Budjir, who was chivaning alongside. The soft-voiced squire replied solemnly that the skin on the prisoner's back was of no interest to anyone, so long as his mouth remained operative.

Considering the mood of the group, Ethan decided it wasn't the time for him to insist on civilized treatment of the captive. He had enough to do keeping his balance as two other Tran pulled him over the ice.

He glanced at his wrist. It was sixty centigrade below.

Happy embraces and greetings were exchanged *en masse* when the little group reached the ship, greetings made doubly fervent at the news that the party had suffered not a single casualty.

Ethan had been expecting furious cries and shouts from behind for the past ten minutes. Evidently the guard still hadn't been changed back at the unsuspecting fortress. Or if it had and Elfa's escape had been discovered, the inhabitants were still debating what to do. By the time they made up their minds to attack again, if they did so, the *Slanderscree* should be far out of reach.

Ta-hoding was already directing the recovery of the anchors. While the captain didn't like the idea of maneuvering the great ship at night and grumbled about it unceasingly, for once his icemanship took second place to military necessity.

Questioning of the captive began the following morning, when the icerigger was far from the cliffs of

Arsudun Isle and the glaring sun showed only clean bare ice behind them.

Though Ethan was interested in most aspects of Trannish culture, he elected to remain far from the bow where the inquiry was taking place. The wind swallowed most of the screams that deck distance didn't. As he fought to ignore those faint, ululating cries he found himself unable not to think of the gap that separated him from his Tran friends. That gap would not vanish, for all that he would have given his life for Hunnar and vice-versa.

Possibly Ethan's great-grandfather many generations removed would have been more empathetic, would have participated in the questioning process with the same cruel indifference of Elfa and Balavere and the others. Such barbarisms were common enough to man's past, up through the twenty-first century, old calendar.

On reflection, though, he was forced to admit that the differences between modern Commonwealth civilization and the feudal methodology employed by the Tran were not so very great. All that distinguished the former from the latter were some informal, mutual understandings known as morals and a few encoded as laws.

There were plenty of citizens in his society who ignored the first while trying to subvert the second. He ought not to raise himself too high, lest the hypocrisy of current civilization make him fall too far. At least the Tran's methods had the virtues of directness and simplicity, even if they were messy. One particularly lengthy, quavering moan reached him across the deck and he found himself unable to repress a shudder.

Troubled, he mounted the steps parallel to the ice-path ascending the helmdeck. Ta-hoding, as always, stood like a part of his beloved ship close by the great curve of the wheel, staring forward. Occasionally he would snap a command to his helmsmen and the wheel would move, or he would shout to the nearest mate some instructions which found their way up the rigging to the sailors working there.

He was the fattest Tran Ethan had encountered, an easy-going, pacifistic sort, less blood-thirsty in manner than the common sailors or professional knights and squires.

"What are they doing to him?"

"The captive?" Ta-hoding kept his gaze on the ice far ahead, sliding beneath the bowsprit. "They are questioning him, friend Ethan."

A faint hissing as of frying bacon sounded above the wind, the noise produced by the five huge duralloy runners slicing across the ice.

"I know that, but . . . how?"

Ta-hoding appeared to consider the question seriously before finally responding. "I do not know how it is with your people, or with the people here, but in Wannome and its neighboring cities the procedure for interrogating a war prisoner is quite standard ritual.

"To demonstrate his bravery and the strength and honor of his family, the captive will lie eloquently or refuse to answer at all. Thus he issues a challenge to his captors that he is more resourceful and courageous than they. Questions will be put to him, or her, with increasing intensity until the captive can no longer resist. He will then provide proper answers.

"The amount of time and effort the captors must employ to finally force those correct, honest replies will determine how much merit the prisoner earns for use in the afterlife."

"What happens when there are no more questions?"

Ta-hoding looked surprised. "The captive is killed, of course."

"But that's inhuman!" Ice crystals scoured his face mask.

Ta-hoding turned his gaze temporarily from the ocean ahead. "We do not lay claim to virtues of being human, friend Ethan. We are Tran. I saw your own sword turned red at the battle of Wannome. Tell me, how do you obtain answers from someone in your own culture who does not wish to cooperate with his captors, or authorities?"

"He's put on a stress analyzer," Ethan replied. "A machine. It monitors his answers *painlessly* and can always tell when a subject is telling the truth."

"Suppose," said Ta-hoding thoughtfully, "the prisoner refuses to reply at all?"

84

"In that case he's bound over under constraint . . . locked up until he decides of his own accord to answer."

"And if he decides never to answer?"

"He stays under constraint, I suppose."

"And you never obtain the answers you require. Very inefficient. Our way is better."

"Just a second," Ethan said. "How do you know his final answers aren't lies? That he's only pretending to tell the truth after you've tort—questioned him?"

Ta-hoding's surprise was greater than before. He looked and sounded deeply shocked. "A captive would lose all the merit he'd gained by his resistance. He would die without merit to carry him through the afterlife!"

Ethan changed his own questioning. "After he has answered all the questions put to him, honestly and truthfully, if what you claim actually is the case, then why kill him?"

"Not all are killed."

"Well, why kill this one?"

"Because he deserves it." Was there a note of pity for Ethan in the captain's voice? Nuances of Tran speech could still give Ethan trouble.

He decided to say something, changed his mind. Better to drop the discussion when the subject of it was still undergoing ordeal.

Or was he? Ethan strained, heard only the rush of wind and sizzle of runner against ice.

September and Hunnar made their way onto the deck. Ethan wondered if his oversized companion had actually watched the procedure. At times he felt a tremendous fondness for the giant, for his easy good humor, his utter disregard for danger and willingness to risk himself for a friend. At other times . . .

Skua September, he reflected, was kin to the Tran in ways other than physical size. When those ways manifested themselves, they made Ethan and Milliken Williams more than a little uncomfortable. He viewed September's personality as an apple. The skin of civilization was bright and polished, but very, very thin.

"Well, young feller-me-lad, we've learned what needed to be learned."

85

"I'm sure you did," Ethan replied, trying to keep his voice neutral. But he couldn't keep himself from asking, "Who did the final killing? You, Sir Hunnar?"

The Tran knight looked upset. "I, friend Ethan? I would not break courtesy so! It was not my place, the honor of dispatching one who had gained much merit not rightfully mine. That was left," he added casually, "to the one most offended in the matter."

Refusing to allow Ethan to ignore the obvious, September finished with fine, indifferent brutality, "The girl did it. Who else? She wanted to do it slowly," he continued conversationally, "but Hunnar and Balavere overruled her. Since the captive held out long and bravely, she had to be satisfied with cutting off his—"

Ethan put his hands over his ears beneath the suit, moved them only when September's mouth stopped moving. He felt sick.

"You didn't hear," the giant said gently, "how they treated her."

"What items of enormous value did you beat out of him?" Ethan muttered disconsolately.

September moved to the railing, looked down at the lightly snow-dusted ice whisking past beneath the ship. "That attack on us was about as accidental and unpremeditated as the one back in the tavern in Arsudun.

"Our prisoner held a rank somewhere between knight and squire. The commander of the fortress was not quite a full knight. They received orders—the prisoner didn't know exactly when—to assault the *Slanderscree* as it rounded the island's southern headland and take it if possible."

"He did not know," Hunnar broke in, "who sent the orders. His commander never told him. But when it was mentioned that you and friend September were aboard, human outlanders, there were questions from the common garrison. They had been taught that humans were not to be harmed."

September, turning from the railing, continued. "For the purposes of this one attack, it seems that that special admonition was to be ignored. Such instructions suggested to our prisoner and to us that the order for the attack came from someone very important and in-

86

fluential, perhaps even the Landgrave of Arsudun. The prisoner refused to believe this.

"I suspect something more than that, feller-me-lad." The railing groaned with his weight. "The *Slander-scree*'s a rich prize for any locals. But for the local Landgrave to countenance the murder of us happy hairless ones, he must feel pretty confident of his position. Matter of fact, he'd have to be almost positive that if the attack failed and word of it got back to Brass Monkey, he wouldn't be subject to reprisals from the local Commonwealth authorities. Which suggests to me that there's collusion between this Landgrave and someone mighty important inside the station hierarchy."

"Trell?"

September considered Ethan's suggestion uncertainly. "I dunno. He was nice enough to us. I'd think someone immediately below him, maybe even that portmaster Xenaxis. He supervises every kilo of trade. It could be anyone with a stake in maintainin' the present monopoly on Tran trade.

"What's important is this means we can't expect help from anyone in Brass Monkey while we're outside the station confines. It's open season until the next Commonwealth ship arrives in orbit. That's two months away. If we return and report now, we'll spend two months fending off assassinations in one form or another. Now that we've been openly attacked, whoever's covering for the Landgrave or high Arsudun native official will take steps to cover his tracks." He glanced down toward the central cabin, where Eer-Meesach and Williams were engaged in frenetic conversation.

"I'd like more discussion, though, before we decide for sure."

Ethan had to give September that. He wasn't afraid to ask for another's opinions, and to change his own if their arguments proved better.

"I think our best bet is to proceed with our original plan and try to get this confederation of island-states started. If we go back to Brass Monkey and present Trell with a fait accompli, I don't think he or whoever's behind all this will try anything. No point in

87

killing us when the monopoly's effectively broken. Leastwise, I hope he'll be that sensible."

"Of course, this may all be so much endophin-swill and it may've been a local attack pure and simple." He looked astern, to where the southern cliffs of Arsudun Isle had shrunk to the size of a modest bump on the horizon.

"We would have taken the ship," the half-angry, half-frightened voice insisted, "were it not for the intervention of the sky-outlanders. They had with them the short knives that fight with pieces of sun." Disgust colored the voice now.

"Of what use is sword or arrow against weapons that can pierce shields and set rafts afire?"

Calonnin Ro-Vijar slumped against the back of the massively timbered armchair and gazed out the third-floor window of the castle. From here, he could see down across the irregular roofs of the city and out across the harbor, could see up the strait almost to the open ice sea. By moving to another window nearby he could study the strange, smooth buildings of the humans and the three glassy bowls where their tiny vessels touched down out of the sky, vessels which brought riches beyond conception every time one arrived.

Riches now threatened.

He became aware of the other's waiting stare, turned to face the worried noble who attended on him. They were alone in the Landgrave's private quarters. This was necessary. The words they exchanged now were too dangerous to be overheard even by the most trusted members of his court. Hence he chose to receive Obel Kasin here and not in the chamber of formal audience.

He knew his continued silence was increasing Kasin's nervousness. Still he did not speak, but watched the slim noble, noting the bandage across the side of his neck, the ragged tear badly patched in the membrane of his left dan, the bare places on his body where fur had been cut away.

"Be at your ease, noble Kasin. You did the best you could."

"I am not," the noble asked unsteadily, "to be punished for my failure?"

"I so promise." Using both hands to help himself rise, Ro-Vijar then walked to stand next to the window. The glassalloy pane stretched from floor to ceiling and framed him unintentionally. It was larger than any other single piece of glass either made or imported into Arsudun. It was larger than any piece of glass Calonnin had ever heard of or imagined. Yet it was here, in *his* castle, come down to him from the heavens in one of the humans' sky-ships. And he had been told and had come to believe that though it was no thicker than his smallest claw, it was stronger than the walls that bordered it.

"As you said," he finally continued, "we cannot fight with swords and shields against the sky people's light knives." He looked back over a shoulder.

"But for all that, we will have that ship, Obel Kasin of Arsudun. One day our flag will fly from its stern and masts and it will stand at the front of the Arsudun fleet." He did not add that some day in the future even the *Slanderscree* could be dispensed with. There were dreams he could as yet share with no one.

"We will have to use caution, and time this next attempt better. I will now take charge of this enterprise myself, noble Kasin. On your way out tell my Minister of Appointments—third door on your left, second level —to ready the *Rinstaster*. That is our best ship. I myself will pick her crew. We will dog the stern of this monster craft until the right opportunity presents itself, whereupon I will take it for Arsudun's glory!"

"Yes, your lordship. May you go with the wind." Genuflecting properly, he departed the room.

Calonnin considered the noble's absence. Kasin had tried hard. His wounds proved his loyalty. There was nothing to be gained by punishing the noble. He knew better than anyone the superiority of the humans' technology. Had he known the three on the great icerigger possessed energy weapons, he would not have ordered the attack.

Excused and commended, Kasin would be twice as trustable now. Ro-Vijar would undertake the task of capturing the icerigger and killing her crew and the humans allied with them because he could not trust anyone else to do it. No one else had his reason or fervor.

Until now he had kept himself hidden in this matter. He could do so no longer.

Dreaming, he pictured the huge ice boat, saw again its human-metal runners which did not wear out or crack on the ice as did stone and bone and wood, saw once more the well-made pika-pina sails and rigging. He imagined it as he'd described it to Kasin, sails full of wind, pennants and insignia of Arsudun flying from her high places.

And if his plans came to fruition, some day that great ship would be but a toy to sneer at. For a while, however, it would be good to possess her.

Though he could not hope to overtake the craft, it must eventually stop someplace. That would be the time for capture.

Distasteful as it would be, he had first to talk to the human Landgrave before he departed.

Jobius Trell received the Landgrave of Arsudun in his office. As the temperature inside was adjusted for human norm, the near-naked Landgrave suffered in brutally hot temperatures.

Trell had altered his midday schedule to receive Ro-Vijar. He wore a light orange service tunic open to the waist, light braid at waist, sleeves, and ankles. He greeted Ro-Vijar alone.

The Landgrave had likewise left his personal bodyguard outside the human's building. Both men felt more comfortable that way. It gave them privacy and confidence, since each felt himself more than a fighting match for the other.

Ro-Vijar chose a couch rather than one of the narrow human chairs. Sitting straight despite the invitingly curved back, he ignored the tremendous heat that suffused the office as he regarded his human counterpartner. This was a little game they played. Whenever Trell came to visit Ro-Vijar in his castle, the Landgrave took particular delight in opening all the storm-shutters and windows so that the freezing winds of Tran-ky-ky could pour through whatever room they were in. Since Trell had to lift the mask of his survival suit indoors in order to keep custom unblemished by showing his face to his host, Ro-Vijar could enjoy the human's discomfort as his skin reddened from the chill—though Trell pretended to be as relaxed and at ease as Ro-Vijar did now.

It was a fair exchange of favors. Trell had one slight advantage in detecting discomfort, however. Having no sweat glands, the Tran did not perspire. So Trell could tell that the Landgrave was feeling especially uncomfortable whenever he covered his mouth with a paw, in an attempt to conceal his lolling tongue and his heat-shedding panting. If he tried to go an entire visit without panting, his overheated body would cause him to black out. Very undignified.

"So they got away," Trell was saying, getting down to business after the exchange of pleasantries had been concluded. "That's unfortunate."

"Worry not, friend Jobius," Calonnin said reassuringly. "They have accomplished nothing, nor will they. I myself will follow with a crew of my best and most trusted soldiers. They will have to tie up that great hulking ship of theirs sometime to spread their vicious treasons. When they do, I will let circumstances determine my method. Whatever I eventually choose, it will be quite final and efficient."

Trell was nodding. "Good, good."

"The noble I placed in charge of this first attempt did what he could. He was defeated by the hand weapons of the three humans on the ship." Settling himself into the disgustingly soft couch back, he forced himself to appear monumentally indifferent to Trell's response to his next question.

"If you could provide me with at least a couple of similar devices and instruct myself and my knights in their use, the success of our journey would be assured."

Trell shook his head, smiled paternally. "Friend Calonnin, you know I can't do that. Commonwealth and Church declarations strictly prohibit the distribution of modern weaponry to non-Commonwealth peoples. Even those races that have attained associate membership cannot obtain energy weapons except un-

91

der special circumstances. Ownership is restricted to full Commonwealth members. This is not a rule of my making, but it is one I can't risk breaking.

Trell hoped his friend understood his refusal.

"Until some future date you'll have to make do with the weapons of your own civilization. In your skilled hands, I'm sure they'll prove more than adequate."

"I did not mean to imply thay would not," the Landgrave assured him. "Your light knives would make this business simpler and much quicker, though."

Trell wagged a finger at him. "Patience is another modern weapon which you can obtain for yourself, Ro-Vijar. But when this obstacle to our future plans is removed, who knows what arrangements we might work out? Arrangements whereby even extreme edicts can be bypassed. But not this time, not today."

"I understand, friend Trell." Ro-Vijar stood, panting like an overworked hessavar. "I am leaving my cousin, Sir Das Kooliatin, as ruler of Arsudun during my absence. You may deal as candidly with him as you see fit. He is unimaginative and harbors no delusions about replacing me on the throne—a trusted relative." This last was mentioned not to compliment the absent Kooliatin, but simply to forestall any idea, however faint, which the human Commissioner might entertain about dealing with someone other than Calonnin.

"Let's not delay your pursuit any longer, then." Trell pulled himself up, walked to stand next to the Landgrave. Round pupils met vertical ones. "The sooner this unfortunate business is concluded, the more easily I'll rest."

"I also, friend Trell." Reaching out, he wrapped one huge paw around the Commissioner's hand. Then Trell leaned forward, placed both his palms on the Landgrave's shoulders and exhaled into his face.

"My breath is your warmth. Go with the wind, friend Calonnin."

Ro-Vijar exited, exerting monumental effort to keep from breaking into a run to escape the hothouse hell of Trell's office for the cool breezes outside.

The Commissioner waited until the Landgrave had left the outer offices. Then he resumed his seat. Touching several switches brought out tapes and the rest of the days work. As always, he allowed himself the pleasure of checking several private molecular files and smiling at the hidden bank accounts there. They were listed under numerous names and companies, but the credit was all his. This delightful activity concluded, he passed on to the more prosaic work of Resident Commissioner.

Calonnin would succeed in his mission. The Landgrave was a resourceful and dedicated individual, at least as greedy as Trell. He had great confidence in the native leader, in his imagination and enterprise.

But Calonnin Ro-Vijar was entirely too imaginative and enterprising to be trusted with anything as lethal as modern energy weapons. Nothing like a needler to give a primitive mind delusions of grandeur. No, Ro-Vijar would remain far more manageable, though never exactly docile, if his methods of violent argument were restricted to lance, arrow and sword.

That was important to Trell's blueprint for the future development of Tran-ky-ky. Keep temptations from Ro-Vijar's hands and he'd be less likely to conjure up awkward ideas. He touched a control which automatically imprinted his signature of approval on a request for certain materials for quartermaster division, then went on to the next tape.

Trell was perfectly correct in his overall assessment of Calonnin Ro-Vijar's qualities, but he was wrong on one crucial point. The Landgrave did not need possession of modern weapons to inspire grandiose delusions. He had plenty of those already.

As he chivaned toward the harbor and his waiting craft, Ro-Vijar considered the details of his recent interview with the human Commissioner. If Trell would not provide him with light knives, he would obtain them somewhere else. Were there not three of the irresistible weapons on the persons of the humans he was going to kill? Once that disagreeable task was concluded, he could easily fabricate some clever story for Trell's ears to explain the disappearance of the human's weapons. Trell might be suspicious, but what could he prove?

If a cub could trip over a slithering *megorph,* could

not a human trip over the future? These purveyors of wealth from the sky might be rich and wise. They were not omnipotent.

VII

The object of Calonnin Ro-Vijar's avaricious thoughts was at that moment nearing the equator of Tran-ky-ky. It was near noon. Ethan was studying the ice sliding past below.

No matter where they passed, the sun always seemed to bring out hidden patterns in the ice ocean's surface. But what Ethan noticed now startled him more than any fanciful face or half-concealed monster thrown back from subsurface cracks and discolorations.

In places, a thin layer of water lay on the ice. Widely scattered puddles formed unexpected mirrors. Once, the *Slanderscree* shot through a depression filled with enough water to send spray flying rail-high.

Several hours later, the temperature had dropped enough for the isolated pools to freeze solid again, but the mere sight of free-standing liquid water on Tran-ky-ky was a considerable shock.

It had a much more deleterious effect on the crew. They were used to seeing running water only in their homes, after ice or snow had been melted down for drinking. Their reaction would be comparable to a human watching the ground beneath his feet begin to dissolve. It was overwhelming to learn that one's world was not indestructible.

Williams and Eer-Meesach moved among the jittery sailors, assuring them that their cataclysmic speculations were groundless, that there was no danger of the ice ocean melting more than a few centimeters in this one exceptionally warm place on the planetary surface. Regardless, Williams told them, the *Slanderscree* would surely float.

It took him a while to explain the concept of floating.

As soon as the sun dropped a few degrees and the surface water refroze, however, even the most superstitious sailors were convinced they had nothing to fear.

Several warning cries sounded that afternoon from the lookout baskets attached to the top of each mast. Ethan rushed to the helmdeck, the nerve center of the great icerigger, to learn what was happening.

He found Ta-hoding yelling commands to his mates, directing the reefing of several sails. Pika-pina sheets began to shrink in the forest of rigging and spars. Ethan forbore interrupting the captain when he was obviously so busy and was soon able to make out the cause of their slowing for himself.

A green thread lying across the fore horizon grew to become a ribbon, then a deep, verdant band. It stretched as far as a man could see from left to right across the ice sea. The band became a broad swatch and soon they were sliding over an ocean of green instead of white.

The massive duralloy runners of the *Slanderscree* left parallel grooves in the emerald-rust carpet of their wake. Sir Hunnar moved to stand alongside Ethan.

" 'Tis one of the largest fields of pika-pina I have ever seen, friend Ethan. 'Twould be a good place to live, were there any high land about."

Ethan knew the adaptable, prolific plant could live anywhere it could sink its traveling roots into nutrient-rich soil. The islands hereabouts might be only a centimeter or two above the surface. Or perhaps the fields' taproots went deep through the ice to penetrate subsurface mountaintops.

In places the thick, triangular stalks tended to a deep, rich green, in others the color turned almost red or brown. Hunnar talked on about the agricultural wealth of this unexploited, icebound prairie.

He didn't use a complex collection of consonants, but instead referred to the growth by its most simple, colloquial name, for the benefit of speech-poor humans. Occasionally the passage of the icerigger would stir up clouds of batwinged butterflylike creatures, little knots of black, purple, and gray fur supported by wings seemingly too delicate to cope with Tran-ky-ky's ferocious winds.

Larger arboreals would then rise to pursue. These had long thin snouts, almost half the length of their bodies, which were filled to crowding with curved, pin-thin teeth. Flapping membranous wings, they would swoop in among the bat-butterflies, mouths moving like scythes as they snapped at their agile but tightly packed prey. Pincushion jaws nearly always emerged from the colorful moving clouds with one or two punctured prizes.

Hunnar's attention wandered to Eer-Meesach's more learned explanations directed at the school teacher Williams. Though diminutive and wizened by adult Tran standards, the aged native wizard still towered over his human counterpart, his white-gray fur contrasting electrically with Williams' satin black beneath his face mask.

"So we see that the pika-pina's regenerative powers are so great that though it is cut today, it will have grown in behind us by this time on the morrow." The wizard gestured with a shaky paw at the tracks in the path of the ship.

"If it can regenerate so fast," asked Williams, "why doesn't it spread until it covers every square meter of ice on the planet?"

"It is not that simple, friend Williams." And Eer-Meesach repeated the method of pika-pina growth which Ethan had come to know and marvel at.

Long burrowing roots laboriously melted or wedged their way through the ice just beneath the surface until they located a cavity, usually an ancient air bubble trapped by freezing. The root would expand there to form a thick nodule. Nutrients concentrated in such nodules—which the Tran hungered after—were difficult to locate and hard to excavate. When the nodule was rich and large enough, it would send out four, five or more new roots in quest of other cavities, while the nodule's supply of nutrients was constantly replenished from other nodules and eventually from some distant landmass.

"Thus," the wizard continued, "with many nodules nearby, the pika-pina can quickly re-establish itself behind our ship, since root-paths have already been cut through the ice here. But to expand further into new territory, it must dig new pathways for itself through the resisting ice. This is why——"

A yell from the mainmast interrupted the lecture. Ethan looked forward, to where the field of green was becoming a wall.

"Pika-pedan," he murmured to himself.

Ta-hoding was already studying the forest through a crude but serviceable Tran telescope. "It appears to extend," he told Ethan, in response to the other's question, "as far to east and west as its tiny cousin." He put down the glass, looked worried.

Pika-pedan was the giant relative of the smaller pika-pina, rising to heights of as much as ten meters.

Hunnar appeared on deck, folded his dan and skidded to a stop. "Weather and ice are your concern, Captain. Do what you believe best."

"Poyolavomaar is through this," Ta-hoding pointed out. "We do not know the extent of the field to east and west. My directions do not take detouring into account. If we try to go around, we could become hopelessly lost and never reach our destination.

"Therefore, we must try to go through." He moved forward, to the front railing of the helmdeck. "Hello the deck!" Acknowledgement sounded instantly from waiting mates.

Ta-hoding ordered additional sail put on. There was good-natured grumbling from the sailors on spar duty as the sheets they'd just recently taken in were let out again, billowing taut in the steady wind.

The *Slanderscree* was once again traveling under full sail. She picked up speed steadily, massively.

"What would you have ordered, good friend Ethan?"

Startled, he turned to see Elfa staring at him. He hadn't seen her come up on the helmdeck. Great searchlight eyes shone down at him, competing with the sun.

"We have to go through, of course." He tried to sound as positive as Ta-hoding had.

"The bolder decision, but typical of you." She favored him with a searing Trannish smile, then moved away to ask a question of Eer-Meesach before Ethan could explain that he was only agreeing with Ta-hoding's decision.

Ethan turned, caught Hunnar glaring morosely at him. As soon as the knight saw that his stare had been noticed he turned away, chivaning down the ramp to the main deck.

Ethan considered following him, to explain, and then decided not to. Apparently repeated protests had done nothing to mollify Hunnar's absurd jealousies. Repetition of his innocence would have no more effect than before.

A subtle jar shook the ship, forcing him to clutch at the nearest support. It felt as if the *Slanderscree* had rammed a gigantic sponge. The sweeping panorama of green fields and blue sky had been obliterated by the columnar emerald wall now sliding past on both sides of the ship. Moving at over ninety kilometers per hour, the icerigger had struck the pika-pedan forest and was grinding smoothly through it.

A glance astern showed a lengthening highway unrolling like a ribbon, the pika-pedan stalks cut off four meters above the ice by the speeding mass of the ship. Flat-sided green logs lay strewn across the stumps, fragments from the broom of a chlorophyllic colossus.

Without distant landmarks to measure by, it was difficult to estimate their speed. Ethan guessed the ship had slowed some since impact, but was still traveling steadily ahead at a respectable velocity. Water and pulp spattered his survival suit, and he had to turn away to keep his vision clear. Up by the bowsprit, he knew the situation must be far worse.

It seemed incredible that the dense vegetation would give way so easily before the ship. But while the pika-pedan looked more solid and treelike than its miniature relative, it was equally mushy inside, consisting mostly of water-soaked soft fibres which snapped instantly under the weight of the *Slanderscree*.

A harsh, husky screech sounded just to port. Ethan looked in that direction in time to see a pair of startled guttorbyn—winged, dragonlike predators—take to the air. For several minutes they paralleled the ship, hissing and screaming imprecations at the crew, before veering off southeast. A flock would have attacked.

There being only two, and two surprised ones at that, they chose retreat over challenge.

The furry butterfly-things were abundant in the high vegetation, and once Ethan thought he spied something long and luminous, like a writhing sunbeam, slithering away from the ship's path with incredible speed. Instead of screaming, it sang weird flute notes back at him as it vanished into the dense evergrowth, and Ethan never knew it was not the creature itself he had seen but its radiant shadow.

Below the tops of the pika-pedan, the wind penetrated fitfully. It was unusually quiet on board, not only from the absence of the familiar gale, but because each crewmember was attending to private thoughts as well as cooperative sailing. Ethan knew the Tran did not enter and explore the rolling forests of pika-pedan. They did not do so because of its usual impenetrability, and because of herds of a certain creature which fed within.

Yet this time the Tran had an advantage. The masts of the *Slanderscree* towered above the crowns of the forest. So did the spines of the animals they feared. From the several lookout baskets, those heaving backs could be spotted in time to give the ship a chance to escape.

Perhaps the lookouts were too intent on sighting that particular danger. Perhaps they might not have been able to spot the trouble anyway.

Suddenly the ship lost forward momentum with a violent shudder. Ethan and everyone else not holding on to something was thrown to the deck. Even as his bulging form was rolling around behind the wheel, Ta-hoding was shouting commands.

Accustomed to sudden, unpredictable gusts of wind, the sailors in the rigging had actually fared better than those on deck. None had fallen, though for several minutes a couple of those in the highest spars hung from a paw or two before regaining their footing.

Tilted twenty degrees to port, bow dipping drunkenly iceward, the *Slanderscree* continued to lurch awkwardly forward.

Back on his feet, Ta-hoding braced chiv against ice and bellowed orders toward the deck. The stern ice anchors were released. They immediately gouged a purchase in the ice and pika-pedan stumps astern. Several seconds of screeching, teeth-scraping progress slowed the out-of-control icerigger to a crawl. She came to a full stop when the last sail was finally taken in.

Ethan, September, Hunnar, Elfa and Ta-hoding went over the side, made their way down a pika-pina ladder. Detailed inspection wasn't necessary. Something had knocked the port bow runner badly askew. It hadn't been torn completely away, but the duralloy rods which braced it to the ship's hull had nearly been wrenched from their moorings. Plates and bolts were missing, and the wood they'd ripped free of was torn and full of gaping holes.

While Ta-hoding began to direct repairs, Ethan and the others retraced the path of the *Slanderscree*. They followed the path cut by the disabled runner, forced to walk single-file between walls of four-meter-high pika-pedan stumps, constantly slipping and sliding over gelatinous globules of rapidly freezing watery sap.

They traveled less than a couple of hundred meters before coming on the cause of the crash. Small rocky spires, showing the mark of the broken runner on them, protruded from the ice. It wasn't any wonder the lookouts hadn't spotted them, buried as they were in thick vegetation. They were barely two meters high, too low to rip into the hull of the ship, but high and solid enough to wreck the impinging runner. Only good luck had saved the other runners a similar fate.

Hunnar bent, indicated a whitish groove in one frozen mass of granite. "See . . . 'twas here the ship struck. We were fortunate the islet was no larger than this."

"Islet!" September grunted. "Why, we're standin' atop a mountain, friend Hunnar. These spires go down to the bottom of this frozen ocean we're sailing across."

"We can't be sure of that, Skua." Ethan struggled to visualize, say, six or seven thousand meters of mass below their feet. "These could just be very large boulders frozen in the ice, deposited by glacial or ice action. Or maybe the ocean here is only a few meters deep. We might be traveling across a shallow sea covering an old desert. These could be rocks on a plain."

September looked disappointed. "Mountaintop's better. You sure can take all the romance out of speculatin', young feller-me-lad."

Ethan gave September a look which clearly said, believe what you want. He turned to go back to the ship, and fell flat on his face after taking only a few steps.

No one found it funny. For so short a journey, neither human had bothered donning his skates, but that wasn't what had caused Ethan to fall.

Three . . . no, four, tiny cream-white tendrils had erupted from the ice and locked around his right ankle. Now they were stretched taut, pulling him downward. Ice began to crack in sheets around his prone form. Ethan fought for a grip on the slick surface. His hips were already vanishing beneath the surface when he managed to lock both arms around a pika-pedan stump. It broke off in his arms like rotten punk.

By then Hunnar and September had come up alongside him. Hunnar drew his sword, but September waved him away.

"For God's sake, Skua, hurry up!" Perversely, Ethan clung to his fragment of pika-pedan, though it was no better anchored than he.

September, sighting carefully on a point just behind and slightly to Ethan's left, depressed the stud of his beamer. There was the snake-talk sound of steam boiling away. It was followed, joined by a stench as of rotting pork. The tendrils wrapped around Ethan's leg did not let go, but the pulling stopped.

Meantime, Hunnar had moved around to grab Ethan's wrists. Digging his chiv sideways into the ice and using the stubby braking claw in his heel, he started to move slowly backward. Ethan came free of the hole in the ice. Attached by its tendrils to his leg, the almost-victor came out after him. It had a smoking gash in its side.

Others had heard the cries and the hiss and light of the beamer. A small mob of concerned Tran was bearing down on the three from the ship. Eer-Meesach, helped along by Williams, was among them.

Ethan, panting heavily inside his suit mask, turned

101

on his back, sat up, and gazed in disgust and fear at the creature attached to his ankle. "What is it?"

Hunnar had his knife out and was slicing through the clinging tendrils. Ethan let out a relieved sigh when he saw that the powerful grip hadn't torn his survival suit.

Pale white with gray blotches and spots, the thing was three meters long, not counting the tendrils. It showed four wide, plate-sized eyes, two atop the dorsal side and two on the ventral. The four tendrils were spaced evenly around the blunt end of the head. Between them, slack and open, was a circular mouth lined with triangular serrated teeth. The jaws were protruding outside the lips, showing wet and shocking pink against the whiteness of the epidermis. Ethan considered what those teeth would have done to his leg had he slid just a little farther beneath the surface.

"Tis a kossief," Hunnar replied thoughtfully, studying the ghostly corpse. This translated very crudely to Terranglo in Ethan's mind as an ice worm.

"They burrow just beneath the surface and wait for some unfortunate creature to stumble across their portion of ice, which they hollow out until only a thin layer remains above them." The knight kicked at the rubbery body. "They strike upward, break through the thin ice and drag their prey down into their burrows. Then they exude water through this," he indicated a protruding organ near the creature's rear, "and reform the ice shell over them."

Ethan studied the toothed worm with distaste as he massaged his leg where the beast had grabbed him. "I can see how they can cut their way through the ice, with those teeth."

"Neatly, too," said an admiring September. He was standing in the bow-like hollow that had been the creature's home. His head was just barely even with the surface.

"Are there others that live beneath the surface of the ice?" Williams was examining the dead worm with as much interest as Ethan had shown disgust.

"Many and various, my friend," discoursed Eer-Meesach. "We see them little around Wannome. They are more prevalent at the other end of Sofold Isle,

102

where the pika-pina fields grow. It is interesting to learn that they flourish also here, among the pika-pedan."

"Can we take it back aboard?" Williams looked hopeful.

"Why of course, we must," said the Tran wizard. Ethan said nothing. He gained some measure of satisfaction in learning that he wasn't alone in his squeamish attitude toward the creature. The two men of learning had a hard time cajoling a pair of sailors to carry the rubbery body back onto the ship.

September had concluded his own examination of the kossief's house. Ethan gave him a hand out and thanked him simultaneously.

"I'd feel better about acceptin' your thanks, lad, if it'd been less of a near thing. I missed my first shot. The ice here is pretty clear, but I could see just the barest outline of a shape down there and forgot to allow for diffraction." He glanced back at the ominous hole. "Let's get back aboard—and let's both watch our steps . . ."

It took four days to properly repair the huge runner. They were in a race with the cut-over pika-pedan, which grew in behind the icerigger to heights of six and seven meters and pressed insistently against the bottom of the raft.

Williams paced anxiously about, trying to form botanical and zoological expeditions to search out the secrets of the homogenized forest. Even Eer-Meesach had sensed enough danger to veto those suggestions. No man could tell what lurked in the depths of such dense aggregations of verdure. The horrors that were known, such as the kossief, were enough to keep a prudent man aboard his ship. No need for them to hunt up new, exciting ways to die.

The disappointed schoolteacher still found enough wild life nearby to keep him occupied. Like a child playing with a new toy, he watched fascinated as another kossief living near the first took a six-legged herbivore browsing among the dried-out stalks behind the ship. Its flat crab eyes rolled in terror as dull grinding teeth snapped futilely at the leather-tough tendrils dragging it downward.

Ethan watched also, his a fascination of a different kind. The herbivore's scream was no less pitiable for its alienness. He had a chance to see what his own fate would have been had September not rescued him.

As soon as the kossief had sucked enough blood out of the hapless grazer to immobilize it, the burrower generated heat. Ice melted beneath them both, refroze above them, sculpted and filled by water from the anal nozzle Hunnar had pointed out. Safely protected from scavengers and nonburrowing predators by a meter and a half of rock-hard ice, the kossief settled in to enjoy its meal.

Ethan shuddered. Not a neat way to die. He made a personal promise never to venture alone where either variety of the triangular green plant grew.

On the last day the sailors sped their repairs at the news that a lookout had heard the distant, reverberant cry of a droom. Fortunately, the monster did not come near enough to be seen and the prevailing wind was away from the direction of the cry.

Small four-legged quns the size of Ethan's hand roamed up and down nearby stalks of mature pika-pedan, burrowing and eating their way in and out of the thick trunks like mice turned loose in a king-sized cheese. They began near the crest of a stalk and munched their way downward, leaving nothing to waste. They preferred damaged or sick stalks, thus helping to preserve the vitality of the forest.

Ethan's favorite was a thing Eer-Meesach called a meworlf. It had a sausage-shaped body from which dangled thin, jointed, two-meter-long legs. A sack ran the length of its cylindrical back. When inflated, the sack swelled to balloon size. Maneuvering on the subdued breeze within the pika-pedan, the meworlf would drift from stalk to stalk, anchoring itself with four of its ten wiry limbs to a selected trunk and using the other six to pluck away bits of plant and convey them to the small mouth. When finished feeding, the meworlf would remain bobbing lazily in the breeze or release its grasp and let the wind carry it through the forest, bouncing like a ball from one stalk to the next.

Fascinating as the extraordinary fauna of the pika-pedan forest was to Williams, it soon began to pale for Ethan. By the fourth day, he was as ready as any of the common sailors to be moving again.

But when full sail had been put out, the worst fears of the experienced icemen were realized.

"We're not moving," Ethan observed, concerned. He turned to the captain. "What's wrong?"

"I worried much on this, friend Ethan." Ta-hoding's expression was glummer than usual. "We had no choice, though. The runner had to be repaired."

"Of course it did." Ethan indicated the gently billowing sails low on the masts, the gustily taut ones higher up, above the roof of the forest. "You mean, we don't have the momentum necessary to get us started?"

He saw the problem now. While the *Slanderscree* was traveling at a respectable speed, she had enough energy to plow easily through the soft pika-pedan. But once stopped, with the thick green pseudopods practically growing over the railings, she couldn't get moving.

"So what can we do about it?"

"We cannot back up," said Ta-hoding solemnly, gesturing behind them. "The pika-pedan has grown too tall and thick behind us while we have waited here."

"What about sending out a crew with axes and swords to cut a clear path ahead of us?"

"We may have to try precisely that, friend Ethan. But I wish I could think of another way. By the time our people could cut a path wide enough for the ship, a decent distance ahead of us, the pika-pedan they first felled would be growing up stiff behind them.

"However," he said, executing a Tran gesture indicative of hopelessness mixed with resignation, "I confess I see nothing else to be done." He waddled off to give instructions to Hunnar.

Everyone not immediately concerned with the operation of the icerigger was sent over the side and was soon frantically hacking away at the forest ahead of

105

the ship with axes, kitchen cleavers, anything that would cut. The huge stalks fell easily, squirting water and sap over the frenzied group of foresters, who knew they were racing against the growing time of the stumps behind them.

Even Ethan, using his sword, could cut down a ten-meter tall column of pika-pedan in ten minutes or so, though the constant swinging was wearying to muscles not used to such activity. To provide a path expansive enough for a ship the size of the *Slanderscree*, it was necessary to fell a great many pika-pedan. They couldn't stop. When the pika-pedan behind them reached underbelly deck level of four meters, they would have to retreat and try to break out as best they could.

As it turned out, they had to quit before they wanted to.

All eyes, on board and in the work party, went to the main-mast observation basket, whose wicker-enclosed lookout was screaming while pointing frantically to the east.

"Stavanzer!"

"How far?" roared Ta-hoding, cupping thick paws to his lips.

"Twenty, maybe thirty kijat," the reply came back from the lookout.

"Coming this way?"

"It is difficult to tell, Captain, at this distance."

"How many?"

"Again hard to tell. I am sure of only one." A pause, then, "Still only one."

There was no need to give the order to abandon cutting and return to the ship. At the news of a sta-vanzer in the vicinity, a retreat to the raft was a matter of instinct, not debate. Everyone was chivaning or running through the maze of felled pika-pedan stalks without having to be told.

"What now, Captain?" Ethan asked Ta-hoding when he'd made his breathless way back to the helmdeck.

Eer-Meesach was standing at the railing, peering forward out of old eyes. "To most it hints of death's proximity, friend Ethan. But it could also be our salvation."

106

"How can that be?"

"Consider if the thunder-eater passes close to us, Ethan. You know how the stavanzer travels by pushing itself across the ice. In so doing it smoothes everything in its path as flat as a metalworker's forge."

"I see. So we can go out the way it comes in?"

"More than that, friend Ethan." Ta-hoding, overhearing, elaborated. "Once we build up enough speed traveling back down the thunder-eater's trail, we can then turn the ship and continue in any direction we wish."

"It is the building up of enough speed that is critical," Eer-Meesach finished.

"Kinetic energy," Ethan murmured, and then had to try and explain the unfamiliar-sounding Terranglo term in Trannish.

"It will be not easy." Ta-hoding was talking as much to himself as to his listeners. "Even if we do pass successfully into the trail, there are other dangers to be considered." Ethan didn't press him for an explanation.

"We must make a decision. We do have a choice." He gestured within an arm toward the bow, his dan momentarily billowing with wind. "We have cut a path a kijat or two ahead of us. We can reset sail and make a run at the forest wall. If that fails, we will then have no room to maneuver, and it will be most difficult to try and back up for another run. Also, I should like to keep that option open, should the thunder-eater swerve and bear down on us."

"Seems pretty obvious to me what we do," said a new voice. September mounted to the helmdeck. "We wait and try to slip in behind it."

Ta-hoding's gaze traveled around the little knot of decision-makers. His usual jollity was absent now. He was all business. "It's settled, then," and he moved to the railing to issue instructions.

Twenty minutes of waiting followed the final preparations. All sailors were at their posts, knights and squires ready to assist when and where they could. The quns had vanished into their holes, and a last meworlf battered itself like a crazed mechanical toy against the stalks as it sought to race out of the area.

107

Presently, a deeper sound rose above the wind-choir, a periodic breathy grumble like a KK-drive slipping past lightspeed. From his single previous encounter, Ethan knew the noise was caused by the stavanzer's method of locomotion. Expelling air through a pair of downward-facing nozzles set in its lower back, it could also pull itself slowly forward across the ice on its lubricated belly by means of the two down-thrust tucks protruding from its upper jaw—though that rubbery formation could hardly be called a jaw.

The rumble grew deeper. The *Slanderscree* quivered steadily as the ice beneath it shook to the rhythm of a monstrous metabolism.

Ethan experienced an unlikely urge to climb into the rigging, to get above the wavering crowns of pika-pedan so he could see. But he stayed where he was, out of the sailors' way.

Murmurs drifted down from those in the highest spars, their eyes focused on something unseen. Their companions hushed them. Ethan let his gaze travel forward.

At the far end of the crude pathway they'd so laboriously hacked from the rusty forest a great mass slid into view. It stood perhaps twelve meters above the ice, a black maw inhaling felled pika-pedan with Jobian patience as the horny lower lip/jaw sliced off the nutrient-rich stalks flush with the ice.

Once, the upper jaw lifted and the huge tusks came slamming down into the ice hard enough to make the kijat-distant *Slanderscree* rock unsteadily. Ice, roots, protein-rich nodules were vacuumed indiscriminately into the Pit: proteins and nodules and bulk to be converted into fuel and cells, ice to be melted and flushed throughout the vast metabolic engine.

Tearing unconcernedly into the wall of fresh pika-pedan ahead of it, the massive head vanished from sight. Like an ancient snowbound train, the dark gray bulk slid across their path. Parasites and other growths of respectable size formed a fantastic foliage of their own on the leviathan's sides and back, a private jungle none dared explore. The fluctuating howl from the intake and expulsion of air was deafening now.

108

Fortunately, the thunder-eaters had poor vision and poor hearing. They had no need for these faculties, having nothing to be alert against. The beast slid past, its blunt tail-end vanishing in quest of body and skull, without taking any notice of the *Slanderscree* or its anxiously silent crew.

It was gone, though they could still hear it eating its endless meal as it moved steadily off to the west.

Difficult as it was to be objective when confronted with so over-poweringly grand an example of nature's diversity, Ethan estimated its length at somewhere between seventy and eighty meters. A mature specimen, but from what he'd been told, not an exceptionally large one. He'd seen bigger himself. He doubted this one weighed more than two hundred fifty tons.

They should have waited another half hour, to be safe, before getting under way, but the sailors were growing restless. Fear that the thunder-eater would perhaps change its path (they were notoriously unpredictable in their habits) and charge down upon them poisoned the sailors' blood with fear. Finally, even the patient Ta-hoding could stand the waiting no longer.

"All sail on, snap to the windwhips!"

The ice anchors had long since been hauled in. Ponderously, but with far more grace than the thunder-eater, the *Slanderscree* began to move forward. Ship's bones groaned as the five duralloy runners broke clear their slight accumulations of drifted snow and ice.

The grinding of the runners became a slick abrasive noise as the huge ship picked up speed. Two, four, ten, fifteen kilometers an hour. Twenty. Thirty and a familiar whisking *zing* rose from where duralloy lacerated ice. They were nearing the end of the brief clearing the crew had bought from the forest.

"Hard a'port! Sparmen swing-ho!"

Both helmsmen strained at the massive wooden wheel. Inefficient muscle worked where hydraulics wold better have served. A nerve-scraping screel came from the fifth runner, the steering runner, as it slowly turned. Sailors aloft fought to adjust sail and trim adjustable spar lines.

And steadily, with unexpected sharpness, the *Slanderscree* hove to port.

Both helmsmen struggled to hold the wheel steady as their feet left the deck. September threw his mass on the port side of the wheel and Ta-hoding added his. With four bodies straining, the runner stayed turned and the ship continued to come around even as her speed increased.

Then Ta-hoding and September could let go. The feet of the starboard side helmsman touched wood again as the extreme angle of turn was relaxed. They were racing down a broad avenue of clear ice cut by the stavanzer.

On command the two helmsmen let go the wheel, to allow the ship to settle on her own forward heading. With the westwind directly behind them now, there was no worry of swerving violently from the trail. The wheel turned freely to a halt, spinning fast enough to crush a man's skull. The helmsmen resumed their positions, tested the wheel and found it handled easily once more.

At sixty kilometers an hour they rushed down the slough. Pika-pedan pulp stained the ice below the runners, and the unbroken growth paralleling them became a green blur on both sides of the ship. With the wind behind them, muffled by the surrounding forest, they seemed to fly below the surface instead of above it, submerged in emerald silence.

The quiet made audible to the relaxing crew the horrified shriek of the foremast lookout.

Ethan looked forward, ignorant of the loss of precious seconds. One, no two gigantic black pits like the mouths of caves were coming toward them, completely blocking the trail. As they raced nearer, a mysterious whisper became a fearful murmuring, then a tornado of roaring and bellowing that shook his teeth inside his head.

Ta-hoding desperately shouted instructions to the mates and the men in the rigging, trying at the same time to direct his helmsmen.

Again the steering runner turned, terror lending the Tran at its spokes a strength normal minds and bodies never possess. Again it dug and chewed at the ice.

The *Slanderscree* angled to the south, slamming into the forest with a deck-sloshing spray of shattered stalks and sap. But now the ship was moving so fast the forest offered no real impediment. Pika-pedan trunks vanished on all sides as the weighty bulk of the icerigger slashed through.

They were off the occupied trail.

And several gray curves showed above the crest of the forest like islands in a pea-green sea.

"Turn!" Ethan found himself pounding the railing and yelling till his throat hurt. *"Turn!"*

There were commands, but the experienced sailors knew the chance they had to take and the action to make it happen. Everyone on the deck and in the rigging rushed as fast as he or she was able to the starboard side of the ship.

With the steering runner hard over until its bolts creaked, the sails properly trimmed, and all movable mass shifted to one side, the *Slanderscree*'s portside runners lifted with infinite slowness from the surface of the ice ocean.

A few centimeters, a half meter, two meters. A few sailors wrestled their way back to portside. The ship held, heeling dangerously far over on its right side, balancing now on two runners. The duralloy would hold, but what about the iron and steel bolts and wooden braces holding the runners to the ship? All sailors aloft held on for their lives. If they fell overboard now, into the forest, they knew they could expect no rescue.

Ethan saw wood and sky as he looked toward the left side of the ship. A voluminous black gullet like an empty place in space loomed over the far railing. There was the sound of an intimate thunder, and suction tore at him, then was gone. Two tusks, each thicker than the *Slanderscree*'s mainmast, caught the sun and sent it tumbling into his mask, temporarily blinding him.

"By the Servants of the Dark One, she'll go over!" someone howled.

The tusks came down, fourteen meters of solid ivory, tons of beauty in the mouth of a demon.

But by that time the ship had already shot past.

111

Ethan leaned over the railing to look back, saw the tusks strike ice and send ten-kilo splinters flying. A tiny wild eye, set back of that monstrous maw, rolled dully at him and he fancied he could see through it and into a ridiculously small brain.

Dimly, he was aware of mates shouting orders. Spars were realigned, sails trimmed. Slowly the ship settled back to an even keel. A dull *thrrrump* sounded, like a titanic belch, as the port-side runners smashed back onto the ice. A wooden brace somewhere below deck cracked audibly, but both runners held.

Everyone had expected the impact, held on through the violent jarring. No one was shaken over the side.

"Too close," Hunnar muttered as he mounted the helmdeck. The knight was panting steadily, Ethan noticed. As for himself, he was sweating heavily despite the survival-suit's compensators. Thermotropic material can adjust only so fast.

Ethan moved carefully down to the main cabin. Anything still intact in the galley and capable of being heated would taste good just now.

He encountered Eer-Meesach at the doorway. They entered together.

" 'Twas a herd guide we first encountered, not a solitaire or rogue." The wizard, for once, did not appear excited by an interesting encounter. "In a herd, the stavanzer will proceed and eat in parallel line. We ran back along the guide's trail, right into their line, and barely did we miss the end guards."

Ethan saw too clearly in his mind's eye the final bottomless gullet they'd just avoided. It was probably only his fevered imagination, distorted in his memory by fear and terror, but the last stavanzer had looked big enough to swallow the entire ship and use the mainmast for a toothpick.

He'd done very little real work, but his body had burned plenty of calories. In any case, there was something reassuring and normal about eating.

He'd had enough of the extraordinary to last him for a while.

VIII

The next time the lookouts cried out, it was in a more normal voice, tinged this time with excitement of a pleasured kind.

Minutes later, without warning, the green forest vanished and began to shrink behind them. They'd emerged from the pika-pedan and were traveling across pika-pina once more. Soon Ethan could no longer look astern and see the gap where they had emerged.

Three days more and they left furry butterflies and green ice fuzz behind and were again chivaning across open ice. Ta-hoding's relief was palpable, that of his men almost too intense to bear.

When they passed a small trading raft, its single small deck piled high with strapped down goods, the cheers of the crew would have led an onlooker to surmise they had reached Trannish heaven. They had not, but the normal world of free ice and other ships was as much as the lowliest hand could wish.

The trader's crew crowded its railing to stare in awe at the enormous icerigger. Clearly, they'd never heard of it, a measure of how far from Arsudun the *Slanderscree* had come. Both crews barely had time to exchange a few brief shouts and queries before the impatient wind separated them.

"Where are they going?" Ethan asked Hunnar.

"Not to Poyolavomaar," said a disappointed Hunnar. "We will try to make more time for asking with the next ship we pass."

That ship turned out to be another trader, one twice the size of the first they'd encountered, nearly thirty meters long. It even boasted a central cabin. Its crew's amazement at the sight of the *Slanderscree,* however, was no less than that of the first raft they'd passed.

Although traveling on a course similar to that of the icerigger, the trader was not proceeding to Poyolavomaar. But its crew gladly gave confirmation that the great ship was traveling in the right direction.

They passed other vessels. Commerce here was not heavy, but it was steady. Several rocky islets grew, slid past. A couple showed signs of habitation. Eventually they grew so numerous that Ta-hoding ordered some sails taken in.

They were traveling through a region of many tiny islands. Smoke curled from chimneys of steep-roofed houses clinging like brown barnacles to miniature harbors or crawling antlike up talus-strewn slopes. Neatly laid out and carefully cultivated fields of pika-pina huddled in the lee of sheltering islets. Startled Tran would glance up as the *Slanderscree* flew past, set to murmuring by the wondrous ship they might or might not have seen.

Two weeks later, after negotiating undulating archipelagos and dangerously low-lying islands that were scattered like reefs in the ice, they reached Poyolavomaar.

Needle-topped crags and spires towered out of the ice, rising to some of the most impressive heights Ethan had encountered on Tran-ky-ky. A few rose three thousand meters into the clear blue sky. The sharp arrogant angles indicated a geologically youthful region, for such spires could not long retain their glory under the ceaseless assault of the planet's eroding winds.

The lofty islands that formed the near-circle Ta-hoding's captain friend had spoken of nearly touched the *Slanderscree*'s flanks, titanic stone dancers frozen forever only an earth-beat apart. Twisting around the granite needles, the wind acted strangely, as if conscious of the unusual setting it played in. Ta-hoding's task looked difficult, until he saw they could simply follow one of the numerous rafts converging on the island necklace and trail it in.

Homes and other structures, including armed ramparts, crowded the afterthought slopes which muted the cliffs where they entered the ice. Connecting the visible islands, and probably all of them if the garrulous merchant back in Arsudun was correct, were high stone walls built onto the ice. Each had a wide gate in its middle to permit entry or egress. Fortunately, no arch covered the one they approached, or both masts and masonry would have suffered. As it was, there was barely enough room for the icerigger to squeeze through, while guards in the flanking towers gaped or shouted orders.

They made their way inside the ring of towering islands. Near the center of the frozen enclosure lay a seventh island, as unlike its companions as they were unlike Arsudun or Sofold. It was almost flat, rising to a peak of barely fifty meters at its highest point. All around, docking piers extended onto the ice from its shore.

Ethan had noticed docks on the surrounding islands also. But judging from the vast number of rafts tied up here, this had to be the center of commercial activity.

Crowning the high point of the island was a three-tiered stone castle as impressive as that of Wannome. Smoke drifted to the west from flues and chimneys.

"What a magnificent place," Ethan murmured. He searched for better words, but they escaped him. Occasionally he wished for the tongue of a poet instead of a huckster.

"Aye, young feller-me-lad. A more perfect settin' for a harbor would be hard to imagine. And all they've got to do is defend those connecting walls. No enemy's going to climb over those mountains."

Williams was studying the heavily forested slopes. "Lumber rich, too. Without transportation problems. They need only cut a tree down and it will slide most of the way to the ice."

"Truly Captain Midan-Gee did not deceive us." Ta-hoding was already hunting for an open landing. "This is a wealthy, powerful state."

"A good place to begin the confederation," Ethan added.

Hunnar snorted skeptically, stalked away. He still held only the slimmest of hopes for the human's bizarre idea that the Tran could agree on anything except their hereditary fear, suspicion, and hatred of strangers.

Williams suddenly clapped his hands together, starting like a little boy who'd just found a coin in the street. The survival suit gloves muffled the sound of the clap and what wasn't smothered was carried away unheard by the wind, but Ethan saw the movement.

"See something interesting, Milliken?"

"Not that, not that, Ethan. I just realized what this place is!" That unspecific announcement rekindled Hunnar's attention. "Poyolavomaar is a caldera."

"A what?" Hunnar, naturally, did not recognize the Terranglo term. But neither did Ethan.

The diminutive teacher tried to explain. "Some time in the past, Sir Hunnar, these peaks we see now rose even higher, and this circular harbor we now traverse was a solid mountain several *satch* high. It was a volcano, like the smoking mountain you knew as The-Place-Where-The-Earth's-Blood-Burns.

"And like that volcano, this one too blew up in a cataclysmic explosion, leaving only fragments of its outside wall. A central cinder cone started to build a new mountain inside the hollow left by the old one, but never got started before the flow of magma—molten rock—stopped. The soft cinders wore down quickly, leaving the central island we're heading for now. The original volcano was probably more than twice the height of the surrounding island peaks."

It was discomfiting to realize they were traveling through the throat of a ghost mountain and that somewhere far below, plutonic pressures could even now be building up enough energy to erupt unexpectedly. Ethan was glad when the small, streamlined ice raft pulled up alongside them. It gave him something else to concentrate on.

One of the *Slanderscree*'s mates exchanged words with the operators of the small vessel, then reported to Ta-hoding.

"Harbor pilot," said the captain with evident satisfaction. "They are sophisticated here, though the pier they have assigned us is barely half our length. No matter. 'Tis a trouble we'll likely face wherever we go."

116

As sails were taken in, the great icerigger followed the pilot raft toward the northeastern side of the central island. Other ships gave them plenty of room, their crews crowding railings to stare as the huge raft chivaned past.

Once more the anchors were released, and the docking procedure employed successfully at Arsudun was repeated. The *Slanderscree* was pushed slightly westward by the wind before the anchors brought her to a complete stop.

Ethan, September, Hunnar, Williams, Elfa, and a soldier named Tersund assembled to greet the harbormaster, who didn't take long to appear. He was short for a Tran, almost Ethan's size, and wore a strange coat of archil and argent done in diamond patterns, the diamond shapes varying in size. Like all Tran torso-wear it was slitted at the sides to permit the dan to move freely, and fastened with silver braid at shoulders and upper thighs. Belts of some snakelike skin formed an "X" across his chest. He picked absently at his left elbow.

"I hight Valsht," he said in a thin, reedy voice that nevertheless carried an air of authority, "master of Poyolavomaar commerce. I extend warmth and greetings." He performed an elaborate weaving of paws which Ethan didn't recognize.

Hunnar launched into introductions and explanations.

When the redbearded knight had finished, Valsht responded almost as if he were anxious to be rid of them, though it was probably only his naturally nervous character reacting normally.

"This confederation you speak of and the reasons for it are not for a simple servant like myself to ponder on. 'Tis a matter for Tonx Ghin Rakossa, Landgrave of Poyolavomaar, Bringer of the Fair Wind and Solace of the Six Peaks, to decide. I am instructed to conduct you immediately to the grand presence."

That little speech, which sounded rehearsed despite Valsht's evident attempt to make it appear extemporaneous, tickled warning thoughts in Ethan's mind. He shrugged them away. Tran-ky-ky was making him suspicious of every stranger they met. If he'd been able

117

to see that thought in Ethan's mind, Hunnar would have enjoyed a knowing laugh.

The harbormaster relaxed slightly, straining to see into every corner of the icerigger. "You appear to have been on a long voyage."

"A modest journey," admitted Hunnar.

"We are a state of much commerce." Valsht said this matter-of-factly, without boasting. "Ships come from many thousands of *satch* distant to trade and exchange their goods here in Poyolavomaar. We have," and he rolled his brilliant yellow eyes in a manner which Ethan had come to know as the Tran equivalent of a sly wink, "many facilities for weary travelers. Reasons why our city is such a popular place to trade, for is not trading a tiresome business and respite after a hard day a necessity rather than a luxury? I am sure your crew would enjoy the sights and availabilities of our city."

"Your hospitality is most welcome. We accept." Hunnar turned, called up to the helmdeck. "Captain, we are given invitation! Give three-quarters of the crew leave to visit the city. They have earned it. The remaining fourth may go when the first quarter of leave-takers returns."

Ta-hoding indicated his agreement. The order was relayed to the mates, who in turn dispersed it among their subordinates. Prolonged shouting and cries of delight echoed from various sections of the ship as each knot of sailors received word of their permission to go ashore and relax.

The decision to grant liberty having been made, the greeting party followed the harbormaster up the pier and into the town, Tran traveling on icepaths while the humans elected to leave their skates on board and walk alongside.

Shouts and insults, hellos and damnations, promises and lies filled the freezing air around them. They issued from booths, stalls, cabarets and cloaked doorways, knots of huddled Tran and isolated craftsmen and children. Even the beggars appeared well fed. Signs of prosperity and ruthlessness coexisted, and the average expression was one of mellow avarice.

"Something wrong," September said with a grunt.

118

Pessimism was part of September's natural reaction to anything unfamiliar, and Ethan knew it. He didn't mention his own initial suspicion of Valsht's seemingly prepared greeting, having already dismissed that as unwonted.

"What's bothering you, Skua?" He strayed onto the icepath, slipped, regained his balance while glaring at a covey of cubs who'd witnessed his clumsiness.

"Not sure, feller-me-lad. That's what's botherin' me most." He didn't elaborate and Ethan, excited at the prospect of finally trying out their confederation proposal on a prospective government, didn't pursue the conversation.

The slope they were climbing never turned steep, and the main approach to the castle was placed from the western side of the island so that the prevailing wind blew always from the back of anyone approaching. Thus, the Tran did not have to tack uphill, but were swept upward effortlessly while Ethan and September struggled to keep pace.

A central gate of dark wood bound with brass fittings admitted them to a wide courtyard. Guards stared at the humans and pointed, all the while chatting among themselves. The group passed the armory, which seemed unusually large to Ethan, then entered the main structure. A long iced ramp led to a floor, a hallway, and finally into a circular domed chamber.

It was quite different from the throne room in the castle of Wannome where Elfa's father held court. Placed on a raised central dais instead of at the far end of the room were three high-backed chairs. The dais was mounted on a huge, carved stone disk which cleared the floor by a centimeter or two, leading Ethan to suspect it could revolve. Decorative mosaics and reliefs filled curving walls, alternating with windows that looked out onto island and harbor. They depicted the six surrounding crag-crowned islands.

Undoubtedly the Tran slumped into the center chair and staring at them was Rakossa, Solace of the Six Peaks and so on. Compared to the ruling Tran Ethan had encountered thus far, he seemed to be very young. There was no white in his gray fur, no crinkling of the skin beneath. He guessed the Landgrave to be, in human-equivalent terms, younger than himself.

Of the two other Tran seated on either side, one was an older male, the other a young female. Advisors, he mused, or perhaps queen and father. He examined the gargoyle-lined stone disk again, wondered at the mechanism that powered it.

All three were in turn studying their five visitors with obvious interest, though different expressions.

Valsht approached the throne, halted a correct distance from it. "Your pardon, sir, but I have duties I must return to." The young Landgrave dismissed the harbormaster with a diffident gesture. Valsht turned, hurried past the visitors. As he passed, he favored Ethan with a brief, complex, inexplicable stare.

No one spoke or moved. Finally Hunnar stepped forward. "My breath is your warmth, sirs and madame. We come to you from a far distant land hight Sofold. We come to forge what we hope will be a union, a confederation of many island-states for the purpose of dealing on fair and equal terms with strange new friends from off-world. These friends," and he indicated Ethan and September.

"They bring great promise and fortune to all Tran who will have the foresight, as your highness surely will, to join in this unifying proposal. I realize that this thought is . . ."

Without warning the Landgrave rose, thrust a trembling clawed finger at them. "Liars! Offspring of guttorbyn! You bring promise of naught but enslavement and poverty!"

Of all the visitors, only September was not so shocked that he couldn't mutter: "That does it."

Ethan whirled, staring dumbfounded at the giant.

"I knew there was something wrong, lad. When the harbormaster was escorting us here, we passed through the heart of town. And we were assiduously avoided. No one except the cubs gave us so much as a curious glance, except the soldiers here in the castle, and even they didn't act too excited. Contrast that with the stares and inquiries we got from the crews of other rafts.

"Means there's been other humans here before you

120

and me. Or else," and he glanced at the third figure seated on the dais, the distinguished looking older Tran whom Ethan had guessed to be an advisor or royal sire, "word of us."

"That is the first truth you have spoken," said the young Landgrave angrily. He gestured to the softly smiling Tran on his right. " 'Twas fortunate that my good friend here, Calonnin Ro-Vijar, Landgrave of Arsudun, arrived but two precious days ago. He told me of your infamous plans to enslave and make servants of the independent peoples of my world, beginning with Poyolavomaar."

Hunnar took a couple of steps toward the dais, his hand going toward his sword hilt. "Ro-Vijar, was it you who had our ship assaulted off your south coast and the Elfa Kurdagh-Vlata kidnapped?"

The older Tran stood, looked imperiously at them. He acted as cool as the air blowing through the open windows. "I did indeed wish you on your way to the afterlife, traitor, to prevent the spread of your evil intentions."

If the confrontation had begun badly, it was still capable of deteriorating. Ethan moved toward the throne. "Your highness," he said desperately, "it's Ro-Vijar, who lies to protect his own monopoly and trade with my people, to poison your mind against us. He trades truth for money."

"Silence and quiet!" Rakossa looked nauseated. "We will not credit the broken words of a hairless k'nith who masquerades as a true person. Your falsehoods do not touch us."

Ethan saw the eyes of Rakossa, wild and fearful, dangerous and cunning. Yellow with cat-pupils, they were not human eyes, but there is something in the gaze of a madman that transcends shape, reaches across genetic distances. There was nothing to be gained by arguing with Tonx Ghin Rakossa. His mind was made up. Logic and reason would only antagonize him.

Only in the near-neutral expression of the female consort, who had not spoken, was there a hint of something else. It might be sympathy, it might be sadism. Ethan couldn't tell.

121

Hunnar's sword came half free of its scabbard.

Several of the mosaic walls moved inward, revealed compartments behind which disgorged dozens of armed Tran. Hunnar stopped.

"Fight and die here," said a tight-voiced Rakossa, "or wait 'til you are properly judged."

"Sounds like that has been done already," Tersund murmured softly.

The Landgrave continued; he looked vastly pleased with himself. "Your ship is already taken, the sailors aboard already imprisoned. As are those who scattered themselves thoughtlessly throughout my city. You will greet them again in the dungeons below."

Meanwhile Ethan was counting the surrounding pack. They filled the circular chamber until they stood shoulder to dan. Better to die here than . . .

He felt a hand cover his beamer as he moved to draw it. "No, young feller-me-lad. There are too many and likely more behind these. Life is chance, death the absence of opportunity. We've nothin' to lose by waiting and hoping."

"What chance will we have without beamers, Skua?" But he left the weapon at his waist nonetheless.

Ro-Vijar stepped off the dais and approached them. Without hesitation he unclipped Ethan's beamer, then September's, lastly Williams'.

Other guards began disarming Hunnar and Tersund. Then they were escorted from the room. Tran bodies were packed so tightly around them they could hardly move without stepping on sharp-chived feet.

"Ro-Vijar's the liar, your highness!" Ethan shouted over a shoulder. "He has money in place of a soul!"

Trying hard not to smile, Ro-Vijar whispered to the Landgrave. "Do not tilt your ears to the words of the sky-outlanders, mighty ruler of mighty state. They are truly more advanced than we poor Tran—in matters of falsehood and deception. You must constantly beware their subtle intonations."

"Do not worry, friend Calonnin. We do not intend to pay the slightest attention to their degrading speech."

"Why not," the Landgrave of Arsudun suggested casually as the captives exited from the chamber, "kill them now and save space in your prison?"

With his usual unnerving quickness, Rakossa turned on Ro-Vijar. "We have listened to you because we believe in your good advice, friend and fellow ruler Calonnin. Do not think that because of our youth we will be impetuous instead of methodical. They will be granted fair trial."

"That is only just," Calonnin responded, barely hiding his disappointment. He was anxious to be on his way back to Arsudun. This distant trading city held only crude delights and he wished the more sophisticated comforts Trell had provided for him. "I meant no disrespect. It is merely that I despise these pale tricksters so."

"No offense is taken." Rakossa looked to the door where the prisoners had been taken, spoke thoughtfully. "They will be tried and judged fairly. Only then will they be killed."

Calonnin had a pleasing thought. "There is a thing to be considered, your highness. There is much to be learned from those Tran who have been corrupted by the hairless devils. It might best be learned by myself, who has had the most experience with them. I would have one of the prisoners to question."

"As you desire. Which of them do you wish?"

Calonnin permitted himself an ugly grin. It is amazing what unpleasant thoughts can be communicated between two decadents of similar mind by a mere gesture or grimace. The girl still sitting silently on her chair was able to divine Calonnin's intent from her Landgrave's responding smile.

She did not smile.

Hunnar temporarily lost his control when Elfa was separated from them and hauled off by a cluster of soldiery. Fortunately, their own escort was evidently under orders not to damage the prisoners, since they only knocked the raging knight unconscious.

Ethan counted three, perhaps four, underground levels as they descended. The location of the lowermost dungeon had an unexpected benefit which neither of the humans had considered.

Since their cells were located far below the surface, they were unaffected by wind or severe changes in air temperature. So the dungeon was actually warmer than the castle above. This made imprisoned Tran uncomfortable, the local concept of a miserable dungeon being one that was too warm rather than too cold.

The lowest stone and mortar level was filled with large barred cells. The bars were made of polished hardwood instead of valuable metal. Ethan tested one, using the waist buckle of his survival suit. It would take a long time for him to cut through the treated, supertough wood with the stelamic buckle. A prisoner using a bone knife would die of old age before completing the task. Each bar was as thick as September's thigh. They were laid diagonally across the cell entrance.

Cries of recognition and despair greeted them when they reached the lowest level. The cells contained the crew of the *Slanderscree,* as Rakossa had intimated.

During the next several hours, other groups of protesting, complaining sailors were bought in. Some were wounded, some drunk. No matter their condition, they were shoved and kicked into fresh cells to join their sullen companions.

Ta-hoding landed in the cell apparently reserved for officers, knights, and hairless devils. He drew himself up and counted off the assembled prisoners. The entire crew was there. That meant no hope of outside rescue and little hope of inside escape.

"Where's our better chance, our opportunity, Skua?" Ethan couldn't keep the bitterness from his voice, even though he was fully aware that fighting in the throne chamber would have meant his death hours ago.

"We're still alive, feller-me-lad," September replied without rancor. "Patient you can be, if optimistic feels uncomfortable. Me, I've been in worse situations. A time with my brother, now . . ." He paused a moment before continuing again.

"We're alive down here. That's better than bein' dead upstairs."

"Ro-Vijar was behind everything all along: the fight in the tavern in Arsudun, the attack on the raft, and now he's telling this Rakossa lies so he'll do his killing for him."

"You've got to admire the beauty of it," said September. "If any peaceforcers come snooping around, Ro-Vijar can blame our passin' on this Rakossa fellow, who doesn't strike me as dancing with both feet."

"But how," Ethan asked morosely, "could he win Rakossa over to his way of thinking so quickly?"

"I fear 'tis not difficult to imagine—*sief*, my head." Hunnar, having regained his senses, sat wearily against a cold wall. "Ro-Vijar is a Landgrave himself. If he could prove such to another ruler like this Rakossa, as he evidently has succeeded in doing, it would give much credence to his claims. His opinion would be much respected. The more so since he is older than Rakossa.

"Also he is Tran. Though it pains me to admit, my people are more likely to believe one of their own than some strange being such as yourself, friend Ethan, who could as likely be a daemon or a servant of the Dark One." He shrugged, suddenly tired.

"Then too, it is not hard to imagine the creature Ro-Vijar offering this creature Rakossa a share in Arsudun's offworld trade. So he is safe both ways, to his way of thinking. He strikes me as ambitious and a bit mad."

"He doesn't need to do even that," September said. "Rakossa already has gained the *Slanderscree*. Oh, Ro-Vijar will argue that it's rightfully his, but he'll let Rakossa argue him out of it, in return for killing us. He's after bigger stakes, Ro-Vijar is. Don't forget, he's got three modern hand beamers. They're worth a damn sight more on this planet than *two* ice riggers."

Hunnar crawled over to the bars, stood, and kicked at them. His sharp chiv barely produced three parallel scratches in the wood. There were many, similar sets of scratches.

"What do we do now?" Ethan couldn't stand to watch Hunnar stubbornly, hopelessly expending his strength on the bars.

"Young feller-me-lad, I don't know."

The giant moved to a back corner. Though of considerable size, the cell floor had been well matted with pika-pina fragments. September stretched out on them, put his hands behind his head, and stared at the ceiling.

"Fer now, I'm going to sleep."

"How is it," Ethan said wonderingly, "that you can always sleep when your life's in danger?"

September closed his eyes, shutting out cell and companions. "Well for one thing, lad, if they chose that time to kill you, you'd never know it happened."

Ethan would have argued, but he was as exhausted as he was discouraged.

The old matting proved unexpectedly comfortable.

IX

"Wake up."

Rolling over, Ethan opened one eye. He was lying by himself near the bars. Who could be talking to him in the middle of the night?

"Wake *up!*" The voice was more insistent.

Dried pika-pina fiber crackled like burning bugs as he got awkwardly to his knees and stared out into the dim light of the passageway. Torches illuminated cells and walkway between.

The voice hadn't sounded like that of the cellkeeper, a phlegmatic Tran who appeared periodically to make certain the outland daemons hadn't burrowed free of their prison by some unknown magical means.

But a dimly silhouetted shape was pressing against the bars close by. It was a Tran, which was expected. It was also female, which was not. Yellow cat eyes glowed by torchlight.

"Please," the voice said anxiously, the eyes turning briefly to glance down the corridor. "There will be a change of cellmaster before too long. We must use every minute."

Having decided that he was not dreaming, Ethan climbed to his feet. As he approached the bars, he finally recognized the speaker.

That gave him his biggest shock yet.

"But you're Rakossa's queen ? . . ."

The girl expectorated, following it with a degrading word. "He calls me his concubine. The court refers to me as royal consort. I am his chiv-stool, for he wipes his feet on me." Her voice held more hatred and bitterness than Ethan imagined possible. Each word was soaked in vitriol, every sentence washed with venom. Yet she spoke quietly and with control.

"I hight Teeliam Hoh, outlander. I was purchased to be less than a pet. Queen?" Fury kept her from laughing. "I am a thing he uses, plays with, like a favorite sword, yet the sword is cared for and treated better than I."

Ethan was looking down the corridor himself now. "You mentioned a change of cellmaster. What about the one on duty now? He'll be coming—"

"Nowhere," she finished for him. "He and the other guard are dead. I cut their throats."

Her hands fumbled at the old metal lock which sealed the cell. Mumblings and questions sounded behind Ethan as the noises and activity woke others.

"Then *you* believe us," Ethan said excitedly, watching her hands work the heavy, ornate key. "You know Ro-Vijar for the liar he is."

"I do not know the Landgrave of Arsudun for anything but the trail a dung crawler leaves behind itself after a meal."

"If you don't know whether he's lying or not, then why are you doing this for us?"

Her bared teeth shone at him. "You think I do this for you? I do it for her." She gestured up the corridor, returned to the lock and key.

Ethan looked in the indicated direction, made out the shape of a second figure. "Elfa." Something clicked and then the door swung open easily. Tran in other cells were awake now, watching and murmuring tensely. Teeliam moved to free them.

Ethan moved toward Elfa, smiling happily. He stopped a meter away, and stared. Just stared. His disbelief was too great for him to curse the reality of what he saw.

The beautiful cat face was bruised and marred, one

127

eye swollen almost shut. There were large patches of smooth fur missing, and places singed and blackened as if by fire. Elfa did not smile at him. In fact, her attention seemed rooted on the floor, though it was in a different place altogether. She held both arms tight around herself. The clothing she wore was simple, not what she'd been wearing when taken away from the rest of them.

Teeliam Hoh, having given the keys to other Tran, had come to stand next to Ethan. He turned a wordless, open-mouthed gaze to her.

"I know the inner passages of the castle," she said, less bitterly now. "I knew one of you had been brought for questioning. Through a chink I saw how this Ro-Vijar asked questions, how nothing he said or did could be credited to a true Landgrave-protector.

"While I could not know the truth of what he said about you, I did know that everything else he claimed should be treated as a lie, for he lives and that is an untruth of itself." She looked away from him, at the floor, then at Elfa.

"Rakossa was with him, watching, relishing the spectacle. After a while, he deigned to participate." She shuddered. "I have had to endure his foul imagination for two years. Would that I could have gone mad."

"Why." Ethan swallowed, tried again. "Why did you stay here? Why didn't you try to escape him?"

Now Teeliam found reason to laugh. "I do that several times a year, sky-outlander Ethan. Always I am caught, or bought back from those who find me. What Rakossa then does to me drives out all thoughts of escape for day-times. As will doubtless happen again after this. If I did not resist him, he would tire of me and kill me, for none can have a woman that Rakossa has had. And when I resist, he . . . imagines things."

"It won't happen again, woman," said a deep, angry voice. September had come up behind Ethan and was staring compassionately at Teeliam. He had already examined Elfa professionally and chose not to stare at her.

"It does not matter. I would have done this only to anger him no matter what you do for yourselves or me, no matter what had been done to her." She indicated Elfa, who had not moved.

"There is another thing. I believe you would wish to have these. I stole them." She swung the small pack from her back, brought out their beamers.

"How long until the new cellmaster comes on duty?" Ethan clipped his own weapon back to his waist, tried to peer through sooty darkness up the corridor and stairs. Teeliam mentioned Tran time-units. "Maybe that's long enough for us to slip up the stairways and fight our way back to the ship."

"Are you offworlders truly the fools Ro-Vijar claims?" Teeliam eyed him disbelievingly. "You cannot go back through the castle. There are soldiers on every level above. You could not reach the courtyard before every warrior on the island had been assembled. I do not think your magical weapons which Ro-Vijar whispered of to Rakossa would be enough to repulse a thousand or more fighters in close quarters."

"Gal's got a point." September bent his white-maned head down to her. "What you have in mind as an alternative?"

"I will cut the face of my father into his back and he will curse his manhood," said a voice cold enough to match the atmosphere above ground. Elfa spoke at last.

"Surely you will." Sir Hunnar had been standing in the shadows for an indeterminate length of time, watching Elfa. Now he moved into the light, speaking gently as he took her arm. "But not now, later. We must free ourselves first."

She tried to pull free of his grasp. For a moment the green cloak and wraps she was wearing slid loosely aside. Ethan saw scars and markings he wished he had not.

"I will remove his fur one hair at a time," she continued, in a tone that chilled Ethan's heart. She made no move to cover herself.

"Yes, but later, later. I promise." Hunnar fixed her cloak. How he kept his voice low and easy was something Ethan was never able to figure out. Now he slid an arm around her shoulders.

With an effort, Teeliam replied to September's

question. "Faint hope lies this way." She started down the corridor, toward the cells farthest from the stairway. Ethan and September followed. With Hunnar's support, a glaze-eyed Elfa stumbled uncertainly in their wake.

At the far end of the dungeon they found another doorway. It was low for a Tran, blocked up with masonry and cordoned off with braided pika-pina cable.

"It is told that in ancient times the worst offenders of the laws were put through there. A tunnel lies beyond. Where it leads to is not spoken of. But it is a place far from here."

"Good enough for me," said September, approving the plan. "Why is it sealed up?"

"Four Landgraves ago, the histories say, it was decided the punishment was too severe for even the murderers of children."

"Wonderful," Ethan murmured, eying the doorway as if some inconceivable horror might at any moment burst through the stones to devour them.

"Where does it go?" A prosaic query from the *Slanderscree*'s reluctant, but ever-curious Captain Tahoding.

Teeliam turning, told him. "It goes down to Hell."

"Fine." September smiled. "Then I don't expect we'll be followed. At that moment he looked a bit like a daemon of the underworld himself. "Stand away."

After adjusting his beamer, he turned it on the sealed portal. The blue energy beam dissolved stone, cement, and pika-pina cable alike. There were mutters of awe from the *Slanderscree*'s sailors. They had seen the light knives of the outlanders in action before, but they hadn't known they could burn through the unbreakable, fire-resistant pika-pina.

Once he'd cut several horizontal lines in the barrier, September turned off the beam to conserve its charge and kicked out the remaining stones. They fell through with surprisingly little effort, though, as the old knight Balavere Longax commented, there was no reason for a really solid barricade, since no Tran would want to go through that doorway of his own free will.

Ethan took one of the torches from its wall holder,

stuck it through the opening. "It looks higher inside. There's a tunnel, all right. It slopes downward."

An uncertain susurration sounded from the tightly packed crew-members. Hunnar faced them. "To stay here is to die. All who wish certain death may remain. Those who desire a chance for life, and revenge, may follow. Our human friends say there is no danger. They have not lied to us before. I do not believe they do so now."

Turning, he took a second torch and ducked beneath the low lintel.

"I never said there was no danger," Ethan told him.

"Nor did friend September or Williams," Hunnar replied, moving his head so as to see further down the tunnel. "I am not worried about danger ahead. Our sailors and knights will fight when they have to, but it is more dangerous to let them stew in their own imaginings."

The two started downward. They were quickly followed by September and Williams, Ta-hoding, Balavere, and Hunnar's two squires. When Teeliam and Elfa went in turn, the murmuring among the crew changed from fearful to embarrassed. In twos and threes, they grabbed torches, muttered of lost hopes, and followed after.

The tunnel was just high enough to permit an adult Tran to walk upright. Though an icepath led steadily downhill, the crew did not take advantage of it to move rapidly. They picked rather than chivaned their way downward and were quite content to follow the cautious pace of the chivless humans. Huge stone blocks formed walls and ceiling.

Without references, time rippled—it became blurry and indistinct. "How deep do you think we've come?" Ethan asked Williams later.

"Hard to say, Ethan." The schoolteacher missed a step, caught himself, and stared meaningfully at the ceiling. "Sixty, maybe seventy meters below the castle. Maybe more. And we've come a fair linear distance as well."

Continuing to descend sharply, the tunnel showed no sign of ending. They stumbled on and on. No mysterious spirits of the underworld materialized to

131

torment them. A breeze blew steadily at their backs, pungent with the odor of the now distant dungeon.

Unexpectedly, the character of the tunnel changed. The roof overhead and the walls flanking them gave way from hewn stone to a material the color of creamy ceramic. Ethan touched the wall nearest, scraped at it with a gloved finger. It came away in reluctant splinters: ice.

He could see the stones behind the layer of ice. Once again the sailors began conversing worriedly among themselves. They were a brave group, but they were walking into the nightmares of their cubhood, and it shook the most stalwart among them.

"Nothing to be gained by going back," said September quietly. He pulled his beamer and they continued downward.

Several times the marchers paused to rest. Hunnar and Balavere were convinced it was safe to do so. Even if their escape had been discovered, the Poyos were unlikely to organize pursuit, convinced that the denizens of the underworld would rid them of their former prisoners. That belief was shared by the majority of the *Slanderscree*'s crew.

Before long they began moving again. "No telling how deep we are now," Williams muttered to himself. "Pressure appears unchanged."

September halted abruptly, his head cocked to one side. He had his face mask open and appeared to be listening intently. The line backed up behind him.

"Hear something, feller-me-lad?" Ethan strained to pick out an unknown sound from the background noise of several hundred respirating humans and Tran.

The sound he settled on was difficult to distinguish because it sounded something like breathing itself. A faint, distant groaning and gurgling. "We can't go back now." He took over the lead, extending his torch ahead of him. The noise grew louder. Despite knowing better, he had to admit it sounded very much like a sleeping daemon softly snoring.

They reached a bend in the tunnel, turned it. The pathway leveled out. Ethan stopped. Anxious queries came from behind him. Turning his beamer on, he set it for the widest possible, most diffuse beam. It lit up an incredible sight.

At some unguessable time past, tremendous heat had melted out the vast cavern they gazed upon. Columns of ice did not so much support as decorate the ceiling, which was festooned with dead icicles. The roof itself was only five or six meters above their heads, but it stretched off into distances unreached by the blue glow of the beamer.

No snuffling efreet or djinn lay waiting to greet their eyes. The sound came from black water—unfrozen, liquid, free-flowing water that stretched off to merge into a black horizon with the far reaches of the ceiling. It lapped gently, echoing through the cavern, against an icy beach a few meters away. Ethan identified the subtle odor that he'd been smelling for the last several minutes: salt.

Williams' gaze was focused on the ceiling formations. "We've come down through the ice sheet and emerged outside the island proper. There must be one or two hundred meters of solid ice above us."

Terrified, childish mewings were coming from some of the crew members. A few dropped to their knees and began imploring whichever gods they believed in to take pity on them. Ethan saw resignation and the anticipation of death in several furry faces.

Even the knowledgeable, unsuperstitious Eer-Meesach was shivering with fear. It is one thing to dismiss stories and legends of fanciful places as inventions utilized by adults to frighten and compel children. It is quite another to confront them as reality.

Balavere Longax, Sofold's greatest general, announced easily, "We shall all die."

"Not unless we have to swim." September's habit of confronting danger with humor hadn't left him. The greater the threat, the more irreverent his comments. He left the tunnel and strolled carefully across the ice to the water's edge. "Maybe it's hell to you, but I find the quiet and openness kind of attractive."

To his surprise, Ethan had discovered he was also trembling. The giant's words brought him back to normal. This was a Tran conception of Hell, not his. It was only a cold, dark place.

133

Holding his torch firmly he moved to join September. A glance over the frozen berm showed nothing but fluid blackness. It was as if he were staring upward at the night sky instead of down into the bowels of some primeval ocean. And like the night sky, this subterranean sea blazed with stars and nebulae of its own.

Thousands of tiny luminous creatures darted and jerked their way through the inky water. Green, hot pink, bright yellow, crimson, and cherry red—every imaginable color indentified some small blazing bit of existence. Compared to this well of magnificence, where every creature no matter how small was cloaked in gems, the atmospheric world above seemed drab and dull.

Ethan grew aware of another figure come up alongside him, but did not shift his gaze from that shimmering palette of life. "How can they live down here, Milliken, beneath the ice?"

"Perhaps there is vegetation which releases oxygen slowly, or volcanic production of gases." The teacher shrugged. "Evidently there is enough to sustain a multitude of forms."

"It is very beautiful." Ethan spun. Elfa was standing behind them, peering almost shyly into the glassy blackness. She smiled hesitantly at Ethan. He couldn't help but smile back. She was not fully recovered, but she was no longer in shock.

His gaze traveled to the glistening icicles, false stalactites, to the columns that exploded torchlight into a thousand tiny replicas of its source, none of which could match for diversity and beauty the swimming bead-shapes of the water dwellers. How lovely is Hades, he mused, when it is other than one's own. Why, it was neither hot nor fearsome here, and there was no wind at all.

A whirlpool of luminescent life eddied ecstatically in the pale blue light of his beamer. He turned it downward, piercing the water to a depth of several meters. It was as if the beamer were a vacuum, sucking up ever more delirious dancers from the depths below.

The water erupted, sent them stumbling or falling backward.

Ethan saw a mouth. Rubies and emeralds, tormalines and topazes, ozmidines, ferrosilicate crystals mirror-bright decorated the cavern within a cavern. Stalactites and stalagmites of vitreous, transparent teeth lined the jaws. Around it was a face wide and fat like a toad's, with a single searchlight of a mad vermilion eye above the bejeweled mouth. Black, slick flesh rippled in folds around eye and mouth, a pulpy envelope to hold organs loosely in place.

Whatever it was, it had been drawn from familiar depths by Ethan's bright beam. Brave as they were some of the sailors fainted in place. Others forgot discipline and command in their rush to squeeze themselves back up the tunnel.

September and Williams already were firing at the apparition with beams tighter and more deadly than Ethan's, while he strove frantically to readjust the setting on his own. Each time a blue beam touched the creature's flesh the hallucination-made-real produced a gargantuan grunt. The humans fired as they retreated back toward the tunnel.

Mouth and eye rose roof high above the water and hunched after them. Several more bolts struck it. The tumorous shape came down on the ice beach with a crash that echoed energetically 'round the cavern, generating a low splintering sound. It lay still and unmoving, quartz teeth shining in the torchlight, the single round eye with its absurdly small black pupil staring blindly at them.

Screaming still sounded from up the tunnel, however, Hunnar had his sword out and was trying to force his way through the panicked mob.

"Cowards of Sofold! The daemon is dead, slain by the light knives of our friends who are half your size!" The mad rush upward slowed, ceased. Screams became anxious or uneasy murmurs. "When you are finished whimpering, you may rejoin us." He sheathed his sword and deliberately chivaned downward at top speed, showing blatant disregard for what might await him within the cavern.

Gradually the sailors drifted after. They spread out

135

below the tunnel mouth to gaze in delicious horror at the hellbeast resting on the ice. It was no less fearsome and not the least bit comical for having a body that was one-third head.

Displaying utter indifference to post-dying reflexes, September strode up to the creature which Eer-Meesach had already dubbed *Kalankatht* (which translates from the Tran roughly as "beast-which-is-all-teeth-and-no-tail") and stuck his head into the gaping mouth. Frozen open, the upper jaw was still a meter above his hooded head.

Though two meters long on average, the transparent teeth were no thicker around than a man's finger. There were hundreds in the chamber-sized maw. Short, delicate-looking fins projected from back and sides, while the blunt tail was flattened vertically for swimming and steering. It could not be very fast in pursuit of its prey, but it could bite at a lot of ocean.

Williams was examing the corpse with fine scientific detachment, though as a strong believer in the lingering independence of certain muscular functions he chose not to stray so near the jaws as had September. "Eye, mouth, and stomach. No waste space or organs." He moved behind the nightmare, out of sight.

Ethan and Hunnar had joined September before the gaping mouth. "What more natural than that there be devils in Hell?"

Hesitantly, the knight reached out to touch the wet black skin. "Then you believe it a daemon of the underworld also?"

"Skua likes to fancify," said Ethan. "There are similar, natural creatures living in the deeps of my own world's seas. Some are bigger than this one, though none quite as outlandish." As life-fluids ceased flowing within the body, the phosphorescences around mouth and sides were beginning to fade, lights and life going out together.

"This water is only part of your liquid ocean, the same kind of water that forms the ice above us, the ice that rafts chivan across, and that surrounds Sofold." Ethan touched his torch to the floor, tasted of the water it produced. "Ice to liquid, just as you drink it aboard ship or back in Wannome."

136

"Then the philosophers are right," the knight said. "The inside of the world is fluid."

Ethan smiled. "Oddly enough, that's right, but the liquid is metal and not water. Williams can explain it better than I can." He turned, called out. "Milliken?"

"This ends our exploring the sea." September clipped his beamer back to his waist. "Next cousin of this mobile mouth we lure up is liable to be bigger still. What're you yellin' at, young feller-me-lad?"

"We can't find Milliken. I thought he'd be studying this body, but . . ."

"Over here!" They looked to their right. The teacher was standing at the far edge of the cavern, where the ice gave way to sloping rock. As they moved toward him, he ducked back out of sight.

"Another cavern?" Ethan wondered aloud. Other Tran moved to follow them.

When they turned the bend he'd vanished behind, Milliken was still further ahead. The ice remained several meters from the gravel and stone.

"What is this?" September looked at the nearby ice wall curiously. "Another tunnel?"

"No." Puffing, the schoolteacher had run back to rejoin them. "It seems to continue endlessly in a general northwesterly direction. In places the ice draws nearer to the island, in others it moves farther out. It may run around the entire circumference of the island." He gestured back toward the now hidden cavern.

"At this depth, in this particular region anyway, volcanic heat from the island's interior has spread outward instead of upward. We are probably at a level parallel to some horizontal flow of magma."

"Then if we follow the curve of the island," September pointed out, "we could come out under the harbor where the ship is moored."

"Of what good is that?" asked Hunnar.

Ethan checked his beamer. "Our weapons are still three-quarters charged, Hunnar. We can cut our own tunnel upward. We couldn't manage it through solid rock, but we've plenty of energy to melt ice." He faced Williams. "Think you can judge when we've come near the *Slanderscree,* Milliken?"

137

"Dear me. I don't know. The angle of our descent from the castle . . . I really don't know."

"Do the best you can. No matter where we come up, we'll have a chance."

When communicated to the rest of the crew, strung out back into the cavern, this information raised spirits considerably. Tran who had long since conceded soul and spirit to the Dark One found hope in the prospect of again confronting flesh and blood enemies.

The open corridor wound its way around the sunken shore. In one place the earth was so warm that the ice turned to black water nearby but the sailors refused to wade through it. Ethan and September had to use precious energy to cut a dry path upward through the ice, then down to the corridor again. They proceeded carefully. It wouldn't do to lose contact with solid land and start cutting their way out into the enormous ice sheet which covered the ocean.

They rested, some of the Tran feeling confident enough to express a desire for food. Hours later, Williams said cautiously, "Here." He raised his left hand, pointed upslope at a modest angle. "Cut here. If we melt our way upward at forty-five degrees we should come out beneath the ship."

"How sure are you, Milliken?"

The teacher looked glumly at Ethan. "Not very."

"An honest answer. I'll start the cut, feller-me-lad." September adjusted his beamer. After several tries he located the setting which best combined a fairly wide beam with enough power to melt the white ceiling overhead rapidly. Water ran beneath their feet, uncomfortable to Tran and human alike, if for different reasons.

Following immediately behind September, Ethan discovered his heart pounding harder than the climb demanded. His breathing was quick and heavy, his eyes darting around the circular tunnel. He found that shutting them relaxed his breathing and the hammering in his chest. Williams touched his booted foot and he jerked.

"Claustrophobic?" Ethan, looking back without opening his eyes, nodded vigorously. "Try not to think about it. Don't think about anything. Think music to yourself."

Ethan did so, dredging up a lilting popular tune from his adolescence. His heartbeat fell to near-normal and he discovered he could breathe without effort. Concentrate, he told himself. Concentrate on Merriwillya night a burning, a-burning, Merriwillya a-yearning. Not on the tons and tons and tons of ice over your head, below your hands and knees, pressing in on your sides, pressing, pressing . . .

He couldn't take his turn at cutting. He didn't freeze or faint, but the sight of solid ice in front of him while knowing there were hundreds of anxious Tran blocking any retreat was too much to handle. They showed Hunnar how to use the beamer and he took Ethan's place, saying nothing as he crawled past the half-paralyzed salesman.

Fortunately, the tunnel lengthened as fast as they could climb. Intense energy kept the little stream flowing steadily around ankles and knees.

The time came when September turned off his beamer, started to trade places with Williams, and then paused to glance upward. "Light above . . . there's light coming through the ice!"

Joyful shouts rang deafeningly through the tunnel, until the knights and ship's officers thought to quiet their men. September looked sympathetically at Ethan.

"It'd be better, feller-me-lad, if we break surface after the sun's well down. If you can't take it, we can—"

Ethan settled his back against the tunnel wall, hands clasping knees, his head resting between them. "I can wait," he said curtly. September merely nodded.

The information was passed back down the tunnel. Sailors settled themselves for fast sleep in awkward positions, while others worked overlong on cleaning claws and chiv, the only weapons they had.

Hunnar was talking in low tones with Elfa and below her, with Teeliam Hoh. Ethan, catching an occasional word, decided they were talking about what had transpired back in the castle. He turned his attention away from them, having no desire to learn the methodology of certain barbarisms. It was enough to have

139

seen the scars and bruises on Elfa's face and body, to have listened to the mental scarring of the royal consort. Bad dreams enough plagued him already.

When darkness above was assured, the sleepers were shaken awake. All torches were extinguished. "Let me." September looked appraisingly at him, then exchanged places.

"Keep your beam short and low, feller-me-lad."

"I'm not completely helpless, you know." Ethan turned to the ice above, began melting with barely a suggestion of blue issuing from the lens of the beamer. September did not reply, in doing so saying much.

A kind of petrified illumination showed ahead. Ethan turned off his beamer, raised both gloved hands, and pushed hard. Splinters fell past his face mask as he broke through the surface.

Cautiously, he raised his head out. Like a vacationing friend now returning, ever-present wind buffeted the back of his skull.

A low wooden wall lay ten meters or so to his right, lining the shore of Poyolavomaar. He twisted around. Piers lay ahead and behind him. A couple of small ice rafts were tied up to each. There was no movement, and lights on only one. With the temperature already a brisk minus thirty C. and falling, sailors and merchants alike would seek refuge in warmer taverns and cabins.

Huddled together in the distance above the shore wall, the lights of the town flickered brightly. An occasional shout rose above the wind.

Ethan looked back, ducked down into the tunnel. Anxious faces, masked or furred, stared back up at him expectantly. "We're in the harbor, between the ends of two piers. But I don't recognize anything, and I don't see the ship."

"Let me through." With much squirming and wiggling, Hunnar slipped past Ethan. Elfa, Teeliam, Tersund and another sailor followed him, their musk strong in the confined corridor. Hunnar looked back down at Ethan.

"My strangely clothed friends, you must remain here. Both you and your wondrous weapons are too

140

conspicuous." Then Hunnar spread his dan, hunched over, and let the wind take him away.

Minutes became hours of worry. What if they were captured? Worse, what if some wandering Poyo soldier discovered the hole in the ice? These and a dozen other deleterious scenarios played on the stage of Ethan's mind before Hunnar's voice whispered above him.

"We've found the ship. 'Tis two piers over. There are but a few sentries aboard her and they sleep the dreams of the bored and ordered-about. Some sleep sounder than that. Come."

Remaining silent, but obviously glad to be back on the surface again, the crew of the *Slanderscree* emerged from the tunnel. Ethan knew that the sentries who were "sleeping sounder than that" were the ones who had unwittingly provided Hunnar and his companions with the swords and lances they now carried.

The prisoners assembled beneath the low underside of a thirty-five-meter merchant raft. It was broad enough of beam to conceal the entire crew.

"We could do no better than to chivan as fast as possible for the ship and raise sail before the city patrols can react." Hunnar hefted his sword. "We have weapons enough."

" 'Tis so!" growled a sailor nearby, flexing furry fingers armed with sharp, stubby claws.

"This meets your approval, my friends?" Hunnar looked at the three humans.

September nodded. "I'm not much for subtle strategies either. Let's do it."

All three readied their beamers again, hoping they wouldn't have to employ the revealing energy weapons. Hunnar moved out into the moonlight, and then in groups of five the crew raced silently across the ice toward the waiting icerigger.

With their skates lockered aboard, the three humans used the simplest method of making the dash across the slippery surface. Sitting down, each extended his arms back over his head. A sailor grabbed a wrist in one hand, a second the other. Spreading their dan, they took off across the open stretch of harbor.

Ethan could only lament his undignified position

and pray the tough material of the survival suit held. It did so, but even the friction generated by such a short journey raised a portion of the suit's temperature above what its compensators considered comfortable.

All boarding ladders were still draped invitingly over the railings. Spreading out beneath the vast underbody of the icerigger, her crew commenced a half hysterical climb upward, utilizing every available ladder.

There wasn't a soul on board. "Apparently," September murmured, "they decided freezing out in the night a bad choice with so many inviting taverns nearby. But wouldn't they wonder at their companions whom you dispatched, Hunnar?"

"I imagine," the knight said with a wolfish grin, "that they left for warmth and drink because they assumed their absent fellows had already done so."

"The Landgrave has great confidence in his dungeons." Ethan relaxed gratefully. There would be no fighting here.

"Why should he not?" said Teeliam, looking around for someone to kill and evidently disappointed at finding no one. "None have ever escaped from them in memory."

"No one has ever traveled through Hell before, either." Elfa spoke in a way that indicated she was referring to more than just their journey through ice and ocean.

"Quick now!" Ta-hoding gave rapid orders to his crew. "Up sail and quiet about it!"

With the prospect of imminent freedom to energize them, the sparmen assaulted the rigging like birds. Sails began to unfurl, filling silently.

Spreading his dan, which in the light night breeze were barely adequate to carry his porcine body up the iceramp, the captain chivaned his way to the helmdeck. From there he shouted in low tones to the sailors astern to hurry in with the ice anchors. Other crewmembers were at work on the pier, quietly and with feverish efficiency slipping pika-pina cables from cleat and capstan.

Though the Tran moved with the silence of a tribe of sock-footed ants, so much activity could not remain

142

unnoticed forever. Before long a voice called out in the darkness.

"Who's there? Who's on board the prize?"

Sailors on deck and shore desperately tried to spot the caller. A minute passed, and then it did not matter.

"Help! The prisoners have escaped!" There was as much astonishment as urgency in that cry. "Guard to the ships, guard to the ships, and ware devils the—"

There was a twang. One of the sailors had armed himself with a crossbow from the ship's armory. Now he let fly from the mizzenmast and the alarming words changed to an indecipherable gurgling. There was the faint, distant *flump* of something striking the ground.

Too late. Other voices sounded now on shore, called querulously to one another and to the unresponsive shapes moving about the great raft. Ta-hoding, dropping all pretense of concealment, moved to the helm-deck railing and roared instructions liberally laced with invective at the crew.

Ponderously, with adjustable spars turning, the *Slanderscree* began to gain sternway and back clear of the pier. Sailors still on the dock saw armed figures chivaning at them, jumped aboard. There was not enough time to loosen all the cables.

A concatenation of bizarre clangings, rips and tears, groans and inanimate protests sounded from the dock. The incredible pika-pina cables held, but the dock did not. Pinions and cleats ripped free of their sockets, flew toward the massive raft, while Poyos on the pier turned about and tried to protect themselves from flying bone and wood.

On board the *Slanderscree* the boarding ladders were brought in, several with sailors still clinging to them. Looking as if they would sweat if they could, Ta-hoding's helmsmen threw the great wheel hard over. The icerigger continued to move backward, her bow swinging steadily around to the north. As soon as it cleared the outermost pier, the spars would shift and the westwind would fill the sails from behind.

They could see oil lamps massing along the shore, spilling out onto the ice. Shouts of outrage and confusion flared as unevenly and brightly as the flames. A

143

few arrows and a couple of spears flew at the great, ghostly shape of the icerigger. Most fell short, a pair stuck into the rear of the helmdeck as it swung landward.

Within the waking city, horns were droning like undertakers. Drums howled more urgently, and edgy soldiers loosed arrows at the moons.

"Over spars!" Ta-hoding bellowed. "Over spars!" echoed his mates. The *Slanderscree*'s sails came around, there was a whiplike crack, sheets plumped out like the prow of a woman September had once known, and the icerigger began to move ahead, picking up speed with every second.

Her crew was much too busy to shout with joy.

Both moons were high adrift in a cloudless sky. The sextuple crags of Poyolavomaar's circling islands cast quilted shadows across the harbor as the foremast lookout yelled a warning.

"Pilot raft ahead!"

Ta-hoding looked grimly at Ethan. "Small pleasure would it be if Valsht the harbormaster, excrement in Trannish form, were to be aboard it."

Seconds later Ethan heard a faint crunching sound and rushed to the edge of the helmdeck. Shards of cut wood were sliding beneath the ship. The rear runners further reduced them to splinters. His gaze shifted aft, to show tumbling bits of wood and softer fragments strewn in the wake of the icerigger.

"The gate is closed!" shouted the lookout again.

Ta-hoding stood his place, simply reminding the helmsmen of their course. They held a touch tighter to the wheel, as everyone else on board braced himself as best he could for the expected collision.

Ethan imagined disapproving, forbidding faces frowning down at them from the flanking mountaintops. He fell to one knee as the deck shimmied beneath him. Then they were through, and he rushed back to the railing for a look astern.

Angry lights danced futilely on the walls linking the two isles. A pair of huge wooden gates lay smashed and fragmented on the moonlit ice. Four huge blocks of stone bounced lightly in the icerigger's wake, their unbroken pika-pina cables still firmly secured to each.

144

Damage reports came back from the bow. The *Slanderscree* would have to do without a bowsprit for awhile. If their maneuverability was slightly impaired, their speed was not. They were flying across the ice now, the powerful westwind shoving them with a giant's hand from behind, their first attempt at initiating a union of Tran island-states a dismal failure that receded rapidly astern.

X

"You must go after them, your highness." Calonnin Ro-Vijar filled his voice with urgency as he addressed Rakossa of Poyolavomaar.

Crowded around him in the Landgrave's personal quarters were the high knights and generals of the city. Most of them would rather have been anywhere but within verbal range of their storming, blood-thirsty ruler.

Rakossa seemed not to hear his royal counterpart. "They *must* have her! Her body is not in the dungeon or on the ice, not in the hell place or the tunnel —the tunnel wrested by the devil-weapons she stole."

A subordinate officer, in charge of the castle's armory, was not present to confirm or deny what most in the room knew to be true. For his laxity in allowing himself to be seduced and then knocked unconscious by the absent royal consort, he had already been returned to his family. As the officer's family was scattered about five of Poyolavomaar's seven isles, it was necessary for him to be returned in the equivalent number of pieces.

"When we catch her this time, we will . . ." Rakossa unreeled a long list of imaginative and shuddersome proposals. While doing so he waved his longsword about with complete disregard for where it might impact, much to the discomfort of those officials in the forefront of the attending crowd.

"It seems incredible, my lord, that they dared travel out through the old bore," the chief jailer observed, wondering why he had not enjoyed the same fate as the armory guard.

One of the knights safely concealed near the back of the group murmured, " 'Tis unwise to pursue those who can kill demons in Hell."

"She will wish she stayed her hand from aiding them!" Rakossa swung his sword, destroying a priceless ivory carving adorning the back of a chair. "We are through playing with this one." He showed gleaming fangs. "She shall not return to embarrass us further. We will make a hell for her she will not have to climb down to, a new hell every day, different and stimulating!"

"Would it not be simpler, my lord," asked the same knight who'd spoken a moment ago, "to take a new and more willing consort?"

"Who speaks? Who tells Rakossa what to do and how to judge?" The knight did not answer, bent his knees to sink a little lower into the crowd.

"No sheslug defies us or gains our better. We will instruct her in the meanings of Hell."

Another official whispered that after serving as consort to the Landgrave for several years, the vanished woman no doubt knew the meanings of hell already. Fortunately, Rakossa did not hear or he might have been inspired to begin a mass murder of all assembled merely to insure the disposal of his single insulter.

"It is only just that you pursue her—and them," said a comfortingly aquiescent Ro-Vijar. Rakossa's anger subsided somewhat, the Mad which had held him fully let clearer thoughts have room in his twisted brain.

"That is truth, friend Ro-Vijar. We must follow her and those who aided her." How neatly, thought Ro-Vijar with distaste, he changes things in his mind to fit his mind's bent. Now it is the escapees who are guilty of assisting the woman, not the other way around. Then he grew tense, aware that the madman was eyeing him coldly.

"We have taken your word in much of this, Land-

146

grave of Arsudun. Of the three offworld devils' intentions and of their Tran friends."

"I tell only the truth, sire, of what needs doing. You defend all of us. Your name will be remembered as mighty."

"We wonder," Rakossa muttered calculatingly, while Ro-Vijar strove to appear unaffected by his ferocious stare, "just whose purposes are truly being served in this."

"However," he said more briskly, taking his gaze from the silent Ro-Vijar, "We will have that witch back. As she is served by those you believe need be destroyed, it seems to pursue one we must pursue all."

"They are devils and destroyers, Lord Rakossa."

"Devils they are. Destroyers seek destruction, not escape. Yet only a few died in trying to prevent their flight. We wonder—we *will* have her back!"

He turned on a stiffly posed officer. "Talizeir, ready the fleet for pursuit. All ships, all officers, all crew to the ready, for we leave by first light."

"As my Landgrave commands," the tall, dignified Tran replied. He pushed through the others toward the door.

"You are dismissed," Rakossa told the rest. "Those who are to chase, prepare yourselves."

"We will have her back," he murmured, alone now in the ornate chamber. "And we will have that ship, that magnificent ice ship for our own, though this strange Landgrave Ro-Vijar wishes it for himself."

As for the outworld devils, perhaps when they were recaptured he would listen a little more to their words and a little less to those of the Landgrave of Arsudun. He was older, this Ro-Vijar, more experienced, his words as devious as his true aims. His purposes clashed somehow with his speech.

Blood and bone awash in a sea of shrieks inundated his thoughts, and he thought again only of the consort Teeliam Hoh, as the thick blood bubbled from her laughter.

Wind howled mournfully across the deck of the *Slanderscree*. Ethan blinked behind his face mask as he emerged on deck, shutting the cabin door tightly behind him. Elfa, Hunnar, and September stood conversing near the mizzenmast. As he drew nearer he saw Teeliam among them, hidden partly by September's bulk.

"Warmth and wind this morning to you, friend Ethan," Hunnar called happily. "We debate on what to do next."

"We still can't return to Arsudun." September spoke through the diaphragm of his own mask.

"Our first try at establishing a confederation certainly didn't work out very well." Ethan sounded depressed.

"What confederation speak you of, friend Ethan?" asked Teeliam. He explained their idea to her.

"That gives meaning to the lies of the false Landgrave Ro-Vijar," said the former royal consort of Poyolavomaar. "The only Tran he seeks to protect is himself."

"We could return to Wannome," Hunnar suggested. Everyone looked to him with varying expressions of dismay or shock and he hastened to protest. "Not I, 'tis not I who wishes to do so. But I felt it but fair to certain of the crew to relay their desires.

"For myself, I admit I was skeptical at first, my friends. Now, the more we travel across my world and the more I see how such as Ro-Vijar and Rakossa conspire for their own benefit, pitting Tran against Tran, state against state, the more convinced am I of the rightness of this plan. This union you have outlined is a worthy end to be fought for of itself, no matter what distribution of trade and benefits it also produces with your government, friend Ethan."

September commented approvingly. "Nothin' like some outright treachery and double-dealing by politicians to convince the citizenry they need a new form of government."

"There are still many good men and women of the crew who feel differently." Hunnar gestured at the ship around them, the populated rigging above. "They became homesick long since and talk more of mates and cubs and mistresses than confederations and politics. Adventure is growing wearisome to them, nor has our failure at Poyolavamaar inspired aught but despair. They wish for familiar faces and home hearths."

148

"They're not alone," Ethan said, feeling a tug toward a hearth more distant than the knight could imagine. "Are you suggesting the possibility of mutiny?"

Hunnar executed a violent Tran gesture indicating absolute negativity. "Ta-hoding is too observant and too good a captain for that. Never would he permit dissension to advance that far. Where other captains might put disgruntled crew members in chains, he can disarm them with a laugh or a sailor's jest.

"I wish merely to say that for this journey to show profit, we will have to have some success capable of raising the spirits of our less far-sighted shipmates."

Ethan studied the parallel grooves the runners cut in the ice behind them. "We can outdistance any pursuit from Poyolavomaar. The question is, where do we go now?"

"Your pardon." All eyes turned to Teeliam. "I care not whither you go so long as it is not back to Poyo. But I have listened well to your talk and believe you have the best interests of all in mind. As you have failed at Poyolavomaar through the wiles of its ruler and not its people, so should you try another state at least as wealthy and powerful, if not as aggressive." She nodded forward.

"I am no sailor, but I know directions and locations." She made a spitting sound as she spoke. "This is necessary when escape to elsewhere becomes one's obsession. Less than two hundred satch to the (Tran equivalent for south-southwest) lies fabled Moulokin."

"Two hundred satch—a fair journey to seek a myth." Hunnar laughed and even Elfa looked dubiously at her savior. "There is no such state as Moulokin."

"You've heard of this place?" Ethan eyed the knight in amazement. "You never heard of Arsudun, yet this place which sounds still farther from Sofold is familiar to you?"

"Moulokin is a mystic name on Tran-ky-ky, friend Ethan." The knight was still grinning. "Many of the finest ice ships were supposedly built there, in its shipyards. Yet not I nor any I know of have conversed with has ever seen Moulokin, nor even a Moulokinese."

"If they're only a myth, what about the ships?"

"Friend Ethan," Hunnar said as one to a cub, "all

149

owners are proud of their vessels. The finer the vessel, the greater the pride. To claim Moulokinese origin for a raft is to claim a credit few dare to match. 'Moulokin' may be naught but an honorary title given the best ships built in many shipyards and bestowed at their launching."

"Moulokin *is* real." Teeliam refused to be dissuaded.

"You have been there?" asked Hunnar.

"No," she said, suddenly subdued.

"Do you know anyone who has been there?"

"Not of myself. I do know of some who say they have traded with some who have been there." Hunnar made a disgusted sound. "Its direction is known," she said defiantly. "Moulokin must be more powerful even than Poyolavomaar, for it is said never to have been sacked by a horde."

"Absurdities, friend Ethan," Hunnar added gently. "The richer a city, the more attention it would draw from the ice nomads. They would band together temporarily until no city could stand against them. Not Poyolavomaar, not Arsudun before your people granted it protection, not Wannome my own. They could not withstand greater and greater attacks forever. The more attacks a state withstands, the wealthier it grows, and the wealthier it becomes, the larger and more frequent the attacks it invites.

" 'Tis kind of you to try and help us, Teeliam, but Moulokin can not lend us the help it does not have."

"What do you propose we do instead?" Elfa asked, challenging him.

Hunnar seemed a bit taken aback by the vehemence of her query. "There should be other states we can try, elsewhere."

"In lieu of the most powerful?" She turned that uncomfortable feline stare on Ethan. He turned to Teeliam.

"How sure are you of this Moulokin?"

"Myths do not have directions." She raised a furry arm, pointed just south of the bow. "There lies Moulokin, if it lies anywhere. Does it not behoove us to try for it?"

September watched a distant gutorrbyn glide by, eying them hungrily. "We can do both. If Moulokin exists, we'll find her. If she doesn't, we might as well search south for our next potential ally as any other direction."

"I agree," said Ethan. He looked back at Teeliam. "One more question, though. Two hundred satch is a long way from Poyolavomaar. Long, but not impossible. If Moulokin is so worth visiting, why hasn't anyone from your city gone there?"

"It is a dangerous journey." She paused, then added more quietly. "I would not hide that from you."

"All journeys across the ice are dangerous," Hunnar cut in emphatically. "How so is it known dangerous to Moulokin?"

"It is told that devils work between Poyolavomaar and Moulokin."

"You've seen devils before." Ethan patted the beamer clipped to his waist. "You've seen what our beamers can do. We can kill any devils."

"Perhaps, but you cannot kill the sea."

"What?" He frowned.

"These are *sujoc* devils who are invisible. They too live mostly in Hell. But between here and Moulokin they cavort close to the surface. Where they do, they bend the ocean." She looked frightened now, for all her hard-shelled bravado.

"That's not possible," said Hunnar.

"That is what is rumored."

Elfa looked accusingly at Hunnar. "If Moulokin be real and not a myth, why should not a bent ocean be equally real?"

Deductive logic was not Sir Hunnar's strong point. "I do not know," he replied angrily, "but the ocean cannot bend."

"We'll find out, because I guess that's the way we'll keep going," said Ethan.

"As always, Sir Ethan, you choose boldness over caution." She all but purred at him. Hunnar growled noticeably and stalked away sternward.

The good knight took it personally every time Elfa supported one of Ethan's decisions over one of his own. But perhaps this time the redbearded warrior was right.

Ethan found himself puzzling over Teeliam's words

151

as he relayed the course to Ta-hoding, found himself repeating her comments over and over again in his mind as he hunted for a flaw in his translation.

Of course there was no such thing as a bent ocean, anymore than there were devils who caused it. But he had seen a "devil" and fought it.

Suppose this other myth also had basis in fact?

Hunnar lay in the sun out on the new bowsprit, tracing lines in the wood with one claw while contemplating the ice shushing past below. Days had passed since they'd swung around to follow the girl Teeliam's imaginary course toward its imaginary destination. The sun was not yet much above the horizon. Early morning cold chilled even a Tran.

Light turned gray, solemn ice to a more cheerful white as the sun rose. His attention lay on the sun's ascension only vaguely. Nor was he thinking of the strange mission to which his off-world friends had converted him.

Instead, his thoughts were for the daughter of the Right Torsk Kurdagh-Vlata, Landgrave and True Protector of Wannome and Sofold. On the way the wind rippled her fur, so thick and smooth. On the noble gray down of her brow, which crested above eyes capable of more expression and emotion than most women's lips.

Inside himself he knew well that the friend Ethan meant no harm toward his desires and surely harbored no intention toward the lady. Certainly Ethan had voiced such of himself, many times. Yet it seemed that the two of them were thrown into argument often and that the tiny but incredibly heavy (*solid* bones, the wizard Eer-Meesach had said, not hollow like the Tran) human won all of them when Hunnar wished most to impress his lady. And Elfa would end up congratulating and cooing approval of the hairless dwarf instead of himself.

More than all the glory of battle, riches of trade, or the accolades of the Tran he led, he craved a few words of praise from her.

The grooves in the wood grew deeper with his thoughts. What was she trying to do by favoring the alien over him? Perhaps Ethan's disclaimers were spoken honestly, but could Elfa have some unnatural attraction to a male of another race? To a being who expressed his hatred of fighting whenever given the chance, who without his artificial chiv-skates would fall flat on the ice like a newborn cub?

He growled under his breath. No matter how he approached the situation, no matter the angle or fore-thought, he could not see the childishly simple explanation.

Double eyelids flicking, he found himself staring curiously at the horizon. An unusual ridging serrated the far-distant surface. They must be nearing another island. He performed some slow calculation in his head. It could not be Moulokin, if Teeliam's estimate of two hundred satch were correct. They were still too far away by a third. Yet whatever was there grew larger as he stared. Another island, and the morning light glowed most oddly bright on its slopes.

Elfa faded from his mind, far enough anyway for him to concentrate ahead. It was as if the rocks and soil of the growing isle were polished like a mirror. Sunlight shattered crazily from it as from jewels in the Landgrave's formal scepter. In this equatorial region snow was usually absent from surface lands. It had been so in Poyolavomaar, but did not seem to be that way here.

There was no sign of an end to the island as the icerigger raced nearer. Indeed, the ocean appeared to blend without a break into the island itself. A few minutes later his eyes widened in sudden realization of what was about to happen. With no land expected, the lookouts had grown lax. But now the one in the foremast basket saw the approaching mass and roared a warning to the ship.

"Come down speed . . . collision course!"

Hunnar was already chivaning back the portside icepath toward the helmdeck, yelling instructions as he went. The rigging began to quiver like a spider's web as sailors swarmed aloft.

One sailor lay asleep across the path. Hunnar bent, kicked. and soared over the prone figure to land on the icepath beyond.

Ta-hoding was not yet awake and on deck, but a second mate named Fassbire was. He relayed instructions of his own as he coordinated with Hunnar's information. Sails were trimmed and spars angled. The *Slanderscree* commenced to slow. A worried glance forward showed Hunnar that it was fast enough. Ice anchors would not be needed.

Dream-dull eyes showed as the morning crew stumbled out onto the deck. Cries of consternation came from those emerging from the fore cabin as they saw what was bearing down on them.

Ethan appeared on deck, followed closely by September. So acclimated to Tran-ky-ky had the humans become that their hoods were off and face masks down, exposing them to the chilly morning air, twenty-five below with a sixty kph tailwind. They soon had hoods and masks up, however, the danger of frostbite being too real to tempt.

Hunnar noted that Ethan was panting as he sealed his face mask, and had to remind himself for yet another time that the humans panted because they were short of wind, not to cool their bodies.

Spying Hunnar in the captain's position, he ran toward the helmdeck. "What is it, Hunnar?"

The knight, all thoughts of ludicrous romantic competition now forgotten, pointed forward, then to starboard and port where the phenomenon extended.

"Teeliam's myth is correct thus far, friend Ethan. 'Twas fortunate I was awake and . . . alert, for the lookout was sleeping or looking elsewhere, I think."

Ethan ran to the railing, sliding across the icepath, to study the remarkable barrier ahead and the quilted reflections it shot at his eyes from wrenched and tortured ice. "The bent ocean," he murmured in amazement. He repeated it to Hunnar after mounting the helmdeck.

"You find it pleasing, friend Ethan? Would it not unsettle you to see the ocean of your own world bent and twisted so abnormally?"

"A liquid ocean can't be bent, Hunnar. Not in this fashion, anyway. I don't know what it's called, but I've seen fax . . . pictures of it on other worlds. Maybe some were taken on my own. I don't know. It's ice, exactly like the ice we've traveled so many satch across." They continued to slow as they came close to the ridge of jagged ice blocks and spears, frozen girders and sparkling white boulders.

"But the ocean is *bent*," Hunnar insisted, with the tone of someone describing a round globe as flat.

"Not exactly bent," explained Milliken Williams from the other side of the helmdeck, "as much as compressed. This is a pressure ridge. Ages ago, this must have been one of the last areas of open water on Tranky-ky. Last minute freezing by two bodies of ice moving toward each other created this wall of broken floes. Clap your paws or hands together in a bowl of water and it will shoot up between them. That's what has happened to the ocean here, Hunnar. It was created by hydrophysics and not by devils or daemons."

"Did I say it was created by devils?" Hunnar spoke with great dignity. "Do you take me for a superstitious fool of a common sailor?"

"I'm sorry. I meant no insult," the teacher replied plaintively. Hunnar accepted the apology gruffly, then quickly changed the subject.

"The concern should not be what name to give it, but how to pass through."

Ethan studied the eerily regular ridge. "It can't be more than twenty meters high. Surely we can get across somewhere."

Scouting parties were sent out east and west, to locate a break in the ice the *Slanderscree* could navigate. Reluctant knots of sailors left the ship to explore the ridge itself, but only after being presented with anti-devil amulets rapidly sculpted by Eer-Meesach.

The icerigger lay facing the ridge, sails furled, awaiting their return. When the first explorers came chivaning back, Ethan and the others awaited their reports anxiously. They were not encouraging.

According to the scouts the ridge ran in an unbroken line almost due east and west. It extended as far as a Tran could see to the distant horizons. In some places the monstrous chunks of ancient ice rose considerably higher than the twenty meters they presently faced.

Having met no devils, the ridge climbers returned

155

equally unharmed and equally discouraged. While the ridge was barely a hundred meters wide, it was as solid as the ship's runners.

"We can't go around it, and we can't go over." Ethan was standing on the crest of the ridge, staring at the inviting expanse of open ice ocean on the far side. "We certainly can't go through. The *Slanderscree*'s no thermprow."

"What's a thermprow?" Hunnar asked, his chiv digging deeply into the ice, holding him steady against the wind.

"In the arctic regions of other worlds they have ships with powerful heat elements built into their bows and sides to melt the ice. I've seen pictures on the tridee." He glanced back at the icerigger. Sailors were moving listlessly about on deck and aloft, trying to keep busy to stave off discouragement. "If we had sufficient recharge capacity we could melt our way through with our beamers."

"Come now, young feller-me-lad." September indicated the massive ice blocks surrounding them. "It would take us a hundred years using these bitty little beamers to melt a *Slanderscree*-size traverse through this ridge. What we need is a proper shipyard torch." He gazed westward, ice particles buffeting his mask. "All to move a few blocks of ice."

"Blocks." Ethan stamped a foot. "How much would you say this one we're standing on weighs? Ten tons . . . twenty?"

September eyed his young companion, then looked back at the anchored *Slanderscree*. "Might be possible at that. If the wind holds steady."

"Have you learned naught of my world?" Hunnar spoke critically, but gently. "The wind is always steady, day and night, year and shayear. If the wind dies, Tran-ky-ky turns upside down."

"Never mind the theology, Hunnar. Do you think it can be done?"

" 'Tis not for me to judge, friend September. Best to put the question to the Captain . . ."

"If Ethan and September and Williams believe this thing is workable, who are we to disagree? Besides, I think it a most excellent idea," said Eer-Meesach.

Ta-hoding made a gesture of concurrence to the Tran wizard, then set about giving the necessary orders.

Pika-pina cables were wrapped tight around the lowest boulder in the ridge opposite. Meanwhile several intricate maneuvers had turned the great icerigger stern-first to the ice barrier. Cables were tied aboard, back of the helmdeck, made fast to the members of the raft's hull.

Ethan and September stood with the cable party on the ice nearby, watched as spars and sheets were adjusted to catch maximum wind. The *Slanderscree* strained, groaning and creaking like an old man. Cables hummed in the wind, dug at a single chunk of ice that weighed a good fifteen tons.

"Think they'll hold?" Ethan spoke without turning, watching the ship.

"The cables?" September snorted. "From what I've seen of pika-pina properties, it ain't the cables I'm worried about. The cables'll hold, but the ship's only wood."

Timbers moaned within the ship as the icerigger remained motionless. Her runners might have been welded to the ice for all the progress she was making.

It made the glass goblet splintering sound of the ice block all the more startling when it suddenly loosened from the ridge. Towing a mass the size of a shuttle-craft, the *Slanderscree* began to move ponderously northward.

Those sailors not immediately occupied let out a cheer. Sails held. So did the cables and the deck to which they were bound.

The icerigger started to slow. Ta-hoding bellowed a command. Spars were shifted. Now the ship swung ten, fifteen degrees north-eastward from its initial heading, putting pressure on the ice block from a different angle.

With a crackling that sounded like a headstone being uprooted, the block came free of the ridge, following in the wake of the icerigger. It was several minutes before Ta-hoding could order sails furled and spars reset to cut the *Slanderscree*'s mounting speed.

Humans and Tran skated and chivaned to examine

the enormous frozen mass. White and irregular, it rose as high as the underside of the raft.

Williams was gazing at the extensive gap in the pressure ridge. Ethan was reminded of a tooth knocked from its socket.

"Better than we could have hoped for," the teacher was saying. "In pulling free this block from the bottom we dislodged a not inconsiderable quantity of ice above."

Indeed, several other massive white monoliths had fallen onto the flat ocean surface. They could be towed aside far more easily than the first block.

The Tran worked cheerfully at looping and securing the cables around the next chunk, now at least half certain that the ridge was not the road traveled by Jhojoog Kahspen, Daemon Lord of the open ocean, as some particularly imaginative members of the crew had first tremblingly suggested.

XI

Several days later a path wide enough for the *Slander-scree* had been nearly completed through the ridge. A few last blocks of intervening ice were all that kept them from the open ocean beyond.

Ta-hoding worried some about his ship and the strain the constant break and tow was placing on her superstructure, but he'd gained confidence as block after multiton block was torn free and pulled clear without any visible damage to the raft's stern.

Three or four more tows of comparatively modest-sized chunks and they would be through. Cables were being readied for securing to one of those last blocks when work was interrupted by a frantic cry from the mainmast lookout.

"*Rifs!* North northwest!"

Working with the cable-setting crew, Ethan heard that threatening word too. Like his nonhuman companions, he stopped working as if stabbed, whirled and glanced in the direction from which the danger approached.

They'd encountered a rifs only once before, one time too often. A rifs was a meteorological anomaly peculiar to Tran-ky-ky, the manifestation of extreme weather forming over an ocean that was cold and solid instead of liquidly warm. September had described it as a linear hurricane, packing winds of over two hundred kph force.

Moving awkwardly on his skates, September followed the rest of the cable crew back down the path through the ridge. By the time he emerged, a black line made innocuous by distance was visible off to the northwest. As he watched, it grew larger, overwhelming the horizon.

That black line was the aerial equivalent of a tidal bore, a sooty sky-swelling wall of wind compressed like an atmospheric sponge. It could scour the ice clear of life save for tightly rooted vegetation such as the pika-pedan or massive life-forms such as the stavanzers.

Neither well-rooted nor massive, the *Slanderscree* had to do what all other life-forms did before a rifs—run.

" 'Twill never be cleared in time," complained one of the anxious Tran standing by the stern port runner of the ship.

Ethan slipped free of his skates, mounted the nearest boarding ladder. He found Ta-hoding, Elfa and Hunnar in animated discussion on the helmdeck. Williams and September were nowhere around.

"We must loose the cables and run 'til the rifs blows itself out," Elfa was saying.

"A rifs can blow for many days. We waste time," Hunnar argued.

She sneered at him. "Better to waste days than the ship."

"Perhaps," put in Ta-hoding, desirous of serving as peacemaker while keeping one eye on the rapidly nearing storm, "But I think Sir Hunnar has another suggestion."

"I do." The knight gestured back aft. "We must

159

move off, gather our speed, and try to break through."

" 'Twill be the ship that breaks, not the ice." She noticed Ethan watching nearby, changed her tone completely. "What do you say, Sir Ethan?"

Abruptly he was aware of many eyes on him, sailors and captain, squires and knights. They did not cease their frenzied work, but they listened for his reply nonetheless.

Good. They'd all hear. "I think we should do," he said loudly enough for everyone to understand clearly, "whatever Sir Hunnar decides. The rifs is a foe to be fought, and in matters of battle his judgment is always best."

Hunnar stared at him for a long moment, mumbled almost as an afterthought, "We have no choice. We must try to break through."

" 'Tis settled, then!" Ta-hoding looked relieved, set about giving the appropriate orders. The crowd which had edged its way to the helmdeck scattered to stations. Hunnar and Ethan continued to eye each other for several minutes, until Hunnar half-smiled and broke for his own favored position.

Was he grateful—or angry at some suspected condescension? Ethan had no time to reflect on the knight's state of mind. There were cables to stow, lines to straighten, sailors to reassure.

Commands reverberated around the deck. The ice-rigger commenced making a wide circle. Their course would take them in a curve eastward, then north, into the front wave of the storm. With its wind at their backs, they would hurtle back toward the nearly completed gap in the ridge and smash through the remaining ice blocks.

There were other scenarios, other possibilities, which Ethan preferred not to consider.

As raftsmanship, the plan made excellent sense. Emotionally, it did not, for the storm seemed to reach out for them as they neared the halfway point of the circle.

So close to the bore front the sky was a vast sheet of black cast iron looming ominously on their left, ready to tumble down and smash soft wood and softer creatures to multicolored smears against the ocean. If they had miscalculated and the rifs struck the ship broadside, it would surely capsize her, splintering masts, cabins, deck and crew.

Like gold thread in a velvet cape, lightning found its way downward through the boiling darkness. Rumbles and crashes, the war cries of inimical weather reached the crew and impelled them to faster work, stronger efforts to bring the ship around.

The first touch of the rifs fumbled for the ship. Not violent yet, but not like the steady, friendly every-day winds of Tran-ky-ky. No longer did they blow steadily to the west. Disturbed zephyrs slid in confusion around Ethan. Idle gusts scudded dismally past him, twisting and darting in and upon themselves like frightened rabbits hunting for a hidey-hole.

"We're going to cut it mighty close, feller-me-lad," said September in as grim a voice as Ethan had ever heard him use. The giant had both arms wrapped tightly around a pair of mainstays. Ethan chose the more solid wooden railing, locking a leg around one supportive post, arms around the railing top.

As the *Slanderscree* came full around onto a southerly heading, the rifs, in a desperate grab for its prey, jumped onto them.

The sky turned from blue to black. Thunder battered ears curved and pointed. Great shafts of electric death hunted for the fleeing raft. They reminded Ethan of nothing so much as the pulpy, luminous cyclops-creature they'd fought below the surface when escaping from the dungeon of Poyolavomaar. Glowing eye, gigantic black mouth filled with jagged teeth. Only now the teeth were kilometers high and yellow-gold instead of transparent.

Ethan's gaze turned with difficulty from the nearing ice ridge to the helmdeck. Looking more like a chunk of gray granite than their fat captain, Ta-hoding stood braced against the center of the huge wheel, struggling to aid his two helmsmen. They were already racing along at close to a hundred twenty kph, he guessed. Another blast of the full body of the rifs struck the ship, punching the sails still further outward and accelerating the craft's motion.

If they missed the gap at this speed, they wouldn't

have to worry about the rifs any longer. The icerigger would smash itself against the ridge. There wouldn't even be smears left of her crew. Even if they struck the gap but angled too far to one side or the other, jagged ice boulders could tear away stays, bring down the masts on top of them, or even shatter the sides of the hull.

There was black overhead and white rushing toward them. Windborne particles of ice and snow whizzed like projectiles from a million tiny guns across his mask, making vision difficult. By then the roar of the storm seemed to originate somewhere between his ears, numbing his senses, playing tricks with perception. Hadn't they reached the ridge yet?

A chalcedony tunnel obliterated much of the blackness as the *Slanderscree* entered the gap. He braced himself for the ultimate impact as did everyone else on board. There was a horrible crunching noise. Whether the ship had struck the jagged walls speeding past on either side or had been struck by lightning, he couldn't tell. The icerigger rocked crazily for a second.

Then they were through, the white ramparts gone, clear ice vanishing beneath the ship's runners. Fighting the wind, he looked astern and saw the pressure ridge from its southern side, receding behind them. His gaze went forward, toward what he knew he would see. Somewhere, the fates had determined the *Slanderscree* should not travel with a bowsprit. Otherwise the icerigger seemed to have handled the impact well. Masts had not fallen, no crevasse had appeared in the deck.

Something irritated his mouth. He parted his lips, sucked in salty fluid. With his face shielded from the wind, he nudged open the mask. Icy-gloved fingers probed at bare skin, felt the flow of blood from his nose. It did not feel broken. It felt worse, and the blood was making a mess inside his suit.

Looking around he saw other members of the crew picking themselves off the deck where they'd fallen or been thrown by the impact of smashing through the remaining ice blocks: How those aloft had kept from being thrown from the rigging was a miracle he chose not to question.

Sails straining to hold to the spars, spars to masts, masts creaking in their deck sockets, deck groaning on its five runners, and crew straining in prayer to whatever personal gods they worshipped that the whole should not return to the parts of its sum, the *Slanderscree* flew southward at a hundred sixty kilometers per hour.

A Tran knelt in the gap in the pressure ridge. Furry fingers collected several nonwhite, nonice fragments. They were mostly slim and irregular. One pricked his finger and he cursed. He had enough anyway. Raising his arms parallel to the ice, he tacked his way back to the group of Tran waiting impatiently at the far end of the passage.

There he dropped his arms, closed his dan, and slid to a neat stop. It would not do to stumble or fall before so many important ones.

"These were a few of what I found, sirs. There are many other such fragments at the far end of this passageway."

Tonx Ghin Rakossa, Landgrave of Poyolavomaar, accepted the several bits of shattered wood. He studied them, avoiding the one which had pierced the scout's finger.

"Many such fragments? Enough to comprise part of a large ship?"

"No, sire. I saw no such large amounts of debris."

Rakossa threw the splinters angrily to the ice. "They have escaped the rifs, then." He gently fingered the bandage over his left eye. "Though not undamaged."

"The five grooves of their runners continue southward outside this passage, sire," the scout added helpfully, currying favor.

Rakossa ignored him. "Would that we knew the extent of their damage. Yet it took them time to make their way through this ridge." The masses of ice nearby showed how the icerigger had made that passage, and Rakossa marveled greedily at the power of a ship that could move such weight.

"They are delayed." He knelt, brushed at the powdery ice lining the runner grooves. "This has not blown away completely, even with the force of the rifs. They are very near, and yet will now widen the distance between us once more."

"Nevertheless, we will catch them, your highness," said Calonnin Ro-Vijar.

"Yes. We will catch them, and the mocking strumpet as well."

Rakossa turned to gaze at the ships waiting behind them. They were a reassuring sight, with sails half-furled and pennants flying. They pursued with a small forest of masts—those that hadn't been torn away by the storm. And they had caught only the fringe of the rifs.

"But we will catch them with thirty ships instead of thirty-five. Three are so badly damaged their captains inform me they will never sail again. Two are nearly as bad off, but they can limp home with the crews of the abandoned three. Five ships lost already, Ro-Vijar."

"All the reason more to seek revenge upon those responsible, my friend," responded the Landgrave of Arsudun, trying to turn calamity to mental advantage. It was Rakossa's emotional state that was critical, not the condition of his ships.

"Perhaps." Rakossa spoke thoughtfully. "We waste time here." One foot descended, three chiv sectioned a fragment of wood the scout had recovered and marked the ice beneath.

Two weeks after leaving the pressure ridge, the *Slanderscree* came upon the plateau. A hundred meters of sheer cliff, it stretched off to east and west in unbroken basaltic glory. It was a barren-looking place, devoid of rim-clinging trees such as decorated the cliffs of Arsudun.

Teeliam was brought on deck, shown the impenetrable ramparts reaching across the ice ocean. "There lies Moulokin," she said with evident satisfaction.

"Moulokin? Where?" Hunnar didn't try to hide his sarcasm. "I see naught but ice, rock and sky. In that order, without exception."

"Nevertheless, this is the region of Moulokin."

"And where is the fabled city?"

"Could it be atop the plateau somewhere, Teeliam?" asked Ethan softly.

"No, that is absurd." The former royal consort of Poyolavomaar took little notice of Ethan's courtesy, as opposed to Hunnar's skepticism. "How could a state famed for the ships it builds be located many kijat above the ocean?"

"The thought had occured to me," said Ethan drily. "I was just pointing out that I see no sign of any city."

"Moulokin is here somewhere." Teeliam's conviction was unfazed. She faced the stone barrier. "Somewhere within this land."

Ethan and Hunnar exchanged glances. Then Ethan asked, "Which way? We must be off in our calculations."

Teeliam considered stories and rumors and legends. " 'Tis told the sun sets late in Moulokin," she muttered to herself. Then she pointed westward. "I would suppose that way."

"As you will." Hunnar executed a Tran shrug. " 'Tis this way or that, as well one as the other." He relayed instructions to a mate, who conveyed them to another, who shouted them to the helmdeck.

The icerigger turned laboriously to the west, commenced making difficult progress into the wind.

Despite Ta-hoding's best efforts, their progress was slow. Cliffs grew near, then receded as the *Slanderscree* tacked away from them, though never so far that land was out of sight. It wouldn't do to slip past their destination while making distance into the wind.

Occasionally there would be a sharp dip in the crest of the plateau where a hanging valley emerged. When the icerigger was on a starboard tack, the lookout in the mainmast basket could see into such gaps in the rock wall. Some held trees that apparently shunned the top of the plateau itself, but none showed any sign of habitation, not of the fabled ship building city of Moulokin or of a single Tran hermit.

Days became a week, the week two, without a break in the cliffs. From time to time the plateau would reach outward or ripple inward, forcing them to alter their heading slightly. But never did it vanish or vary its general east-west orientation.

165

By the beginning of the third week, however, the plateau began to curve gradually southward. Ethan mused on the distance they had come to the west. Nor was there any way of telling how far the cliffs extended westward.

"According to the mestapes I took long ago, back on the ship traveling here," Ethan was telling September, "survey work had been very limited on this world. Arsudun was the largest populated island the first team found, so they put the humanx station there. But this," and he gestured expansively at the towering ramparts, "it's either an island-sized continent, or a continent-sized island."

"It's plain enough, feller-me-lad," the giant commented, "that we've found no mere mountaintop stickin' its head above the ocean."

Hunnar joined them, braking to a halt on the starboard icepath, turning his chiv at the last moment so as not to shower them with ice. His excitement was evident from his expression and the fact that he almost forgot to lower his dan. September caught him as he stumbled forward, nearly fell. He was so preoccupied he forgot to produce an excuse for his clumsiness.

"We have found the tracks of a ship! They travel parallel to this high land also, but they approach from the east before turning south."

"Maybe someone else's calculations were a little off," said an equally animated Ethan.

"Mayhap." Hunnar regained some of his usual dignity. "This may mean only that another raft is exploring or lost."

"Sure. But if the Moulokinese do most of their trading with peoples to the south and west away from that pressure ridge we crossed, it would explain why we've encountered no tracks before now, and why they're so little known in Poyolavomaar." Hunnar's excitement had proven infectious. "Not to mention in far-off Arsudun."

"All possible, all possible." The knight's eyes flashed in the midday light. "We shall see."

The next day they came across two additional sets

166

of ship tracks. Like the first, these approached from the east before turning south.

"If Moulokin does lie along this plateau," Ethan was saying, "then any shipmaster knows he only has to encounter it before turning south or north."

The actual discovery, when it occurred, was anticlimactic. One moment the *Slanderscree* was racing southward, its speed faster now that it wasn't running into the wind. The next, the fore lookout was yelling loudly to any who could hear.

Off-duty crew rushed to the port rail for a glimpse of a myth become real. From the day they had first encountered the cliffs of the plateau, it had taken them nearly a standard month to reach their present position. Ethan couldn't estimate how far they'd come. But it was far enough to convince him that Tran-ky-ky could now boast at least one true continent in addition to its thousands of islands scattered spice-like across its endless ice seas.

At the same time he understood why those islands rather than this landmass of considerable but inexact extent were chose by the Tran for their towns and cities. Islands offered easy access to fields of pika-pina and pedan, access to the ice ocean on which all commerce moved. Everything they had seen of the broad plateau hinted at an interior as barren as the lowliest tundra.

Like everyone else, the cries had roused Ethan from his cabin and sent him running to the deck to learn what all the shouting was about. As he snapped his suit closed he noticed sailors up in the rigging taking in sail.

"What is it, Skua?" he shouted at the giant as he ran to the railing. Then he didn't have to ask because he saw it for himself.

As though cleft by the axe of a god, the cliffs had been split from rim to ice just off the port bow. As they drew nearer, the extent of the chasm could be estimated. Ethan guessed it was not quite two hundred meters across. It maintained that width as far down the canyon as he could see.

There was no sign of a city, but there were numer-

167

ous signs of its nearness. September leaned over the railing, pointed wordlessly down to the ice.

Despite the light dusting of ice particles and snow, Ethan could clearly make out many sets of parallel grooves running through the smooth surface. They were the tracks of ships which had passed this way. While they crossed and cut over one another, all converged on the chasm in the plateau wall.

September had his tiny monocular out. He'd flipped up the protective mask of the survival suit and was holding the compact telescope to one eye.

"What do you see, Skua?"

"Sheer rock, feller-me-lad. Rock no different from that forming the cliffs we've been pacing for weeks. Not a sail, not a building, nothing. Maybe the canyon takes a tight turn and hides the town." He slipped the monocular back into the sealocket in his suit, squinted at the plateau. "One thing's certain . . . all these tracks lead somewhere popular. I wonder at the clouds inland, though. Even if the wind's less there, you wouldn't think they'd linger so thick in one place."

It did seem that the interior of the plateau immediately behind the canyon was home to a dense mass of oddly whitish clouds. Blue sky around and above made the cloud-forms stand out sharply. Ethan thought briefly of volcanic smoke, such as could be seen from Sofold's steady-burning peaks. Only this smoke was much too light to be volcanic in origin.

"If it's such a busy port, why don't we see any other ships?"

"That gal Teeliam did say this Moulokin's primarily a ship-building and manufacturing center. Poyolavomaar, Arsudun, Sofold—they're all trading ports. Maybe no one visits here unless they've a finished raft waitin' for them. Or maybe the Moulokinese are superstitious and only trade certain times of the year. Be interestin' to see what they make of us."

Cries sounded from the helmdeck immediately behind them. Ta-hoding was gesturing busily to mates and assistants. Gracefully, sails were drawn up and tied to spars. The *Slanderscree* continued its cautious approach to the canyon.

Something pressed against the face mask of Ethan's

survival suit. He raised it cautiously, then shut it fast. His suit thermometer indicated it was minus twenty outside, but it wasn't the cold that made him hastily shield his skin.

They were traveling almost due east. That meant the untiring westwind was directly behind them. Yet they were making little progress. The icerigger rocked slightly, and he saw that Ta-hoding was tacking. That was crazy: nobody tacks away from the wind!

"Strong gale blowin' down *out* of the canyon," observed September with interest. A glance upward showed the sails flapping uncertainly against the spars. Occasionally the wind off the plateau was strong enough to shove pika-pina sail material back against the masts. At such moments the ship shuddered as if reluctant to continue. But under Ta-hoding's careful and expert guidance, they kept making steady progress forward. Very soon they entered the mouth of the canyon.

Walls over a hundred meters high towered on both sides of the ice ship. As they progressed up the chasm, the sheer stone ramparts rose steadily higher, though the canyon showed no sign of narrowing.

At a hundred seventy meters high the cliffs leveled off, only then the canyon walls began to press inward slightly. There was less room to maneuver. Ta-hoding and his crew worked hard to keep the zig-zagging ship from smashing into unyielding canyon sides. He was making shorter and shorter tacks, threatening terribly if a sail crew was seconds too slow in shifting a spar.

Once, the sailors manipulating the foremast tops misinterpreted a mate's order and swung their spars starboard instead of port. With a lurch, the *Slander-scree* continued on course to starboard instead of swinging around to cross the expanse of ice in the channel. Ethan stared, frozen, as they lumbered steadily toward the nearing gray cliff.

Sailors fought frantically to correct the error, compensate for the mistake. There was a dull, patient grinding noise. Fortunately the icerigger was now traveling so slowly into the headwind that the impact did no more than crack the railing and splinter a couple of deck planks.

The ease with which the planking splintered turned

169

Ethan's attention to the treeless rims high overhead. How stable were they? In the event of a slide there was no room to escape in the narrow confines of the canyon.

He was worrying needlessly again. The crash of ship into stone hadn't loosened as much as a pebble from the clifftop.

Strong comments were relayed from helmdeck to foremast crew via the midship's mate. They were intended to relax the atmosphere on board while chastising the foremast sailors. Instead, the invective only added to the general tension, did not produce the laughter it would have in less threatening surroundings.

The mystery of the mythic city-state, the narrowing canyon walls that shut out the clean sky, the skate-scarred ice they were traversing, in conjunction with their unfortunate experiences at Poyolavomaar, combined to test the mental stability of the crew. Ethan knew it would be better if they encountered *something* —hostile, friendly or even inexplicable—before many more minutes passed.

It occured to him to wonder what they would do if Moulokin proved as unreal as it had proven elusive and the canyon simply continued to narrow, perhaps to a lonely rock-face dead-end. The many ship tracks might signify nothing more than a convocation of religious worshippers at a favorite shrine, or indicate a well-used refuge from storms.

Such visitors would have no trouble turning their ships around and racing back down the ice-filled canyon with the inland wind at their backs. But the canyon was as narrow as the *Slanderscree* was long. She could not possibly be turned 'round in so slim a space. They might have to backsail, traveling stern-first and steering in a fashion unthought of.

September had theorized a bend in the canyon. All at once it turned sharply southward. The crew had to struggle with lines and spars to swing the icerigger safely around the twisting walls.

The wind continued to buffet them from off the plateau, but it was gentler now. The ice raft could preceed up canyon on a softer tack.

Except that the canyon was blocked.

At first he thought it a landslide, tumbled down from those cliffs so stable in appearance. As they drew nearer it was clear that the obstacle was Tran-made, its great stones and blocks neatly piled with mortarless masonry to form a wall stretching across the ice strait like a granite web.

It was perhaps thirty meters high, deeper than he could casually guess without a higher view. As was the custom on Tran-ky-ky, the colossal double gate was constructed of wood. It rose nearly as high as the stone walls themselves and was flanked on either side by a triangular tower.

The structure puzzled him. Impressive as they were, these could not be the gates to fabled Moulokin. Behind the barrier the cliffs rose high and close together as ever. There was no room for a city behind the wall. And if any such did exist there, he reminded himself, surely it could be seen from the lookout cage on the mainmast.

The wall itself was a typically solid piece of native engineering. It looked well-nigh impregnable. But something lay behind that gate. The quilt of grooves in the ice now ran straight toward the double gate.

They were very close when the sound of a horn reached them. It brayed three times and then was silent. Ethan ran for the bow, discovered Elfa, Teeliam, Hunnar, September and many others already there, staring forward.

A voice from one of the towers hailed them. Its tone, so crucial to the precise meaning of many Trannish phrases and words, was neither hostile nor openly inviting. "Who are you, in the great ship? From whence do you come and what do you wish of the peaceful folk of Moulokin?"

This development produced an excited muttering as word spread through the crew, made its way up the masts and into the cabins. Moulokin existed; Moulokin was real! At least, an unseen presence on an impressive wall had laid claim to the reality of a rumor.

Hunnar replied. "We come from a far state, Wannome, to the northeast of you. We desire to parlay with your Landgrave and council on a matter of

171

great importance to all Tran. And we have three important visitors with us."

"Step forward, lad. Time to show ourselves." September slid back his mask so those hidden in the wall would have an unobstructed view of his furless visage. Williams and Ethan duplicated his movement.

"They are from a world other than Tran-ky-ky." Hunnar pointed skyward. "A world from the ocean of black ice."

All at once there was movement on the ramparts. Ethan could see Tran soldiers emerge from concealment, gesturing at the icerigger while talking among themselves with apparent excitement.

So the appearance of the three humans was a surprise to them. Now he could relax some. Calonnin Ro-Vijar had not conjured up a skimmer or other modern vehicle to carry him here in advance of their arrival, to stir up trouble and spread the lies he'd sown so effectively in Poyolavomaar.

"They have much of importance to impart to you, as they have imparted to us," Hunnar continued. "Important things which can benefit all Tran."

"These Tran are of Moulokin and for Moulokin first," responded the voice from the tower, sounding noncommital. "But . . . we will talk with you and mayhap even listen.

"As to your own plans and desires, know that many have tried to sway Moulokin with weighty promises erected on thin ice. We make no promises of our own. Will you still talk, given these words? We will open the gates to you." A pause, then, "I believe your vessel will pass between. Marvelous as are the shipwrights of the city, they have created nothing half so grand."

"Happily will we share our knowledge with all." Lowering his voice, Hunnar faced those grouped around him. "What think you, friend Ethan?"

Uncomfortable as always with so many eyes on him, Ethan replied softly. "Everything points to the real Moulokin lying somewhere beyond that gate. Whether it exists or not, we seem to have found some Tran with self-confidence and a willingness to listen. That's a valuable combination we should try and enlist."

172

"Leastwise they haven't told us to turn around and take off back the way we've come." September was gazing expectantly at the wall barring their path. Shrouds and stays snapped around them, singing in the down-canyon breeze. "We should be careful, and we should go in."

"'Tis settled, then." Hunnar called out the command to the midship mate, who relayed it crisply to the helmdeck. A prompt reply came back. Ta-hoding felt he could negotiate the narrow gateway in the wall.

"We will come in," Hunnar shouted back to the listeners assembled on the wall and in the two towers, "and with thanks for your friendly welcome." The last was offered as much in hope as certainty.

Like the snores of a restless giant, the thick wooden gates drew back on stone slides. Ta-hoding rumbled cautious orders. The *Slanderscree* started forward, tacking minimally under slight sail.

Ethan was too busy to decide whether the anxious expressions of the guards gathered on the walls were due to curiosity, awe, or nervous tension. The stone wall contained a surprise. It was much thicker than he'd expected, varying from ten to twenty meters in depth. Cabins and barracks were built into and on top of the immense rampart.

Ta-hoding employed his fanciest maneuvering to turn the ship to starboard once her stern had cleared the wall. As the icerigger began to edge slowly around the sharp rightward bend in the abyss, a cry of dismay sounded from the bowsprit lookout. Other cries sounded from the bow.

Intending to discuss the difficulties of negotiating the slim channel with Ta-hoding, Ethan heard the shouts, stopped, and reversed his course. By the time he reached the bow, the *Slanderscree* had come to a halt. A glance showed the cause of the crew's consternation.

Around the canyon headland and before them lay a second wall. It looked just as impregnable and well-tranned as the one behind them. There was a double gate in it, and the gate was closed.

A creaking noise turned his attention to the stern. Working frantically, the guards on the first wall had succeeded in closing the portal they'd just passed through, after having oiled the stone slides to keep the ponderous gates from screeching and warning the icerigger's crew. Now they were draping thick green-red cables across the gate and securing them to the bracketing towers. Spears, lances, and bows formed a threatening fringe along the wall top. Expectant yellow eyes gleamed behind them, shining brightly in the dim canyon light of afternoon.

"So much for local hospitality." September studied a furious Sir Hunnar. The knight was showing clenched teeth, examining the armed walls, instinctively gauging an opponent's strength. "Much as it pains me to admit it, friend Hunnar, I'm tempted to come 'round to your way of thinking'. First Poyolavomaar and now here. Doesn't look like Tran folk even like to speculate on cooperatin'."

"Raft coming!" called the mizzen lookout, stimulating a rush toward the stern. Everyone clustered at the icerigger's widest point, over the starboard stern runner.

A very small icecraft was fluttering toward the *Slanderscree* from behind, having emerged from a dock attached to the inside of the first wall. It looked like a brown leaf scudding uncertainly across the hard whiteness. Three Tran manned it: one steering, one handling the single sail, the last standing at the bow-point gazing curiously at the icerigger which towered above him.

One of the sailors peering over the railing growled. "They carry no weapons."

"And fly no pennant," said Hunnar, adding admiringly: "They said they would let us past *this* gate, and that we would talk. Talk we will, though 'tis not the setting for a parley I would prefer." He glanced over at one of the assistant mates. "Vasen, what are our chances of backing sail and breaking through that gate?"

The mate replied as if he'd already considered the question carefully. "As thick as the wall is, Sir Hunnar, I would care not to try. We might crack the wooden gates despite lack of room to build up proper speed. But the pika-pina cables appear well secured to the stone towers. They would not snap, and I would not care to chance pulling their moorings free from the wall." He thought a moment before speaking further.

"With the aid of our crossbows and the light weapons of our human friends, we could perchance overpower the guards on the wall. But we would still have to unkey and drop the cables barring our retreat." He gestured toward the bow and the second wall up canyon. "I cannot judge how many soldiers might be waiting out of sight behind that wall. They could attack us from behind and overwhelm us with numbers." He executed a Tran gesture of disappointed negativity. " 'Twould be prudent to talk first. We can then always slit the envoy's throat before attempting to escape."

Hunnar responded with a snarl. He disliked having to wait. Patience was not a Tran trait. The humans had chided him about that before. Well, he could be as patient as any hairless human, and would chat pleasantly and politely with this envoy.

As Vasen said, they could always cut his throat later.

Someone finally thought to throw over a boarding ladder. It clattered against the side of the icerigger. The tiny raft pulled up alongside. Clasping the ladder cables in both hands, the Tran in the bow climbed toward them, moving smoothly for a biped balancing awkwardly on three sharp chiv instead of a flat foot.

Then the Tran was standing on the deck, confronting half a hundred hostile stares with an aplomb and air of assurance Ethan could only admire.

He was skinny to the point of emaciation, being no broader than Ethan himself, though he appeared healthy enough. After surveying his audience with a rigorous half-smile, his gaze settled on the three humans. Double eyelids blinked against winddriven particles of ice.

" 'Tis true? You are truly from a world other than this?"

"It's so," Ethan shot back. "We prefer not to be thought of as strangers, however. We'd much rather

175

be thought of as friends, though appearances suggest you feel otherwise."

"Contraryso, offworlder. We would wish it similarly. I hight Polos Mirmib, Royal Advisor and Guardian of the Gate."

"Which gate?" Hunnar's tone made his response sound like much more than a question. "The one we were invited to pass safely through, or the one that has been used to entrap us?"

"The gate to Moulokin, of course," replied Polos, appearing unaffected by Hunnar's hostility and avoiding his insinuations diplomatically. "That is a gate made not of stone or wood, but a gate mostly of the mind."

A belligerent voice sounded from close by Hunnar: Suaxus-dal-Jagger. "I'd heard that the Moulokinese were famed as shipbuilders, not philosophers."

Mirmib executed a smile. "Recreational metaphors are a personal affectation. Do not ascribe such word-play to my people as a whole. They are for the most part stolid, honest, not especially imaginative folk, who wish nothing more of life than to enjoy a good day's work, a hearty meal and warm fire at day's end, and the love of their mates between days."

His voice took on a slight sharpness as he continued. "To outsiders, Tran and otherwise, these things may seem a peasant's way of life, simple and uninspiring. We enjoy being uncomplicated." The sharpness disappeared. "Enjoy we also guests, visitors who bring to us news of the strange places to which we of Moulokin rarely venture."

"Because you're afraid to?" challenged a voice from up in the rigging. A mate shushed the sailor.

Mirmib had the control as well as the diction of a diplomat. He did not grow angry, as he would have been justified in doing. "We do not travel because we find in the stories travelers tell to us all we wish to know of far regions. As none we are told of sound superior to fair Moulokin, we see no reason to leave it. Better to remain and let others perform the arduous task of travel for us."

His gaze focused on Ethan. "As travelers from a

176

place so far distant I cannot comprehend it, you must have still more exciting tales to tell us." Ethan started to reply, but Mirmib raised a paw to forestall him.

"Before that can be done, before we can greet you freely as guests and friends, that simple way of life I have described to you must be insured against violent disruption. So that the second gate may be opened to admit you to our home, to my home, I would ask that you pile your weapons here before me where they can be collected and stored safe for you by the gate patrol, to await your departure."

He added a few additional words, but they were drowned out by the angry and uncertain outcry this request produced among the sailors who had gathered about.

XII

Balavere Longax finally stepped forward. His presence quieted the crew. "From where I was raised and have lived a long life, no Tran will enter yea even the home of a neighbor without retaining at least a knife."

"You must be mistrustful of your neighbors." Mirmib sounded unperturbed, but did not modify or drop his demand.

"Suppose," Hunnar ventured pragmatically, "we refuse?"

Mirmib made the equivalent of a shrug. "I will be saddened by what might happen. You are trapped here between walls even this wonderful vessel cannot break. In seconds I, or others if I am unable, can call on large numbers of waiting soldiers to rally against you. You may still be able to escape, though I think not. In any case, many would die, of mine and yours. I would rather not speak of such unpleasantness. As Guardian of the Gate, I give my warmth in promise: none of you will be harmed and you will be welcome as proven friends."

177

He turned to near-pleading. "Surely this custom seems strange to you. 'Tis a requirement for strangers we insist upon. On subsequent visits to Moulokin such will be not required. You are an unknown and judging by this ship, powerful factor. My people are insular and suspicious. This request has preserved us in the past when prevaricating, jealous visitors would have pillaged us. Please, I implore you, execute this gesture of good will! We wish your friendship, not your blood."

Hunnar seemed ready to reply. Ethan hastily put a restraining hand on the knight's arm, felt the tenseness beneath the fur. "It's time for us to take a chance, Hunnar. If they really wanted a fight, why send a single unarmed representative to advise us of their intentions? That's poor salesmanship. They could have attacked as soon as we passed through the first gate."

"Why attack if they can win the *Slanderscree* without a fight?" the knight protested. "This thing is unheard of. To enter a strange city is difficult enough, but to do so without weapons is to invite justified murder of all of us, fair retribution for such stupidity." He growled at the human. "No, it is not a thing to be considered!"

Ethan spoke anxiously. "Hunnar, this whole long trip we've taken together, from Sofold to Arsudun to here, was not to be considered either. Yet we've done it. The idea of a confederation of Tran city-states was not to be considered, and here we are trying to implement *that*. Each day you, Balavere and the rest of the crew do things none of your people imagined doing.

"Now is the time for boldness and risk-taking, not for reverting to primitive superstitions and dying customs." He paused, aware that Balavere, Elfa, and the rest of the assemblage were watching him steadily, some without affection. He kept his poise, and kept his eyes on Hunnar's.

Mirmib spoke into the ensuing silence. "I understand not all of what you refer to, offworlder, but your position I can naught but concur with. I believe strongly that we will be friends."

"Spoken firm if not well." Hunnar shook Ethan's clinging hand off, turned to glare at Mirmib. "Be this

178

an excuse for treachery, know that my companions and I have walked into Hell itself and have returned after spitting at the inside of the world. Even unarmed, we would not go like k'nith to the slaughter."

"You talk too much of slaughter." Mirmib looked sad. "Having much to protect, we of Moulokin are no strangers to killing. But we are less fond of it than outsiders seem to be."

"Where do you want them?"

Mirmib looked across at Elfa. She had her own sword out, ready to turn it over. The diplomat's voice turned deferential.

"Here will be sufficient, noble lady." He indicated the section of deck in front of him.

Sailors and knights trooped by, dropping off bows, crossbows, swords, axes, weapons of every kind. Tahoding invited Mirmib to inspect cabins and below-decks storage holds for additional weapons. The Moulokinese declined politely, accepting Hunnar's word that the entire armory of the crew was being deposited at his feet.

Ethan reflected that while Polos insisted he belonged to a simple working people, they were more than sophisticated enough to have evolved an inflexible, efficient procedure for dealing with potentially bellicose strangers. He didn't doubt the diplomat's claim that his people were no strangers to killing. Mirmib had likely overseen this turning in of weapons many times in the past.

As steel and bone rattled unmelodiously on the ever-mounting heap, Hunnar moved to stand next to Ethan and whisper. "Your proposed confederation and your own life may end with your blood steaming on the streets of this city, Sir Ethan."

"Even in my business, you eventually reach a point where you have to trust someone, Hunnar."

"You speak highly of trust, Sir Ethan," Hunnar said wryly, "yet I notice that neither you nor your companions have stepped forward to place your weapons of light on the pile before us."

"As long as this fellow doesn't recognize them as weapons, there's no need to overextend ourselves where we don't have to." Ethan's rationalization

179

sounded unwieldy as he muttered it. "In my business, it's also a good idea to have an ace in the hole."

"Would that we had a hundred such aces," Hunnar agreed, expanding on the analogy without understanding it. " 'Tis interesting to note that you do not regard trust as an absolute, but as a term with definitions which vary according to the situation."

"I didn't mean——" Ethan started to argue. But Hunnar, trying hard to conceal his evident pleasure at this revelation of human morality, walked away before the salesman could reply.

Polos Mirmib studied the imposing heap of weapons as the last sword was laid atop the metal and bone pile. Edges and points gleamed in the dim canyon light.

"For those who profess to offer naught but friendship, you travel well-armed."

Elfa offered a candid response. "We also have much to kill for."

"Well put, my lady." Mirmib executed a light gesture of modest admiration.

"What now?" September's impatience made him sound nervous, which he wasn't. "We just push the lot over the side? Or do you have somebody waitin' to come pick them up and tag them for us?"

"Neither." Mirmib showed the giant his widest nontooth smile. "Your willingness to so comply with a custom of gravest imposition is sufficient proof of your good faith and, I hope, true intentions." He gestured idly at the armory. "You may repossess your weaponry. Your actions have told us what we wished to know." While those of the crew standing around stared stupefied at the diplomat, he turned and walked to the railing. A mild gust of Tran-ky-ky's unceasing, arctic winds made him stumble and Ethan reflected again on the other's fragility. Like many sentients of great character, Mirmib wore his steel and iron inside.

He shouted to the two Tran waiting on the tiny raft alongside. Ethan caught only isolated scraps of sentences. The accent used here was thick and slippery.

One of the Tran blew several indelicate notes on a horn. This mournful baying was answered by a jubilant blare from a horn on the first wall. Another horn sounding from the second wall, up ahead, was followed by several more, until the canyon reverberated like a thranx concert at mating jubileejee.

When the final mellow flat had retreated into crevices too small to return it with audible force, Ethan was able to make out cheers from the Moulokinese soldiers lining the massive walls ahead and behind. The small raft moved away from the *Slanderscree*'s shadow to assume a waiting position near her bow.

"Where is your captain?" Mirmib asked. Sliding his own sword back into its sheath, Hunnar used his free hand to point to the high helm deck. Ta-hoding stood staring curiously down at them. "I will join him, to aid in directing you to our city."

Ethan joined several others in following Hunnar and Mirmib up to the wheel. While Ta-hoding received instructions and conferred with Mirmib, Hunnar drew Ethan aside.

"See, the cables barring the gates fore and aft have been taken in. We could break the gate behind us and escape."

Ethan eyed his massive, hirsute friend. "Is that what you wish to do?"

"I do not. You accuse with your questioning, friend Ethan." It was Hunnar's turn to walk away for a different reason.

Ta-hoding had the necessary sails reset. Slowly the icerigger moved toward the second gate, swinging delicately through the tight bend in the canyon. As they squeaked through the gate, the soldiers on the walls studied the ship and its occupants intently. Unlike the *Slanderscree*'s passage through the first gate, however, the watching warriors jostled one another and chattered freely among themselves. Their weapons hung easily from paws or lay forgotten against walls and rocks. A few even exchanged hesitant questions with members of the icerigger's crew.

The canyon grew no shallower as they followed Mirmib's raft up the ice. Sheer basalt walls towered steadily higher above them. Before long the canyon wound around to the east and started inland again. The walls hemming them in seemed to lower slightly, and breaks where a man might climb upward began to appear in the hitherto vertical cliffs.

Now that they were facing the interior of the plateau once more, Ethan could see over the bow the dense clouds they'd found so intriguing from out on the ice ocean. They continued to hover persistently in one place, succumbing to the dispersing effect of the wind only with reluctance. Their initial familiarity now came home to him.

Similar clouds clung possessively to the plutonic highlands of Sofold, Hunnar and Elfa's home island. That puissant grayness was a great upwelling of steam, not smoke. Issuing forcefully from volcanic fissures and vents, it would renew itself as fast as it could be blown away. That explained the illusion of the "hovering" clouds.

Volcanic heat provided the base for Sofold's foundry and much of its wealth. So in addition to a reputation for fine shipbuilding and an impregnable canyon locale, Moulokin also enjoyed this additional important resource.

He moved to stand next to the diplomat Mirmib. " 'Tis true there are foundries up there," the emaciated Tran admitted, "but they are neither owned nor operated by us." In response to Ethan's look of surprise and consternation, he explained, "We have an agreement with the people who operate the foundries."

"They're not Moulokinese?"

"No." And he formed a peculiar expression Ethan could not interpret.

He intended to pursue the question, except the *Slanderscree* abruptly turned hard to starboard. They were proceeding up a side canyon. Sailors fought with spars and sails, but for a new reason. Now that the icerigger was traveling southward and no longer heading inland, the wind from the plateau all but vanished as soon as the ship had fully entered the branch canyon.

The wind faded to a gentle, almost earthlike breeze. Tentatively Ethan cracked the mask of his survival suit, hastily shut it again. There was no paradise ahead. The wind might have died, but if it was warmer than minus fifteen outside his protective cloth-

182

ing, the outraged cells on his face had lied to him. Moulokin would be no Trannish Shangri-la.

The canyon took several twists and turns. Ten minutes later it opened into a vast natural amphitheater. The dark cliffs arced out to east and west before curving smoothly southward again. They were moving across a cliff-walled bowl at least a dozen times wider than the mouth of the canyon.

Ahead lay Moulokin, looking very real.

At the southern end of the canyon the cliffs had crumbled and eroded away, mounting upward in uncertain stages, forming levels. Much of the city was constructed on these levels, giving Moulokin a terraced look.

Several thousand roofs shone in the sun. Ice-paths were filled with black specks like splinters of chocolate which darted up and down the white streets. Far back from the harbor's edge, built into the topmost level with a thirty-meter-high wall of sheer rock behind it, was a substantial-looking fortress.

There was ample room now for the *Slanderscree* to maneuver. The magnificent ice harbor could easily have contained as many ships as that of Wannome. To the west, docks marched like brown worms out onto the ice. Ice canals and strange buildings dominated the far western edge of the harbor, running up to the cliffs themselves.

"Our shipyards," Mirmib explained with a touch of pride in his voice.

"I'm beginnin' to understand why this place's never been taken," September rumbled. "A few could hold those two walls we passed against an army. No way up the plateau from outside to outflank 'em. And the way that wind blows down the canyon, any attacking rafts would have the devil of a time trying to tack up-canyon against them while carryin' on a runnin' fight."

As the icerigger edged toward a long, deserted dock under the joint direction of Mirmib and Tahoding, Ethan's attention traveled to the southeast. Between the city and the western canyon wall, the cliffs gave way to a gradually rising sub-canyon filled with the densest growth of coniferous-type trees they'd yet encountered on this world. No doubt they matured to such heights here because of the protection the canyon provided from the steady eroding winds that scoured the rest of Tran-ky-ky. Seedlings here could add height and breadth without being torn loose by hurricane-force winds, and seeds might find accumulated soil in which to take root, while larger trees would not have the earth ripped away from their surface roots. In that immensely valuable stand of mature timber lay Moulokin's greatest source of wealth.

As they maneuvered into the dock, Ethan saw Mirmib temporarily free and asked him again about the operators of the distant, steam-shrouded foundries.

The diplomat appeared uncomfortable, tried to divert Ethan's attention to the neat storehouses and homes cut into the cliffs forming the harbor.

"Is there some reason why you can't tell me?"

"None written. They guard their privacy and . . ." Mirmib stopped, his expression changing to one of reverence. You are friends: there is no reason I can think why you should not know of the Saia."

"The Saia?"

"People of the Golden Saia, offspring of the fires they tend. They know of things ordinary people do not. Ordinary people they are not."

"You worship them, consider them gods?" Ethan pressed. If he'd hoped to get a revealing reaction from Mirmib, he failed.

"I did not say either of those things. No, they are not gods. They are simply different. To know them is to respect them. This is a tradition as old as Moulokin. We pride ourselves on our independence." For the briefest instant, Ethan detected a hint of the rabid tribalism of which all Tran seemed to be guilty.

"But we keep the bargains they set."

"Out of fear? Why not just take the foundries from them? Or at least strike your own bargains."

"It is not a question of fear, my friend. You know naught of the Golden Saia. We fear them not, but we respect them mightily. And we would gain nothing even could we wrest the foundries from them, for we could not run the mines and smelters as well as they do, nor fashion such intricate metal parts for our homes and rafts.

"Where they live and play, it would be death for one of us to work. 'Tis difficult enough but to go briefly to trade with them."

"It's warmer where they live, then?"

"It is not to be believed," said Mirmib solemnly. Of course, what was unbearably hot to a Tran might be wonderfully comfortable for a human or thranx.

But if that was the case, then what were the people of the Golden Saia?

"There are plants and creatures living among the Saia which would interest a curious traveler, did he not die of the heat while examining them. They grow nowhere else that we have heard."

"What kind of plants?" Ethan and Mirmib looked to their left. Milliken Williams stood there, the diminutive teacher reluctant to interrupt but finally too intrigued to forgo a question or two.

"I will not describe them to you. I cannot describe them to you. They are pieces of dream." Mirmib looked thoughtful. "I have been to the head of the main canyon but twice in my life, and have no desire to go again. When I finished conversing with them, though they met our party on the very outskirts of their lands and the region of fire, I was so exhausted and weakened that I lay unconscious for two days each time before my body had recovered."

"Dehydration," murmured Williams.

"And now, if you mind it not overmuch, I would rather talk no longer on them." He indicated a group of staring Tran making their way toward the ship via the dock icepath. "There are matters of official greeting to be taken care of. My presence is required."

Mirmib left them to join Ta-hoding, Hunnar, Elfa and September. While Moulokinese protocol was conducted in the universal fashion of such matters—which is to say, with teeth-clenching slowness—Williams and Ethan spent a few relaxed moments watching two cubs as they chivaned dangerously but gleefully in and out among the runners of the busy icerafts in the harbor, ignoring imprecations hurled in their direction by disapproving adults and tired sailors.

185

There were few such vessels to play among. As the legends had insisted, Moulokin was a center for building and manufacture, not commerce. Trade here was in intense bursts rather than a steady flow.

Williams slowly raised his face mask, letting his skin grow accustomed to the near-windless cold. In the absence of the usually omnipresent blinding ice-whiteness, he also popped out his protoid optical contacts and exchanged the high-glare configuration he normally wore for regular implants from a small black case. He had to wear the implants anyway, and they saved him the necessity of bothering with the regular goggles that the others wore beneath their suit masks.

A few lost snowflakes touched lightly on his dusky skin. "Ethan, what does this canyon remind you of?"

Carefully Ethan examined the surrounding harbor. Moulokin lay ahead, the canyon opening behind them. To either side, the locals who dwelt in the caves chivaned down icepaths cut into the lower cliff sides with breathtaking disregard for the precipitous drops lining each path. Blue sky overhead and thick wool-gray clouds toward the interior completed the scene. None provided an answer to the teacher's question—except perhaps the terraced topography of the city itself.

"I'd guess it reminds me of some old river canyons I've seen, where the water level had dropped drastically."

"Yes, a river canyon, certainly. Only parts of it don't fit." Williams spoke with a curious intensity. "That's not enough, somehow." His gaze turned to the canyon exit. He rested his elbows on the high railing, his chin in cupped hands, and did not go into what parts he was referring to.

Ethan shrugged. Williams's obsessions differed from his own and September's. Then as if on cue, a familiar bellow sounded from the main deck. He moved to the helmdeck edge, stared down to see the giant beckoning to him.

"Come on, young feller-me-lad. The local Land-grave deigns to chat with us. 'Pears we're going to get

186

our chance to enlist the second state in the union of ice."

Leaving Williams alone at the railing, contemplating ancient geologies, Ethan joined the party assembling on the dock.

Moulokin was much like Wannome, save that it rose in steps instead of the smooth incline of Hunnar's home. Icepath switchbacks formed the way from one level of the city to the next.

As expected, curious crowds came to stare at the newcomers. Black pupils expanded on yellow fields as the humans passed, looking more alien than ever in their brown, shiny survival suits.

"Tell me, Mirmib," Ethan inquired of the diplomat leading them, "you and your people have done well for yourselves here. Apparently these Golden Saia have done likewise up at the canyon's end." He gestured hesitantly at the cliffs surrounding them.

"But what of all the land around here, behind the Saia? The forested canyon on our right looks as if it runs right up to the edge of the plateau. There are no cliffs there barring settlement of the interior. Who lives on all that land?"

Mirmib regarded him with surprise, great furry brows twisting. "Why, no one, friend Ethan. That is to say, no one to the knowledge of Moulokin. And Moulokin," here he gestured at the city, "has been here as long as there are records to read and legends to precede them."

"Then you can't be sure no one lives in the interior?" He smiled at the antics of several fascinated cubs fumbling along in his footsteps and eying him as if he were a refugee from a bad dream. "Has anyone ever been in there?"

Mirmib spoke gently. "Friend Ethan, you question me thus in your search for others to join in your idea." Ethan nodded, added a yes when he remembered that the gesture would be unfamiliar to Mirmib. "You will find none in there. Yes, we have been above the canyon's rim. There are no natural ice paths up there, no ice ocean." He raised one foot off the ice to show his sharpened chiv-claws.

"How would we travel and explore? We could melt

187

ice and let it refreeze to form icepaths as we do here in the city. But to journey any significant distance inland would require more labor than 'tis worth."

"But you said some of you had been above the rim?"

"Yes. Despite the difficulties. They tell of flat, barren lands with little vegetation and no game. There is naught to eat but a low, thin form of plant, not nearly as rich as the pika-pina we harvest outside our own upper canyon. Nor are there trees worth cutting. They are stunted and scattered. There is little enough ice to melt for drinking, let alone to spread out and form paths to travel upon." His voice dropped and he looked away.

"Besides, there are spirits that haunt the inlands. They feast upon the minds of those who venture within, and it is told that the farther one goes from Moulokin, the faster his thoughts melt like drinking water. Enough."

They had reached the castle. Ethan forced aside the visions of the inner continent his considerable imagination had conjured up. They had another new Landgrave to confront, and they'd best have better luck here than in Poyolavomaar.

Smoke and distance had obscured their view of the castle from the harbor. Up close, Ethan found it unexpectedly modest in dimension. It was not built on nearly so grand a scale as the stone massif in Poyolavomaar nor even as that of Elfa's father back in distant Wannome. Its location high above the city lent it a grandeur it would otherwise not have had. Also, it was far wider in proportion than it was deep, basically a long rectangle of cut rock.

So shallow was it that the thirty-meter high cliff rising to the edge of the plateau which backed against it appeared ready to tumble and demolish it at the first strong wind.

The guards lining the entrance in expectation of their arrival looked more solid than the structure they defended. A high main gate admittted them to a narrow courtyard. From there they entered the main interior building. Only after they'd walked a substantial distance without stopping, and windows had given way long since to torches, did Ethan and his companions realize that most of the castle was hewn out of the cliff face.

They'd hardly adjusted to this surprise when Mirmib directed them into a room distinguished only by its lack of ornamentation. A few furs covered the walls, torchlight adding to their exoticism. Hunnar, Elfa and Ta-hoding looked unimpressed. When informed by Mirmib that they stood in the throne room, the visiting Tran could not believe it.

The barbaric magnificence of Elfa's father's throne room in Wannome, with its brilliant banners and dominating stavanzer tusks, was absent. So was the spacious ostentation of the throne chamber of Tonx Ghin Rakossa of Poyolavomaar.

The feeling here was intimate instead of overpowering. In addition to the pelts and torches, the only color was in the floor. It was a crazy-quilt pattern of pentagrams, triangles and other geometric shapes, each made from a different wood. The inlays ranged from a rich, almost space-black through the darker shades of brown to one deep-grained square that was nearly yellow.

The throne itself bore closer resemblance to the Trannish version of an easy chair than that of an impressive seat of state. Ethan, having absorbed his impressions of the room in a few seconds, now directed his attention to the figure seated in that chair. It raised both paws and slid back the hood which had been shadowing its face as it stood to greet them. Finely woven robes clung to unexpected curves.

Never intimidated by position, September murmured an appreciative comment. There was no real reason for the surprise Ethan experienced, he told himself. The power positions of women within the Commonwealth were so commonplace that they were never remarked upon. Anything else would have seemed unnatural. But it was not so in many primitive societies, particularly those of a feudal/barbaric inclination.

Yet had not the leader of the Horde which he and September and Williams had helped Hunnar's people to defeat been female, the repelling Sagyanak the

Death? And wasn't Elfa the one who would inherit title as Landgrave of Sofold?

Leaving the throne, the Landgrave of Moulokin came to exchange breath-greetings with them each in turn. Mirmib performed the individual introductions. The Landgrave did not hesitate or shy away when she came to the two humans.

The Landgrave (Landgravess? Ethan wondered) was named K'ferr Shri-Vehm. She had the typical broadness of all Tran, though was slimmer than the other females present, Elfa and Teeliam. Perhaps the Moulokinese ran to unusual thinness. They did if their Landgrave and guardian of the gate were any indication. Her slimness by Tran standards made her appear almost human, save for her height. She was nearly as tall as Hunnar or Skua September. September might find her attractive, in a bizarrely alien fashion, but to Ethan she was merely intimidating. Her sequinned dan could envelop him completely.

Her smile when she greeted each of them seemed genuine. Despite her beauty and presence, reflected in the admiring gazes of Hunnar, Ta-hoding and Bala-vere, nether Teeliam nor Elfa appeared apprehensive. Possibly it was due to K'ferr's aura of authority. She seemed neither male nor female so much as Land-grave. This despite being the youngest Tran in the chamber, excepting Teeliam.

For reasons he never quite understood, it fell on Ethan to tell the tale of their accidental arrival and crash-landing on Tran-ky-ky, of the presence of a humanx outpost at Arsudun, their various adventures in reaching this point and their joint interracial decision that the best way for all Tran to improve their status was to form a Trannish government including many city-states which could then petition for admittance to the Humanx Commonwealth.

K'ferr absorbed this barrage of new ideas and concepts quietly, listening with both pointed ears cocked intently at Ethan. Occasionally she would make a small gesture of agreement or disagreement, or mutter something softly to Mirmib, who stood close on her right. She said nothing to anyone else until Ethan came to the part of their story where they were greeted and then betrayed and imprisoned by Rakossa of Poyolavomaar, who acted in collusion with the Landgrave of Arsudun, Calonnin Ro-Vijar. Before Ethan could finish, K'ferr rose and began pacing the open area between her throne and the assembled visitors. Her chiv clacked on the wooden floor, making her sound like a nervous tapdancer. Ethan studied the inlaid wood, wondering if the chiv marks were polished out after each audience or if the chamber was simply little-used.

When Ethan related the lies Ro-Vijar had employed to sway the mind of the unstable Rakossa, K'ferr's soft voice angrily launched into a list of old grievances Moulokin held against Poyolavomaar.

"But Moulokin is a half-legend in Poyolavomaar," said Hunnar.

"And their mendacity is legend in Moulokin! 'Tis true," she continued furiously, "we have no contact with them. But they have contact with many peoples who trade with us. Though they cannot match the skill of our shipwrights, out of jealousy they try to keep others from contracting for our rafts. Their merchants are known as arrogant and their traders bully many who would deal with us. They are fat with power, from cheating at every opportunity. Yet we are told others are afraid not to deal with them. The capriciousness and evil of their Landgrave is well known to us." Teeliam Hoh murmured a comment which none could hear clearly, but Ethan could guess at its substance.

"This Rakossa is famed for the taxes he wrings from his people. However," she said more easily, lowering her voice, "you are here and not in Poyolavomaar."

"And grateful for it, my lady," added Hunnar.

K'ferr slid with a remarkable hirsute sensuousness into her chair, leaned on her left arm. The claws on her right paw appeared, vanished, reappeared, a nervous Tran habit Ethan recognized immediately.

"Tell me of this idea, this plan you have for our world, outlander-man. This—what did you call it, Mirmib? This confederation you call a union of ice." She glanced sharply at Hunnar. "I have never heard of this Sofold, nor know any who have. Yet you subscribe to this proposition made by a few of another race. You can speak for your city and assure me that you will keep the peace if we eventually agree to become part of this union?"

Confronted abruptly with the reality of an idea coming true, both Hunnar and Elfa looked questioningly at Ethan. He said nothing. Finally, Hunnar replied. "We had not considered that we might so soon have to commit our state to this proposal, my lady,"

"So you are willing to agree in principle, but not with your own selves."

"I did not say that," Hunnar hastily corrected her. " 'Tis only that I . . ." He paused, drew himself up impressively as he could. "I am a knight. I have no authority to make treaties."

"I can."

K'ferr turned lidded eyes on Elfa. "And you are also a knight of this distant land of Sofold?"

"I am the Elfa Kurdagh-Vlata, daughter of Torsk Kurdagh-Vlata, Landgrave of Sofold. One day I will be Landgrave, upon confirmation of the knights and nobles of Sofold. I give my warmth as forfeiture in the event Sofold should ever act belligerently toward our friends in union, the people of Moulokin. We will join in peace forever, for the betterment not of two small city-states, but of all the people of all Tran-ky-ky." Aware everyone was staring at her, she continued less imperiously, "In so doing we but implement a larger vision from friends who exist in a greater universe than our own."

K'ferr came forward, grabbed Elfa's wrists with her paws. Elfa did likewise to her counterpart, and they exchanged breath, to brief but animated cheering from the others. It had all happened a bit fast for Ethan, used to dealing with the intricacies of Commonwealth bureaucracy. Once more, the informal nature of Tran government had shown its value.

It did not at all feel like a critical moment in the history of an entire world.

XIII

"There is Jinadas, which lies forty-three satch south-west of Moulokin," Mirmib was telling the now relaxed visitors. "They might well be willing to join in this union, especially if we send representatives along with you to assure them of its efficacy. And we have good friends in Yealleat, a most powerful state lying some hundred satch to the west."

"We forget ourselves, Polos." K'ferr Shri-Vehm looked solemn yet pleased with herself. "You must all remain several days now. An event of this magnitude and importance cannot be consummated properly without much feasting and celebration." Topaz eyes flickered in the torchlight. "We Moulokinese seize readily upon any excuse for a holiday."

"I don't know." Ethan tried to sound apologetic. "It might be a good idea if we hurried on our—"

"We'd be *glad* to stay awhile," September cut in anxiously, with a sharp look in Ethan's direction. "After the last couple o' months, we could do with a bit of celebratin'. Couldn't we, feller-me-lad?"

"Skua, don't you think we ought to—"

"That's settled, then."

" 'Tis agreed." Mirmib entwined his fingers in a gesture indicating extensive satisfaction. "Preparations will commence. Meantimes, I would inspect this wondrous vessel of yours." He directed his next query to Elfa.

"How did you manage such an enormous raft?"

" 'Twas made possible by the special metal which our human friends call dur'loy, and which Sir Ethan insists can be supplied to us in quantity and at fair trade rates."

The diplomat swung his fur-framed gaze toward Ethan. "Is this truth. outlander Ethan?"

"Commerce is the life-blood of the Commonwealth,

193

friend Mirmib." As he spoke it, Ethan wished for something less trite than that ancient government aphorism. He was better dealing with specific items than generalities. At the same time he wondered at Polos Mirmib's title. He'd called himself Guardian of the Gate, but his presence as K'ferr's sole advisor here hinted at a much more powerful role. Was he chief minister, perhaps? Or father, or consort? Given the uncertainties, Ethan thought it best not to risk a breach of courtesy by inquiring. At least, not until the new Trannish confederation had been in existence somewhat longer than a few minutes.

"I'm sure something can be worked out," he added.

"It promises abundances for the peoples of Moulokin and Sofold," the Lady K'frr agreed. "And to our friends in Yealleat and Jinadas if they too will join, as I believe they will." Her easy-going manner and beatific expression lulled Ethan completely, so that her next words were twice the shock they'd have been if he'd been expecting them.

"There is one thing, an obvious trifle, that all should agree to, of course. The treacherous inhabitants of vile Poyolavomaar must naturally be excluded from this."

Ethan's heart skipped a beat. Hunnar shook his woolly head and regarded the salesman with eloquent silence. The slant of his lips, the narrowing of double lids, said as plain as words, "See now? No matter how accommodating or friendly these folk of Moulokin are toward us, there will always be hatreds among the Tran which a mere idea cannot obliterate."

"Details of the confederation can be worked out later, my lady." It was a desperate attempt to forestall a possibly crippling argument. "For now we should return to our ship and prepare properly for Sir Mirmib's visit."

Either K'ferr sensed his discomfort or else he'd genuinely taken her mind off the subject of Poyolavomaar. "There is no need for you to trouble yourselves with special preparations for us, for I am coming also." Mistaking his attitude of discomfort, she added, "But if you desire to rest yourselves and warn your crew, I fully understand. We will await word of your readiness."

They made formal gestures of leave-taking and were preparing to exit the room when a Moulokinese soldier came running in.

The mere action was indicative of the importance of his message, for the Tran disliked running and avoided it except in extreme situations. Their sharp, long chiv were magnificently adapted for chivaning, or skating, across the ice. Running was awkward and dangerous, but this soldier came clip-clopping into the room at an impressive pace.

While the visitors stood grouped to one side and politely pretended to ignore the soldier's anxious words, Ethan strained to overhear. Not only the soldier's method of locomotion, but his manner and the rapidity of his speech hinted at news of some urgency.

As was the case with all Tran they'd observed thus far, the panting soldier did not prostrate himself before his ruler, or perform other time-consuming obsequious gestures. He simply approached the throne and began talking, pausing every so often only to catch his breath.

"My Lady—outside the first gate . . . a ship. And beyond, near the mouth of the canyon, many ships!"

"Conserve thy warmth, soldier," said Mirmib quietly. "Now, how many is many?"

"Twenty to thirty, minister," the exhausted messenger poured out, ignoring Mirmib's admonition to relax. "All filled to the railings with armed soldiers."

Ethan's imperative whisper broke into the conversation between Hunnar and September.

"What is it, feller-me-lad?"

"Just listen." He gestured surreptitiously toward the throne. Elfa, Teeliam and the others also stopped chatting, strained to hear.

"They say they come from Poyolavomaar," the soldier continued.

"Speak of the devil." September looked atypically upset.

"They say they know that—" he looked around the room and finally focused on Ethan and his companions, "—they are here."

"How can they know that?" K'ferr's nape hairs were bristling.

"From the depth and sharpness of the marks their

ship's runners leave in the ice, my lady." Mirmib nodded sagely. "They demand that these visitors, their great raft, and the woman among them hight Teeliam Hoh be turned over to them. This done, they will quit their position and leave us in peace. Otherwise, they threaten to take the city." At the close of this the soldier's voice, despite his evident fatigue, took on a note of disbelief.

K'ferr stood abruptly, raked the left arm of her chair with sprung claws. "The *arrogance*. To come thus to our gate and demand by virtue of arms that we surrender *any* visitor. I would not turn over to such children an injured k'nith!"

The soldier unabashedly admired his ruler's stand. "It seems incredible, my Lady. He insists he will destroy us if we do not comply."

"He? Who is he?"

"Their Landgrave, Tonx Ghin Rakossa, leads them, my Lady."

"Does he deign to allow us time to consider his generous offer?" she asked sarcastically.

"Four days, my Lady."

"So much time? Why do they grant us so much?"

Taking her question literally, the soldier explained. "They realize, their representative told us at the gate watch, that it may be a difficult decision for us to make, going as it does against traditional laws of hospitality. We should be permitted time to consider. However, it was made clear to us that as long as their fleet blockades the canyon entrance, no ship of ours nor any other can move in or out to trade."

"Or to escape," added an unperturbed Mirmib. "Tell me, soldier, what is your name and profession?"

"Cortundi, minister. I am a leathersmith by trade."

"What would you do, Cortundi?"

Common soldier regarded ruler and minister. His paws tensed into digging mode. "I wish only to return to the first gate, my lady and sir. I expect I will be needed there."

"A siege would be long Cortundi."

The soldier-craftsman smiled, showing pearly fangs. "There mayhap be better hides to cure, sir."

"A pleasant thought." K'ferr returned the panther-grin. "Wait outside, Cortundi." The soldier turned and left.

"My fault, 'tis on me alone." Ethan heard the disconsolate whimper, turned to see its source—a downcast Teeliam standing back against the wall. Torchlight turned the fur on her head and shoulders to singed silver.

"I should not have come with you when I helped you to escape," she continued. "I ought fair to have killed myself cleanly then and prevented this. Rakossa is mad."

"He is mad indeed," said K'ferr, "to think he can take Moulokin. He cannot reach the city, nay, cannot breach the first wall. Truly he is driven not by common sense but by insanity." Ethan forebore from mentioning that some of Terra's greatest generals, ancient and modern, had been thought quite mad.

"'Tis me alone he seeks out," Teeliam went on sadly. "He cannot stand the thought I may finally have escaped him. I would kill myself here save that he would be more furious still at being deprived of the pleasures he doubtless has spent these past days planning." Fur rippled nervously as muscles tensed.

"Come what will, in fairness I must go back to him." Her gaze rose, traveled from human eyes to Tran. "If I do this, he may depart."

"I do not understand," said K'ferr slowly, gaining more knowledge from something behind Teeliam's eyes than from her words. "It was said that Rakossa demands also crew and ship of you."

"Yes, he desires them, but will be satisfied with me."

"He may be," Ethan admitted, sounding more heartless than he intended, "but Calonnin Ro-Vijar will not." He tossed a brief explanation over his shoulder to the staring Mirmib and K'ferr. "Ro-Vijar is Landgrave of distant Arsudun, an ally of Rakossa's in spirit if not material."

"It is not right that an entire city risk war for one person." Teeliam sounded resigned. "I will suffer whatever Rakossa has concocted for me." She made the Tran equivalent of a resigned shrug. "It cannot be worse than what I have endured before."

"We will not," Hunnar said tensely, "turn you over

197

to the madman. Sofold does not sacrifice the innocent for the sake of expediency. Besides, as Ethan says, doing so may not sate Rakossa anyway. Of course," and he turned to face the throne, " 'tis not properly our decision to make."

K'ferr had left the throne and was pacing once again. Almost absently she said, "This business of turning over your companion to Rakossa is a waste of time. We would never consider such a thing, nor permit you to do it even should that be your wish. There are more important matters to discuss." She looked to her minister.

"So the Poyos would challenge us here, at our own door, in our canyon, on our ice. Further proof of this Rakossa's insanity. Arrogance dilutes sense as *vouli* thins strong drink. If they are in truth foolish enough to attack the gate, we will give them a welcome they will not outlive."

"If you're determined to fight, we'd better ready our own people," Ethan said. "With your permission, and our deepest thanks, my Lady, we'll return to our raft."

"Do we permit them to enter the first gate and trap them between, or stop them at the first with arrows and spears?" The compassionate Landgrave was deep in discussion of life-shortening methods with her minister. Mirmib had presence enough to dismiss the visitors.

Ethan rose from his place at the long table in the *Slanderscree*'s galley-cum-conference room. "We can't let them have Teeliam, and it doesn't seem right to let the Moulokinese fight and die over something they've had nothing to do with." Teeliam was not present to object to the first part of his statement, having been excluded from the meeting over her protests. She was too biased to render objective suggestions, Hunnar had informed her, a bias which even extended to condemning herself to death.

"Me, I'd rather welcome a chance to dally with this Rakossa and his pack." September leaned back in his Tran-sized chair. Not designed for his greater weight, it creaked alarmingly beneath him. He rubbed his pinnacle of a proboscis.

"I know you would, Skua. Sometimes you act more Tran than human."

September grinned, moving the hand from nose crest to white mane, and scratched. "Lad, when you've seen as much of the galaxy as I, you'll know there's nothin' especially flattering about laying claim to being part of mankind."

"No, friend Skua." September looked with surprise at Elfa. The Landgrave's daughter had seemed anything but pacific. Now was an odd time for appeasing attitudes to surface.

Appeasement was not what Elfa had in mind, however. "Ethan is correct when he says this is not the Moulokinese fight. We cannot ask them to die for us."

"But didn't you see the way that K'ferr cat was actin'?" September argued. "She's spoilin' for a confrontation and bloodshed."

"Surely, my lady," said a disbelieving Hunnar, "you cannot be thinking of turning Teeliam over to the monster?"

"Quite so, noble knight. I cannot be." Elfa's eyes swept over the table. "But suppose Rakossa and Calonnin knew the *Slanderscree* was not here?"

"Not wishin' to appear condescendin', gal, but you heard what that soldier said back in the throne room." September's nails were mere stubs compared to Tran claws, but he etched a shallow groove in the hardwood table nonetheless. "No ship could make the chiv marks in the ice outside the canyon that the *Slanderscree* could."

"No known ship," admitted Elfa. "Yet there are many regions of this world that the Poyos, much as ourselves until recently, know nothing of. This would be true also of distant Arsudun. How could they be certain our tracks are not those of another ship, say a great towed barge long since dismantled for its wood by the Moulokinese?"

"Not impossible, my lady," put in Ta-hoding. "But how could we convince the attackers of this?"

Elfa looked embarrassed. "I had not considered that far. Could we not hide our craft while representatives of the Poyolavomaar fleet inspect Moulokin's harbor?"

199

"Hide this vessel?" Hunnar executed a high Trannish laugh.

"No, let's think this through, Hunnar." September appeared thoughtful. "The lady, she has a point."

"What if," Ethan said after a moment of introspective silence, "we took the ship apart. Yeah, took it apart and put the sections up on the plateau. The Poyo representatives would never think of looking up there."

"And with good reason." Hunnar tried hard not to sneer. " 'Tis a most marvelous proposal, friend Ethan, save that it would take the whole population of the city in addition to our own crew working several weeks to accomplish such a task, even if the Moulokinese have heavy engines enough to raise the large timbers and masts. We have but four days."

"No, wait a minute, now." September leaned forward, speaking with controlled excitement. "What the lad suggests makes sense, but in a different way. We need to get the rigger up on the plateau, and a really fair distance inland in case the Poyos *do* insist on lookin' there, something this Rakossa is likely to try. Since we can't do it in sections, we need to move her intact."

Murmurs of polite astonishment came from several of the Tran seated around the table.

"Suppose we sail her to the upper end of the main canyon, Captain." His attention was directed at the intent Ta-hoding. "I'm kind o' curious to meet these Golden Saia folks myself." Ethan threw him a questioning glance. Had Skua, despite his initial disclaimers, been as intrigued by the mysterious Saia as Ethan and Milliken Williams?

"Now with all the forces actin' on the land there, it's a fair assumption that the land of these Saias slopes fairly gently inland."

"Given that it does, friend September, and I intend no disrespect, but—what of this?" Hunnar waited to be convinced of he knew not what.

"I was on a world once," the giant said reminiscently, "similar to this one. Only the oceans were covered with grass—sort of an anemic pika-pina, Hunnar, like they say grows inland here—and there were sailin'

200

ships akin to the *Slanderscree*. They sailed easy over those green oceans, on wheels instead of skates."

"What," inquired Hunnar blankly, "is a wheel?"

Ethan sat stunned. The Tran had achieved such a high level of civilization that he'd taken an invention as basic as the wheel for granted. Now that he thought back on it, nowhere in Sofold could he recall seeing a wheeled vehicle; not a cart, not a wagon, nothing. Everything traveled on chiv, or skates. Dry land transport was by means of sledges, used as little as possible. And they had no need for wheels, after all, in a land where icepaths were easily constructed and frozen seas surrounded every city-state.

He finally found an example to serve as illustration. "Like the millstones, Hunnar, you use for making meal from dried pika-pina and juice from its pulp. Like the," and he had to use the Tran term for steering control to refer to the *Slanderscree*'s own great ship's wheel. "You place them apart like so, with a supporting beam between like those that connect our ship's skates and they carry you smoothly across unfrozen lands."

"This is surely an awkward way of traveling," Hunnar admitted, brows contorting in confusion, "yet if you say the thing works, it must be so."

"It's a proven method," replied Ethan without smiling. At least Hunnar and the other Tran had the idea now.

"We will need," Williams began, already drawing designs and measuring stresses in his head, "additional axles to place beneath the ship. While the five duralloy skates now positioned beneath us are sufficient to support the icerigger's mass, I have less confidence in stone or wooden wheels, and that is the best the Moulokinese could construct. They have good quality timber. Perhaps they can be metal-reinforced, if the work of these Saia is as fine as they claim."

"Why not just make metal wheels?" wondered one ship's mate.

"Assuming these Saia are indeed not gods, they would do extraordinarily well to manufacture one wheel of such size in only four days," Ta-hoding pointed out gruffly. Gentle of demeanor when speak-

ing to his superiors or the three humans, the icerigger's captain could be harsh whenever he thought one
of his own crew guilty of stupidity.

"With stone or wooden wheels then," the teacher
continued, calculating all the while, "we'd need additional axles for additional wheels."

"Plenty of trees big enough," September agreed.
"They'll be a lot easier to cut and attach than takin'
the ship apart would be. Of course," and his excitement grew tempered by thoughtfulness, "this is all assumin' the Moulokinese are willing to make 'em for
us. I expect they will. I'm sure most of 'em would prefer to work a little harder rather than fight. A saw
usually sheds less blood than a spear."

"You speak a truth which I suspect extends beyond my own world, friend September." Hunnar regarded the giant somberly. "There are those who do
not share your opinion and mine of fighting." He
looked around the table. "There is also the question
of obtaining permission from these Saia, whatever
they may be, to travel through their lands. Given all
this, I will defer a personal desire to shed Poyo blood."

K'ferr Shri-Vehm also had to be convinced. It took
considerable persuasion by minister Mirmib to talk her
out of opting for the bloodthirsty path. That accomplished, orders were issued for an orgy of work to
commence.

The industrious Moulokinese took the enormous as-
signment as a challenge to their skills. When the first
evening fell, lights were brought out to permit the
work to continue. The central shipyard reeked of old
oil. From a distance, it looked as if the *Slanderscree*
rested in a pool of fire.

Huge trees, cut and stored for use as masts on other
rafts, were already available to serve as subsidiary
axles. Metal bolts made by the Saia were brought out
and used to help pika-pina cable secure axle to ship.
Four new axles were emplaced between the fore and
aft pairs of duralloy runners beneath the motionless
icerigger.

Hours passed, became days. The metal-sheathed
and reinforced wheels were bolted onto the four new
axles. Then the runners were removed, first the pair

fore and then the two aft. Wheels slightly larger than the eight already attached were placed on the runner shafts. Finally, the fifth runner, used for steering, was replaced by a steering wheel.

As expected, a brief experiment revealed that the resultant hybrid was as maneuverable on ice as a greased two-year-old. There was no way it could make any distance upcanyon against the steady, powerful winds that blew down off the plateau. The wheels would simply spin in place as the icerigger was shoved into the first cliff behind it.

Seven of the largest rafts in the harbor—and the Moulokinese built respectably big ones—were detailed to tow the helpless *Slanderscree* upcanyon, to the end of the ice. To the land of the Golden Saia. From there it could begin its slow journey inland.

Mirmib, however, could not give assurance to Ethan and the others of safe passage through the thermal regions. A representative hastily dispatched to acquire such assurances had returned, typically dehydrated and exhausted, to report that the Saia chose not to comment on the question. They had not given guarantee of safe conduct, nor had they denied it. Their sole response had been an indifferent silence.

In the absence of denial, it was decided to proceed.

"They have strange powers and commune regularly with the spirits of the interior," a solemn Mirmib informed the readying travelers. "You would do well to treat cautiously with them, and to avoid conflict at all costs. In addition, they might offer much more information on the true conditions you can expect inland, though they abhor it more than we do."

It was night as Mirmib addressed them. They were standing on the long dock paralleling the almost-finished, almost converted icerigger. Ethan and Hunnar were alone among a rushing current of preoccupied craftsmen.

Winches were carefully loading the last of the five removed duralloy runners aboard the ship. Hopefully, they would find another sloping canyon far away. Ethan found himself shivering as the minus sixty temperature pressed at his survival suit's adjustive potentials. On locating another such canyon they would once more replace the duralloy runners, remove the wheels, and set off for a new location, perhaps distant Yealleat. As Ta-hoding had pointed out, the stars were a Tran icemaster's principal guide to navigation, and the stars remained constant over land as well as ice.

They were loading final stores the next morning when a small raft came racing into the harbor, heeling dangerously to port as its crew hiked to maximum for top speed. She disgorged a single officer, who hauled himself up a boarding ladder with impressive speed despite the blood filtering through the fur over his left eye. The four sailors sprawled exhaustedly on the deck of the little raft looked equally battered.

"The Poyos have not waited," the officer explained to the rapidly growing group of listeners clustering around him. "This is the fourth day and they attacked two *hoid* ago, no doubt hoping to catch us offguard and by surprise." The bleeding soldier permitted himself a vicious smile. "They did not, though they are stronger than we thought." He recognized Hunnar among the assembled Tran.

"It would be well for all if you were on your way as soon as possible." He took in the seven jostling tow-rafts, the cables stretching taut between them and the icerigger. "I must return to my post. Our warmth is with our new brothers. Go with the wind." He was over the side before anyone had a chance to ask questions.

Ta-hoding was already heading for the helmdeck. Cranes and lift cables were disengaged in a flurry of commands. *Slanderscree* mates and harbor pilots of Moulokin took up positions in the bow. Sails began to billow, a blossoming of blue-green and gray, flowers of speed.

Word of the Poyolavomaar attack spread rapidly among the icerigger's crew and those of the towing vessels. The Moulokinese hurried their last-minute preparations. They wanted to return as quickly as possible, to help defend their city.

Settled in arrowhead formation around the *Slanderscree*'s bow, the seven tow rafts exchanged signals and orders. Sailors stationed astern of each turned single-minded attention to the braces where the thick cables ran out to the icerigger. Pika-pina cables had never been known to snap, but they'd never been employed to pull so massive an object as the *Slanderscree*. If one did break, given the tension that would exist between dead weight and tug, the flying cable could decapitate an unwary sailor. Those stationed to watch the cable braces were all volunteers.

Ethan worried more about the effect of the plateau winds on the huge icerigger. Even with her sails furled, if the winds obtained a grip on her, she could be smashed against a down canyon wall.

Raft by raft, each of the towing craft let out its own sails, adjusting position to catch the gentle breezes sweeping down Moulokin's protected canyon. The cables grew taut, hummed. There was the sound of pottery breaking beneath a heavy weight which muffled even as it broke. The icerigger ponderously started forward, sliding out of drydock as neatly as any clean birth.

Ta-hoding was in constant verbal communication with relay mates stationed along the length of the ship. Shouts rang out constantly, darting from towing raft to icerigger to raft as all concerned fought to maintain equal tension on all cables. It seemed an impossible task, but the Moulokinese proved themselves as skilled on the ships they built as they were in the shipyards. The cables thrummed and sang of uneven pressures, but none snapped—not even during the most dangerous maneuver, when the seven towing craft turned up the main canyon and the forceful interior winds struck them and their massive ward.

Tacking as one, they pulled the great raft steadily inland.

Ethan rushed to the portside, found to his relief that the second wall which barred passage downcanyon showed no sign of warlike activity. That meant the Poyos were still being stopped before the first wall. So far, the confidence K'ferr of Moulokin had displayed earlier seemed justified.

Great walls of dark stone drew close beside them, the roofless hallway of some ancient cataclysm. At times Ethan found himself impatient for more speed, for their progess seemed abysmally slow. It was not a journey that could be hurried, however. Not when seven ships had to maneuver as one.

On the fifth day, the ever-present walls began to shrink. Small side canyons, some hanging above ice-level, began to break the cliff edges. Some were smooth as they vanished into the plateau, while others dropped in steps similar to Moulokin's topography. Their own little canyon-born zephyrs contributed to the difficulty of maneuvering.

Soon they were passing between cliff walls no more than twenty meters high. The lookouts on the *Slanderscree*'s fore and mainmasts could see over them and study the terrain beyond. They reported seeing only yellowish, wind-swept, inhospitable near-desert.

On the frigid morn of the eleventh day, when the canyon had ceased to be a canyon but was instead a river of ice bordered by gently sloping banks, they entered an area where clouds of steam and mist blotted out vision for all but a few meters in any direction. When they slid close to the banks, those on board the rafts could make out thick, towering trees whose crowns were lost in gray water-down, boles more massive than the largest growing in Moulokin's side canyon.

Before long a cry came from the lead raft in the triangular formation. They had reached the end of the frozen river. Cables were cast off and neatly coiled aboard the *Slanderscree*. Finally the last was disengaged and all seven tow rafts had moved carefully downriver from the icerigger.

The wind here was dispersed, indecisive. Quickly, Ta-holding had sail put on as the huge raft slid slowly but aimlessly on the ice. Orders were given, spars adjusted. A sound new to the ears of Tran sailors penetrated the mists: a deep, impressive rumbling. The icerigger was now traveling on land.

It stopped.

Lookouts forward reported that the first two sets of wheels were resting on a gentle beach of gravel and grass-covered rock. Ta-hoding considered. Obviously, they had to put on more sail. But he was still leery of sailing on naked soil. Williams, who was standing

206

nearby on the helmdeck, did his best to reassure him.

The plump captain remained skeptical. "I would rather have good, solid ice beneath my runners than," he made it sound obscene, "bare ground. Still, we must gain more wind."

Additional sail was unfurled, positioned. The strongest, steadiest breeze came from the north. Tahoding ordered the necessary shift in sail position. Fresh sheets of woven pika-pina billowed out to match the captain's belly. An incredible creaking and groaning rose from beneath the raft's hull, startling unprepared sailors who were used to traveling across silent, smooth ice. The crunching of stone under massive wheels was a disturbing new sound to them. It reminded some of a ship's timbers breaking loose.

However unaesthetically, the third, fourth, fifth and eventually the sixth set of wheels moved inland, followed finally by the single steering wheel. There was a modest cheer of appreciation from the watching Moulokinese on the rafts astern as the *Slanderscree* rumbled awkwardly but steadily upslope.

Gaining confidence, Ta-hoding ordered a few additional small sails unfurled. The icerigger picked up speed. There was a cry and gesture of fond departing from the bow of the nearest tow ship. Ethan and Hunnar returned minister Mirmib's arm action.

"I wonder if we shall see them again," said Hunnar fondly.

"Not if, but when," Ethan commented with surprising confidence. "Sofold and Moulokin now belong to the same confederation, the union of ice, remember?"

Hunnar looked abashed. "New ideas take root slowly on my world, friend Ethan. It is still difficult for me to comprehend the meaning of so many new and strange things, all of which have taken place since your arrival in Sofold such a short time ago. I suspect that as we have more and more contact with your people, with the peoples of other worlds, events will change still more rapidly for me and for all Tran."

"I expect they will, Hunnar," Ethan confessed. The knight's words raised conflicting emotions within him. Had they chosen the right course in trying to rush these people into a galactic government? In their own way the Tran struck him as being reasonably happy with their place in the universe. Who could predict what influence some of the less lofty elements of humanx civilization would have on this proud, self-sufficient people? Despite all safeguards, such elements would find their way onto Tran-ky-ky as surely as any parasite infects an unwary host.

And what was the justification for their actions thus far? The threat of a little commercial exploitation on one corner of a vast, frozen globe? Such exploitation would, if unchecked, eventually smother the hopes of this world of course, but still . . .

Then he thought back to the killings, to all the horrors he'd heard about the nomadic hordes of Tran-ky-ky. Of the depredations they made on innocent city-folk, of whole cities wiped out and the intermittent rule of true barbarism on this planet. He considered the individual cruelties practiced by hereditary rulers unfit for their positions of power, Tran leaders the like of Tonx Ghin Rakossa of Poyolavomaar and Calonnin Ro-Vijar of Arsudun.

No, on balance, the ledger rode high on the side of their intervention. He, Ethan Frome Fortune, absolved himself of wrong-doing. What he and his companions were attempting was done not as Counselor Firsts of the United Church, nor as ministers of the Commonwealth, but solely because they were the ones unexpectedly afforded a chance to Do Something.

It was being done by a salesman, himself. By a teacher who was as gentle and considerate a human as he'd ever met. By a reclusive giant who was something more than a cabinet minister and less than a saint. These three were committed to helping the Tran, and the Tran were now committed to helping themselves. If many more meetings like the one which had joined Moulokin and Sofold took place, their personal decisions would all be justified.

Such lofty thoughts kept away the brutal alien cold outside his survival suit, kept him from musing on another likely possibility—that he might die in a lost cause on this distant, unnoticed, and wholly inhospitable world.

XIV

The ice river had long since vanished behind them, and the sailors of the *Slanderscree* continued to exclaim in wonder at the thickness of the mists. They were familiar enough with the phenomenon. Volcanic foundries were located atop the mountain crests dominating their home isle of Sofold. But not in such profusion as this. Boiling pools and streams ran downslope wherever they looked. The quantity of freely flowing water was as alien to the Tran as a river of liquid oxygen would have been on Terra.

To everyone's relief, the terrain, which proved the least of their problems, continued to incline gently upward, smooth earth and gravel interrupted only by the occasional pool or stream. The broadest volcanic fissure they had to cross was less than a meter wide. There were no crevasses or secondary canyons.

As if to compensate for the unexpectedly regular topography, obstacles were provided in the form of occasional trees too massive for the slowly advancing icerigger to push down. These grew thickly enough so that at least twice a day the raft would be forced to halt while a crew went overboard to cut down the upcoming barriers. At least the bottom of the hull was high enough to clear even the broadest stump.

They also either passed over or ground inexorably through a profusion of ground cover as foreign to the Sofoldian Tran as was the running, steaming water. Bushes and small trees, ferns and bromeliads smothered the surface wherever sufficient soil had collected to support extensive root growth. These were the strange plants of which minister Mirmib had spoken to Ethan when they'd first entered Moulokin harbor.

Such vegetation could exist in this place solely because of the heat and humidity furnished by the volcanic springs. Ethan and Williams debated extensively on the origin of the grotesquely anomalous tropical vegetation, as to whether it originated because of the conditions existing in this region, or was some hold-over from a warmer climate in Tran-ky-ky's distant past.

Great wheels plowed through rotted, fallen logs, scattering hordes of tiny crawling things and sending pulped fungi flying. Twelve wheels kept the raft from bogging down in the occasional softer areas.

Williams tried to estimate how much altitude they'd gained, but discovered that the mist and steam made accurate calculation impossible. His guesses at linear distance traveled were more precise. The fog made standard navigation impossible. Ta-hoding simply kept them headed eastward and hoped they were still trav-eling up the main canyon.

In places where the terrain leveled out they en-countered not only bushes and ferns, but berries and the first flowers Ethan had seen on Tran-ky-ky. Though the blooms fascinated the Tran, Ethan thought them pretty but familiar. Williams was utterly absorbed in speculation on how they were pollinated, not to mention explaining the process itself to the Tran wizard Eer-Meesach.

"It is the heat which makes such growth possible," the teacher explained to the elderly Tran.

"So you have insisted. Tell me more about this pol-lination. You still have not fully explained what is a bee?"

As he spoke, the wizard removed his last vestige of clothing. Nakedness had become the norm on board, a general divesture of attire to which crewmembers male and female ascribed without comment. It had become not a question of modesty, but of survival.

In fact, the temperature had now risen to a point where the three humans could move about without their survival suits, which were given a much overdue airing-out. Moving about in underclothing was a pleas-ure for Ethan and his companions, but the heat was be-coming a matter of concern for the crew.

Some of Ta-hoding's sailors began experiencing an affliction with which they were completely unfamiliar: heat prostration. Ta-hoding himself ceased his cooling panting only when he had to speak, and then he kept his orders to a minimum. As one sailor after another had to reduce his work time, schedules were juggled until the *Slanderscree* was operating with a dangerously small crew. If they did not enter a region of cooler weather soon, the time might come when they would not have enough active bodies to control the ship properly.

When the weak cry sounded forward, Ta-hoding and everyone else at first ignored it, thinking it only the frustrated shout of another overheated crewmember. But the second yell: "Ahoy the helmdeck!" was insistent. It was definitely not just the voice of a fractious, heat-logy crewman.

A midshipmate, tongue lolling, relayed the message. Dehydration could not keep the amazement from his voice. "Captain, bowsprit lookout reports there are *people* to port."

Ta-hoding ordered all sails furled. Grumbling sailors aloft struggled drunkenly to comply. Ethan had heard the report, too. Soon a modest crowd had assembled above the first axle, just above the portside wheel.

Standing on the ground below and gazing up with casual interest at the gaping faces lining the ship's rail were three of the Golden Saia. Ethan stared at them without thought of politeness. He was no less fascinated than Ta-hoding, Hunnar, or any of the other Tran.

It put him in mind of their first meeting with Hunnar and his scouting party, after the lifeboat had crashed on Tran-ky-ky. Hunnar had believed Ethan and his fellow humans to be some peculiar, hairless variant of the Tran norm. And here, where they had no right to exist, were those very variants Hunnar had speculated upon.

For while the three bipeds below resembled the standard Tran in most respects, the differences were significant and striking.

All were males, built much as any member of the *Slanderscree*'s crew. But instead of the longer, steelgray fur sported by Hunnar and his brethren, the Saia were cloaked in short, thin fur sparse enough to let bare skin show through in places. The lighter coats were buttery-yellow instead of gray, with isolated spottings of brown and amber.

When one raised a spear and then leaned on it for support, there was a simultaneous exhalation from the Tran lining the rail. These creatures had no dan! The wind-catching membrane all other Tran sported between lower hip and wrist was totally absent. Such a shock made the next discovery seem almost anticlimactic. The Saia stood on sandaled feet. That was an impossibility for normal Tran because of their extended chiv. Instead of the long, powerful skateclaws, the three natives below showed claws on their feet no longer than those on their hands.

Yellow and black cat eyes were identical, as were the pointed, nervously shifting ears atop the head. But the absence of chiv and dan coupled with the short, light-colored fur seemed to suggest a variety of Tran as different from the average as a Neanderthal from Cro-Magnon man.

"Quite astonishing, friend Ethan." The salesman looked uncertainly at the teacher standing next to him. Williams thought a moment, then looked embarrassed. He'd spoken in Trannish, out of habit, and in so doing had used the formal familiar honorific in referring to Ethan.

"They appear to be a specialized variant of uncertain age," he hurried on, "adapted specifically to existing in this hot, thermal region. This may be the only tribe so modified on all of Tran-ky-ky."

Conversation on board was stilled as one of the three below said, loudly but not clearly, "Greetings." The accent was radically different from any Ethan had yet heard, so much so that the word verged on incomprehensibility. It was less guttural, closer to Terranglo than to Symbospeech, than was usual Trannish.

The Moulokinese had not exaggerated the special qualities of the Saia, he mused, as he prepared to climb down a boarding ladder to confront the triumvirate waiting patiently below. Mentally, he scoffed at the suggestion that they might possess mystic powers

212

or knowledge. They were less hairy and less mobile, but that was all.

Even so, Ethan felt better when he touched ground and could turn to face them. Sir Hunnar and Elfa, who followed behind, were less comfortable, though it was the solid ground and not the presence of the Saia that was responsible.

Hunnar walked toward the three, moving like a clumsy newborn on the springy grass. It smashed and ran beneath his sharp chiv, staining them with green juice and giving him a crawly feeling he was hard pressed not to show. When the three offered nothing at his approach, he turned and looked expectantly at Ethan.

Speaking slowly so as to be understood, Ethan ventured the traditional Tran greeting. "Our breath is your warmth." This struck the three onlookers as amusing. They murmured among themselves like people at a party sharing a private joke.

"We come from a far place," Ethan continued firmly, ignoring the local levity he had produced. "We come with the blessings of the Moulokinese, our good friends. They say that you are their friends, and hope you will extend this friendship to us."

All three Saia stared quietly at Ethan out of black pupils that seemed somewhat narrower than those of normal Tran, though it was probably only Ethan's imagination that made them appear so.

Eventually the one in the middle turned to his right-hand companion and said audibly, "What a strange being that one is. So small, and with less hair even than ourselves."

"Yes, and there are two others." The second speaker pointed in the direction of Williams and September, who were among those clustered along the ship's railing. "And how different they are! That one," and he had to be indicating September, "is of proper size, but equally hairless. The other is even smaller than the one who speaks to us, yet his covering is dark brown instead of gold or gray."

It was the last of three who stepped forward. "We welcome you as friends of our friends in Moulokin," he said to Ethan and Hunnar, then glanced disapprovingly back at his companions. "Have you no manners?" He placed both golden-furred paws on Ethan's shoulders, but did not breathe into his face as was customary.

"In many ways," he said, dropping his paws and studying Ethan curiously, "this one resembles us more than our cold brothers."

With a start, Ethan realized the truth of the other's words. Lacking dan and chiv, and with a coloring closer to gold than gray, he and September did look much like the Saia. At first glance, a new observer might take Saia and humans as relatives rather than Saia and Tran. Not that the Saia were anything but a hothouse version of the inhabitants of this world. The duplication of eyes and ears, of body and extremities, proved that.

"We come," Ethan began easily, launching into a by-now familiar tale, "from a world other than this one." The loquacious Saia's immediate response was anything but familiar.

"That is obvious." As if he were discussing something quite ordinary, he leaned on his spear and rubbed idly at the finely woven vest he wore. "From which star, and how far away?"

It was not lack of vocabulary that rendered Ethan momentarily speechless. When his thoughts stopped whirling he thought to gesture at the billowing steam. "Your land must always be like this. How do you know of other stars when you can't even see the sky? And what makes you think other people live out among them?"

"Legends." The Saia shifted his position slightly. "We have many legends. They are our heritage. We regard them properly."

There was truly, Ethan thought, something of a vanished grandeur about these people. They carried themselves differently than the average Tran, as if conscious of their specialness, of a uniqueness that extended beyond mere physical differences.

Had high civilizations once existed on Tran-ky-ky? If so, were these Saia remnants of such civilizations? Or were they perhaps simply recipients of knowledge handed to them by other peoples, now extinct or else from offworld? Did that make Hunnar and his people—and all other Tran—degenerate offshoots of a higher species instead of the pinnacle of Tran evolution?

Manner and alterations in form were not sufficient proof of superiority, however. Hunnar and his companions probably regarded the absence of long fur, dan and chiv as deformities, not as evidence of advanced evolution. And what of the attire of these Saia? Simple vests and skirts, a well-formed but basic metal axe slung at one hip, spears—nothing to hint at knowledge of advanced technologies. They seemed as barbaric in achievement if not attitude as any other Tran.

It was only that—Ethan hunted for the right concept—that they appeared more advanced psychologically. They were open and friendly, instead of as withdrawn and suspicious as other Tran. Many primitive peoples refined the characteristic of seeming to know more than they actually did. It would be to their advantage, especially if they were numerically weak, to cultivate such an impression. Claims of supernatural abilities or lineage to powerful ancestors would help them awe more warlike relatives such as the Moulokinese. Protective coloring can be verbal as much as physical, he reminded himself, without losing its effectiveness.

Not that they were weak and helpless. The axe and metal-tipped spears looked efficient if not advanced. At least their metallurgical skill hadn't been exaggerated by the worshipful folk of Moulokin.

"Whither do you go, strangers?" the middle Saia inquired, after efforts to identify a Commonwealth star or two met insurmountable semantic barriers.

Ethan pointed south westward. "To the interior of this land, and further. To explore and hopefully find another canyon similar to this one."

"Do you know of such a place?" Hunnar sounded harsher than he intended. Alongside these graceful, confident people he felt inexplicably clumsy and overbearing.

"We know of no such." The center Saia was apologetic. "We can travel no more than a few kijat outside our lands. The cold affects us faster than the heat subdues our thick-furred brothers." Ethan noted that they employed the same units of measurements as other Tran.

"We are not equipped to live elsewhere than here. We know naught of the interior by sight of our eyes. By legend we know it to be haunted." At a questioning glance from Elfa, he added, "Foul spirits of the long dead, who died unclean. Did you not know?" He looked in amazement from one companion to the other, then back to the visitors. "Where do you think the spirits of the dead go when they die?"

"*Our* legends," explained Elfa firmly, "say they go to the lands of the dead, where they exist in peace forever. A place of singing and gentle winds."

"Perhaps that is true." Whether the Saia genuinely believed this or was merely being polite, Ethan couldn't say. "If so, it is true only when such peace is not disturbed by the living. That is why we would not venture into the interior even were we able." He regarded them warningly.

"When they are disturbed, the vengeance of the dead is unimaginable." He raised his spear, gestured inland. "Go that way, to the land of the unclean dead where spirits dwell in aimless, milling anger. They may focus on you, the living. Or they may not. We will not stop you. We would not if we could. But we will lament your passing as friends.

"They will not," he concluded significantly, "like being disturbed. Every Tran may choose his or her own death. As for ourselves, the day has light to spend and we have hunting to do. Farewell." He smiled a Trannish smile at Ethan. "Farewell, furless friend. Our legends lie not."

Back on the raft, they were surrounded by excited sailors and knights who had been unable to hear the conversation. When Ethan concluded his brief resume of what had transpired, Williams danced about like a man possessed by a vision—which in a sense, he was. "We've got to follow them! I must have a look at their village, learn how they've adapted to a climate so radically different from the rest of this world. We must record their legends, and interpret—"

216

"We have to," September interrupted him in no-nonsense tones, "get inland and find another way off this plateau as fast as we can, Milliken. This isn't a scientific expedition."

"But a discovery of this magnitude! . . ." Williams wailed. Abruptly, he killed the pleading in his voice. "I must formally protest, Skua." He put his hands on hips, glared defiantly up at the giant.

September weighed more than twice as much as the diminutive schoolteacher. Ignoring the other's belligerence, a product, no doubt, of a year's survival on Tran-ky-ky, September replied humorlessly.

"Okay, now that you've gotten that out of your system, we'll be on our way." When it looked as if the teacher's rising blood pressure might do him more harm than September ever would, the giant added consolingly, "Milliken, I'm 'bout as curious as you are concernin' these folks, but we've considerable more people to try and help, remember?"

" 'Tis true, friend Williams," Sir Hunnar added. "We should be on our way." The teacher turned desperately to Ethan, who half-shrugged.

"They're right, Milliken. You know we—"

"Barbarians. I am surrounded by barbarians. Where's Eer-Meesach?" He stormed away in search of his only intellectual colleague, mounting to the doorway of a second-story cabin like a hyperactive sloth.

Ethan smiled as he watched the teacher ascend the steep rampway paralleling the wider icepath. When they'd first crashed on this world, the smaller man's muscles would have strained to mount that ramp at all, let alone propel him upward at such respectable speed. Tran-ky-ky hadn't done much for their credit balances, but they'd built up other assets.

He had to think thus because the cloying mists, the rich greenery surrounding them here, were all too reminiscent of lands and worlds more receptive to human life. This place was too friendly. Go a few thousand meters or so in any direction, he knew, and the ambient temperature would drop a hundred degrees or more.

"Our friend classes us with you, Hunnar." September regarded the knight expectantly. "Let's be on our way, then. Or are you afeared of these spirits and night-creeps the Saia seem so fond of?"

Hunnar looked insulted. "We will deal with whatever we may encounter, friend Skua. Be it Rakossa of Poyolavomaar or the ghosts of my fathers."

"Those who have traveled into Hell are not easily dissuaded by the tales of heat-softened hunters." Elfa said with admirable confidence. She lowered her voice then, so that only those immediately around her could hear. "Still, it would be as well not to speak of this to the crew."

Ethan and the others agreed readily. Though Elfa and Hunnar and a few of the more educated Tran were equipped to combat superstition and rumor, the average sailor was not. Tell them that according to the Saia they were about to enter the lands of the dead and confront the spirit world, and the *Slanderscree* might find itself moving in the wrong direction. Whether man or Tran, a storm is easier to combat than the fears dwelling in the depths of the mind.

Sails were reset and once again the icerigger commenced rumbling uphill. Two days later the mists started to thin. Once Ethan thought he spied an ellipse formed of neatly crafted wooden houses. They were nothing remarkable, but they were radically different from the familiar heavy-beamed, stone dwellings of all other Tran. He did not mention the sighting or his observations to the still sulking Williams.

The mist did not disperse gradually. They reached a point where it stopped clean, a slightly oscillating wall of steam. From then on they saw no more signs of the Golden Saia. Some day Ethan would return and listen to the long legends of a misplaced people. So he told himself. He was not honest enough to admit that once back in the comfortable hub of Commonwealth civilization, he would likely forget all but memories of Tran-ky-ky.

For now, he forced his attention outward. They had a confederation to expand, a union of ice to cement, and they did not have a lifetime in which to do it.

Grass turned yellowish and scraggly. Trees gave

218

way to bushes, and ferns and flowers vanished behind them. The *Slanderscree* had emerged on a high, rolling plain. As they lumbered across bare gravel and tormented grasses, the wind began to rise, an old companion back from unwilling vacation. Soon it was blowing at familiar strength. The Tran found it comforting.

None of the crew had been lost in the transit, though Eer-Meesach was still treating the most severe cases of heat-stroke in the central cabin. The temperature fell and the humans had long since redonned their survival suits, the Tran their heavy hessavar fur coats.

They received no visits from the spirits of the dead or otherwise. The most notable spirits aboard, those of the sailors, had risen considerably with the return of a congenial climate. The rolling landscape mounted into steep hills to the north and east. After consultation with Ta-hoding, it was decided to turn southward. They would eventually reach the western edge of the plateau. Then they could begin hunting for a way down.

As the wind increased, so did their speed. Before long they were traveling at a pace short of breathtaking but quite respectable. It didn't take long for everyone on board to grow accustomed to the domesticated thunder of the twelve huge wheels.

Yellowish grass continued to speckle the plain, fighting to stay rooted in the sparse soil. The raft's chief cook tried some in a meal one night, and though it was pronounced edible by all who tried it, there was no rush to harvest. It proved tough, tasteless, and hard to digest.

In days of traveling they saw nothing that resembled a tree. The closest approximations were widely scattered, meter-high bushes which looked like umber tumbleweeds. Their tightly intertwined branchlets had the consistency of wire. Ethan wanted to use a beamer to cut a sample and for a change, it was Williams who protested. Eying the isolated, unimpressive clump he said, "Anything that can survive in this desolation deserves to remain unharmed." And Ethan put his beamer away.

The wind was steady and predictable. That gave the sailors needed time. They learned fast, but handling a ship the size of the *Slanderscree* on land was a different proposition from doing so on ice.

Ethan spent much time watching the parade of distant hills and thought of the Golden Saia. Taken theoretically, he supposed it was possible for the spirits of the departed to linger in some outrageously incomprehensible mode—that they would congregate like so many conventioneers seemed impossible. And if they were so inclined, why choose a region as unattractive as this? True, the Saia had remarked on their desire for privacy, and this vast plateau would certainly provide that, but—

He stopped himself in the middle of a thought. Endless days of dull landscape had lulled him into compensating with steadily growing rococo imaginings. There was nothing out there but scattered wire-brushes and poverty-stricken grass.

Nothing.

"Enormous ice-raft? What enormous ice-raft? Truly are your fantasies entertaining, my guests!"

K'ferr Shri-Vehm, Landgrave of Moulokin, eyed her visitors pityingly. "You make senseless demands of me and my people, you attack us at the first gate, and now I find the basis for these actions are only dreams of wandering minds. Your information is false, visitors."

"Hedge not with us." The voice was edgy, nervous, dangerous. "Where have you hidden them?" Rakossa of Poyolavomaar sent quick, jerking glares around the modest throne-room, as if the *Slanderscree* might be tucked in a corner or secreted behind a chest.

K'ferr made the Tran equivalent of a laugh. "*Hidden,* my lord Rakossa? Hidden such a great vessel as you describe? Where would we conceal such a craft?"

"You could have dismantled it, moved the sections somewhere."

"In less than four days? I venture, my lord, you have an imagination second to none."

An officer of the Poyolavomaar fleet chose that moment to enter the chamber. "The ship we seek is not anywhere in the harbor, sires. 'Tis nowhere to be found, nor, as some suspected, is there a cave in the cliffs large enough to hide even part of such a large raft. We also ventured far up the main canyon and saw no sign of it." What he said was true; what he didn't know was that the Moulokinese had used scrapers and torches to obliterate the tell-tale tracks marking the *Slanderscree*'s passage.

"I do not think, sire, that—"

"We are not interested in what you think!" a furious Rakossa shouted.

"Did you not see," K'ferr continued, "the great raft we ourselves are building? That is what formed the tracks outside our canyon you seem to find so absorbing."

"We saw," said a different voice. Calonnin Ro-Vijar stepped forward. "Wooden runners of that size will not support a vessel of a size necessary to make them worth constructing."

"Our profession as a city-state, and one for which we are justly famed, is raft-building." Mirmib stared condescendingly at Ro-Vijar. "What you say may be true, but we often begin such new raft shapes and sizes by way of experimentation. We learn much that is valuable to us in our trade, even if the actual concept eventually proves unworkable. Is this Arsudun from which you come also a specialist in the construction of rafts?"

"No, but—"

"Then do not presume to pronounce judgment on a craft with which you are not conversant."

Ro-Vijar started to say something, then hesitated. When he spoke again, it was in a surprisingly apologetic fashion. " 'Tis evident we have made an error in offending and accusing these people, Lord Rakossa. We may best continue our hunt elsewhere."

"The tracks lead here!" Rakossa threw arms and words about careless of who they struck. "They are here somewhere, magicked or otherwise."

"Do you think they rose into the air and sailed away thusly, my good friend?" Ro-Vijar asked. The comment, made in jest, inspired a horrible thought

221

in the Landgrave of Arsudun. For an instant he thought the humans might somehow have obtained one of their powerful sky-rafts and transported it here. He had been told by the human commissioner, Jobius Trell, that the skypeople possessed vehicles capable of transporting an object even as massive as the vanished icerigger through the air. While he had never seen such a device, he was inclined to believe whatever Trell told him abut human technological capabilities. Trell had undoubtedly lied to him about many things, but not about that.

But if he didn't get this idiot Rakossa out of the throne-room before trouble began, they would waste valuable time in a needless battle.

"She's here somewhere." Rakossa prowled the room, heedless of common courtesy. "We know she is."

"She?" inquired Mirmib puzzledly.

"The concubine, who has bewitched us. We require her. She is present. We sense it!" He took a couple of threatening steps toward the throne. "Where are you hiding her, woman?"

Two burly guards, big even for Tran, stepped forward between the throne and the raging Landgrave. Each held a weighty metal battle-axe before him. One let his sway back and forth just above floor level, a pendulum of death.

"My liege and friend Landgrave," said Ro-Vijar earnestly, stepping forward but remembering not to touch the hypersensitive Rakossa, "we have already heard ample explanation. These good people have ne'er heard nor seen the vessel or woman we seek."

"Again I say, this is truth." K'ferr leaned forward. "Considering your hostile actions toward us, I believe we have been extremely courteous and patient with you. Before any irrevocable insults are exchanged, I suggest you take your leave of Moulokin."

"So it would seem best to do, my gracious lady." Ro-Vijar tentatively reached out, chanced a grip on the wild-eyed Rakossa's left arm. The Landgrave of Poyolavomaar did not react angrily. He turned, seemed to see Ro-Vijar clearly for the first time since entering the throne room. Then he shook off the other's hand, whirled, and stalked out of the chamber, muttering slyly to himself.

"Our pardon for this most grievous mistake, my lady, good minister Mirmib." Ro-Vijar made a gesture of profound obeisance. "It was a matter of great importance to us, and we acted in haste instead of good sense. I am convinced of your sincerity."

"You are excused by your ignorance." K'ferr indicated the now vacant exitway. "The actions of your colleague explain much. May your search continue more profitably elsewhere."

"May your warmth remain constant all the days of your life. Rest assured we will eventually find those we seek." With that, Ro-Vijar turned with the Poyo officer and departed from the chamber.

When they were many minutes gone, K'ferr turned to Mirmib and asked, "What do you think they will do now?"

"If 'twas up to this Ro-Vijar, they would give up and sail home." The minister rubbed the back of an ear, looked thoughtful. "Or perhaps the calmer of the two is in reality the more dangerous. So blinded by hatred, or love, for this Teeliam woman is the other he cannot think straight. If he ever could."

"You saw the woman in question, Mirmib. The scars. Why would this Landgrave risk his power, his armed might, to find and torment her further?"

"Some rulers take not well personal affronts, though rarely do they react in so extreme a fashion as this Rakossa, my lady. Hate can be as powerful an *eldur* as love. Often is the line between the two indistinct." They exchanged a glance unfathomable to outsiders. "I do not know what transpired between this girl and this Landgrave, and can but speculate. One thing I can say confidently, though. Should they eventually meet again, one or the other will surely die of it."

That petty matter did not occupy Calonnin Ro-Vijar's mind. If they returned to Arsudun now, he would have this second failure to report to Trell.

The critical question was: had the *Slanderscree* actually been within the harbor of Moulokin? If so, he could envision several fanciful possibilities to explain what had happened to the great icerigger. Though he

223

badly wanted to, his "escort of honor" had kept him from talking to, or bribing, any of the townsfolk. In the absence of direct information he would have to extrapolate. That was something he was very good at, something which made the games he played with the human Trell interesting.

With stakes as high as they were, he was not about to leave Moulokin until he knew the truth of what had happened to their quarry.

XV

Enough days passed filled with the same rolling gravelly ground and spare vegetation to make Ethan wish for a spirit or two to liven up the journey. Their sole excitement was provided by a two-meter-wide crevasse that ran east and west as far as chiv-sore scouting parties could determine. Numerous methods for traversing the obstacle were proposed. One mate suggested removing the duralloy runners from where they had been secured to the deck and using them to bridge the gap.

For a change it was Ta-hoding who provided the solution. Though he had only modest confidence in himself, he'd come to feel boundless enthusiasm for his new command. Despite Ethan and Hunnar's apprehension he ordered all unnecessary personnel off the raft. The *Slanderscree* sailed in a wide circle and bore down on the crevasse with all sail flying, wind directly behind it.

At the last instant, spars and sails were aligned to obtain as much upward lift as possible. Like some obese bird the front end of the enormous raft rose skyward. Only the two fore axles completely cleared the gap before the bow began to settle surfaceward again, but it was enough. Mass and velocity were sufficient to carry the entire ship across the narrow

224

abyss, though the rear axle and wheels dipped dangerously inward.

Ta-hoding explained that they carried spare axles and, in the event that his ploy had failed, could still repair any damage. The threat of being halted in this chill, moody land was sufficient to inspire even the cautious captain to daring.

They reached the edge of the plateau the following day. The longing of the sailors for the boundless ice ocean out of reach two hundred meters below was evident to all the mates and officers. They felt the ice-pull themselves.

Continuing southward, the icerigger raced parallel to the sheer cliffs. Barren terrain continued to unravel from an infinite brown thread to port, gleaming ice and blue sky above shining daily off to starboard.

Ta-hoding and his crew had grown so skillful in their handling of the ship that Ethan no longer worried or turned away when they hove unnecessarily near to the breathtaking drop. All this activity kept the crew from succumbing to the worst kind of mental fatigue: the kind induced by unrelieved boredom.

"I'm beginnin' to worry a bit, young feller-me-lad." September clung to a yard nearby, his face showing diappointment beneath the transparent mask. "Hunnar and the others are starting to feel likewise, and with reason. We haven't come near findin' another canyon resembling Moulokin's. It just don't make sense, lad." His tone was tense but quiet. "That there'd be just a single canyon of that type cuttin' into this continent, I mean. Got to be others."

"I'm no geologist, Skua, but I admit it seems peculiar to me, too."

September made a face, an expression centering whirlpool-like on that sharp, hooked beak of a nose. "If we do have to circle back the way we've come, it's a good bet the Poyos will've completed their inspection of Moulokin and, not finding us there, gone off elsewhere after us." He brightened somewhat at the thought.

"At this point that just might be our best course. Think I'll go have a chat with the captain and Sir

225

Hunnar. Stay sane, lad." He started to head stern-ward, halted as Ethan gestured toward the bow.

"We may not have any choice tomorrow, Skua."

The steep hills that had marked the north and eastern horizons since they'd emerged from the land of the Golden Saia were growing closer, curving around ahead of them and threatening to cut off easy progress to the south. That left them only the path behind.

The slopes ahead looked more precipitous than the ones they'd been running alongside for many days. Signs of erosion, indicating possibly unstable hillsides and talus falls, were becoming visible. They would almost certainly have to turn back unless a clear pass could be found through these new obstacles. The *Slanderscree* had proven herself landworthy, but she could not climb much of an incline.

As Ethan predicted, they reached the first of the low but steep-sided hills that evening. They decided to make a semi-permanent camp in the sheltering lee of the tallest minimount. Scouts would be sent out on the morrow in wheeled lifeboats to try and find a passage to the west that the icerigger could negotiate. Both scout groups would be gone a maximum of five days. In that time, the crew would busy themselves with making minor but bothersome and necessary repairs to the ship, and try to keep busy until the scouts returned.

Sinahnvor was patrolling his foredeck position, cold in the near cloudless night, when something flickering on the hillside caught his eye. He blinked double lids, but the flickering remained. It looked like a fat eye winking in the night.

Fortunately Sinahnvor was not particularly imaginative. Nevertheless he shivered with something other than cold. Who would be off the ship this time of no-light? There'd been rumors of one of the humans and the Landgrave's daughter, but such tales propelled more rafts than did the winds.

The watchman lifted his oil lamp slightly higher, extending the pole to which it was slung over the side of the raft. It was his imagination after all—no, there

226

it was again! A definite intermittent gleam part way up the steep slope, no higher than the topmost spar of the foremast.

Rumors of a less amusing kind filtered through his brain. If this were truly a land of spirits, might that not be some nightwraith come to snatch him from the deck? And who would know the manner or time of his abduction?

It made him glance around anxiously. The two moons were high aloft, an indication that it was nearer morning than eve-time. He saw no movement anywhere. Would his relief find only lamp pole, clothing, and weapons? Surely a spirit would be interested only in his body.

Monont should be on center deck watch now. He could remain silent and confront that mysterious glint, waiting for his soul to mayhap be stolen out his mouth, or he could seek the comfort of a comrade's company. Lamp pole swinging, he descended from the bowsprit to the deck and moved past the fore cabins.

"Clean ice and wind on your neck," came a husky voice in the darkness. Sinahnvor swung his pole around. It lit the face of a curious Tran.

"What are you doing away from your post, Sinahnvor?" asked Monont, concerned. "Should the night-mate catch you, he could make you—"

"Be silent, Monont!" Sinahnvor whispered hastily. "There is an eye in the mountain!"

The other lookout studied his colleague carefully. "You have been chewing too much *bui* extract."

There was conviction in Sinahnvor's voice, however. "As you doubt me, come and see for yourself."

"I should not leave my post."

"Who is to know? The night-mate will not appear until watch-change time, and our nearest enemies are at least a hundred satch behind us."

"That is true. I will come, but only for a moment. Foolishness," Monont muttered as he followed the other sentry to the foredeck.

Motioning his companion to silence, Sinahnvor extended his light pole over the railing, moved it about slowly as he searched the mountainside. For several seconds there was no sign of the shining and he was more afraid of the story Monont would tell the others come the morn than he was of any spirit they might arouse. But then the spark showed once more, unmistakably. It remained as steady as the lamp pole.

"See? Did I not tell you?"

The more prosaic Monont eyed the speck of light. "Truly is there something, but I think it is no spirit. Who ever heard of a spirit with only one eye? They have at least four each."

"Shssh! Do not insult it!"

"That is no spirit, idiot-friend." Monont mounted the railing, swung a clawed foot over the side. Sinahnvor watched him worriedly.

"Where are you going?"

"To that hillside."

"You are mad! Don't do it, Monont. The spirits will draw you into the mountain and drown you in dirt."

"I thought the spirits of Hell would take us when we went under the ice and down to the inside of the world. The humans and Sir Hunnar Redbeard said such tales were mere superstition. Then they killed the devil that came up from the waters of the night. It stunk like a slaughtered hessavar. I find it hard now to believe as I once did in spirits and daemons."

He slipped over the side, used a boarding rope to drop quickly to the ice.

"Monont—*Monont!*" Sinahnvor raised his lamp higher. In its shallow glow he saw the dim outline of his friend reach the hillside and begin an awkward ascent. The outline faded to shadow, then a memory of a shadow. Moments passed, silent moments broken only by the moan of the tired wind. But while he heard no cries of triumph, neither did any screams drift back to him.

It was with considerable relief that he picked out the returning figure of the other sentry, apparently unharmed.

"What was it, then?" He extended an arm and helped Monont back on deck.

"Here is your spirit eye. I had to dig it out."

Sinahnvor, much to his surprise, recognized the object immediately. "Why, 'tis only a *purras,* a common mixing bowl much as my own mate uses. Odd how it shines. The wood must take a very high polish."

"Take it," urged Monont. " 'Tis not wood."

Sinahnvor accepted the object . . . and nearly dropped it. It was made of thick, dense metal, badly tarnished in places, still flashy in others. He did not recognize the metal.

Both sentries exchanged glances. What people lived here in this iceless desert who could afford to make common, everyday kitchen utensils out of solid metal? Metal was hoarded for use in weapons and nails and tools, not mixing bowls.

Sinahnvor did not understand. Not understanding, he said, "I think we had best wake the night-mate early."

The officer was no less startled by the bowl than the two lookouts had been. He chose to wake the second mate, who in turn roused Ta-hoding, who alerted the three humans and Sir Hunnar and the others of the icerigger's informal decision-making body.

Before long most of the crew was awake and hacking at the nearby hillside, their lamps looking to those remaining on the *Slanderscree* like a convocation of stultified fireflies.

None of the humans took part in the digging. Their survival suits could barely cope with the nighttime temperature of seventy below, with a wind-chill factor nearing instant death. A crude digging tool could make a substantial gash in a survival suit. Insinuating itself into the cut, the outside air could freeze human skin solid almost as efficiently as a spray of liquid helium.

With such a large party working, it wasn't long before several bags of trophies were being examined on deck. Peering through his mask (no need of the secondary goggles during the night), Ethan saw spread out among wood and soil a treasure trove of metal objects. On most worlds these would have been dismissed as nothing remarkable, but on metal-poor Tran-ky-ky they hinted at a vanished civilization of immense wealth. There were knives, utensils of all kinds, buckles and braces, engraved and broken drinking vessels, even metal buttons and pins. Hunnar fingered several of the last. Until now he'd never seen a pin made of anything but bone.

"Enormously rich or enormously wasteful," he murmured, letting oil lamp light create argent patterns on the ornamental steel. "We will dig with more discipline in the morning."

"Who could have lived here?" Ethan wondered aloud.

"Not Tran nor Saia." The knight turned his attention to a delightfully intricate metal bottle wrapped in fine wire scrollwork. " 'Tis too desolate and iceless for us and too cold for the Saia. But this is not spirit work." Cat-eyes strove to penetrate windswept darkness. "Someone lived here . . ."

The next day different sections of the hillside were marked off according to how promising they'd proven the night before. The excavation parties turned up a steady stream of new artifacts. Some were made of familiar materials, wood and bone, but most were various alloys, including several neither September or Williams could identify.

Unexpectedly, the wooden artifacts were what the teacher found most intriguing. When Ethan asked him why, he replied, "Because they mean this region cannot have been deserted very long, in geologic time. While it's true the cold air would preserve cellulose materials for a while, it is not desert-dry. Nor is the soil devoid of minute organisms and bacterial agents, which would also act to break down the wood—though they are scattered through the soil and nowhere very populous.

"This wood is in far too good condition to have lain buried for any great length of time."

They decided to remain several days and unearth all they could. But a new discovery soon altered their plans.

The two scout parties sent out to search for a passage through the hills returned. Their crews babbled out an impossible tale, so laden with gestures, expressions and adjectival phrases that Ethan and his friends were hard pressed to make sense of any of it.

While they debated uncertain terms among themselves, Ta-hoding and his crew launched feverish preparations to get underway. At that point, Ethan cornered Hunnar and refused to let him pass until he explained what was happening.

"Suaxus, my squire, was in the first boat," the knight said, trying to control his obvious excitement. "They found a pass through the mountains. Only, they aren't mountains."

"You're not making sense, friend Hunnar," September prompted.

"They traversed this pass and emerged on the other side of this range. It seems the wind blows harder, or steadier, or both, on the other side. What is buried here lies revealed there." He turned, indicated the partly excavated hillside.

"These are not mountains, they are buildings." And he broke away to perform some important task before Ethan could think to ask anything more.

Only Williams accepted this news calmly. "It makes sense, not to mention explaining the preponderance of artifacts we've found." The icerigger was already racing for the recently discovered pass. "There are similar buried cities on many Commonwealth worlds, Ethan. The same winds which would cover an ancient metropolis could later uncover it."

"Assuming that's what we've found—who built it?"

The teacher eyed Ethan, pursed his lips. "Who knows? The Tran obviously don't, nor do the Saia, who are supposed to know so much about this land. If we're lucky, maybe we'll find out. Perhaps they are people who no longer survive on Tran-ky-ky but who gave the Saia their legends of other worlds."

The pass turned out to be much wider and smoother than anyone had a right to expect. So straight was the gap between hills that unnatural forces were suspected. Ethan wondered if they excavated straight down, would they eventually strike pavement?

Once through the slopes they turned east, inland and away from the cliffs. They did not have to travel far. Dirt and rock were piled here also, but much stonework could be seen rearing planes and angles toward the sky, reminding Ethan of a partially eroded

231

graveyard. Here it was the bones of dead buildings which stood revealed to the air.

The ground rose skyward not in a smooth slope as on the other side, but in graduated levels. "See?" called Williams, pointing out different stone work and designs on each level. "This is not one building, as the scout parties assumed, but new structures raised atop the old. As each older structure was buried, it formed a foundation for the next building erected on the same spot. One town on the skeleton of the old." His hand swept eastward.

"We are looking at an ancient series of cities, not a cluster of monumental buildings. We can only guess at how far it extends. Since we've been paralleling similar rises nearly all the way from Moulokin, it's possible similar towns are buried beneath each of them. They may all form part of a single lengthy metropolis at least several hundred kilometers long."

The crew furled all sail and anchored the icerigger against the wind. Everyone not on watch scrambled over the side to marvel at the colossal architecture.

"One thing I don't understand." Williams tried to rub an eye, remembered his mask, raised it slightly to admit a comforting finger. "It would be natural to expect the topmost structures to be the most sophisticated in design and execution. Yet from what I can see the architecture is nearly identical from top to bottom, town to town."

"I'd like to know who's responsible for all this." Ethan scrambled carefully across the fine but slippery talus. "Now I'm even more positive it's not the Tran. Look at those arches, those wide windows." He balanced himself on a partly buried rectangular block that must have weighed several tons, pointed upslope and to his right.

"And that building almost exposed over there. The roof's too flat to resist snow buildup, and it's lined with what looks like glass to me. A skylight, on Tran-ky-ky? Not with the quality of glass the Tran make. A decent day's wind would blow it to splinters. Unless, of course, it's something more than normal glass."

"Perhaps the Saia did build this after all, and have just forgotten about it, young feller-me-lad," ventured

232

September. "A selective memory about such matters would keep 'em from gettin' embarrassed about letting so much knowledge slip away."

They uncovered one building after another: homes, warehouses, public meeting places, even what seemed to be an open amphitheater. An open stadium, on Tran-ky-ky!

It didn't take thirty years experience or several scientific degrees for Tran as well as humans to postulate a climate completely different from the present.

Having come to that realization, Williams left the archeology to Eer-Messach and others. Using the primitive Tran navigation instruments and the inadequate but useful ones included in each survival-suit's kit, he devoted himself to a night-time examination of the stars. Not the most intricately formed metal cup or detailed inscription cut into stone could dissuade him from his sudden fanatic interest in astronomy. Vacuum-clear skies, Tran navigation charts and old tales seemed to reinforce his determination to keep at his lonely cold night studies. Ethan could imagine what the teacher was trying to prove.

He was only partly right.

The teacher was deep in conversation with Tahoding when Ethan finally sought confirmation of his suspicions. "I don't mean to interrupt, Milliken, but I'd like to know for sure—why this sudden interest in local astronomy? I'd think you'd be grubbing away in the cities instead of freezing out on deck at night. "You're trying to find proof that the climate here was once much warmer, aren't you?"

"Not just here, on this plateau." Williams was only stating what to him was obvious and not being in the least insulting. A less sarcastic human being Ethan had never met. "Everywhere on Tran-ky-ky. The physical evidence inherent in the buried metropolis coupled with what little I've been able to calculate tells me that this was so. More importantly, it indicates to me who built these successive cities."

"Don't keep me in suspense, Milliken. Who was it? The Tran, the Saia, or some now extinct people? I'll bet it was the latter, and when the climate turned cold everywhere, the builders died. The Saia were con-

233

temporary with them and keep their memory alive in legends."

"Plausible, but I think, incorrect." He adjusted the calculator built into his sleeve. "These cities were raised by both the Tran and the Saia."

Ethan couldn't forestall a grin. "That's crazy, Milliken. It's too cold here for the Saia now and if they built these cities, surely they'd remember. And its too desolate now for the Tran and, assuming the climate was warmer, too hot for them before."

"That reasoning misses the point. It's because . . ." Williams paused, took a preparatory breath. "It's not simply a matter of its once being hot, now being cold here, Ethan. I think Tran-ky-ky has a perturbed orbit of predictable periodicity."

"I hardly know what to say."

"I'll try to explain. Any competent astronomer would have noticed it after a week's study, with the proper factual input. But the only astronomer to visit this outpost world was the initial survey drone which first located it. The Commonwealth government would be interested first in the fact that it was an inhabitable planet with a stable climate, flora, and fauna. Relatively long-term alterations will show up in the files on Tran-ky-ky, but there's no reason to act on them until the next period begins."

"*What* next period?"

"Of warm weather. I'd estimate, very crudely, so many standard years of cold, followed by a briefer period of warm weather as it passes nearer its sun. Say, ten thousand years. The transition from cold weather to hot takes place comparatively rapidly, since as Tran-ky-ky swings close by its star, its orbital velocity, would increase, slowing as it swings out into the cold zone again. It's a peculiar situation and I'm not certain of the details or mechanics, but that's what I believe takes place.

"Think what that would mean for this planet." He spoke distantly, his gaze centered on events far away in time and place. "During the hot period the ice oceans melt, and rapidly. The sea level would rise to submerge island states such as Sofold and much of Arsudun. Sofold is in reality built atop a seamount,

234

while the mountain-tops of Poyolavomaar would become true islands." Suddenly he dropped his gaze, looking embarrassed.

"That was what puzzled me so about Moulokin canyon." Ethan thought back, recalling the teacher's confusion over the canyon's geology and his feeling of half-recognizing its source.

"It's not a river canyon at all, though it resembles one closely. Rather, it's a dry undersea canyon, the kind that slices through a continental shelf down to the edge of the abyssal plain flooring the ocean. The cliffs of the plateau we sailed alongside for so long are actually the old continental shelf. Now," he said with satisfaction. "I'm ready to go digging for artifacts. But not in the cities. Right here, beneath the ship."

"Wait a minute. What do you expect to find under the ship? And what did you mean when you said the Tran and the Saia both built the metropolis?"

"Tell you in a couple of days, young feller-me-lad," he said, mimicking September.

It was two days, exactly. What the teacher uncovered were far less spectacular and much more important than any objects thus far uncovered in the buried structures.

He spread them out on a table in the central cabin, where human and Tran alike could see. "Look," Williams began, "insect eggs over there." He pointed to a pile of eddy-shaped, tiny white beads. "Try opening one. The casings are tough as stelamic. I had to use my beamer to assure myself of the contents.

"Animal eggs." He pointed to some similar objects, only they were larger and multi-colored. "Seeds, I think." He indicated a vast array of black and brown objects, mostly spherical. "Those I could barely singe with the beamer set for fine cut.

"When the temperature rises and the oceans melt, you'd have ample rainfall. In addition to enhancing an explosion of vegetation on land, such a drastic change would kill off the pika-pina and pika-pedan. Despite such changes, some plants have managed to survive the cold periods. Witness the yellow grass and occasional wire-brush we've passed these past days. Those grasses and the unknown varieties contained in

235

these seeds take over the land. The pika-growth would retreat to the poles, waiting for cold epochs to return. We've seen how fast it grows. It could expand down from the poles, and perhaps from isolated surviving pockets on the shores, to become the dominant vegetable species in a very short time.

"I wish I had a decent laboratory here. These eggs . . . Somehow they survive thirty thousand years before the land warms and frees them. That's important, because there are pretty disorganized people wandering around at that time, looking for food.

"The Golden Saia are not a different variety of Tran, nor are the Tran a species of Saia." He gestured at Hunnar, at Elfa, at Ta-hoding. "You and the Saia are the same people."

A mate made a disgusted noise.

"The Saia are the warm-weather mode of the Tran. During the onset of cold, those who survive the radical weather change develop thick fur. Wing dan appear and podal claws expand and grow to become chiv for traveling across the ice." He sat down behind his table of living fossils.

"Think what such cataclysmic change would do to a developing but still primitive society. Famine, death from exposure, the near instant destruction of familiar food supplies. Sea travel obliterated, cutting off intercontinental and interisland communication. A drastic reduction in population—which explains the extent of these cities compared to the size of present Tran communities.

"It explains, Hunnar, why your people retain no memory of your warm weather ancestors. Survival would be more than enough to occupy every mobile minute of the dazed remnants of that hot climate civilization. How to make a fire, how to cook food, those would be the important things to hand down to shivering children. Not history. Given the frequency of the warm-cold weather cycle, you never have the chance to catch your racial breath."

"No ice—free-flowing water for oceans?" Hunnar's expression showed both horror and disbelief, as if someone had proved unequivocally that the world was flat.

"No ice," said Ethan slowly. "And probably no real winds to speak of, either. Rain instead of snow and ice particles—good-water-falling-from-the-sky," he translated awkwardly, remembering that the Tran had no word for rain.

"No ice." Hunnar seemed unable to pass beyond that incredible concept. "One could fall all the way through to the center of the world."

"Water can support you, Hunnar, though not as well as ice." Ethan forbore trying to describe what swimming was.

"The more reason for this confederation." September brought them back to the present, back from speculations future and past. "If this information can be conveyed back to a few Commonwealth bureaucrats in the right agencies, it could mean a change so big and important here that—well, I can't put into words what it would mean to your people, Hunnar.

"More o' less, it'd mean that the next time your world warms up and you develop a nice, burgeoning society, get yourselves growing good and proper, then when it turns cold again, Commonwealth technology will be there to help you cope. Assumin' the Commonwealth stands. I don't make predictions for *any* government. They've got a disconcertin' way o' self-destructing.

"And you'd be able to develop a true planetary society for the first time, gain a continuity of racial development and history your world's knocked down every time its gotten started.

"But it won't do anybody any good unless we get this knowledge to Commonwealth authorities and show them there's a world here cryin' out for associate status and some honest recognition."

XVI

It was several days before they broke into the Assembly. The impressive domed chamber was buried beneath a huge slide. That unstable ground made Ethan and several others reluctant to enter, despite the apparent stability of the intact ceiling. Williams and Eer-Meesach could not be restrained, however. They were followed by others, reluctantly, into the largest enclosed space they'd found on Tran-ky-ky.

Built of stone and metal so solid that it supported the cumulative weight of dirt, rock and structures above it, the dome was filled with engravings and mosaics which proved conclusively most of William's assumptions.

"You were not entirely correct, my friend." Eer-Meesach ran a gnarled finger across one wall bas-relief. "The yellowish grass does not drive out the pika-pina but rather is a warm weather variety of it, as the Golden Saia are warm weather versions of us Tran."

Williams was examining the carvings, nodding slowly in agreement. "Probably the nutrients concentrated in the pika-pina and pedan are moved landward and help to revive the dormant grasslands."

"But what are these?" The elderly wizard indicated a profusion of small carvings, each different from the next. Remnants of ancient dyes still clung to the bare stone.

"Do you not remember them from the land of the Saia?" said Elfa. She turned to Ethan. "What did you call them?"

"Flowers." He walked over, avoiding rocks and broken stone which littered the floor. "So the pika-pina flowers before it gives way to the grasses. Milliken, maybe every creature that flies, swims or chivans on Tran-ky-ky has both cold-and hot-climate

238

varieties. That creature on the wall over there, isn't that a stavanzer?"

"No," Hunnar insisted from nearby. "Those strange things on its front—"

"Gills!" Ethan shouted it. "The stavanzer does look vaguely like a beached whale. Dormant gills don't show themselves until the oceans turn to water. A stavanzer could never support its own weight on land."

"I'm sure," added Williams, "that the creature could exist as an amphibian for as long as was necessary to complete the transition to a watery existence."

"I would much like to see these things you call 'ghuls'." Hunnar took a knife from his belt, handed it handle-first to Williams. "Go and kill a stavanzer and I will help you do the looking inside." Laughter human and Trannish resounded in the chamber, producing echoes that were anything but eerie.

A week later the *Slanderscree* was filled with a cargo as unusual as it was diverse. There were hundreds of kilos of carvings, artifacts, sections of mosaic and wall. Enough proof of Tran-ky-ky's erratic history both sociological and climatological to convince the stubbornest bureaucrat or Landgrave of The Truth.

September and Ethan were once again discussing the Tran's future and history as the last of the cargo was secured in the spaces within the deck.

"Likely in the Saia mode all the Tran lived together on a few continents, lad," the giant said. "Raisin' a new civilization until the cold wiped it out, forcing 'em to disperse to the islands to survive. The harsher the climate, the more territory it generally takes to support folks.

"Now that we can prove they all used to live together and cooperate, it ought to be easier to get 'em to do it again." He punctuated the comment with a reverberant grunt.

When they produced the evidence many days later, back in the steaming lands, the Golden Saia accepted the unarguable with typical lack of visible emotion. Their words betrayed their true excitement. Here was proof of most of their legends, solidified with a knowledge hitherto unsuspected. Listening to the legend-

239

spinners, Williams and Eer-Meesach were able to fill in portions of the history that silent stone and walls had been unable to tell.

In contrast to their difficult ascent of the canyon, returning was mostly a matter of keeping the ship on a single heading. Motive power was no longer a problem, not with the wind off the plateau shoving insistently at their stern.

On reaching the edge of the ice, the captain brought the ship to a halt, whereupon Hunnar and a small group of sailors chivaned off toward Moulokin. They were expected to return with shipwrights, cranes and tools to aid in removing the wheels and axles and to help speed the installation of the five massive duralloy skates.

Their arrival in that busy shipbuilding city provoked a good deal of surprise. Neither the Landgrave Lady K'ferr, minister Mirmib, nor any of the others who knew where the *Slanderscree* had gone ever expected to see her crew again. They were certain the spirits of the dead who lived in the great high desert would claim the healthy bodies of the sailors for their own, to enable them to wander the spirit lands in more corporeal form.

Sir Hunnar's hurried, none-too-precise explanations of what they'd uncovered created more confusion than enlightenment. He finally gave up trying to explain something he didn't fully comprehend himself.

The following day he returned to the landlocked *Slanderscree,* accompanied by a large party of craftsmen from the city's yards. Eer-Meesach provided a better explanation of their discoveries. Thus assured of old friends and a new heritage, they set to work making the great raft iceworthy again.

"What of the fleet from Poyolavomaar?" Ethan hesitantly interrupted the chief of the Moulokinese work crews.

The burly Tran left the final installation of a duralloy runner to his colleagues. "They remained a ten-day after your departure to the land of the Gol 'en Saia, Sir Ethan, thence departed themselves. There have been but few ships put in to Moulokin since. None report sighting them, though two mentioned a

240

large number of runner tracks extending northeast-ward."

"Toward Poyolavomaar." Ethan couldn't quite convince himself that mad Rakossa and Ro-Vijar of Arsudun had conceded so quickly, despite this evidence to the contrary.

" 'Tis so. Nor have any of our own vessels seen signs of them, though two still search further out to make certain they have truly taken their leave. 'Tis safe I think to say that, finding you not here, they betook themselves elsewhere."

"I doubt that." Ethan looked around to see who agreed with his own private opinion. Teeliam Hoh watched the repositioning of the fore portside runner, while the crew leader watched Teeliam. Her thoughts, though, were not on the delicate operation taking place over the side.

"Tonx Rakossa would not leave me alive while he remains so. While I live free, his thoughts will be on naught else."

"Maybe he and Ro-Vijar had an argument," Ethan half-joked, "and he lost."

"I hope not."

"What? But you've said . . ."

She stared at him, cold cat-eyes dark as the waters beneath the ice sea. "If he should be slain by someone unknown, far from here, if he should perish before we again meet, then I will be barred the delicious opportunity of killing him myself." She spoke calmly, as if discussing the most ordinary, obvious thing in the world.

"Of course. I should've thought of that."

She continued to stare at him, her head cocked slightly to one side. "You fancy you know us, do you not, Sir Ethan?"

"Know you?" Ethan felt glad of the expression-distorting face mask and the goggles behind. "Teeliam, I've lived among you for more than a year now."

" 'Tis true then, you indeed believe you know us. I've seen it in your gestures, in the way you converse with your companions from this distant land of Sofold. But you do not understand us. When I spoke of killing

241

the Thing, it showed in your body and your way of forming words.

"You are . . ." she paused, half-smiled, "much too civilized, in the sense I believe you use that term. For all that you have shared with such as the magnificent Sir Hunnar and my good friend Elfa, they are still not part of you, nor you of them. They are part of me and this world. You will never change that." There was pride in her tone, and a hint of arrogance.

"Perhaps not." He knew better than to argue with such a recalcitrant customer. "I can only try to help as best I can, the people I've come to care for so strongly."

Teeliam grunted noncommitally, chivaned away. Ethan was unable to tell whether she was voicing a deeply felt opinion, or if such challenge and gruffness were traits forced upon her by the actions of Rakossa. The results might simply have made her resentful of anyone who happened to be happy or optimistic.

Or male.

Still, he considered her words apart from their emotion-charged source. How well *did* he know any Tran? He counted Elfa, Hunnar, and many others his friends. But he had to admit there were occasions when he could not puzzle out their reasoning, or they his. Might they be doomed to exist forever as psychological pen-pals, able to communicate but only across a vast mental sea of alienness? So indeed he might not know them as well as he thought. As to never getting to know them, that he hoped was the brash opinion of one used to dealing only in absolutes.

Of one thing he was certain. Despite Teeliam's insistence, contact with and membership in the Commonwealth would change the Tran, and their world. It had happened to other primitive peoples. Several had already risen to coequal status with human and thranx, and had been raised to full membership within the government. Others were working hard. Perseverance coupled with safe and benevolent supervision by the government and the United Church would aid any less sophisticated society in making the transition to a modern space-traversing technology with as little pain as possible.

That there sometimes was pain he could not deny, even to himself. That pain would be lessened considerably as soon as they returned to Brass Monkey and conveyed news of their discovery to the proper authorities—doing so took precedence over adding new states to the Trannish confederation. He had no doubt they could swing wide around Poyolavomaar and return to Arsudun uncontested.

He lost a mental step. What could they do, what should they do, on reaching the distant humanx outpost? Who could they report to? He was still unsure of Jobius Trell's exact involvement with Calonnin Ro-Vijar. There was a possibility that Trell was operating directly with the Landgrave of Arsudun. September seemed to think so, but they had no firm proof.

Not that he was inclined to shrug off the giant's opinions. More than once September had hinted that he was used to dealing with a higher echelon of power than was Ethan, that analyzing the motives and actions of power-wielders was not new to him.

Consider that Trell was the Resident Humanx Commissioner, that he had knowledge of every aspect of outpost operation. Brass Monkey had a few peaceforcers, stationed there more to protect the natives from the humanx than vice versa. Were they in league with Trell, or with Ro-Vijar directly? And what about the customs handlers, or the portmaster Xenaxis, not to mention the computers and processors?

Who within the modest complement stationed at the outpost could they entrust with such a momentous set of discoveries? Who could not only record and preserve such information against a possibly hostile bureaucracy, but could also transmit that knowledge to incorruptibles offplanet, where they would quickly become so widely disseminated that neither Trell nor anyone else could conceal them?

He took the problem to September. The giant was sitting on the frozen shoreline, his white hair blending into the background of sea and land.

September was not moving, simply staring motionless at the sheet of snow-dusted white where it ran up against the walls of the canyon. It was unusual to see him in such a reflective, downright pensive mood.

"Still in the egg?" The thranx phrase had long since entered the burgeoning roster of interspecies colloquialisms.

"Mmmm? Oh, hello, young feller-me-lad." How oddly quiet he was, Ethan thought, as he turned his attention back to the ice. "No, not in the egg."

"What are you thinking about?"

"My brother. Leastwise, the man who was my brother once."

"You mentioned him before, a long time ago." Ethan sat down alongside the mountainous form. "You said, 'I had a brother, once.' I didn't understand what you meant by 'once.'"

September's mouth relaxed into a grin. He was watching the antics of two furry beetle-sized creatures. They were performing a miniature ice-ballet, skittering smoothly about where the shore met the frozen river.

"I suppose technically we're still brothers. Once born one, I guess you're stuck with it. Haven't seen him in twenty, twenty-five years. I've done a lot of growin' up since then. Sometimes wonder if he has, though I doubt it."

"If you haven't seen him, then how do you know he hasn't, as you say, done any growing up?"

"You don't understand, feller-me-lad. Sawbill, he was born bad." Long minutes of quiet passed. September raised his gaze from skate-bugs to skating clouds racing overhead. "Got himself into a rotten, stinking business much too soon. That's a part of it."

"What kind of business?" September hardly ever talked about himself, and then always in his joking manner. To find him both loquacious and introspective was rare enough that Ethan forgot his original reason for seeking out the big man and probed on.

"He dug too deeply into . . . well, put it brief, he trained himself to become an emoman."

Ethan knew of the men and women and thranx who sold emotions. Their status was only marginally legal, and what they sold was usually best left hidden away in the darker sections of hospitals. Commonwealth law guaranteeing so much freedom kept them from being closed down, though it could not prevent the occasional killing of one who grew too bold, or remained in one place too long. The social side-effects of their profession being what they were, few chose it as a life's work. An emoman (or woman) rarely grew rich. There were other satisfactions to the profession, however, which induced a few to practice it. That gave rise to the saying that the most likely candidate for an emoman's trade was himself.

"There was a girl," September continued, rushing the words as if anxious to be rid of them. "There's always a girl." He chuckled in a bitter, bad-tasting sort of way. "I was interested in her, too much so. I was very young then. Sawbill was also interested in her . . . as a customer, and in other ways.

"We argued, we fought. I thought . . . anyhow, Sawbill sold her something he shouldn't have. She wanted it—it's a free galaxy. But he shouldn't have done it. She was—repressed, I think's the best way o' puttin' it. What Sawbill sold her made her unrepressed. Anyways, she overdosed herself. She—" his expression twisted horribly, "became somethin' less than human but more than dead. Voluntarily turned herself into a commodity. Not a lynx or somethin' decent like that, but something lower, beneath vileness, who—" He stopped, unable to continue.

Ethan wondered if he dared say anything. Finally he spoke as softly, gently as he could. "Maybe if you could find her now. She might've changed, tossed what she was engulfed by, and you could—"

"Lad, I said she overdosed herself. She didn't follow instructions. Happens all the time to those who make use of an emoman's merchandise." There was a mountainous sadness in his voice.

"When Sawbill finally stopped supplyin' her, she hunted up others who would. I can't find her because she's dead, lad. To me and most o' the worlds, anyway. She just sort of got eaten away from the inside. Not physically. That I might've been able to cope with. The body did just fine, 'til it got used up too. By the time that started, her mind was long gone." He turned his attention back to the ice.

"I hope she's dead, Ethan. Should've done her a great kindness and killed her myself. I couldn't, but as

245

I told you, I was very young then. Everything Sawbill did was perfectly legal. He was always very careful about that. Probably still is, whatever he's doing."

"But couldn't you have stopped him, legal or not? The man was your brother. Couldn't he see what he was doing to the girl?"

"Feller-me-lad, emomen have their own code, their own set o' morals. 'Cording to his way of thinkin', he wasn't doing a thing to her. She was doin' it to herself. Commonwealth law sides with him. Emomen's drugs have never proven addictive, not like something such as bloodhype, say. They're big on legality. Not morality."

"How can you act legally and not morally?" Ethan wanted to know.

September laughed, looking with pity at his young friend. "Feller-me-lad, you don't know much about government, do you? Or law."

"Government—that reminds me." Ethan hastened to change the subject. He'd tunneled too deeply into another's soul and had entered hollows he now wished he'd stayed out of. "How are we going to make our discoveries known to proper Commonwealth authorities without letting anyone cover them up?"

"So you're finally as suspicious of Trell as I am, feller-me-lad?"

"Almost."

"Good enough. Never trust an official who smiles that much."

"He knows everything that happens in Brass Monkey. We need someone who can command a closed beam for off-world transmission."

"Isn't anyone," September grunted. He seemed hard at work on the problem, having already forgotten the moody discourse of moments ago. "Wait now." He rose, towered over Ethan. "Ought to be one office that can send closed messages."

"Don't keep me guessing, Skua. Trell's Commissioner, and he can—"

"Think a second, feller-me-lad. Brass Monkey's large enough to rate a padre."

Being only an occasional church-goer, and less religious than most, Ethan hadn't thought of the local representative of the United Church. No one, least of all a comparatively minor functionary like Trell, would dare tamper with a sealed Church communication.

"Now that that little gully's crossed, let's go back and see if we can't help put our ship back together, eh, young feller-me-lad?"

They left the shore and headed toward the ice-rigger. The fifth and final duralloy runner, the steering skate, was being hoisted into place at her stern. Ethan snatched a surreptitious glance at his companion. The patina of indestructible confidence had returned to his expression, only slightly tarnished.

Skua September had turned out to be as vulnerable as any human. His huge frame simply gave him greater depths in which to hide his passions.

With typical lack of formality, the Moulokinese prepared no noisy demonstration to greet the return of the *Slanderscree*. The townsfolk went about their everyday business and the shipwrights who'd helped replace wheels with runners returned to their yards. Officially, the sole ceremony consisted of minister Mirmib and two aides meeting them at dockside.

"Landgrave Lady K'ferr Shri-Vehm bids you welcome again to Moulokin, my friends. Our breath is your warmth.

"There will be a feast tonight to celebrate your unexpected but nonetheless welcome return, at which time you may further enlarge on this wondrous history you have made for us."

"Wondrous isn't the word," Ethan addressed the minister. "Significant would be better. Among other things, it shows that your new confederation isn't as far-fetched as we first thought, because all Tran once lived within a far stronger union."

"A union repeatedly scattered by weather stranger than I can believe, or so go the rumors our shipwrights have told me," Mirmib replied.

As it developed, the feast of the night extended in various incarnations for several days, during which time the crew enjoyed the hospitality of Moulokin. Their tales engendered considerable, lively speculation and discussion among the townspeople. Some of the stories lined up neatly with local religions, which grew at once stronger for the confirmation and weaker for the reality of it.

When it was adjudged time for the *Slanderscree* to embark on its circuitous return to Arsudun, the Moulokinese finally abandoned their casual reserve. They took leave of their work to crowd around the harbor and voice enthusiastic, spontaneous wishes for the safe journey and good wind of their new friends and allies. With the last shouts of the watch patrolling the outer gate adding to the wind pouring down the canyon, the icerigger raced out onto the frozen sea.

Instead of paralleling the cliffs, Ta-hoding set a course northward. They would cross the endless pressure ridge of ice at a different point, to avoid possible confrontation with any lingering Poyolavomaar forces that might be guarding their first passageway through that broken, jumbled barrier.

Ethan stood on the helmdeck, watching the canyon that concealed Moulokin recede behind them. Ta-hoding animatedly waddled around the great wheel, happy as a pup. His steersmen also looked pleased at nothing in particular.

When asked to explain his beatific expression, the captain replied, "Why should we not be happy, friend Ethan? We sail with smooth, clean ice beneath us instead of unpredictable rock and dirt. I know now that if I order the mastmen to port a spar one jahn, the *Slanderscree* will react precisely so," and he outlined air with a sweeping motion of one long arm.

"No longer need we guess at the results of our maneuvers. No more must I . . ."

"Below the deck!" came a shout from the mainmast lookout. "Sail five kijat to port!"

"Must be a merchantman, headed for the city." Ta-hoding strained to look in the indicated direction. The horizon remained uninterrupted.

"Below the deck!" A note of urgency in the lookout's yell sent idle sailors chivaning to the rail. "Four sails more traveling with the first . . . no, five! More still!"

"Do you suppose, friend Ethan . . ." A worried Ta-hoding let the sentence trail off. His jovial manner had faded.

Dan spread wide, Hunnar came shooting onto the helmdeck via one of the ice ramps leading up from the main deck. He dropped his arms and dan, lost speed, and braked in a shower of ice, then skated impatiently to join the captain and Ethan.

"Turn about, Captain." His tone was grim. "They could be an unusually large group of merchants traveling together for protection, but we'd best not take chances."

As if to confirm their worst suspicions, the lookout sounded again. "Eight, nine . . . I count at least fifteen sails, possibly more!"

"Must be the Poyolavomaar fleet. So they haven't given up. They've waited all this time, hoping we'd return. Damn!"

"The girl Teeliam was right." Hunnar's gaze was fixed on the portside horizon. "Who should better know a madman's desires than one who was subject to them? Turn about, Captain."

But Ta-hoding had already begun unleashing a river of commands to all within earshot. When he concluded, he returned to stare in the same direction as Hunnar and Ethan.

" 'Tis difficult to say what may happen." The plump captain looked concerned. "We cannot swing to starboard, for it would take us into the cliffs. To make headway against the canyon winds, we need the westwind behind us. Yet they are already positioned to make use of it themselves. We have no choice but to swing toward them, catch the westwind on our starboard side, and swing back to Moulokin." He stared up at Hunnar. "We may run into their point rafts before we can swing 'round to the west again."

"Take care of your ship, captain friend. I will take care of other considerations." Hunnar raised his arm and slid back toward the main deck, already organizing in his mind ways to repel potential boarders.

Off-watch crew came pouring onto the deck. Some of the sailors were buckling on swords and armor while double eyelids blinked away sleep.

Ethan continued to stare, looking forward as the

prow of the icerigger began to come around and point directly at the onrushing Poyo rafts. By then the opposition had drawn close enough for the lookouts aloft to distinguish markings and pennants. The faint hope that the vessels might constitute part of some huge merchant fleet vanished.

A stocky, wizened Tran had mounted the helmdeck, stood alongside Ethan. Balavere Longax, Sofold's most respected senior warrior, gestured to their left with a clawed finger. The claw was pitted and dull, a fragment of worn feldspar set on the tip of a gray branch.

"Infantry," he grunted. "Slower than rafts but more maneuverable. They seek to cut us off before we can gather the westwind behind us." He fingered the sword slung at his waist, a weapon far younger than himself. Turning, he shouted toward the main deck. "Ware bowmen! Keep to your shields, men and women of Sofold!"

Arbalesters, carrying the crossbows devised by Milliken Williams to aid in the defense of Sofold against the assault of Sagyanak the Death and the Horde over a year ago, took up positions high in the *Slanderscree*'s rigging.

Balavere studied the rush of infantry, now curving slightly toward the raft. "We must pass through them, but they will not stop us." He glanced back at Ethan, grinned unexpectedly. "Their archers will concentrate their fire here, my friend, to try and pick off our wheelmen. Best you get yourself below."

"If you don't mind, I think I'll stay right here." His own confidence shocked him. Little more than a year on this harsh world had transformed him considerably. Contact with the Commonwealth would surely change the Tran. Contact with the Tran had already changed at least one human. He patted the sword slung at his side. It felt familiar, comfortable there. But it was the hand beamer he raised and checked.

"Charge is way down," he told Balavere, squinting to read a tiny gauge through mask and ice goggles. "I expect Skua's and Milliken's are low also. But the first

250

bowman who comes too close is going to get a strong dose of modern technology."

"I had forgotten about your knives that fight with the long light," the general said. "Good. Remain then and help protect our mobility." He walked over to talk with Ta-hoding.

"I worry not overmuch about their arrows," Ethan heard the general tell the captain. "They could do worse, if this Rakossa has good advice. Himself I think incapable of much tactical subtlety. Their rafts sail with discipline, so keep the wind and try not to cut us off overfast. They may try to jam the steer runner with cables."

"Think you I've not been in battle before?" Anxious and concerned as he was, Ta-hoding wasn't about to let Balavere or anyone else tell him how to handle his ship. "Keep any cables out from our stern and I will deliver all safely to the harbor." He muttered a Trannish curse. "Had we but a few hours longer, we could have outrun them. Only a—"

He was interrupted once more by a cry from the mainmast. "Ten ships, eighteen kijat to port!"

By then the icerigger had swung around to where westwind was beginning to fill her sails. She picked up speed, but the sailors of the main Poyo body were visible on the decks of their rafts. A new threat.

"They have cut us off, then," Balavere observed.

"Not yet." Ta-hoding bellowed new orders. Painful creaks sounded above them, and Ethan anxiously looked upward. The adjustable spars had been twisted around so far that they were holding the sails almost parallel to the raft's keel line.

"Think you they'll take the strain?" Balavere was also gazing up into the webwork of singing rigging. The foremast groaned, appeared to bend slightly from the vertical.

"Did I not, I would never have given the order," replied Ta-hoding. "If we did not try it, we would truly turn straight into these ten new rafts.

Continuing to accelerate, the *Slanderscree* curved tightly around back toward the canyon. When it became apparent to the infantry on the ice and the ten flanking rafts that their quarry was going to slide past instead of into them, the bowmen unleashed a rain of arrows in the icerigger's direction.

One stuck tautly into the hessavar hide shield Ethan had been given. He stared at it for a second, then ducked back behind the railing as another shaft whizzed close by overhead.

A small group of Poyo infantry had managed to gain slightly on their companions. Now they were chivaning parallel to the ice-rigger. A few had even managed to slip beneath her hull, where they could not be seen. As Balavere had guessed, thick pika-pina cables were slung on the backs of several of the attackers.

Hunnar, looking tired but not worried, appeared on the helmdeck. "We will have to put men over the side." An arrow landed at his feet, stuck quivering in the deck. Both Tran ignored it. "Our crossbowmen cannot pick them off quickly enough before they get beneath us."

"Any we send over who fall behind would be lost instantly," countered Balavere. He gestured at the swarming Poyo infantry, who were gathering in steadily greater numbers around the icerigger. "We cannot afford to lose many of our complement."

"We cannot afford to have them jam our steering!" Young warrior confronted old.

A commotion forward temporarily brought the argument to a halt. Despite the danger, Ethan rose so he could see over the bow. A brown-gray arrowhead was streaming toward them from the vicinity of the nearing canyon.

"Looks like a sortie from the city." Hunnar was standing close by him, gazing with satisfaction at the widening silver river pouring from the canyon mouth. "Our new brothers and sisters have come to help."

With the Poyolavomaar fleet close behind and infantry preparing to ensnarl the *Slanderscree*'s steering mechanism in green cable, the arrival of forces from Moulokin saved Balavere and Hunnar further argument. The Moulokinese exploded into the unprepared Poyo troops. With the canyon wind canceling out the westwind, the Moulokinese soldiers now had the ad-

252

vantage of speed and maneuverability. They had timed their charge perfectly.

Half the Poyolavomaar infantry succumbed to that initial surge, whereupon the Moulokinese arrowhead formation split, the soldiers curving around to left and right to race back toward their canyon. Some of them, in making the turn, came under fire from the nearest Poyo rafts and were cut down. Most were soon flanking the *Slanderscree* to port and starboard, exchanging victory yells with the sailors on board.

The canyon had become a familiar, gaping slash in the cliff wall. The icerigger slowed as she fought the powerful winds racing off the continent and down through the canyon, but so did the speed of her pursuers.

The Poyolavomaar infantry who remained made it a difficult last few moments, however. Shielded from the strong headwinds by the *Slanderscree*'s bulk, they were able to overtake her. However, between the escorting Moulokinese and the accurate fire of arbalesters positioned on the huge raft's stern, no cable-carrying enemy soldier was able to close nearer than a dozen meters to the vlunerable steering skate.

They were within the towering walls of the canyon then, making slow progress inland with the Poyo fleet close behind. Once, one of the smaller pursuing rafts came almost within bow range. It mounted a pair of small catapults, one on each side of its single mast. Both were soon throwing skins filled with flaming oil at the wooden icerigger.

The Poyo catapulters had not compensated for the tremendously powerful headwind, however. Not only did the dangerous, fiery sacks fail to reach the retreating raft, but the wind held them up and carried them back to fall behind the catapult-mounting craft. Infantry tacking behind it scattered frantically as the flaming skins burst on the ice, sending burning oil in all directions.

The second Poyo ship hit sections of ice temporarily melted by the hot oil and slid awkwardly sideways as its runners lost purchase. Two more rafts piled up behind it, doing their best to avoid smashing into their out-of-control companion.

253

All this contributed immensely to the enjoyment of Moulokinese and sailors, who added hoots of derision and some especially choice Trannish insults to the confusion taking place in their wake.

Balavere permitted himself a crusty smile. "If all their attacks prove as ineffectual, we will have no trouble with these."

" 'Tis clear—I mean, it's clear now why the Moulokinese didn't report the Poyo fleet's presence," Ethan said thoughtfully. "Any neutral merchant raft was likely captured or frightened off, and those two rafts Minister Mirmib said were still out scouting will probably never return home."

Balavere's smile disappeared at Ethan's words. He studied the scene behind them. Their pursuers were untangling and beginning to tack laboriously upcanyon after them. "They still owe much, friend Ethan. I fear that once we are safe behind the Moulokinese walls, they will give up for good this time."

Ethan happened to see two figures conversing by the entrance to the main cabin: Teeliam and Elfa. "I don't think so, Balavere. So long as this Rakossa has control, I don't think they'll ever give up. We may be here for a long, long time."

XVII

The *Slanderscree* and its Moulokinese escort slid in through the massive gate in the outer wall. Word of their return and the Poyo attack had resulted in full mobilization of the city. The wall was packed with armed Tran. Others waited in casual but still disciplined formation on the ice between the two walls, while rafts shuttled supplies out from the city itself.

Ta-hoding brought the icerigger to a halt, reefed in most of her sail. "Why are we stopping here?" Ethan asked.

"Sir Hunnar has conveyed to me a wish to disembark, friend Ethan."

Moving to the railing, Ethan saw that the knight and a majority of the icerigger's crew was swarming iceward. To help defend the wall, naturally. Ethan ran to join them. September was already on the ice, moving awkwardly without his skates. Williams looked up as Ethan neared a boarding ladder.

"Aren't you coming too, Milliken?"

"No, Ethan." The teacher didn't look at him. "You know I'm not much good in a fight."

"I've seen you in combat, Milliken. You handle yourself as well as anyone."

The teacher smiled gratefully. "Better one of us retain a partly charged beamer. Sure, I can fight with it. But when the charge is gone, I'd be an encumbrance. Swordplay's not for me, Ethan."

Unable to decide whether Williams was making a good strategic point or merely an excuse, Ethan said, "You're probably right, Milliken. We'd better keep a beamer in reserve. Maybe you and Eer-Meesach can think of something to help."

The schoolteacher appeared relieved. "We'll try our best, of course."

Ethan went over the side, bumping against the hull of the raft, the soft *chunk, chunk* of a sailor's chiv sounding above him. His friend Williams, he knew, was no coward. He was perfectly right in insisting they keep a beamer aboard the ship. And he wasn't much good with a sword.

Then he was down on the ice, where he promptly fell flat on his fundament, much to the amusement of the nearby Moulokinese. Elfa dropped down the ladder ahead of him. She held a crossbow. Sword and bolt quiver were slung at opposite hips. She smiled at his fall but did not laugh.

In the midst of a situation where he might soon find his throat slit, Ethan found himself staring deep into those topaz Tran eyes and thinking unthinkable thoughts. Here and now, he scolded himself, hundreds of kilometers from the nearest outpost of humanx civilization, parsecs from the closest civilized world.

What better place to think uncivilized thoughts?

"Thank you, Elfa," he said as she gave him a hand up, for once not caring what Sir Hunnar made of his words.

Looking down the canyon from the crest of the wall, he could watch as Poyo rafts and soldiers formed a solid line across the ice. Arrows began to fly from the ranks of Poyolavomaar archers kneeling on the ice, from their counterparts aloft in the rigging of many rafts. All sails had been furled and ice anchors held the attackers' rafts steady against the down canyon wind.

Military sophistication wasn't necessary to identify a completely untenable position. Those Poyo arrows which did have enough force to reach the top of the wall had been slowed by the wind to where they could do little more than nick flesh. On the other hand, having the wind behind them drove crossbow bolts and Moulokinese arrows out and down with sufficient power to penetrate a hide shield.

The officers aboard the Poyo rafts quickly realized the hopelessness of their present position. Drawing in anchors, they let their rafts drift downcanyon and out of range.

Soon shouts of "Down, down!" sounded along the wall.

"That must mean catapults," Elfa explained from nearby. Ethan was acutely conscious of her proximity. While the Tran did not sweat, they exuded a powerful musk which was individually distinctive. None was more so than Elfa's.

" 'Tis to be hoped they are as accurate with stones as they were with oil sacks." She grinned a battle grin, showing delicate, pointed fangs.

That ferocious, toothy smile was enough to erase the absurd scenarios he'd been dwelling on for the past half hour. At the same time he discovered that the tension which had gripped him during the same period had less to do with combat than he'd thought. Now he relaxed a little.

Some distant heavy *thumps* sounded muffled by the wind. Ethan chanced a glance over the wall. Several man-sized boulders lay on the ice below. The massive stone rampart was barely chipped. War cries and

256

obscenity-flavored laughter were the defenders' response.

An audible *whoosh,* and a slightly smaller boulder sailed over the wall to land on the ice behind. After a few minutes. Ethan recognized the futility of his new assault. With perfect accuracy and no misses it would take the Poyos a dozen years to breach the wall which was far too massive to succumb to bombardment from such modest-sized stones. Nor could the Poyo fleet carry an endless supply of such ammunition, and bone and primitive metal tools would not suffice to cut new material from the dense basalt cliffs.

In the crowded canyon, they could not bring enough catapults to bear to drive the defenders off the wall. They had ample time to spot each arriving stone and get out of its way on the rare occasion when one would actually land atop the parapet.

When the Moulokinese arrived from the city with their own artillery and began using catapults to hurl wind-blown boulders back at the attacking rafts, the despair of the Poyo soldiers could almost be felt. They retreated again, still further down the canyon, and sat there. Meanwhile the Moulokinese soldiers and the sailors off the *Slanderscree* held an informal competition to see who could concoct the most degrading insult to hurl in their attackers' direction.

Despite the situation, the Poyo rafts gave no sign of departing. It was to be a siege, then.

"I don't think they'll try that again for a while, young feller-me-lad." September's leathery skin was flushed, giving him the look of a man generating an internal sunset. No doubt he'd enjoyed the brief battle. Privately, Ethan suspected the giant was disappointed at the absence of any hand-to-hand fighting. His enormous battle-axe dangled from one burl-sized fist.

"Their arrows got here slowed down enough to pluck out of the air," he commented, sitting down with his back against the wall. "Can't hurt this wall with their rocks, and they don't know enough ballistics to put every stone on top."

"What do you think they'll try next?"

"If I were them, lad, and foolish enough to continue this, I'd make a try at breaking in the gate. Since they

257

can't sail a ram into this wind, that means bringin' up a hand-carried log or something or usin' oil to try and burn it through."

"The Moulokinese cables will still stop any raft from sailing through, Skua."

"Right, feller-me-lad. That means they'd have to get enough infantry through to take over the wall and lower the cables themselves. I don't see they've got a chance. We can have archers and arbalesters pick 'em off outside the gate, and can mass fifty soldiers behind the gate for every one who fights his way in. Be suicidal to try. That doesn't mean they won't. Humans have been known to try similar stunts."

"They can keep us bottled up here in Moulokin indefinitely, though."

"That's so." He fingered the gold ring in his right ear. "Don't bother me much. I like Moulokin. But it will keep us from gettin' our important discoveries to the padre in Brass Monkey. More important is what it'll do by blockading all commerce. Traders and ship buyers will go elsewhere rather than fight their way into Moulokin. Rakossa's officers probably know that, even if he can't think of anything but gettin' his hands on Teeliam. I don't think our friends the Moulokinese will crack, but too many wars are decided by factors economic instead of military.

"Now me," and he fingered the haft of the huge axe, "I'm hoping the Poyos get frustrated and try another frontal attack. It's more likely they'll get frustrated and sneak off, ship by ship, for their homes and hearths.

"Meanwhile, we might as well lean back and enjoy the hospitality of our hosts, 'till the Poyos decide which way their frustration's goin' to drive them." He put both massive hands behind his head and closed his eyes. After a few minutes, he indicated to Ethan that he hadn't fallen asleep by popping one eye open.

"Barbarians against us, barbarians with us, and we three supposedly civilized folk helpless to influence 'em one way or the other. Think about it, lad."

Then he did fall asleep, oblivious to the cold and the noise of a thousand alien soldiers chattering around him.

"With all due respect, my lord, we cannot attack."
The Poyo officer looked uncomfortable under the glare
of his mercurial ruler, wished he were back on his
own raft instead of here in the royal stateroom.

"Oduine is right, my lord," said another of the assembled captains. "To have a normal wind before us
would be disadvantage enough. But the wind in our
faces here would give pause to a god! At their whim,
they could sally out and do us much damage. Their
weapons outrange us badly. And these peculiar small
arrows," he held up a Sofoldian crossbow bolt, "are
fired with a force greater than our best archers can
muster."

"Their catapults have the wind behind them too,
sire," a third officer added. "I was with the group
that entered the city many days ago to search for this
accursed great raft. The wall before us is fully half a
suntt deep and solid as these cliffs around us. It cannot be breached by any siege weapon I know of."

Tonx Ghin Rakossa, Landgrave of Poyolavomaar,
slouched in his chair at the far end of the triangular
table and quietly regarded his commanders. He let
the silence grow until many were shifting nervously in
their seats.

"Do you have any more good news to give us, my
soldiers?" They looked at one another, at the walls,
their chairs, anywhere but at the dangerously soft-
voiced Landgrave. Most of them despised their hereditary ruler, only a few shared his perverse dreams.
There had been mutterings of disloyalty ever since the
erratic Rakossa had ascended the throne following the
suspicious death of his older brother, but the Poyos
were a tradition-minded people. There was no outright rebellion then. There was none now.

None, however, could deny the wealth (however
questionable the methods) which Rakossa had brought
to their city-state. Many felt guilty at accepting wealth
obtained by devices so callous, yet there were none
who brought themselves to refuse it when their share
was offered them.

Having spoken with quiet control, Rakossa now
leaned forward and screamed at them. "Do you think
we are blind, like the doublebody *Gilirun* who

259

travels the ice by feel? Do you believe that as we face the refuge of that unmentionable woman and those off-world interlopers and that knot of fat merchants we cannot feel the wind blowing hard in our face?" He sat back, dropped his voice to an insinuating purr.

" 'Twas not we who failed to jam with cable the steering runner of the coveted ice ship."

One of the other officers held up another crossbow bolt. The tip and shaft were stained brown. "My lord, this came out of my back this morning." A murmur of support sounded from the other captains.

"We ourselves were also wounded, T'hosjer," said Rakossa. He had always to be careful. As ignorant and stupid as these warriors were, they were all he had to make reality of his dreams. Though devoid of vision, they could still be dangerous.

"Our soldiers would have jammed that raft's steering, my lord," said T'hosjer emphatically, "would have sent it crashing into the cliffs. Would have jammed it so it would have taken forty men a ten-day to untangle it . . . save for these!" and he snapped the bolt angrily in two.

" 'Tis truth sire, save for that—and for this!" A sub-officer guarding the door into the cabin shouldered his way into the assemblage. Facing the Landgrave, he stood on one of the chairs and slammed his right leg onto the table. Triple chiv stuck in the hard wood.

A black line only a few millimeters wide ran from just below the furry knee around to the back, which was bulkier than any human calf. "The offworlders did this."

Several of the other captains leaned forward, examined the remarkably symmetrical wound. Fur and skin had been burnt away.

"They have strange weapons which shoot pieces of sun," the subofficer was saying. "They are long and thin and will go through the thickest shield.

"I had a woman in my command hight Zou-eadaa. A good fighter, afraid of nothing. She chivaned almost near enough to throw her cable at the raft's huge runner. I myself saw what happened next, for I was closest to her.

"One of the offworlders pointed a tiny piece of

metal at her. There was a flash of fire, blue instead of red, that was for a moment brighter than the sun." An awed murmur rose from several officers. "It went through Zou-eadaa's shield, her war coat beneath, her chest, to come out her back and strike the ice, which melted under it to a deep puddle.

"After the fight today, I went out on the ocean to retrieve her sword and armor and cut a muzzle lock for her family." He held up his right paw, extended the index claw. "Were this finger long enough, I could have passed it completely through her body, through the hole the light weapon made. I did not watch myself enough this morning, and received this." He brushed his palm sharply, bitterly, across the black line on his leg.

" 'Tis no clean way to fight, against a weapon that makes one's own leg smell like cooking meat." He pulled his leg free of the table, stepped down off the chair. "Can we fight those who magic with the sun?"

Angry agreement came from several of the most disgruntled captains. Rakossa let them jabber on for a decent period, then said quietly, "Idiots."

Conversation ceased, though there remained barely masked stares of rebellion. Rakossa stood up. "Did you know that, that you are all fools and idiots? Your mothers gave water!" He held up a paw. "Before you babble cubbish objections, we will tell you something else. We have already won this battle."

Strange expressions greeted this ridiculous pronouncement. All knew, even his supporters, that the Landgrave was not the sanest Tran in Poyolavomaar. They wondered if he now might not have entered the region of the humored dead, a development many would have welcomed.

That was not the case. "We have won, because these detested creatures returned here to where we awaited them. We did not know if they would do so. We could not circle this enormous land to find where they might leave it and return decently to the ice. We had thought they might fly off through the sky, as Calonnin Ro-Vijar has told us the offworlders can. But he also assured us that they most likely would not."

That last prompted a query from the officer who'd

261

first spoken. "Where is the brave Landgrave of Arsu-dun?"

"Yes," shouted another "where has he taken himself now that we must fight with blood instead of words?"

"At least you have the brains to note the absence of our valued friend and ally. Now, strain your tiny minds but a little further. Where can he have gone to? Think a moment!" He savored the sudden consternation visible on their faces. "Think of what we just told you, of the offworlders flying through the air."

Someone finally said, in a stunned voice, "He has gone for offworlder help of our own."

"A sensible man among you." Rakossa marked the one who'd spoken for future promotion, provided he continued to behave with proper humility and deference toward the royal person.

"Ro-Vijar has allies among the offworlders, even as that accursed woman does. When it became clear to us that the iceraft and its cargo were elsewhere than in the city of the merchants we dispatched Ro-Vijar at his own suggestion back to his own country. He assures us he can procure offworld help. When he returns, it will be with weapons of battle so terrible that the puny hand knives of the offworlders on that raft will appear as a wooden sword beside one of steel!"

Sitting down, he let the officers mull over that bit of news. "Meanwhile," he interjected, "the merchants and their offworlders cannot come out. If they dare attack us on the open ice, we will retreat past their wind advantage and cut them up on the sea despite their strange weapons. If they vanish again, they will be found when the Landgrave of Arsudun returns with his aid. They cannot escape us!" He slammed a paw down hard on the table.

"Then will we possess not only the great iceship, but all the riches of this bloated merchant city, which we will strip and then burn to the ground."

The cabin rang with cheers. Rakossa sat back, smiled inwardly. Once more he had them. Maintaining the loyalty of such peasant was a disagreeable game, but one which great men like himself necessarily had to master.

Yes, he would have the raft with its beautiful, tall runners made from metal of the offworlders. He would have the mysterious short-arrow bows of its crew as well as their blood. His soldiers, who had grown too thoughtful for responsible citizens, would now have the chance to forget idle speculations and drown themselves in the flesh and wealth of Moulokin. His name and the name of Poyolavomaar would spread a little farther over this portion of the world.

There was something still more important he would gain. More vital than the conquest and rape of the city, than gaining the greatest iceship on all of Tranky-ky, than the power and prestige the coming destruction would bring to him. His eyes narrowed and double lids nearly closed, giving the Landgrave of Poyolavomaar a glazed, sleepy look. He would have the concubine Teeliam.

Let his officers and men gain the riches of the city. His desire was for a possession much smaller. He could not live knowing a possession had defied him.

The excited buzz of conversation around him faded to a dull hum as he envisioned for the thousandth time what he would do to her when his paws again touched her skin.

It would be her last escape.

One of Mirmib's underlings was showing Ethan and Skua the outskirts of Moulokin. They were on the far southewestern side of the city now, where dense stands of coniferous forest ran inland up the shallow subsidiary canyon. Looking behind them they could see small rafts skittering back and forth within the bowl-shaped harbor. Smoke drifted from stone chimneys. Gentle breezes muffled distant shipyard and city sounds. The blockading Poyolavomaar fleet and the possibility of violent death seemed very far away.

"These trees," the official pointed out proudly, "are among the oldest and largest in the canyon. We do not cut them indiscriminately, but reserve them for special endeavors, such as the mainmast of an especially large raft. They serve also to break the rare severe winds that come off the plateau above the city."

The official dropped his arms, slowing his speed on

the ice-path to a crawl to accommodate the two humans who plodded uphill alongside him. But they never did get to visit the saw mills and lumberyard which lay further upcanyon.

A shout sounded behind them. An anxious-looking young Tran was chivaning uphill after them. He came to an abrupt halt, tongue lolling, panting like a winded runner. Throughout his subsequent monologue his arms gesticulated wildly, usually in the direction of the harbor.

"More—more skypeople have come." Ethan and September exchanged glances, said nothing. "They say . . ." He looked at both humans warily as he paused for a breath, "they say that you are renegades among your own people, evil ones come to work evil among us. That the Tran of Poyolavomaar are but doing all Tran a service by trying to take you into custody, and that we of Moulokin should surrender you immediately."

"I see." September regarded the downy-maned messenger easily. "What do Mirmib and the Lady K'ferr say to this?"

The other grinned in that peculiar Trannish way. "Many things that it would not be right to say in the presence of young cubs. They believe you. All we of Moulokin believe you. Those who could join with the treacherous Poyos could be naught but liars, no matter their powers or origin. A faster raft or stronger sword does not make a stranger's words right."

"I think," September said approvingly, "you folks are gonna make good additions to the Commonwealth. Did you happen to see these new skypeople yourself?"

"I did."

"Was one of 'em just a little shorter than myself, with a self-important manner about him?"

"I know naught of the mannerisms of you offworlders," the messenger replied honestly. "I was sent only to inform you. But there were three skypeople and the one you may describe gives orders to the other two. They have come in a craft most marvelous and magical. It has no runners at all," he murmured in astonishment, "but floats above the ice the height of my chest."

"A skimmer," explained Ethan, adding, "they can come right over the wall with that if they want to. But three?"

"Trell wouldn't leave Arsudun without a bodyguard of some sort," September said reasonably. "Probably peaceforcers. They'll take orders from the Resident Commissioner without question, unless we can talk sense to 'em. And if Trell's told them we're dangerous criminals or some such, we won't have a chance to get near them. But a skimmer doesn't frighten me. Trell would guess that much. Let's go see what else they've brought."

Trell had indeed brought much more than a skimmer. Ethan and Skua stood on the wall sealing off the canyon. In the distance they could see the furled sails and masts of the Poyo fleet. Considerably closer, floating two meters above the ice, was a rectangular metal shape with a curved prow. The back third of the object was irregular and composed of the same dull-antimony-hued metal as the body, the bumps and rises giving it the look of a diseased animal. The front two-thirds were normally encased in a metal and glass-alloy canopy, which was presently retracted. A steady, mellow hum came from within the skimmer.

One survival-suited man sat at the controls. Trell stood behind him. Slightly to the left and still further back a third figure sat in a flexible seat. The seat was attached to a device consisting of a narrow, tapering tube two and half meters long that nested in a webbing of opaque ceramics, glassalloy, and spun metal. Ethan experienced a sinking feeling. The abstract sculpture was a beam cannon. One of modest size, but of sufficient capability to turn any fortification of Tranky-ky to a mound of molten rock.

Its operator was sitting easily in the seat, running a hand through her long red hair and waiting for instructions from the Commissioner.

The proximity of the skimmer rendered the use of voice amplifiers unnecessary. "Ethan Frome Fortune, Skua September, Milliken Williams!"

Ethan recognized Trell's voice immediately. "Where's Milliken?"

"Off with the wizard someplace. Never mind, feller-me-lad." September roared over the wall. "We're here, Trell!"

"You are engaged," the Commissioner began officiously, "in unauthorized, unpermitted, and illegal diplomatic endeavors among the natives of this Class V unstatused world."

"We're trying to help them form something resembling a planetary government," Ethan yelled back, "so they can make the jump to Class II. That's a good thing. You said so yourself, Trell."

"You do not have official permission," Trell replied sweetly. "As Resident Commissioner I share your concern. But I cannot countenance unauthorized activities of such delicacy."

"We're willin' to cooperate," countered September. "Give us permission."

"I'm not empowered to do so, Mr. September. I'm only an administrator, not a policy-maker. If you will return with me to Arsudun, I will help you fill out the proper forms and put the request through correct channels."

"That would take years." Ethan didn't try to hide the sarcasm. "You know how the bureaucracy works. We're not recognized diplomats, missionaries, anything but private citizens. We'd never get permission."

"That is not for me to say. But you must go through official channels! As Resident Commissioner I am empowered to enforce the law. No law permits amateur meddling in native affairs."

"You call it meddling. We call it somethin' else."

"Evidently, Mr. September. However," and he nodded toward the waiting cannon, "whatever lies you've managed to foist on your native allies will not resist modern weaponry. For the last time, I implore you to return peacefully to Arsudun—."

"Where we might get our bellies slit . . . accidentally," September cut in.

"—to pursue your endeavors through proper authorities."

"If we don't?" Ethan asked.

Trell managed to look pained. "If I am compelled to employ modern weapons against primitive peoples it will go very harshly with you."

"What he's sayin'," September muttered, "is that if we and the Moulokinese resist, he can blow the whole city to fragments and blame it on us. If we go back with him, you know what'll happen. If he doesn't kill us outright, he'll just have us put on the next ship out-system. That'd be the end of any attempt to organize the Tran and lead 'em out of their self-destructive feudalism. You know how far any official request will get."

"What say you, friends?" They looked back, saw Hunnar standing expectantly behind them. Ethan switched from the symbospeech he and September had been speaking back to Trannish and repeated most of their conversation for the knight and for Mirmib, who had chivaned over to join them.

Hunnar hefted the crossbow he'd taken from the *Slanderscree*'s armory. "What happens if I put a bolt through the chief human's chest? Will he not die quickly as any Tran?"

"Just as quickly," September admitted. "But we'd have to kill all three of them simultaneously." He glanced over the wall. "Near impossible. If one of 'em survives, they'll move back out of range and reduce the whole city, or worse, return to Brass Monkey and report what happened here. Then Moulokin would be listed as an outlaw city full of belligerents, and Ro-Vijar and Rakossa would go down as the finest leaders on all Tran-ky-ky. Too risky except as a last resort. Like jumpin' a crevasse, it's an all or nothing proposition.

"Besides, Trell's no dummy. He knows we've got a couple of beamers. Probably the skimmer's beam-shielded right now. Anything we fired at 'em would just get bent into the ice."

"We've got one other thing to fight with, Skua." Ethan looked from man to Tran. "The new history of an entire race."

September let go a derisive sniff. "I'm not sure Trell's the sort of man to whom that would make much difference, feller-me-lad."

"Don't judge him too fast, Skua. You said yourself once you're used to dealing in extremes. Let me try and sell him, first. Before we try any all or nothings." September looked undecided.

"Maybe I'm wrong, but I think he might be the sort of educated functionary who likes to steal so long as it can be done quasilegally. There's a difference between a professional killer and an immoral opportunist."

"You spin words mighty fine, lad."

"It's my business. Let me at least try talking to him. If he ignores me, well," he shrugged and eyed Hunnar's ready crossbow, "we can always try blunter methods."

"Why not slay him," Hunnar suggested blithely, "when he comes to parley?"

"In the first place, Hunnar, we're not that kind of folks," September replied sternly. "In the second, Trell will come by himself. May sound paradoxical, but he's safer with his bodyguard behind him, runnin' the skimmer and the gun. Kill him and we lose."

"We agree then. Friend Ethan, try your words." Hunnar's tone left no doubt what he thought Ethan's chances were.

He showed himself at the wall's edge. "Will you meet us at the gate? We have a lot to tell you that you don't know, Trell."

"I will," came the response, "provided I can bring a couple of bodyguards!"

September's jaw sagged. If Trell were fool enough to leave the skimmer and cannon unattended . . .

He was not. When the towering wooden gates were lugged slightly askew, the opening admitted Trell, two huge Tran, and Calonnin Ro-Vijar, looking like a great gray cheshire cat.

Trell had come thoroughly prepared. He wore skates similar to those manufactured for Ethan and his friends.

"So you and Trell were together in this all along," said Ethan.

"In what?" Trell looked as innocent as the man who claimed his garrote was a handkerchief. "As Landgrave of Arsudun, naturally Ro-Vijar would be interested in anything affecting the peoples of his world."

"Such as personal profit?"

"We are all businessmen and traders here." Ro-Vijar did not sound offended by Ethan's intended insult. "As a trader, I would be most gratified if this could all be resolved quietly, with no dyings. You should do as your leader requests and return with him to your outpost."

"That might settle things between outworlders." Hunnar leaned against the wall nearby and inspected the edge of his sword. "After the humans depart, there would remain many things to be settled among people."

"As you wish, so may it be." Ro-Vijar gestured imperceptibly in the knight's direction, and Hunnar stiffened angrily.

"It doesn't matter," Trell said hastily. He pointed to Ethan's waist. "In case you're wondering, the skimmer's not beam shielded. No need for it to be so on this world. But we're just out of range of your hand beamers. They can't reach a tenth the distance of that cannon.

"While I'd dislike having to kill you, if you refuse to return peaceably with me and persist in these illegal actions, I will regretfully do just that. Now what is it you wish to tell me?" He sounded impatient. It was cold in the shadow of the wall and his survival suit did not fit properly.

Ethan gestured to Sir Hunnar. The knight went to the door of a chamber built into the base of the wall. Several sailors from the *Slanderscree* trooped out. They carried pika-pina fiber sacks. Carefully the contents of the sacks were removed, laid out on the ice in front of Trell. Knives, plates, bas-reliefs, all manner of relics removed from the buried metropolis they'd discovered inland.

Wishing Williams were present to offer a more scientific and comprehensive explanation, Ethan launched into an analysis of what they had discovered. His narrative produced a more pronounced reaction from the Tran bodyguard and Ro-Vijar than it did from Trell.

That didn't mean the Commissioner was unaware of the significance of the artifacts spread out before him. He knelt, examined a strange tool made of native steel finer than any he'd ever seen. "I admit I've seen nothing like this before. All this means is that these Mulkins of yours are superb craftsmen."

"You don't believe that, Trell. You don't have to be an expert to tell how old this stuff is. With Commonwealth help, the Tran would be able to preserve their accomplishments and heritage from one warm cycle to the next."

"These Golden Saia you spoke of . . ."

Ethan continued enthusiastically. "Warm weather versions of the Tran we see around us, survivors in their thermal region of the previous warm period. Plants and animals from that era have survived there also. Living proof, Trell, of what I've told you. The Tran live together on the continents in large social organizations during the warm cycles. Give them communications technology and you'd have a real planetary government. Only the periods of terrible cold force them into city-states competing for habitable territory.

"Don't you see, Trell? There's much more than just Associate Commonwealth status at stake for the Tran here. They'll have full status in a few millennia, and they'll keep it, once they're assured of a cultural foundation that's not going to be shattered by a new ice age every time it gets started." He paused, continued with more solemnity than he thought he possessed.

"If you take us back to Arsudun, shunt us off on the next ship through and forget all this, you're condemning an entire race, hundreds of millions of sapient beings, to an existence of periodic crisis, starvation, and death that can all be avoided. You'd be personally responsible for denying them their rightful heritage."

"Leastwise you got a simple choice, Trell," September said pointedly. "A few credits in your own account against the future of an entire world. 'Course, if you decide for the former, you wouldn't be the first to do so."

Ethan could see the Commissioner was sweating inside. It was one thing to skim a little illegal profit off the trade of a quarrelsome, primitive people, quite another to do so at the expense of an entire civilization's

270

future. Trell was just moral enough, just civilized enough, in fact just enough of a Resident Commissioner to be thrown into a real quandary by the problem.

Sensing uncertainty, Ethan searched desperately for some additional semantic weapon to throw at Trell. "You'd still be in charge, still be Commissioner. You could still take a legal percentage, however much smaller, of the local trade. Think of the boom in that trade when the Tran organize themselves on a planet-wide basis. We've already started them on that path here in Moulokin.

"And if that's not inducement enough, consider the fame a few stolen credits can never buy. You'd go down in the Church histories as the Commissioner who recognized the cyclic nature of this world's civilization and its importance and took the first steps to aid a climactically impoverished people. How much is a footnote in immortality worth, Trell?" He went quiet. Having appealed to Trell's morality and now to his ego, Ethan had nothing left to fight with.

"I don't—I'm not sure . . ." Trell's unctuous manner had vanished along with his confidence. He'd come in expecting to hear pleas or defiance. Instead he'd been confronted with artifacts and a new world history. He was badly shaken, needed time to recover his balance.

"I've got to think on this, consider it carefully. We—" He halted, turned abruptly to Ro-Vijar. "Let us go and talk, friend Landgrave." Ro-Vijar simply gave acknowledgement, accompained Trell to the opening in the gate.

The Commissioner looked back at Ethan. "I'll give you an answer in less than an hour."

"All we ask is that you consider the obvious," said Ethan. "We'll give you our answer at the same time." Trell didn't appear to have heard the last, sunk in thoughts deeper than outside communication could penetrate.

"What do you believe he will do, friend Ethan?" asked Hunnar as the wooden walls ground shut behind the departing four.

"I don't know. I really don't know. Usually I can

271

tell when I've got a customer bubbled—when I've convinced someone of something—but Trell's too numbed to read. Skua?"

"I don't know either, young feller-me-lad. Trell's tryin' to decide whether immortality's worth the pleasures of the present. It's the old human dilemma: do you live for today or work for a place in heaven? Problem is, we can't counter with the threat o' Hell. We'll know in an hour."

"Assuming he refuses, Skua . . . what *do* we do?"

September said nothing. His expression was answer enough.

XVIII

The skimmer hovered alongside the royal raft of the Poyolavomaar fleet. Within the central cabin Trell, Ro-Vijar, and Rakossa conversed. The two peace-forcers stood nearby, chatting idly to each other and ignoring the curious stares of the Tran around them.

"Friend Calonnin," Trell said wearily, "I keep telling you but you refuse to understand. I no longer have a choice in this. Events have taken it beyond my control."

"You are right," replied Ro-Vijar tightly. "I do not understand why you say you have no choice. Why do you not use your light weapon to make hearth-ashes of those three outworlders and scatter their ashes upon the ocean?"

"It's not a question of three people any more." Trell sat in the too-large Tran chair and worked his fingers. They rubbed, scratched, entwined and folded upon one another.

"Everything they said about the future of your people is quite correct, given the accuracy of their interpretation of the discoveries they made. I'm inclined to accept both. Besides, I like the idea of having my name in the history tapes. You will, too."

"Your history is not mine."

"It will be."

"That remains to be seen."

"Neither of us will sink into poverty because of these developments, Calonnin. You'll still be Landgrave of Arsudun. As the port of Brass Monkey expands to handle increased trade from the rest of Tran-ky-ky, Arsudun and you will benefit."

"In how many of your years?"

"Soon, soon," Trell insisted.

"What of other, new ports?"

"There might be one or two," Trell conceded. "But Arsudun will still be foremost."

"I am little interested in what will occur after I am dead, friend Trell. I am interested only in what will happen tomorrow, perhaps also the day following."

Trell glanced across the room at a figure standing in shadow. "What about you, Rakossa of Poyolavomaar? What do you want?"

Rakossa stepped out into the light. "We have wealth enough to satisfy us for all our future days. We have position and power. As to what happens to our name after we die we care not a k'nith. We do not even care what happens tomorrow, but only today. What do we want? We want justice! These merchants who dare to defy us and!—"

"Yes, I know, I know." Trell sighed, exasperated by the childish obsessions of these ignorant primitives. "Calonnin explained to me about the concubine. Your desires are as limited as your vision, Rakossa."

"You think us beneath you, offworlder. Our vision," he said in a way which started a funny prickling at the back of Trell's neck, "may not be so limited as you think."

"Meaning what?"

"We attempt to foresee all," Rakossa explained obtusely. "That is how we have been able to survive as long as we have in a court filled with intrigues and crafty enemies all about us. They too think we are foolish and mad, that we are blinded by silly desires. But obsession is not blindness, and we are not so obsessed that we cannot see possible futures. Cannot see all possibilities."

Trell's right hand began sliding cautiously toward the pocket in his survival suit, opening the interior heat seal to admit the hand into the coveralls beneath.

"First you said you care only for today. Now you claim to look into the future. You're inconsistent if not truly mad, Rakossa."

"'Tis our way of protecting our desires of today, offworlder."

Trell had a sudden thought. Hand still moving, he turned a stunned gaze on Ro-Vijar, who had moved to stand against a far wall. "Calonnin, what is . . . !"

The first arrow struck the Resident Commissioner just above his pushed-back ice goggles. It glanced off the skull and so failed to kill him outright. Subsequent arrows did not.

Both Ro-Vijar and Rakossa had ducked from the line of fire, Ro-Vijar out the door he'd ambled so casually toward, Rakossa behind the table and into shadows. Trell had just enough foresight to get off a shot. His beamer pierced only the cabin roof.

As soon as their task was completed, the sailors who'd been hidden in the rafters above and outside the doors and windows returned to their usual tasks. All save a few who were directed by Rakossa.

The bodies of the three dead humans, for the peace-forcers had fallen as well, were rendered almost unrecognizable by the profusion of arrows sticking from them.

"Were so many necessary?" inquired Ro-Vijar, eying the corpses a mite uncomfortably.

"'Twas yourself, Landgrave of Arsudun, who told us you could be not certain of the location of their vital organs. We do not take chances. Wait!"

The procession halted, their grisly cargo staining the clean wood of the deck. Rakossa walked to stand next to Trell's limp form. Reaching through a small forest of arrows he lifted the vacant-eyed head by its hair, stared into it with blazing black and yellow eyes.

"Think you still so much smarter than us, Trell of the offworlders?" He grinned a bloodthirsty grin at Ro-Vijar. "Odd. He does not answer. Perhaps we have changed his mind for him." He let the skull fall with a loose-jointed bobbling, a rotting apple in a stream. The sailors carried the bodies from view.

"Are you certain you can operate the offworlder's great weapon?" he asked Calonnin.

"I tried in many ways most subtle on our journey here to induce Trell to show me, but he was too clever for that. However, when we confronted the humans before the wall, I watched intently as the female prepared the machine. I am sure she was ready to protect Trell, so the weapon should have been ready to fire. I memorized the procedure required as best I could."

"Excellent. What will happen now that we have slain the offworlders' leader?"

"He is but the leader of the single small town they maintain on our world," Ro-Vijar explained thoughtfully, scratching at one ear where a persistent mite had been troubling him for days. "If you or I were to die, the knights and nobles would rise our offspring or one of their own to the throne. I suspect it is much the same with the skypeople. They will choose one among them to replace Trell until a new leader can be sent from beyond the sky to take his position.

"Whoever they send will know naught of what transpired here. Those in their outpost who know me will believe me, will believe my account of his death and that of his companions, as there is naught else for them to believe."

"And you will remain secure as the only go-between twixt skypeople and Tran."

" 'Tis truth, friend, Rakossa." Ro-Vijar has sloughed off a slight feeling of apprehension. He knew to a certain extent the powers the offworlders possessed. But what of powers he knew nothing about?

Trell had bled and died as readily as any Tran when the arrows transfixed him. No offworlder had arrived to save him or revenge him. It seemed likely none would. He was feeling much, much better now.

"I will control all the trade. As promised, you will receive your recompense for this day's work."

"And the raft. Do not forget the raft."

"Yes, the great iceraft shall be yours also." Ro-Vijar conceded the ownership of the icerigger easily. And why not? There was the skypeople's skimmer which needed no runners to travel across ice or land faster than any ice ship. There were doubtless other devices he could purchase or steal from the human traders. He could blame any such thefts on others. The Poyos, for example. All knew of their ruthless treacheries. What need had he of an iceship, no matter its size?

"We will still strive to persuade the three offworlders in the city to surrender," he told Rakossa. "They have the small light weapons."

"Do we not have three of our own now, in addition to the great one in the sky raft?"

"True, friend Rakossa. But we are not experienced in their use. Best to avoid trouble if possible."

"If they surrender, we will have six instead of three. They will inquire about Trell. Then they must die."

"That is obvious," agreed Ro-Vijar calmly. " 'Tis good that we agree."

Ethan leaned against the wall. He was watching several Moulokinese soldiers play a game familiar in a thousand manifestations throughout the galaxy. On ancient Terra it had been known as sunka, kalaha, and in a dozen other incarnations. One soldier had just collected seven of his opponent's pebbles when the horribly familiar sound of paper tearing was heard.

Across the gate from his present position a gap had appeared in the top of the wall. It was roughly three meters long and three and a half deep, almost perfectly circular save for the jagged edges of a few stones sticking into it. Within that circle everything: stone, soldiers and weapons, had vanished. Or more properly, had become either part of the molten debris lying at the bottom of the cut or of the ashy vapor drifting downcanyon. Mist formed above it as the cold air of Tran-ky-ky contacted the superheated rock.

He hadn't seen the bolt from the cannon, not that he had to. A frantic look over the wall showed the skimmer still floating in place in front of the nearest Poyo raft. September put a hand on his shoulder, stared alongside him.

"Feller-me-lad, that's no man at the controls."

As the skimmer started toward them, moving awkwardly in fits and jerks, Ethan was able to confirm the giant's observation. The skimmer held several Tran, but no survival-suited humans.

"I recognize Ro-Vijar. He's the one operating the gun."

The skimmer halted just out of hand beamer range. The Landgrave of Arsudun rose behind the weapon. "I do not form phrases so pretty as offworlders. You will all surrender: now. Or I vow every man, woman and cub in Moulokin will die."

Ethan shouted across the ice. "Where's the human Jobius Trell?"

"Trell has traveled the path destined for all traitors, offworld or otherwise. He cannot help you now."

Several Tran chivaned forward. They carried between them three feathered bodies, which they unceremoniously dumped on the ice. The corpses were not so far away that Ethan and the others on the wall couldn't distinguish the limp forms of the former Resident Commissioner of Tran-ky-ky and his two attendant peace-forcers.

An anxious voice sounded behind him. "What means this, friend Ethan?"

He did not try to evade minister Mirmib's question. "It means that our enemies now control weapons more powerful than our own. They've killed the humans who brought those weapons. I had doubts the man Trell would use such power against you and your people. I have no such doubts about Rakossa and Ro-Vijar."

"We cannot surrender." Mirmib looked adamant and worried simultaneously. "We cannot let them into the city."

"I know." Ethan considered. "Maybe if we three gave ourselves up . . ."

"Easy, feller-me-lad. Ro-Vijar might be sittin' behind the convincer, but it's that fella Rakossa who's in control out there."

"Teeliam would give herself up to save the city. She's already tried to, once."

"Use your head, lad. We didn't let her do it before for the same reasons we won't now. Rakossa's got control of something that can level this whole town. He's

277

tryin' to control a bunch of angry, embarrassed and bloodied troops. Do you think he's going to let Ro-Vijar leave anyone alive here, maybe to tell the next Commissioner what really happened? Not a chance. We've got to fight."

"Use your own head, Skua." Frustration made Ethan sound angrier than he was. "We can't fight a beam cannon."

"Let's fake a retreat. Pull back, maybe even let 'em into the city proper. We can split up, some of us head up the main canyon and hide in the mists, then come down and try and take the cannon on the chance they'll relax. A few thousand would die, but better that than the whole population."

"I have a better idea, gentlemen."

Ethan and September turned to see a puffing Williams mount the last of the ramp leading to the wall top.

"Where the hell have you been, Milliken?" September growled.

"We thought it best to keep one beamer in reserve," replied Milliken, ignoring the big man's tone.

"I've been working on an idea with Eer-Meesach and some of the local craftsfolk," the teacher continued, "ever since the Poyolavomaar fleet began their blockade." Williams's shyness passed for self-control at a time when everyone around him exuded an air of imminent defeat.

"I ain't too proud o' mine," said September. "Let's hear yours."

"Have you forgotten the battle of Sofold? Have your forgotten, Sir Hunnar?"

"Nice thought, Milliken, but that won't work this time." September jerked a thumb back in the direction of the waiting fleet of rafts. "There was no beam cannon at Sofold, and Sagyanak traveled by raft, not on a skimmer above the ice."

"I am aware of that," Williams replied, with just a twinge of reproval. "I did not think we could repeat the battle of Sofold here."

"Then why ask us to remember it?" wondered Ethan confusedly.

Williams proceeded to explain.

"We have waited long enough." Rakossa stood in the bow of his craft and yelled to Ro-Vijar on the skimmer. "Let them die if they wish and die if they do not. Our soldiers would let out their heat. We have promised them Moulokin and they shall have it. If at this moment you have become fainthearted and uncertain like the offworlders . . ."

"Calonnin Ro-Vijar hears his friend Rakossa. Time enough has passed. It shall be as you wish."

Turning, the Landgrave of Arsudun squirmed down into the too-small seat and repeated the sequence he'd memorized while watching the human female earlier. There was a crackling and a narrow shaft of glowing azure jumped from the end of the weapon. It struck the left side of the massive wooden gate at the place where it was hinged to a stone tower. A gaping hole appeared in the base of the tower. Slowly, accompanied by a tired groaning noise, the tower collapsed, bringing half the gate down with it.

An expectant, humorless cheer rose from the assembled soldiers on the rafts as they saw the heretofore impregnable gate go down so easily. In tumbling, the fallen tower had also pulled down the pika-pina cables behind it, opening the way to the inner canyon.

Ro-Vijar had to try several times, but finally succeeded in adjusting the attitude of the weapon so that it was pointed at the other half of the gate and its still-standing supportive tower.

"I can reduce the whole wall, if you wish to watch," he called back to Rakossa.

"No. The stones left behind would cause my ships more trouble than the wall itself. We waste time. Make but a proper entry for us and we will do the rest."

Gaining confidence in operating the weapon with each burst, Ro-Vijar fired again. Splinters of unmelted stone flew in all directions as the other tower was undercut and collapsed. Several additional bursts cleared the ice completely. Then he issued careful instructions to the young squire who was at the skimmer's controls.

A little more smoothly, the strange offworld sky raft moved forward. Unfurling sails, the Poyolavomaar fleet commenced to follow.

Ro-Vijar raised the barrel of the gun, fired again at the top of the wall and blew another impressive circular gap in the crest. Following that, the shields and weapons lining the rampart began to disappear.

"They abandon the wall!" shouted one of the officers on Rakossa's raft excitedly. "This will be a day long sung of in the city's taverns and halls."

Rakossa did not comment. As he'd told the human Trell, he cared nothing for histories.

Soon they would be within the city. He prayed devoutly that Teeliam would not kill herself. She should have enough sense to do that, or have another do it for her, but in the past she had clung tenaciously to life. Perhaps she would remain alive in hopes of killing him, as she had so often promised to. Little fool, little fool. She played so poorly at the game.

The faster they moved, the less time she would have to think. The less time she had to think, the better were his chances of finding her alive. He had no wish to toy with a corpse.

His lead raft sailed cleanly through the gap in the wall. Other rafts crowded close behind, soldiers lofting arrows at the retreating Moulokinese.

The last of them had vanished behind the false protection of the second wall as the Poyo rafts rounded the tight bend in the canyon. The fleet slowed, waiting while Ro-Vijar prepared to reduce this second obstacle to ash and slag.

He took his time. Powerful winds rocked the skimmer, despite its compensating stabilizers, and Ro-Vijar did not know how to adjust for the gale. No matter. His first bolt passed high over the wall. Snarling to himself, the Landgrave of Arsudun lowered the angle of the barrel. Crossbow bolts and tiny flares of blue light from the human's hand beamers reached for the skimmer, falling laughably short.

There was a dull rumble above. A storm would dampen but not slow their entrance to the city. He looked skyward curiously—saw a few clouds, harbingers of the nearing storm no doubt. The rumble sounded again, then a third time. It was peculiar thunder, deeper yet not as reverberant.

Then the sky narrowed at the edges and he began

screaming at a panicky squire, "Back sail, *back sail!*"
He did not remember in that last brief moment that the
offworld ship had no sails.

Jammed together as the rafts were, it was impossible
to turn them quickly. The rumblings continued to echo
through the canyon, some louder, some softer, coming
in rapid succession now. Ro-Vijar leaped over the side
of the skimmer, landing on the ice with an impact hard
enough to crack one chiv. The wind at his back, he
raced for the first wall fast as the downcanyon breeze
would carry him.

Hundreds of meters above, Malmeevyn Eer-
Meesach, wizard and advisor to the Landgrave of Wannome and Sofold, supervised the execution of Milliken
Williams' plan. The last of the powerful gunpowder
charges were set off in the holes so laboriously drilled
into the cliff tops. Then he and his assistants retreated
as the upper portions of both sides of the canyon caved
in.

Blocks of basalt and granite weighing a hundred
tons or more tumbled majestically into the gulf. They
struck hard enough to splinter the ice, though not
crack it all the way through to the bottom of the solidly
frozen inlet.

One gigantic irregular stone, a black iceberg that
must have massed a hundred fifty tons, landed with a
thunderous *broom* on the ice. It bounced once, rolled
over and made the rear half of a Poyolavomaar raft
into matchwood. Screaming sailors abandoned their
craft in mindless panic instead of trying to navigate an
escape.

Only a few rafts located at the rear of the fleet managed to back sail fast enough and with sufficient discipline to retreat. Then two rafts became jammed in
the ruined first wall entrance, sealing the single path
of escape.

A different roar sounded as the massed militia and
sailors from the *Slanderscree* came chivaning through
the gate in the second wall to engage the remaining
demoralized and scattered Poyo troops who hadn't
been killed outright by the awesome power of the col-
lapsing cliffs. Their only thoughts were of flight. They
scrambled over rocks, ruined rafts and ruined com-

281

rades in their haste to flee. Moulokinese and Sofoldians pursued with bloodthirsty delight. Arrows, crossbows, and spears rapidly gave way to swords, axes, and other more intimate methods of destruction.

Ethan recognized one figure in the forefront of the carnage: Teeliam Hoh, wreaking murder with more enthusiasm than any warrior. He knew September would be out there also, slipping and sliding on his skates as he butchered alongside Sir Hunnar and the rest of the Tran.

He didn't share their appetite for slaughter. Thanking the Tran who'd given him a tow, he skated over to where a gleam of light on metal showed beneath a boulder. From the looks of it, the huge stone had hit the ice, bounced once, and struck the skimmer broadside. Not having been designed to handle that kind of impact, the flotation craft's compensators had blown and it had fallen to the ice.

Circuitry protruded from numerous gashes in the skimmer's flanks, and molecular storage modules lay like dead bugs on the ice. Several smaller rocks had made scrap of the beam cannon. For an overview, he clambered up the chill sides of the stone.

Standing atop the boulder, he was able to see down the canyon—no longer a smooth white river, but a landscape of isolated dark shapes resting on a plain dusted with smaller rock fragments. His gaze went higher. Smaller bits of stone continued to loosen and fall from the cliff tops, which were no longer smooth and regular but deeply notched for a thousand meters on each side. Explosives were among man and thranx-kind's oldest weapons. They still had occasional uses.

Williams had reached the cliff top opposite Eer-Meesach. Below, ants slaughtered one another among pebbles.

One of the Moulokinese chemists who'd helped him stood nearby. " 'Tis a marvelous thing you have conjured for us, Wizard Williams."

"I'm not a wizard, and I certainly didn't invent or conjure the powder. We didn't get as much out of the charges as I'd hoped to. If we can find purer nitrates I'm sure we can manufacture a better grade." He was performing calculations as he spoke.

Watching him, the Moulokinese was at once awed and afraid. The distance between scientists and the sometimes destructive results of their science is often more terrifying to the average being than the inventions themselves.

Williams noticed the Tran's expression. To his great horror, he discovered it made him feel good.

It was late afternoon and the temperature was falling with the sun when the Moulokinese fighters chivaned wearily back to the canyon. Blood had frozen in copious quantities between the two walls, giving the inlet the look of quartz littered with crystals of vanadinite.

" 'Twill require much time and effort to clear our canyon so that ships may travel it again." Landgrave Lady K'ferr looked quite magnificent in battle dress, Ethan thought.

"We shall rebuild the damaged outer wall," said one of her officers from nearby, "higher and stronger than before, with the same stones that have crushed our enemies."

" 'Tis truth. We will have the help of our friends of Sofold." K'ferr gazed fondly at several weapon-laden sailors from the *Slanderscree* as they returned with prizes from the massacre. "I wish only," she continued, looking saddned, "that I could congratulate your Sir Hunnar Redbeard, friend Ethan. Of all who fought, he was bravest."

Ethan stared down the canyon at the stragglers returning to the canyon. "He could still be out there, cutting down one last Poyo."

"I'm afraid not, feller-me-lad." September had skated over to join them. "I was out on the ocean with him. Saw him go down myself. He didn't get up again."

There was a wail from behind them. Ethan wished the Tran were capable of fainting. Then he wouldn't have had to see the look of anguish September's words had produced in Elfa Kurdagh-Vlata's eyes.

September laid down his heavy, stained axe, pulled his beamer from his waistband and tossed it to Ethan. After inspecting the reading on a certain small gauge, Ethan nodded, handed it back to the giant.

"Mine's dead too, Skua. I don't know about Milliken's, but I think he used it up drilling holes for the charges."

"Well, let's hope we won't need 'em on the way back to Brass Monkey, feller-me-lad. We'll take Trell's body and the two peaceforcers back with us. Been thinkin' on what we ought to tell the port authorities. No need to get complicated about it. Unfriendly native attack, wandering bandit types." Ethan nodded slowly, eying the three gashes on the left side of the giant's neck. Someone had patched the survival suit with local materials. Since September chose not to mention the wound, Ethan ignored it.

"They'll accept that story because they won't have a choice, lad. Just as they'll accept the artifacts and new interpretation of this world we'll bring 'em. The next Commissioner sent here won't have any ideas about illegal profit skimming, not with a civilization to help organize. But we'll play it safe and tell the padre first anyway."

"Once the Church stirs a theological finger in here, the bureaucracy will monitor its people more tightly," concurred Ethan. "Poor Trell. He created the conditions for his own murder."

"Sorry, feller-me-lad. I got no sympathy for him. I've seen this sort of thing happen on too many primitive worlds. And he made the old mistake of forgetting that primitive folks can be just as crafty-treacherous as the most jaded technological sophisticate."

"You said the portmaster and others will accept our story because they'll have nothing to compare it with. What if Ro-Vijar managed to get away?" Turning his face away from the blast of ice crystals streaming down the canyon, he looked toward the distant frozen sea. "I didn't go looking for his body, but I didn't notice it among the dead."

"Assumin' he ain't lying under one of these rocks, we'll just have to deal with his lies when we get back to Arsudun," said September. "Be our word against his. I'm inclined to think Xenaxis will side with us."

"That's not what worries me, Skua. Ro-Vijar's clever enough to settle for maintaining the status quo on Arsudun. By telling some story about his last minute alliance with us, for example. Xenaxis may not believe him, but he hasn't got the authority to prosecute a native leader on our word alone."

"I hadn't considered that, lad. Be tough to prove anything if he agrees with us instead of attackin' us. Let's worry about that on the way back to Brass Monkey. We've a long way to go. Maybe we'll get lucky and overtake him."

Far out on the ice ocean, five battered rafts hove to a halt. Thunder, natural this time, sounded to the northwest and the captains of the five rafts knew they would have a difficult time making headway homeward if the storm did not skirt 'round them.

Furthermore, not only were their crews depleted, but of those who remained many were wounded too badly to work the sails.

A small group of sailors and officers had gathered on the stern of one raft. A single figure stood in the center of the circle they formed.

"You cannot put me off here," the Landgrave of Arsudun insisted, frightened for the first time since they'd escaped Moulokin. He looked over the side, at the ice now lit an eerie blue-white by the twin moons of Tran-ky-ky. "Not without food and weapons."

"We have carried you far enough, Ro-Vijar of Arsudun." Rakossa fingered the fresh scar running down his sword arm. "Mayhap you can make it back to Moulokin and your offworld friends."

"They are not my friends! You know that." Fear lent force to Ro-Vijar's protests. "Did I not help kill three of them with you, among whom was one partly my friend?"

"Ah. Then you may throw yourself on the mercy of the compassionate people of Moulokin." There were unfriendly laughs from the circle of sailors, few of whom wore no bandages. One of them jabbed viciously at Ro-Vijar, his spearpoint piercing the Landgrave's vest and starting a trickle of blood.

Ro-Vijar clutched at the puncture. Looking now like a terrified cub instead of the leader of a powerful island state, he scrambled over the railing and onto the single pika-pina boarding ladder there.

"I beseech you, Rakossa, do not do this thing to one who befriended you! I ask mercy."

"We *are* being merciful," said Rakossa nastily, "by not killing you slowly this moment." He spat at the dangling Ro-Vijar. "Because of you we have lost most of our fleet, all of our best fighting men and women. When we return home, we will be pressed because of this disaster merely to retain our rightful throne.

"But worst of all, *worst of all,* that woman is safe!" He was quivering with rage, his fur bristling from ears to feet. "Safe among offworlders, whose 'irresistible' weapon you had us put our trust in."

"Who could foresee the magic they would use to bury us beneath the canyon tops?"

"We tire of your excuses, Landgrave-no-more." Several sailors moved threateningly toward the rail. Ro-Vijar hurriedly slid down the ladder. As it was drawn back aboard he stood shaking on the ice, staring up at the equally cold faces lining the railing.

"You cannot leave me thus, you cannot! Give me a weapon. A spear . . . even a knife!"

"You fought well with words, Ro-Vijar of Arsudun. Do battle with them now."

"Offspring of a k'nith!" wailed Ro-Vijar. "Your mother mated with a root! I will follow you all the way to Poyolavomaar and thence travel on to Arsudun, where I will mount a fleet to raze your unspeakable city! You will die a death more horrible than you can imagine!"

Rakossa made a gesture of disgust. "There is no death we cannot imagine." He turned to the squire standing next to him. "We would not inflict this vexsome babble upon the creatures of the ocean." He put a paw on the squire's lance. "Best to kill him now and spare the roamers of the ice." He tugged. The squire did not let go of the lance.

Rakossa regarded the wounded soldier with a stare of disbelief. "We will gift you with another spear, subofficer, unless you wish to kill the thing on the ice yourself." When the squire did not reply, Rakossa tugged again, harder. Still the Tran didn't let loose of his weapon.

"You wish to join him?" Rakossa's voice was

touched with incredulity. "Give us your lance, squire, or we will—"

"You will do nothing," a tight voice said. Rakossa spun, confronting the speaker of the unbelievable words. Surely he recognized the young officer. It was one who had not cheered as loudly as others when Rakossa had first announced their intention to pursue the escaped offworlders from Poyolavomaar. And had he not seen this one in council since that time . . . ?

"I hight T'hosjer, son of T'hos of Four Winds, of a line who have served Poyolavomaar many generations." The moonlight gave his youthful features a sinister cast, shone on the slim sword the officer held to the Landgrave's chest.

"Be that so, T'hosjer, you are an officer no longer." His voice rose. "You are not even a squire; you are nothing!" He reached up a paw to shove the point of the sword aside. T'hosjer leaned forward, penetrating the other's chest just above the sternum. Rakossa froze.

Looking around the circle he saw the fixed expressions on the faces of sailors and officers, wounded and spared. No one spoke.

"What is this? Have you all gone mad?"

"No, Rakossa of Poyolavomaar. We have gone sane." T'hosjer gestured with his free paw toward the slight, silhouetted figure of Ro-Vijar down on the ice. "You blame all that has happened on that one. 'Tis not his fault. We of Poyolavomaar always prided ourselves on making trade or war on our own, without the help or interference of others.

"You have sought the aid of those who are not even Tran, have taken the advice of one not of the Seven Peaks. Because of that my brother T'sunjer and many friends of my cubhood lie dead on the step of a strange city that meant us no harm, their hearts pierced by arrow or sword, their bodies broken by rocks."

"You fought as fiercely as any other," said Rokassa accusingly.

"I fought for the city of the Seven Peaks, for Poyolavomaar my home and for my friends and companions. I fought because the alternative was to run. An officer of Poyolavomaar does not run and leave his friends to fight and die without him. There will linger on us no disgrace from this defeat, for we fought blind." A mutter of agreement came from the surrounding soldiers.

"We were blinded by your words and the position you inherited. We partook of your madness. This, and not the defeat in battle, is the shame we will carry with us to our own passing. It has been long said that you were mad, Rakossa of Poyolavomaar. Those who disagreed or argued too strongly with you disappeared too often these years past."

"We are your Landgrave," said Rakossa angrily. "We stand before you as rightful ruler and liege!"

"You are no longer ruler or liege. From this point," and he mimicked Rakossa's own words of a moment ago, "you are nothing."

Rakossa studied the circle of glowering soldiers, male and female. "A thousand metal *pled* to the soldier who kills this traitor!" No one moved. "Two thousand!" Then, "I will mate and make my coruler the woman who kills this one!"

That produced the first sounds from the group— mewling laughs from several of the female soldiers. One said, "To live the life of horror you visited upon your concubine Teeliam Hoh? I believed not the rumors that came of what you did to her. Now I think they mayhap were understated."

Rakossa still could not comprehend what was happening. "Officers, prepare to set sail. Soldier-sailors, to your posts."

"Over the side." T'hosjer jabbed a little harder with his sword. Blood trickled faster through gray fur. "Join your ally and friend."

Dazed, Rakossa crawled over the railing. "We will follow. We will see all of you spitted over hot fires in the kitchens. We will have your mates and cubs disemboweled before you!"

T'hosjer leaned over the side of the raft, made certain the no-longer Landgrave of Poyolavomaar dropped to the ice. Then he turned, exhausted, to the mate who had become captain of the raft and spoke a single word.

"Home."

As members of the circle moved to their posts and

signals were exchanged with the four remaining rafts, T'hosjer slid his sword back into the scabbard tied to his right leg.

"What of Moulokin?" asked one of the sailors. "Will they not come seeking revenge?"

"When we have regained some of our pride, we will come back to the canyon of the shipbuilders and make peace with them, as should have been done long ago. There will be changes in the way Poyolavomaar relates to its neighbors."

As the pitiful remnant of the once grand fleet began to gather wind and move northeastward. T'hosjer moved to the stern. Two figures were receding behind them, dark blots against the ice.

"What see you, T'hosjer captain?" It was the one of the female fighters who'd laughed at Rakossa's bizarre, desperation proposal.

"I expect they started the moment we prepared to leave," he told her. He squinted into the moonlit distance. "I believe Ro-Vijar of Arsudun is on top, but it is becoming hard to tell." He grunted, turned away as the two flailing figures became merely another blur on the blue-white ocean.

In the canyon of Moulokin several shapes moved against the wind and cold. Scattered among the boulders and the dead, they gathered the personal effects of the soldiers of Moulokin and the weapons and armor of the enemy not already scavenged by the victorious soldiery.

One figure did not move. She sat on a wooden beam splintered from some shattered raft and stared out toward where black cliffs gave way to shining ice sea. Since the sun had dropped behind the west rim of the canyon she had been singing in a high, keening wail that was part growl, part rhyme, part something no human could put a definition to.

A voice sounding tired and a touch irritated called to her from among a cluster of stones which had been torn loose from the outer wall by the offworlder energy weapon.

"With all due respect, my lady Elfa, I implore you

289

to have mercy on a wounded soldier and cease that awful caterwauling."

Her head came around sharply, eyes strove to pierce the night.

"Who . . . who calls the Landgrave's daughter?"

"And give us some help," the voice added, ignoring her request. Two figures limped out from behind an enormous boulder. One promptly slumped to a sitting position. The other figure fell atop the first, rolled off to one side and lay panting on the ice.

"I have a broken leg and torn dan, and this soldier of Moulokin is sorely hurt. I sewed up his belly as best I could, but I am no seamstress or physician."

"Hunnar? Hunnar Redbeard?" She slid off the section of ruined mainmast, chivaned recklessly toward the two shapes.

Tonx Ghin Rakossa did not die easily. The same forces that powered the demons within him refused to let him perish.

He snugged the too-small cloak more tightly around his torso, leaned against the howling wind. Curse the leperworm Rò-Vijar for the damage he'd done before he died! Rakossa's dan were too badly torn to give the wind purchase, and his left arm dangled uselessly from the shoulder.

But the former Landgrave of Arsudun was worse off. Rakossa warmed himself with the memory of Ro-Vijar's neck snapping beneath his fingers. The Arsudunite had been weak in the end, weak from the softness inflicted on him by offworld luxuries.

When we return to Poyolavomaar and reclaim the throne, he thought venomously, we will deal with these offworlders once and for all.

His return to the city-state would provoke much consternation on the part of T'hosjer and the other traitors. How he would enjoy that confrontation! His allies remained safe at court and his lineage as Landgrave was unchallengeable. His claim would hold, and his very presence make liars of the traitors. To salvage their own precious necks, many of the common soldiers who survived would suddenly have second thoughts about any tale T'hosjer could conjur. Then he would have the pleasure of watching those traitors toast over low coals, until their fur blackened and their bare skin began to peel away.

But first he had to get there.

The walls of the plateau were growing gradually nearer, despite his arduous means of traveling by use of his legs alone. He was safely distant from vengeful Moulokin and should encounter no soldiers this far from the city. Within the lee of the cliffs he should find some shelter from the nightwinds, and likely some scattered pika-pina or other vegetation to eat.

Trading vessels should pass this way soon. He would hail one leaving Moulokin. Of his ability to pass himself off as a survivor of the battle he had no doubt, for words had always been his most effective weapon. While not clad in Moulokinese attire, his adopting of Ro-Vijar's would not mark him as a dangerous Poyo either. The brotherhood of ice sailors being what it was, he would likely be treated kindly and carried to the merchant's home port.

Once there, he could eventually buy, steal, or cajole a raft to carry him home to Poyolavomaar and revenge.

Something moved on the ice to the south. He froze, until he saw it was no roving carnivore but a ship, and a tiny one at that. Too small to be a merchantman, it probably held ice gleaners searching the cliffs for edible plants or animals. Simple hunters and gatherers, now able to ply their trade outside the secured city. In Ro-Vijar's cloak he should not immediately be regarded as an enemy. If they were not of Moulokin he could retain his first plan. If they were of the city, he could feed them a formidable tale of shipwreck and woe.

Either way, he could gain their confidence long enough to give time to dispatch them, despite his one useless arm. That would give him a raft far sooner than he'd dared hoped. Why, it was not inconceivable that he could reach Poyolavomaar ahead of the traitors. How gratifying it would be to stand at the harbor front and greet T'hosjer upon his arrival!

The little raft drew nearer. He slumped to the ice. Let them think him more sorely afflicted than he was, the better to lull any suspicions they might have of

291

him. Stone chiv braked to a halt nearby. There was the noise of someone stepping onto the ice. Slow chivaning sounds reached him, then stopped. He waited patiently, but no further indication of movement came. Only the everpresent wind, skipping and moaning over the ice like a mournful spinster.

Best to show them he was alive. He made his voice a weak croak. "Blessed are those who give succor to the wounded in time of trouble."

The chivaning started again, but moved not toward him. Instead, it seemed as if he was being slowly circled.

"Blessed are those who deal in justice, to reward the persistent."

That voice sounded half familiar, despite the wind's distorting. He rolled over, wishing for a sword. A glimpse of his hoped-for savior made his wide yellow eyes bulge wider.

"YOU!"

For the first time in several days, screams rang across the ocean. They lingered, growing progressively fainter, for three days before ceasing altogether.

No one thought to question Teeliam Hoh when she sailed her tiny raft back into the harbor of Moulokin many days after the Great Battle, and none dared ask the source of the terrible content that shone in her face. She became a much-respected member of the Lady K'ferr's household staff and lived a long and fruitful life in Moulokin. She had many pleasurable affairs and encounters, though she never mated, since relationships always faded whenever any male grew close enough to see what remained forever fixed within her eyes.

"What will you do now, friend Ethan?" Hunnar rocked awkwardly on his crutches as the *Slanderscree* heeled slightly to port.

They'd left Moulokin several days ago, promising to return and complete formal documentation of alliance between Sofold and the canyon city at first opportunity. Meanwhile the Moulokinese would sail out to spread the gospel of the Union of Ice and the confederation of all Tran among surrounding city-states and towns.

"I still have a job to return to." Ethan spoke ruefully. "At least, I think I do. I'm a bit overdue at my next scheduled stop."

Skua September stood nearby, his suit hood back, enjoying the minus twenty-five degree wind blowing in his face. He had one foot up on the railing and held himself steady with a massive hand entwined in the pika-pina rigging as he gazed out across the ice ocean. They had many satch to travel before reaching Brass Monkey.

"You really goin' back to that business, young feller-me-lad?"

"It's what I know best. If I'm lucky, I might be promoted to a management position in a few years."

September made an impolite noise.

"M'nag, what is that, friend Ethan?" Hunnar looked curious.

"I would direct others at the job I'm doing now, supervise them. When the next Commissioner arrives here and begins recruiting a network of Tran to act as Commonwealth agents for Tran-ky-ky, he'll be delegating similar jobs. You'd be a good candidate for one such important post, Hunnar."

"He is candidate for no post," said Elfa Kurdagh-Vlata, laying a possessive paw on the knight's shoulder. With his broken leg, Hunnar was unable to draw away —not that he wished to. "Upon my father's passing, he is to be my ruler-mate in Wannome."

"Well, that's a pretty good management position too," Ethan admitted with a smile. They could see the smile through his survival-suit mask. Copying September, he slid it back, gasped as the cold air struck him.

The shock passed quickly. The wind was blowing no more than a dozen k.p.h. Coupled with the gentle temperature, it made the day seem positively tropical. He watched the white sea skim by beneath the icerigger's duralloy runners. Perhaps he would doff the survival suit altogether, plus the clothes beneath, and enjoy a sunbath in the shelter of the central cabin.

He considered other options besides the obvious. What of the distant, wealthy Colette du Kane? By now he had acquired almost enough self-confidence to deal equally with that massively composed woman. It was a possibility he should reconsider.

Especially if he had lost his job.

"Will you come back, Sir Ethan?" Hunnar asked hopefully.

"I'd like to."

"Me also, feller-me-lad."

Leaving Hunnar and Elfa locked in more than just conversation, the two humans moved off across the deck.

"We've made a lot of friends here, Skua."

"Oh, I wouldn't come back just for that reason, lad." The giant grinned that knowing grin which gave him the look of a man half devil, half prophet. "I've friends scattered all over the Commonwealth, on more worlds than I can remember. Fact is, I've other places to visit.

"There's this gal on Alaspin, she's an archeologist thinks she's onto somethin'. Been wantin' me to come 'round that way for a couple o' years and help her out on some big dig. As I've only been to Alaspin once before, I think I might just drop down that way and look her up again."

"Then if not for the friends, why would you want to come back?"

"Why, young feller-me-lad?" September's smile widened. "You saw the carvings and inscriptions and mosaics in the mountain-city, and you heard our teacher friend Milliken hypothesize a different ecology, where the predominant color's green 'stead of white.

"Yes, I'd like to come back allright. In about ten thousand years or so when this world swings close by its star again and the cycle shifts from cold to warm. I'd like to sail these same oceans again in a real boat, though the ol' *Slanderscree*'s got her points." He tapped the wooden rail affectionately.

"Think on those carvings again, feller-me-lad. Ten thousand years from now, why, it'd be nice to be here. Because when those frozen seeds thaw out fast, there's gonna be a few hundred billion flowers all bloomin' at once."

About the Author

Born in New York City in 1946, Alan Dean Foster was raised in Los Angeles, California. After receiving a Bachelor's degree in Political Science and a Master of Fine Arts in Motion Pictures from UCLA in 1968–69, he worked for two years as a public relations copywriter in a small Studio City, California firm.

His writing career began in 1968 when August Derleth bought a long letter of Foster's and published it as a short story in his biannual *Arkham Collector Magazine*. Sales of short fiction to other magazines followed. His first try at a novel, *The Tar-Aiym Krang*, was published by Ballantine Books in 1972.

Foster has toured extensively through Asia and the isles of the Pacific. Besides traveling he enjoys classical and rock music, old films, basketball, body surfing, and karate. He has taught screenwriting, literature, and film history at UCLA and Los Angeles City College.

Currently he resides in Big Bear Lake, California, with his wife JoAnn (who is reputed to have the only extant recipe for Barbarian Cream Pie), three cats, three dogs, two hundred house plants, assorted renegade coyotes and raccoons, and the ensorceled chair of the nefarious Dr. John Dee.